ADVENTURES OF LEWIS AND CLARKE: THE BEGINNING

THE FIRST THREE STORIES

ADVENTURES OF LEWIS AND CLARKE

KITTY BUCHOLTZ

Daydreamer
Entertainment

Adventures of Lewis and Clarke: The Beginning

Published by Daydreamer Entertainment

Copyright © 2017 Kathleen Bucholtz

ISBN: 978-1-937719-16-6 (ebook)
ISBN: 978-1-937719-17-3 (print)

Cover design: Stephanie Shackelford at SaRose Design
Unexpected Superhero cover design: Najla Qamber Designs

INTRODUCTION

Tori Lewis and Joe Clarke have been living in my mind and heart for years now. I've known their secrets, their fears, and how their families feel about them as a couple. But I believe their big adventure began — as it does for so many couples — when they came home from their honeymoon. That's why *Unexpected Superhero* was the original first book in the Adventures of Lewis and Clarke series.

But then readers started asking me questions like "How did they meet?" and "Did anything interesting happen at the wedding?" So I wrote those stories, too, both for you because I like to write what you want to read, and for me because I love hanging out with Tori and Joe and their friends.

Unfortunately, that made numbering the series a little complicated since "book one" was already out. Calling the other two stories "Prequel 1" and "Prequel 2" made it difficult for people to read them all in order, if that's what they wanted.

So, my friends, I put together this three-story set for **you**. I hope you enjoy reading the entire beginning of their adventures from, well...the beginning. Enjoy!

SUPERHERO IN DISGUISE

For John,
Our meeting wasn't this cute, but our happily ever after is even better
than the most blissful of fictional characters.
How lucky are we?!

SUPERHERO IN DISGUISE

Kitty Bucholtz

SUPERHERO IN DISGUISE

Finally, *a place where I can be myself. No more hiding.*

Tori Lewis grinned as she and her sister Lexie dropped Tori's mattress on the floor. She put her hands on her hips and caught her breath. For only a double size mattress, that sucker was heavy. Especially when they got it stuck in the doorway of her new house.

A place all her own, even if it was only studio sized. There was a time Tori would never have believed she'd have her own home. When she'd moved in with Lexie three years ago, she was sure that was how her life would end—two old women bickering good-naturedly with each other in between visits from the nephew/son who adored them, no other men in sight.

Yet here she was, totally psyched about her new digs. The first time she'd seen the place, the *Hallelujah Chorus* had sounded in her head. It was a tiny little building in the backyard of another house, a few blocks deeper into a not-so-great area of the city than where she and Lexie lived now. Peach stucco with white trim on the outside, peach and white paint on the inside, it was totally cute without being girly-girl. The main house, a three-bedroom ranch, sat at the front on the street, and another little one-bedroom house leaned up against the alley.

Now Tori had her own bathroom, two—count them, *two*—parking spaces in the trash-filled alley, and a little patch of actual green grass. Well, browning grass. Halloween in Northern Michigan, and no snow in the forecast. *Awesome.*

Tori glanced out the rear window at the empty lot next door. Weeds the size of small trees and a dozen feral cats added a bit of Halloween spookiness even though it was still daytime.

A shiver tingled down her spine. Was she really going through with her plan, Operation Freedom? Or was she just pretending?

But a look through her front window showed a well-kept, if tiny, lawn with struggling rosebushes lining the sidewalk. The rosebushes were the reason Tori had signed the lease. If they could survive and thrive, so could she, right? Okay, so maybe they weren't *thriving*. They just needed some tender loving care. She would nurture the roses, and somehow they would help her grow stronger, too. She'd just have to mimic the front yard of her new home, not the backyard.

Tori sighed happily. She used one foot to maneuver the mattress up against the rear wall between two windows. "Well, the bedroom's all set up. Let's get started on the living room and office."

Lexie laughed with her and took in the entire house in one not-so-long glance. "A three-hundred-square-foot room, huh? It's not much."

"Three hundred and forty-three," Tori corrected. "And it's all mine." She threw her arm around Lexie. "For the first time in twenty-seven years, I don't have to share a bathroom. I don't even have to worry about the neighbors hearing the TV through the walls. It's a little *house*, not an apartment, and it's all mine!"

Tori squeezed her sister's shoulders to keep from clapping her hands. But the excitement came out through her feet, and she bounced on her toes. Her face was going to hurt if she didn't stop grinning. Her plan was a good one.

"Well, if this is what you want," Lexie said with a shrug, "I'm not going to rain on your parade."

But Tori could feel her sister's disappointment. It gathered and ebbed in the air as Lexie tried to hold it in. It was a weird Lexie-thing that no one could explain. Whenever she suffered a strong emotion, it radiated out. People nearby would begin to feel what Lexie felt, sometimes to a debilitating degree. It frightened their mother, Dixie. Their stepdad (who was really just "Dad") and younger siblings seemed more curious than frightened, but Dixie wouldn't allow anyone to talk about it. It was one of the elephants in the room at the family zoo.

Tori had learned to push back against the overpowering billows of Lexie's emotions, and she did so now. Pretending her sister's feelings were behind a movable glass wall, Tori focused on pushing the wall away, giving herself some emotional space. Lexie's disappointment eased back, and Tori's excitement returned.

She gave her sister another squeeze and kissed her cheek. Lexie could feel what Tori was feeling, too; that was the counter-balance. Tori focused her enthusiasm until Lexie gave in. A warmer sensation flowed between them, and Tori felt her sister relax. Much as their parents loved them, both girls had always known there was only one person they could count on: each other. Tori was determined never to let her sister down.

She grabbed Lexie's hand and dragged her back to the rented U-Haul in the alley. Today was the most exciting day of her life, and nothing was going to ruin it. One item at a time, they unloaded Tori's life. First came the computer desk Tori had bought at IKEA when she graduated from college and got her first "real" paycheck. Then came two bookcases, a TV stand, and an office chair—IKEA, IKEA, Office Max—and the little studio was already crowded.

"Are you sure about this?" Lexie asked, permanent worry lines etched across her forehead. "We haven't even brought in any boxes yet."

Tori pushed against Lexie's anxiety. Her own fear could wait until the dark night brought strange noises. She tried not to think about how creepy it might be to sleep here alone for the first time on Halloween night. "I'll have my own bathroom," Tori reminded her. "No plastic potty, no Elmo bath toys. I can light candles and take a bath for more than ten minutes."

Lexie laughed. "Okay, okay, I get it. It's paradise." She started out the door, then paused and asked, "Can I take a bath here?"

Tori chuckled as she pushed her sister through the doorway. "I'll give you a key." She couldn't remember ever feeling so good. Would she feel even better when she stole back other freedoms? Imagine—no more shrink, no more medications, no more thinking of herself as broken and in need of fixing. She couldn't quite wrap her head around what that might be like.

For twenty-two years, Dr. Huntington had been an unwanted authority figure in her life. Weekly visits and innumerable pills hadn't given Dixie the "normal" daughter she wanted, nor Tori the reassurance of unconditional love from her mother. An incident at this year's annual Labor Day family reunion had pushed Tori for the last time, and she'd begun changing her life in secret.

As she climbed up and down the three steps to her front door, bringing in box after box from the truck, Tori's insecurities rose and fell. Was this move a bad idea? She and Lexie had been doing so well living together. Lexie hadn't reverted to any of her old patterns, even early on when they were stressed about paying the rent and buying groceries. What if things took a turn for the worse and Lexie ended up back on the street, this time with her two-year-old son Ben? What would happen when Dixie found out Tori decided to stop going to the shrink? Would Tori's choices help her grow as a person or drive a wedge between her and the people she loved?

The way she went from acting strong and courageous to scared witless and back again, maybe she *should* continue with counseling. Maybe she should've waited until Ben was in school before she moved out. That way—

"Stop!" Lexie came up behind Tori, her arms full of boxes. She dropped them against a wall and turned to Tori with that "mother" look she'd almost mastered. "Stop worrying! What's the worst thing that can happen? You move in with me again." She studied Tori's face for a moment. "And if you're worried about what Mom thinks, just..." Her voice softened. "Just stop. You're a grown woman, you need to make your own decisions."

Tori sighed and opened a box. Their dad, Danny, assured them that everything Dixie did or said was because she loved them. But a great divide existed between mother and daughters. Tori wondered if their half-brother and -sister, Kevin and Samantha, ever had to be reassured of their mother's love. Dixie doted on her two younger children.

"I don't want to make the wrong choice," she said as she put books on a bookshelf.

"Well, get over it." Lexie put Tori's little TV on the TV stand and plugged it in. "Life is full of wrong choices. Look at me. But then there are the unexpected blessings, like Ben, so...I'm not convinced wrong choices always turn out so bad."

Lexie didn't talk about "blessings" much, but when she did, her son was usually the focus of the discussion. Tori didn't know if Lexie still believed in God, but she'd changed a lot since Ben came along. Maybe if moving out wasn't the best choice for Tori, it would still turn out okay in the end.

Tori hesitated, afraid to tell her sister about her other plans.

As usual, Lexie picked up on her emotional vibe. "You're trying to decide if something else is the wrong choice?" Lexie stacked DVDs on the shelf under the TV. "You're still taking your medication, right?"

This was the reason people often thought Lexie was a mind

reader. She wasn't, but she was scary good at guessing what was going on in your head based on your emotions. Tori wanted to answer the question, "Of course!" But lying didn't work very well around Lexie unless you were *very* good at it. The silence was deafening.

Lexie turned toward her, crossing her arms in big-sister mode. "You're kidding me." She sighed. "Tori..."

"I'm mostly still taking them, but I don't think I need them," Tori burst out. "No one makes *you* take any pills!"

Lexie snorted. "No one *can* make me, that's why."

Tori threw her arms wide. "But I don't have impulse control issues or an anger management problem. I'm fine!"

They stared at each other, feeling the swirl of each other's emotions, pushing and pulling in a wordless argument.

Lexie gave in first. "Fine. You decide what you think is best." She pointed a finger at Tori. "But if anything happens—"

"Like *what*? What's going to happen? No one will ever answer that question!" Years of frustration spilled out. "*Just tell me!*"

Tori watched as Lexie's face crumpled. She seemed to be trying to speak, or not to speak, Tori couldn't tell. She rushed the few feet to her sister and grabbed her shoulders. "Are you okay?"

The emotions in the room swirled with helplessness and secret fears and...was that resignation emanating from her sister? Lexie relaxed with visible effort. Her clenched jaw loosened, and her facial muscles smoothed. She took a breath.

"Remember when you were little, and you had problems at school?"

Sort of. Tori remembered the kids didn't like her. She nodded.

"Do you remember why?"

Tori thought back. "I wanted to play with them, and they wouldn't let me." The memory still hurt.

Her sister shook her head. "No, you *forced* them to play with you. That's what they didn't like."

Tori sifted through memories and old hurts. "I didn't..." She was going to say, *I didn't force them*. But then she remembered being very little, in a store, wanting a toy, and throwing a temper tantrum until her mother bought her the toy...and she remembered Dixie's face.

Her mother was afraid of her.

By the time they finished unpacking and returned the truck, dusk had settled. They picked up Chinese take-out and went to Lexie's to get dressed and hand out candy. Tori loved her Pirate Wench costume. It was sassy and bold and completely unlike her. She'd rented a blonde wig, bought some fishnet stockings, and borrowed a pair of ridiculously high heels she could barely walk in. It was perfect.

Lexie wore an adorable Little Red Riding Hood costume she'd made, and little Ben spent a couple of hours as a cute pumpkin until he screamed to get out of the puffy gourd. Immediately upon his release, he reverted to his usual angelic self.

"Just because you can't talk much doesn't mean you don't know exactly what you're doing," Tori chided him with a mock frown. He grinned at her.

Around 9:30, Tori decided to call it a night. Seeing all the costumes was fun, but tonight she was eager to go home. Besides, she needed to get away from all the little packages of M&M's. Plain, peanut, peanut butter, and pretzel—Tori loved them all. She couldn't decide if they were her kryptonite or her energy source, but she'd eaten at least six packets tonight, probably more. She tried not to let the words "stress eating" settle in her mind. Besides, the half gallon of fresh apple cider counted as a fruit. Several times over.

Lexie had been great about not pressing her to talk, but the swirl of emotions in their apartment—that is, *Lexie's* apartment—

was cloying. Or maybe it was just the swirl of Tori's own emotions. In any case, she wanted to get away. She needed to be able to think someplace where no one could "hear" her thoughts.

"Before you go," Lexie said, and pulled a box out of Red Riding Hood's basket. She handed it to Tori.

Tori blinked at her in surprise, feeling Lexie's delight before she even got the box open. Inside was a keychain with a tiny silver house on the end. She gasped with pleasure and plucked it from the box, dangling it up close for a better look. Everything that makes up sisterly love coalesced into a warm cloud around them as Tori hugged Lexie tight.

"Congratulations," Lexie whispered. "You're going to do great." Her voice cracked at the end.

"Lex," Tori began. If Lexie cried, she'd cry, too.

"Go on now," Lexie pushed her away. "I know it's only a few blocks, but call me when you get home."

Tori smiled. Home. She had her own place to live, and that was exciting. But home is wherever you're loved, that she knew. She squeezed her sister's hand. Sometimes blessings were so obvious. "See you tomorrow."

As she walked home, Tori fished her house key out of her purse and put it on her new key ring. She held it up in the mostly dark and watched it swing. She *wouldn't* be nervous. This was an exciting time. Nothing to be afraid of. Living alone only meant no bathroom schedule and eating whatever you wanted.

She tucked the key into her purse and stumbled a bit. Darn, she'd forgotten to change back into her own shoes. She'd been so eager to leave before the two of them burst into girlish sobs. Oh well. It wasn't that far.

Two ghosts and a ghoul passed her on the sidewalk. A miniature princess dressed in pink satin and lace flashed her a toothless smile. Tori wondered why so many children were still out trick-or-treating, and without their parents. Or their coats. The autumn night had gotten quite cold.

Teen boys dressed as the Angel of Death and the Devil leered at her cleavage as they sauntered by. Tori grimaced and pulled her lightweight jacket closer. *Teenagers.*

As she fumbled with the buttons, the Devil stole her purse.

Honestly, she should have seen it coming. The teenage boys in their hand-me-down, seen-better-days Halloween costumes exuded rebellion like it was cheap cologne. Tori stared for a second in surprise.

Tall and gangly in a red mask and black cape, the Devil took off at a dead run. Losing what little cash she had wasn't what made Tori mad. It was losing the keys to her brand-new home—and the key ring with the little silver house on it! Her first house-warming gift!

Without another thought, she gave a shout and took off after the thief. As soon as Tori began to run, she saw how *this* would end. The girl always picked last in gym class, the one who quit the track team after one day (she'd tripped over the hurdles setting them up), the girl whose greatest aerobic activity was bathing an active toddler—that girl was now running down a broken sidewalk in four-inch heels and the world's tiniest Pirate Wench costume.

A flash of red cape turned the corner ahead. So few streetlights worked in this neighborhood, the kids would get away for the simple lack of her being able to see them. Her chest tightened. She needed to *do* something.

"Drop my purse, you jerk!" she screamed with all her breath, which, granted, wasn't a lot at that point.

The tiny pirate's bodice wasn't made for sprinting, and the material lost its hold on her right breast. A swift downward glance showed an expanse of pearly whiteness bobbing up and down *and* a tree root growing up through the sidewalk. She reached up to cover her boobs at the same time that her left foot missed its jump over the tree root.

The four-inch heel went flying. Her ankle twisted under her.

Tori flailed for balance with her left arm and fell, hitting the sidewalk hard. Her left leg made contact from hip to knee, shredding both skin and fishnet stockings. Both palms skidded across the concrete. Tori felt the sharp sting of skin peeling away and gasped. She landed with a thump on her left hip and bottom, the tulle petticoat under her tiny pirate's skirt flying up.

For a stunned moment, she remained in that undignified heap. Her mind created a mini-movie of what she must've looked like. A quick embarrassed laugh burst from her throat. She winced as she peeled her hands away from the sidewalk. This one needed to be entered in the Falling Hall of Fame. Then, realizing her skirt was no longer covering her lacy underwear, she slammed it down over her thighs, grimacing at the sting in her palms. No need to give the staring trick-or-treaters more of a show than necessary.

She looked toward the street corner where the Devil had disappeared. "Happy Halloween," she muttered.

JOE CLARKE SUPPRESSED the temptation to whistle while he worked. He loved his job as a superhero, even with the long hours and the often negative press, but it didn't seem like work on Halloween. He got to dress up as anything he wanted and wander the streets looking for bad guys. Or more accurately, teenagers behaving badly.

Maybe the city's real villains were at home handing out candy with their villain-in-training children; Joe didn't know. But most of Double Bay's superheroes spent these couple of nights patrolling their neighborhoods against the only immediate threat —tomorrow's citizenry.

Devil's Night, the night before Halloween, had become a free-for-all over the years. Kids had gotten it in their heads that they could do anything they wanted this one night of the year so long as they called it a prank. Even good kids succumbed to peer pressure to become petty vandals.

At one point, things had gotten so bad that chucking eggs at cars had escalated into setting the vehicles on fire. A city-wide crackdown a decade ago had brought the situation under control. Now most of the complaints were about smashed jack-o'-lanterns, stolen decorations, trees and shrubs wrapped in toilet paper, and thrown eggs and rotten vegetables.

Last night, Joe had arrived too late to keep a house from being toilet-papered—a very quiet job that he didn't hear until he was right on top of it. But he'd managed to keep a few cars from getting egged. Of course, most of the eggs had dropped on the sidewalk when he'd scared the crap out of the kids. But better there than on a car's paint job.

This year, Joe dressed as Zorro. The black costume concealed his presence and allowed him to stop more vandalism-in-progress than he'd managed last year. Fewer smashed pumpkins and stolen decorations, less graffiti. Renting the Captain America costume last year, complete with hoodie-mask and metal shield, rated high on his geek meter, but it hadn't put the fear of God into many vandals. Zorro apparently scared them more, no doubt due to the fact that his sword looked real. Joe really liked the sword.

A flock of teenage girls rushed down a driveway and turned toward Joe. Their titters upon seeing him turned to giggling cries when Joe swept off his hat and bowed as he passed. He chuckled softly.

Dry leaves crunched under his feet as he walked the dark streets. The warm scent of woodsmoke curled into the brisk night air. An occasional gust of wind coming off the bay signaled colder weather on the way. Joe almost hoped it would snow soon. He'd bought a new John Deere Snowthrower last spring at an end-of-season clearance sale, and he could hardly wait to try it out.

A woman's scream tore through the night.

Joe swiveled toward the sound and sprinted down the street. He analyzed the night as he ran. The woman didn't sound in pain, or even scared, and she hadn't screamed again. She sounded angry. Possibly a thief then, something relatively nonviolent. He hoped so. Violence against women and children unmasked darker sentiments in Joe's heart that he didn't like to acknowledge. He scanned the empty yards. The leafless branches of the trees made it easier to see, like looking through the bare arms of motionless skeletons. Nothing.

Running feet. He crossed the street to intercept the potential hoodlum. His costumed cape flew behind him. Hoodlums, plural. Two teenagers ran toward him.

"Stop!"

Joe's command caused them to stumble over each other as they changed direction. They hopped a short fence and ran through a dark yard. A dog barked and another picked up the call. One of the teens threw something behind a parked car as he ran.

Protect her.

Joe hopped the fence and paused. He blinked and shook his head.

Protect her.

The feeling overwhelmed Joe's senses like a voice that was more than audible. Team protocol called for him to nab the boys, call the police, and find whatever had been stolen, in that order. He was sure the woman's scream was more of a yell, that she wasn't hurt, but his intellect couldn't overcome the command surging through his mind. *Protect her.*

He took a moment to search near the parked car and saw something fuzzy on a thin chain. The nearest streetlight was broken, so he couldn't see well. Perhaps a woman's purse? He'd never seen anything quite like it. Tucking the chain around his belt, he hustled down the street, looking for the woman who'd been mugged.

Turning a corner, he saw someone sprawled on the sidewalk. His heart raced. As he got closer, though, his steps slowed as alarm warmed into red-blooded admiration. A blonde pirate sat in a tumble of lace, one beautiful breast in her hand.

LEXIE'S COMMENT about Tori forcing her school friends to play skidded through Tori's mind. What were the chances that she'd forced the mugger to drop her purse? Probably not very great. She shook her head. Lexie was exaggerating to make a point. Sure, Tori was unnaturally good at convincing people to do things, but that didn't mean she could *force* them to do what she said.

She carefully brushed the dirt from her fingers, not letting her palms touch, and began to put herself back into her costume. Trickier than it would seem using just her fingertips. She pulled away the bodice with her right hand, then used her left to tuck her breast back inside. But the stiff lace trim pulled at a piece of raw skin and made Tori's eyes water. She snatched her hand back. Sure enough, the lace now glistened with blood.

"Cra-ap!" she muttered. Thoughts of Bactine and Fudgsicles entered Tori's mind. Dixie had always been great about fixing life's little scrapes. Her funny little saying—"Nothing broken, no one maimed"—a smile and a hug, followed with a Fudgsicle or a homemade treat; that would forever be how Tori judged life's small injuries.

It was the big things Dixie couldn't handle.

Still trying to adjust herself properly, Tori used both hands to push and prod. It shouldn't take this much work for a B cup, but her bloody hands were half useless. She heard a soft swish of fabric on fabric, then darkness blotted out the streetlight.

Tori looked up in alarm.

Zorro towered over her. From her vantage point on the side-walk, he looked enormous. Dressed all in black, he had tall gleaming boots, snug breeches, a billowy shirt under a flowing cape, and the perfect Zorro hat complete with a long black feather. *Gorgeous.* Tori craned her neck. He was at least as tall as her dad, and Danny stood at six feet in his socks.

The masked man looked stricken. His mouth worked sound-lessly until the words finally came out. "Can I help you?"

Tori followed his gaze to see both her hands still inside her bodice. She snatched them out. The quick movement undid some of her work, so she hunched her shoulders a bit to block his line of sight, pushed and prodded—bloody hands or no—and sat up straight again.

She cleared her throat. "Thank you, no, I'm fine."

He raised his eyebrows. Even in the darkness, Tori was sure she saw him fighting back a smile. Then she realized what he meant—not her *boobs*, her *situation*!

"Oh!" She felt blood rush to her face. "I'll be fine. I just have to get my purse back." She moved to get up and winced.

Zorro bent to one knee. His cape swirled around them, giving Tori the strange feeling that they were alone together. Her heart raced. Behind the mask, his eyes looked kind but intense.

He held out a fluffy pink heart on a silver chain. "Yours?" he asked. "The kid dropped it. I guess it didn't go with his outfit." Zorro had the same expression her dad and brother got when-ever they looked at her purse. Kind of like they were about to heave.

Tori gasped. Sparing a glance for the dark stranger, she unclasped the heart-shaped bag to find everything still there. The mugger must've dropped it before he could open it.

"Th-thank you," she said, fighting to keep her voice steady. A wave of emotion washed over her. Not a swirl of feelings like when she and Lexie were together. It was more specific...*safe.* Similar to when she was with her sister, but deeper somehow, more stable. She was absolutely and inexplicably safe. She stared into Zorro's eyes, trying to figure out what was happening.

If it weren't for the "no men" rule, Tori would find a way to get to know this man better. She'd never felt safer, but she'd learned her sister's lessons. And her mother's. She needed an exit strategy.

"You're smiling."

Really? So was he. Had she smiled first? If so, only because of that warm, wonderful feeling wrapping around them.

Zorro's crooked smile lifted higher on the left. It made him look young and mischievous. This guy was dangerously cute. Gorgeous she could walk away from, but cute...

Tori cleared her throat and looked away. *Get a grip.* She took a deep breath to clear her head. Oh geez, he smelled wonderful. Something she did *not* want to notice. She pulled away, her nerves tingling.

"Thank you for finding my purse," she said. She pulled her right leg under her to leverage herself up, but forgot about her skinned palms. As soon as they touched the sidewalk, she gasped and curled her wrists toward her body.

Zorro leaned over and picked up Tori's hands. Turning them palm up, he grunted. "Bet that stings."

His quiet, deep voice wrapped around her heart. His touch set her mind and body at ease. She was exactly where she was supposed to be.

Focus! She shook her head and leaned back a few inches. "Not as much as my leg," she tried to joke.

"Let me see." He laid her hands in her lap and gently prodded at her skinned-up leg. "Can you stand?"

Tending to her injuries, he was more focused on her than ever. It was disconcerting, uncomfortable, and fabulous. Tori wondered what it would be like to be the focus of his attention long-term.

"I'll be fine, thank you," she said, pushing his hands away and grimacing as her palms made contact. She should go home.

Rule #1—If you're attracted to them, they're bad for you.

Lexie and Tori had created the rules for their protection. Whoever Zorro really was under that mask, she feared he was the kind of man who would make her forget the rules.

Gathering her legs under her with as little wincing and groaning as she could manage, Tori tried to stand without giving Zorro an eyeful of black lace underwear. Before she realized his intent, Zorro grasped Tori's ribcage and lifted her to her feet. Well, not exactly to her feet; they were dangling off the ground. He held her hundred-and-not-telling pounds off the sidewalk with ease. Too much ease. As if he were holding a teddy bear. How could he do that?

The idea of "superheroes" whizzed through her mind. But no, her parents insisted that the news stories were only publicity stunts by the city and the police department to make them look like they were tough on crime. Tori had never seen a superhero, but her experience with governmental agencies made her believe they'd say anything to look better to the public. Her parents were probably right. Zorro must be a bodybuilder or something.

"See if your ankle will hold your weight," he said, and he lowered her until her feet touched the sidewalk.

Tori put most of her weight on her good foot, the high-heeled shoe holding her four inches above her normal height of five feet seven. Her other ankle throbbed. She needed a minute to get used to the discomfort before she walked home. And it was an excuse to tilt her head back and examine her savior. Oh yeah, much taller than her dad. Gorgeous, deep-brown eyes. Tori couldn't tell if the warmth she experienced came from his hands around her waist, or something else.

The attraction intensified as they gazed into each other's eyes. She wanted more. They leaned closer. Contentment and peace stirred in her heart. He wouldn't let anything hurt her, she *knew* it. She couldn't explain it, but that didn't make it less true. The silence between them turned thick and warm. It wasn't sex on Tori's mind; it was that strange, confusing feeling of safety. Either way, it came down to the same thing—she wanted to be with him.

The thought of getting closer to the electrifying man before her filled Tori's mind until her body followed. She took a step toward him on her twisted ankle—and tripped yet again.

JOE LUNGED for the woman falling at his feet. At first, when he'd held her at arm's length, he'd focused on her features—soft lips, a slender nose, pretty eyes, and was that a velvet mole? He'd gotten distracted with her breasts...soft and plump and touchable, and pretty much falling out of her costume. She looked like the cover of a romance novel. He'd never read one, but he was pretty sure the men in those books got to touch what they were ogling.

But he felt that strange feeling inside expanding. It seemed to radiate out from his chest, similar to the way his super powers gathered just before he used them. He needed to protect this woman.

This woman.

Joe swallowed. Maybe it was something he ate, heartburn from onions. No, he'd eaten lasagna tonight. Freezer dinner. Never had heartburn from frozen lasagna.

Protect this woman.

Could it be something in his superhero blood that caused this reaction? He'd never felt anything like it before, never heard of anything like it. Wherever it came from, the feeling was powerful...and strangely peaceful. He felt stronger with her in his arms right now than he'd ever felt before. Which was ridiculous since he could stop a bullet with his bare skin, but there it was. Was there something about her that was reacting to his powers somehow?

Pirate Girl gazed up at him with a look of wonder of her face. She felt it, too.

Joe chuckled.

"What?"

He tried to hold in his laughter. "Uh...well, you look even more like a pirate now."

Pirate Girl looked down at her torn stockings, spots of blood on the white lace edging of her black satin skirt. She touched her blond wig to see if it was askew. A jaunty felt pirate's hat had been sewn onto the wig.

Joe wondered about her real hair color.

Her fingers found the eye patch still covering her forehead above her right eye. She pulled it down. "Aargh! Good thing you found the little devil before I did, or he'd be shark bait by now," she said in a ridiculous attempt at a pirate voice.

Joe laughed, and Pirate Girl laughed with him.

"I love Halloween," she said. "You can be anyone you want."

The wistful note in her voice hit Joe in the stomach. He'd never wanted to be anyone else. The Clarke family superheroes went back generations. What could be better than that?

"Who do you want to be?" he asked.

The wistfulness crept into her expression and, for a moment, Joe thought she looked sad. Then she said in a low voice, her eyes dropping to his chest, "I think maybe with you I could be...myself."

Joe's protective instincts shifted up a gear and he pulled her closer. He didn't know what to say. "So you'll be falling for me often then?"

She burst into laughter. He could swear she moved further into his embrace.

He grinned. Playing the hero had never been this much fun before. The superheroes in his family had protected Double Bay for years, and Joe took his role as a guardian of the city seriously. It could be hard, lonely work, but tonight...

Tonight, rescuing this woman gave him more than just satisfaction with his work. He loved her laugh, spontaneous, full of warmth and joy. Her smiled bewitched him. He felt as if all the problems of the world were manageable, as if he were more powerful when she smiled at him.

"You have to admit, you're having a lot of problems tonight," he said. "Should I call your keeper?" He wrapped his arms more firmly around her, and she didn't protest. He felt strong enough to stop a train.

Pirate Girl laughed again. "I really should have one."

Joe let one of his hands run slowly down her back, enjoying the feel of her relaxing in his arms. Really enjoying the feel of her breasts pressed against his chest. Wondering how long he could stretch out this rescue. An hour? All night? Every night?

"You need a job?"

Joe's hand stopped moving. Could she read his mind? The job of "keeper" or "keep her"?

"Well, I am a member of the neighborhood watch," he said. "I think I could handle it."

The mole on her cheek caught his attention as she asked, "We have a neighborhood watch?"

"We do," he said to the mole. He could tell now that it was one of those press-on velvet ones, but he liked it all the same. "Unfortunately, I'm the *only* member."

Joe raised his gaze to hers as she giggled again. She did that a lot. He didn't know what she found so amusing, but he liked it. Neither too high nor too low, it reminded him of sleigh bells. Bright, warm, festive. Perfect for this time of year.

"Oh, well," she said, heaving a sigh of mock disappointment. "I guess you better not quit then." She looked around the dilapidated neighborhood. "I think we need you here."

Joe followed the rise and fall of her breasts as she sighed. "Mmm-hmm," he said.

"Hey!" She slapped at his shoulder. "I saw that."

"Wha-at?" He grinned at her. It was hard to be serious when he felt so good. It brought out the tease in him, a skill he and his brothers had developed into an art form living with sisters. "You want help putting those back?"

She shifted in her one high-heeled shoe and pushed her body more firmly into his. Joe realized she was trying to hide her exposed flesh. Her little suede jacket wasn't helping. Women and their impractical clothes. But who was he to complain, especially now?

"Close your eyes," she ordered.

"It's hard to take you seriously when you're laughing," he said, causing her mock stern look to crumble into giggles before she attempted solemnity again.

"Close. Your. *Eyes.*"

Joe obeyed. His mother had raised him with good manners, but he wanted to sneak another peek. "Can I open them yet?"

She moved around in his arms, and he loosened them to give her more room to maneuver without falling again.

"Not yet."

He heard the laughter in her voice and it swirled around in his chest, warming him from the inside out. "Now?" he asked.

"No."

More movement. He could hear material sliding around, and the sound was doing things to his insides. "Now?" he asked, bringing his lusty thoughts in line before he embarrassed himself. "Now? Now?"

"O-*kay.*" She laughed and one arm slid around his neck again. "You must've been someone's little brother."

He opened his eyes and looked down. "Why do you say that?" Aw, she'd even fastened up her coat. It was one of those coats that buttoned to just over her breasts. Still a pleasant view, all creamy smooth skin.

She swatted his shoulder and gave one of those delicate female snorts, the kind that could've meant anything. "Because I have a little brother."

Joe was sure she was enjoying the evening as much as he was. Then she smiled at him again, and he wanted to climb Mount Rushmore, or fly to the moon, or just toss her into the air and spin her around until she was breathless with laughter.

He wondered if she felt the pull of attraction—or whatever it was—as acutely as he did. He thought about the word for a moment and discarded it. He'd been attracted to women before, and it was nothing like this. No, this was a different kind of connection.

Protect her.

The feeling was so compelling, it was as if he were hearing voices. He couldn't explain how or why. Looking at the girl in his arms, he didn't care what the explanation was, he was happy to do his job.

His right hand caressed Pirate Girl's cheek. She sighed and laid her head on his shoulder. He let his cheek rest against her hair for a moment, enjoying the scent of her, the feel of her. And at the same time, wanting to break away.

Joe didn't need complications right now—not blond, brunette, or red-headed. He wanted to work, and he didn't want anyone or anything to make him feel guilty about that. He didn't want to end up like his father, quitting because he had children.

Just one kiss, and then I'll walk away.

Joe leaned down and captured her cheeks in his hands, tilting her face up. Her gasp of surprise brushed against his lips as he kissed her. More surprising than his lack of impulse control was her reaction. After a moment's hesitation, Pirate Girl leaned into him, her hands on his chest, her lips moving with his.

Which only made it that much harder to stop.

Vaguely, Joe registered a dog barking a distant alarm. He ignored it and pulled Pirate Girl off the ground and up into his arms so he could kiss her more easily. Her hands wrapped around his neck, and she kissed him back with gusto.

Okay. Enough. Joe reminded himself of his duties and pulled back.

Pirate Girl blinked up at him, looking dazed. Then she smiled a dazzling smile.

Joe smiled back and gave her one last soft kiss before he lowered her to her feet. A burst of satisfaction spread through his chest.

She felt it, too.

It was one thing to feel safe and protected. It was something else entirely for the world to light up in brilliant colors from a kiss! Tori's perspective on the world changed. Like a crooked window made straight, now everything made sense.

That kiss... She wanted another one. The way he held her now, the way he was looking at her like he wanted to do it again, made her want more. She'd never instigated a kiss with a man in her life. But everything was changing tonight.

Rule #2—If you ignore Rule #1, phone a friend and *get out.*

Lexie had told her to call when she got safely home. Tori knew her sister would want her to call now, to *get* safely home.

But tonight she and Zorro were both costumed, disguised, hidden. Safe. This was the perfect time to act on Operation Freedom. For just one night, she could be herself with no repercussions. She could try out possibilities and see what *she* thought felt right.

Tori wobbled on one four-inch heel. She thought to take off her shoe, but she liked the idea that Zorro would catch her if she fell. Plus, her mouth was four inches closer to his. Taking a deep breath for courage, she leaned against him and slid her hands up to his neck, pulling him closer. If he resisted, she hoped the embarrassment would kill her on the spot. But his mouth came down on hers quickly and easily. Needing no more encouragement than that, Tori poured herself into the moment.

Zorro's lips moved against hers, setting off grass fires throughout her body. His hands swept hot paths up and down her back, her rib cage.

Tori imitated him, moving her lips over his, running her hands over his muscular chest and back. When his mouth opened, hers followed. When his tongue touched hers, she heard a moan escape. Nothing she'd ever experienced in her life could equal this!

She let Zorro lead, but followed his moves like a prodigy. After a moment, Tori tried a few moves of her own. His arms wrapped around her in response, pulling her against his chest and off her feet again. She heard him moan, and the sound rippled over her nerves.

Everything she felt tumbled around her brain without connection—hard, soft, warm, hot, more...

Zorro stopped kissing her. He rested his temple against hers, a ragged sigh escaping into her ear. The sound went straight through her, hitting every nerve all the way to her toes. Could she be wrong? Had he not enjoyed that as much as she had? More than anything, Tori wanted another kiss.

"What are we doing?" Zorro asked, his deep voice rumbling through his chest and into hers. His arms tightened around her.

Tori's senses heightened, waiting to see what he would do. She kept her eyes closed to enjoy this last bit of passion before it was over.

His forehead slid over hers, traced the path of his breath across her cheek, closer to her mouth, closer still, until—

The touch of his lips to hers was magic and fireworks and

s'mores all rolled together. His mouth and tongue fought a give and take with hers.

Rule #3—If you ignore Rule #1 and #2, don't let them see your true self.

Screw that.

She gave herself over to him, no more thinking and imitating. Tori just let go. Her fingers spread through the curls at the base of his neck, soft and silky. One hand caressed his neck, exploring upward to his cheek, smooth and soft and hard. Cupping both his cheeks, she lifted herself up as far as she could go, pulling his head down to put the last of herself into the kiss before she pulled away.

But she didn't know that more begat more. The kiss kept pulling her higher. Out of control.

Zorro pulled away, breathing hard. Tori felt bereft for a moment until he tucked her head under his chin and held her tight.

She didn't know what was happening. It wasn't just the kissing—though that was *awesome*. No, there was something deeper going on here. She shivered and pressed closer. She didn't want to leave him. She didn't want him to leave her. She wanted—

"Have you always been trouble?" he teased.

Tori sobered a bit. He had no idea. "Since the day I was born."

Rule #4—Pretend, pretend, pretend.

She couldn't do this to him. The "no men" rule had been created to protect her and Lexie from the world. They'd created a haven for themselves and it had worked exactly as it was meant to—they were alone and safe.

But even if this man, a man whose name she didn't know, even if he really could keep her safe... Well, she couldn't protect *him*. There was something odd about her sister and her, something that scared people when they found out about it. She didn't understand it, but she and Lexie were better off alone.

He sighed. "I guess I should get you home before you freeze."

Tori hid her face and her disappointment in the folds of his cape. "Of course."

"I'll carry you. Where do you live?"

He lowered her to the ground and, with a flourish, pulled off his cape and settled it around her shoulders. Tori bit her lip to keep from crying. She loved grand, romantic gestures. This would be the last one before he said goodbye.

Zorro tied the strings of the cape around her throat and adjusted the material. Tori swallowed when his fingers brushed her skin. His eyes met hers and his fingers stilled. His thumbs trailed down her throat.

She held her breath.

How could she act wisely when she didn't know which course of action was wise and which was foolish? The rules were for her protection, but Operation Freedom was about exploring what exactly God had in mind when he made her. She needed to know who she was outside of her family, outside of her psychiatrist's office, who she was on the inside.

Lord, give me a sign!

"There's something special about you," Zorro said softly, almost as if he were talking to himself.

Tori felt herself deflate. "Different," she said sadly. "Odd."

Zorro shook his head dismissively. "No, *special.* I'm not sure why, but..."

Tori held her breath. Hope battled fear. Joy began to overtake caution.

"Maybe you'd take a chance on someone like me," he said. "Maybe you'd let me see you again."

Maybe? Did dogs bark and cats meow?

"Yes!" Joy bubbled up from her toes and escaped in a wild giggle. But Zorro didn't seem to mind. He grinned back at her and pulled her close again, right where she wanted to be.

That safe, peaceful feeling overwhelmed her senses. The

connection between them strengthened. She not only felt that no harm would come to her when this man was near, but she was sure she wouldn't scare him off either.

She took a moment to think. No, she couldn't remember *ever* feeling this way before. Surely, it was a sign from God. It was all she could do not to bounce on her toes and clap her hands.

It felt like the weight of the world had been lifted from her shoulders. And not just because Zorro had lifted her off the ground again. He twirled her in a circle. Tori grinned and threw her arms around his neck.

Finally, someone I can be myself with. No more hiding.

A NOTE FROM KITTY

I hope you enjoyed reading *Superhero in Disguise*. This story always makes me smile! I originally wrote it as the beginning to *Unexpected Superhero* in the Adventures of Lewis and Clarke series. But introducing the two main characters on the day they met made the book feel like a romance, and I wanted more action. So I pulled the scene.

One day, it suddenly hit me what I'd been saying with this piece: we're all trying to find out who we are and who were we meant to be, and we'll discover along the way that there are forces at work around us to help and hinder our quest.

Once I figured that out (consciously, my subconscious already knew!), the edits to the newly titled *Superhero in Disguise* were made in just a few days. Exciting times for a writer!

My books are available as ebooks and in print at most online retailers. *Unexpected Superhero* and *Little Miss Lovesick* are also available as audiobooks. All the ebooks, print books, and audiobooks will be added to my own web store over the course of 2024. Purchases there support me and my work in a significantly greater way so I'd love it if you'd like to buy from me directly (kittybucholtz.com/books)!

You can also join my free or paid membership community over on Patreon (links at the end of About the Author). Read chapters early before the books even come out, discuss the stories with other readers, see fun art about the settings of the books, and more!

You might also try my romantic comedies in the Traverse City in Love series and the Strays of Loon Lake series. You can read *Cherry on Top* for free. It's set in the same town as *Little Miss Lovesick* during the famous National Cherry Festival. It's my gift to you when you join my reader newsletter at kittybucholtz.com/freebook.

If you really want to make my day, I'd love for you to post your thoughts about the book in a review. Thanks so much!

And just so you know, I rebranded all my books in 2024 to be "sweet" — so no swear words or overt sex scenes. I hope you enjoy the change.

Happy Reading!

A VERY MERRY SUPERHERO WEDDING

For Debra Holland and Brenna Aubrey,
and all my writing friends —
Thanks for helping me believe I could do it!

A VERY MERRY SUPERHERO WEDDING

Kitty Bucholtz

1

Two things always surprised Joe Clarke in December: the weather, and the people of Double Bay.

Some years the snow would start falling by Halloween. Thanksgiving would be a day to have a plan B in case you couldn't make it to Grandma's house due to blowing and drifting snow. And Christmas would be both beautiful and frustrating with every outing marred by icy roads and fresh piles of snow to clear off the car.

Other years, like this year, there were a few snow showers, but hardly any of the snow stuck to the ground. The ski slopes were covered with machine-made snow. Shopping and traveling were a breeze.

And tracking potential home invaders proved more difficult.

Ah, yes, the wonderful citizens of Double Bay constantly surprised him. The young man he tracked now — that is, that his alter ego Superhero X tracked — really put the "dumb" in dumbed down. Not only was he peeking in windows in the fading light of the afternoon rather than waiting for the full dark that would fall over the city by dinnertime, but he wasn't paying attention to the security signs.

This particular yard sported a bold red and white sign near the front door — MGV Security. The sign wasn't hidden by snow either. What, did the guy think it was a Christmas decoration? Superhero X shook his head and waited. When the young man took out a pocket knife and pried the screen off one of the windows, Superhero X moved closer and cleared his throat.

The man jumped and dropped his knife. His eyes widened as he looked up — way up — into the superhero's face. "Oh! I-I-I was just...I mean, I...I live here..."

X raised his eyebrows skeptically. "What's your address?"

"It's, uh, let me think, I just moved here and..." The man looked around the yard and at the other houses nearby, searching for a helpful clue.

Taking a long black zip tie from a pocket of his super suit, X gestured. "Hands."

The man sighed heavily and sagged against the siding. "You're not going to call the cops, are you?" He held out his hands. "I didn't take anything."

X tied the man's hands, then pressed a button on the wrist of his suit. "Superhero X to dispatch," he said. He gave the address, dispatch assured him that a police car would be there soon, then he marched the would-be Christmas thief to the sidewalk.

Pressing another button, he winced at the time. He'd have to hurry home to change after the police picked up the wannabe burglar. His fiancée, Tori Lewis, would be waiting for him — that is, for *Joe* — to pick her up from her last day at work. He didn't live far from here since this was his regular patrol neighborhood, but he still wanted to hurry.

Superhero X kept his facial expression impassive, but on the inside he could feel a grin. In five days, on Christmas Eve, he would finally marry the girl he rescued Halloween night. He could hardly wait.

Afraid a smile would break through and spoil his stern super-hero expression, he brought his mind back around to work. He pressed a different button on his wrist and recorded a message with the time, the date, and the address of the house that had been broken into. Someone at MGV Security would get the information and call the homeowner to make a report.

"Someone" who was not Joe Clarke. MGV Security was a real security firm, but it was also Joe's cover job. A cover job from which he was technically on vacation for the next two weeks. Owned and operated by Joe's friend and fellow superhero Mickey Valient, a.k.a. Tick Tock, MGV provided professional security services to all of its clients, but there were also more...*discreet*... services they provided the city.

A snowball whizzed overhead.

Superhero X turned to look down the sidewalk. Two boys around eight or ten years old stood frozen in their snow suits, mouths gaping. They'd collected what little snow was on their lawn and made a half dozen little snowballs, piled at their feet. X smiled and gave them a little salute. They whooped and jumped up and down. X grinned. He loved his job.

A Double Bay police car pulled up to the curb. Time to finish up work for the day and hightail it over to get his girl.

Tori Lewis felt butterflies square-dancing in her stomach. In a few minutes, she'd be off work to finish planning her wedding — and then she'd be away on her *honeymoon*. It almost didn't seem real.

For the last ten years or so, she had lived a quiet, semi-solitary life. Her mother Dixie and older sister Lexie were living proof that women in her family didn't make good choices when it came to men. Dixie's marriage to Tori's biological father had ended so badly that Dixie was still angry about it nearly twenty-five years later, even though her second marriage to Danny Lewis was filled with love and respect. Lexie had finally turned her life around a few years ago and found a "good" man to share it with. Then he broke it off and left when he found out she was pregnant. With those examples always on her mind, Tori had been afraid to chance the heartbreak and disaster she was sure would accompany a profession of love.

Until now.

There was something about Joe Clarke that called to a place deep within. It was like he'd opened a tiny door inside her, and Tori was finding all kinds of treasures — a joyful hope, love without worry, a peaceful sense of relief that she could let down her guard and relax and be herself.

With Joe, she felt safe in a way she never had before. Since Danny became her dad, he'd provided a sense of security when the world tumbled crazily around her, but then Joe came along and Tori felt like everything was finally going to be all right.

No, not just all right. *Beautiful.* Her life felt beautiful all of a sudden.

She shook her head a little as she filed the last of the papers on her desk. She was being silly, all head-in-the-clouds like a Disney princess. That's apparently what love did to people.

It wasn't the drugs. A niggling doubt squirmed in her head, trying to get her attention and ruin her day. No, it wasn't only that she wasn't taking her medications anymore. She'd started Operation Freedom in September. She'd been working toward finding her real self when she met Joe just after Halloween. He seemed so strong and sure of himself, it gave her strength to push forward and make new choices.

And when he proposed on Thanksgiving Day, Tori knew the time had come for Operation Freedom's grand finale. No more Dr. Huntington and his drugs. No more kowtowing to her mother.

Yes, she'd been feeling better since she stopped taking the pills, but that couldn't account for how she felt about Joe. From the moment they met, they'd had a connection that was...well, it defied explanation. They both felt like they really *knew* each other. In sync, on the same wavelength, whatever you wanted to call it. And it seemed to grow stronger every day.

Tori let her worries fade as she shut down her computer. It was almost five o'clock. Joe would be here any minute. They had one more quiet evening together before the final rush toward Christmas Eve and their wedding. Her stomach felt the butterfly gymnastics again and she let out a soft giggle.

This was real. She and Joe loved each other with an urgency and earnestness that made people fear they were merely infatuated with each other. But she knew — they both knew — it would last. They saw the world in similar ways. They believed in the same things. They'd prayed, together and individually, about the decision to get married. Waiting would only prove to others that they were ready. And they had nothing to prove.

"Oh, Tori," one of her co-workers singsonged nearby, "Someone's here to see you."

Tori's gaze flew to the doorway. There he stood. She sucked in a breath. His wavy brown hair was mussed, giving him a little boy look. So adorable. A knit cap stuck out of the pocket of his down-filled coat, and his scarf hung a foot longer on one side. Every time she saw him, he looked taller and more muscular than before. Every time she saw him, his smile made all of her nerve endings fire. Every time she saw him, she stopped breathing for a moment.

He grinned his lop-sided grin and chuckled. He always laughed when he saw her looking at him this way. Tori giggled and sighed. She knew he loved it, though. He'd told her no one had ever looked at him like she did.

Joe walked toward her and Tori felt a kind of tunnel vision come over her whole body. Every cell focused on him. And then he kissed her, and every cell burst out with a shout of joy.

Interrupted by the sound of laughter and clapping.

"Hello, beautiful," Joe whispered in her ear before he pulled away.

Tori felt her blood make a mad dash for her face. She'd never been so public in her displays of affection before Joe walked into her life. She'd been taking down Halloween decorations outside when he wandered by on a Sunday afternoon. They'd started talking and laughing and then they went for a walk together. Before she knew it, they were sharing a pizza. Then meeting again the next night, and the next.

And now here he was, staring down at her like he'd found a treasure he couldn't believe was his to keep. Tori realized she was grinning up at him only when more laughter and ribbing caught her attention.

She stepped back and said, "Let me get my stuff and I'll be ready."

"Not so fast, lovebirds," called her boss, Faith Borden. "We need to send you off in style."

Faith pulled out a foil-covered tray and another co-worker cleared a space on a worktable. As Faith pulled off the foil, all the ladies broke into the "Happy Birthday" tune but with the words "Happy Wedding to You." On the tray were homemade Christmas cookies, each with a letter in icing spelling out "Congratulations Tori & Joe!" M&M'S candies, Tori's favorite stress reliever, decorated the tops.

Tori laughed and squeezed Joe's hand before she reached over to hug Faith and the others.

"Thank you, Faith," she said as she squeezed the woman who'd become a new friend. "This is wonderful."

"Good heavens, lady," Faith said in an undertone, "When you said he was gorgeous, I thought you were using hyperbole like every other bride. He's stunning!" She giggled.

Several similar comments followed, all in whispers hidden by the hugs. One woman offered to babysit any time Tori was out of town. Tori laughed and shook her head.

She looked over her shoulder at Joe talking to Faith. It was fun to be the envy of all the women in the room, but she didn't care much what other people thought. She knew Joe was a good man, decent and kind and hard-working and funny. He'd made her laugh more in the last seven weeks than she could remember laughing in the last couple years.

And he made her feel safe. And strong. Kind of like the Zorro character who'd helped her on Halloween after she'd been mugged. Zorro had joked about being a superhero and Tori had laughed and said, there's no such thing as superheroes, it's an anti-crime publicity stunt by the city. He'd argued with her, presumably because he was staying in character as a defender of the defenseless, and Tori had argued back. The spark she'd felt that night seemed to lose some of its fire after that.

Then she'd met Joe two days later. At first, she thought maybe he was Zorro. But when she asked him, he laughed and said he was just an ordinary, everyday, average Joe. She'd thought that was funny. The more she got to know Joe, the less she thought about Zorro. The spark that night was nothing compared to the blazing fire that sprang up between her and Joe.

Studying him now, she knew nothing would ever put out that fire. Not the Lewis women's family curse. Not other people. Not time and old age. In five days, Joe's dad, Pastor Owen Clarke, would say the words, "What God has joined together, let no man separate." And that would be that.

For now, she needed to stop worrying that something would happen between today and Wednesday.

Joe caught her eye and nodded. She nodded back. Time to go. Tonight was the last night they would have alone together before they got married. Between the wedding and Christmas, it had been a busy month, and it would only get busier.

They said their goodbyes, Joe quickly accepted the rest of the cookies, and they made their way out to Joe's truck.

"They seem nice," Joe said. "Too bad you won't be working there again after the honeymoon."

"Yeah," Tori agreed, "I'd love to work for Faith. I hope her business grows enough that she can bring on permanent employees soon. Maybe I'll still be temping and she'll call me."

Tori smiled as Joe opened the truck door for her and handed her in. Such a gentleman.

"Are you sure you don't mind me temping for a while?" she asked when he climbed in the driver side. "I know I should probably get a real job, but I haven't found anything that makes me say, *this* is what I've been waiting my whole life to do. You know? I'm good with people. I'm a fast learner with tech stuff. But I haven't found a good mix yet. Maybe I should get a job at the Apple store," she joked.

Joe squeezed her hand as he pulled onto the street. "We'll manage," he said, "whatever you decide to do."

Tori smiled at Joe's profile. Good man, through and through. She sighed. She was so lucky. So *blessed*.

Joe took her left hand and kissed her ring finger near her engagement ring. He held her hand while he made a turn, then he said with a grin, "You're staring."

Tori giggled. "Where are we going? This isn't the way home." They only lived a few blocks away from each other, so they obviously weren't going to either place right now.

Tomorrow, Joe's friends were going to move her belongings into Joe's house, and she'd stay with Lexie starting tomorrow night. The whole "moving into his house" concept still seemed surreal. She wondered how long it would take before she'd be comfortable saying "our" house.

"It's our last night alone for a few days, so I thought we should enjoy it."

"Um, you remember we have stuff we have to do tonight, right?"

"We still have to eat." He nibbled on one of her fingers until she giggled.

"Yes, yes, all right." Tori pulled at her hand. "Focus on your driving, mister."

Joe drove another ten minutes and pulled into the parking lot of a steakhouse Tori knew he loved. Actually, she wasn't sure if a steakhouse existed that he wouldn't love. Barely half-full at this hour, the restaurant provided quick service and hot, delicious food.

When Joe was nearly done with his steak, he cut another bite and paused. "You know I couldn't love you any less than I do right now. You know that, right?"

Tori put down her fork and lay her hand on his. "I feel the same way. It's crazy how much I love you," she said, feeling her throat tighten. "I can't imagine my life without you now."

Joe appeared to consider her words.

"Are you worried..." Tori felt a spike of anxiety lance her heart. "Do you think we shouldn't..."

It took a moment for Joe to follow her unspoken question. "No!" His startled expression underscored the truth of his denial, and Tori relaxed.

"You still want to, right?" he asked. He put down his fork and squeezed her hand.

"Oh, yes!" Tori chuckled in relief.

"Okay, good. No, I was just thinking...I wanted you to know that even though we haven't known each other very long, there's nothing you could do or say to make me love you less." He looked a little worried again. "Whatever we may learn about each other in the future."

Tori tried to figure out what was going on in his head. Was there something he wanted to tell her? Something he was afraid she'd find out? Something...oh no, something he'd found out about her?

She tried not to pull away. He loved her. She knew it. He'd just said it again, promised his feelings wouldn't change. "Has someone said something?" she asked, trying to focus on breathing evenly. "Told you something about me?"

"Oh, honey, no," Joe's expression changed again, back to his protective look. "There is nothing anyone could say that would change how I feel. I was just thinking that we haven't known each other very long, and...things are bound to come up that may surprise the other, and..." He shrugged. "I'm sure it will all be fine."

Ah, she got it now. He was afraid she wouldn't like something she might find out about him. She tried to lighten the mood. "You mean like if I found out you like country music?"

He made a face. "That is never going to happen. Metallica all the way, baby."

He'd said things before about not liking country. Tori pushed his buttons. "Or if you found out I like country music?"

"Don't even joke about that."

"Would you still love me if you found out I own some Garth Brooks CDs? It's great road trip music. You'll love it."

"That's not funny." Joe put one hand on his chest. "You're killing me."

She giggled. "Rascal Flats, too."

"Stop, just stop." Joe's comical expression morphed into laughter and he kissed her knuckles before letting go of her hand and picking up his fork.

"You're not an ax murderer," she said with a smile. "You haven't bilked thousands of people out of their retirement money, right? I can't imagine finding out anything bad about you."

She meant it, too. Joe was the epitome of Mr. Nice Guy.

"Maybe you'll learn more about my job, wish I were in a different line of work." His voice sounded casual.

Tori tried to soothe his concerns, whatever they were. "You work in security, keeping people safe," she said. "What's not to like about that? I'm proud of you, Joe. You walk your talk. I haven't met a lot of people who can do that. You're my hero." She gave him a flirtatious look.

Joe smiled and took her hand again, pulling it against his cheek. "Like a superhero?"

"No, a *real* hero. Not a Saturday morning cartoon. You really help people when they need it. That's a wonderful thing. I'd like to find a job like that."

Until recently, Tori had worked with the single-minded goal of making enough money to help take care of her nephew. Temp jobs with few benefits paid more than the full-time jobs she'd looked into, and she could take time off if Ben was sick. But now that Lexie was on her feet, Tori could start thinking about what she wanted to do with her life, not what she had to do.

"Come on," Joe said in a teasing voice, "wouldn't you like to meet a real superhero?"

"Like Batman?" Tori laughed. "If I ran into Batman in our neighborhood, he'd scare the crap out of me! Really, if you'd never seen any of the movies to know he was a good guy, you'd take one look at him and assume it was all over. Pearly gates, here I come."

Joe chuckled and shook his head. "Maybe. But I think if you met a real superhero you'd know you were safe."

"*You're* the one who makes me feel safe," Tori said, pulling his hand to her lips and kissing it.

Joe looked like he was going to say something else, but the waiter interrupted to ask if they had room for dessert. Tori thought about the flourless chocolate cake she'd seen on the menu, but Joe told the waiter they'd pass.

"Eat too many cookies earlier?" she teased.

Joe raised his eyebrows a couple times. "You'll see. You want a to-go box?"

With the rest of her meal wrapped up, they put on their coats and gloves and hats and scarves. Even without much snow, the temperatures had dipped into the 20s every night not long after the sun went down.

Joe pulled her close as they walked to the truck. She loved his physical nature. His easy manner helped her to relax and allow herself to be a bit more demonstrative, in public and in private. She normally only let her guard down when she hung out with her siblings, especially with her little brother, Kevin. She'd spent so much energy over the years trying to please her mother, and staying away from men because they might ruin her life, she'd sort of lost herself. Hanging around Joe's excessively huggy family reminded her that she rather liked physical displays of affection.

She sighed happily.

Again Joe drove in a direction not toward home. He made a couple of turns into a residential neighborhood and hit the buttons to roll down the windows partway. What was he doing now?

Tori started to ask when she heard the Christmas music. She gasped in delight as Joe turned right and pulled into a long line of cars driving very slowly through the brightly lit street.

"Christmas lights?" She clapped her gloved hands. "That's one of my favorite parts of Christmas!"

2

Joe grinned. The colored lights from the outside decorations danced over Tori's face. Driving around looking at Christmas lights was one of his favorite parts of Christmas, too. The more he and Tori got to know each other, the more they found in common.

Keeping his foot on the brake, Joe reached behind the seat and pulled several things to the front: a blanket, a thermos, and a plastic food container. He tucked the blanket around Tori's lap, letting his hands linger at her hips. Then he opened the thermos and poured the steaming beverage into the lid-cup.

"Hot chocolate?" Tori asked, reaching for the cup.

"Starbucks hot chocolate. Your favorite, right?"

Tori nodded and sipped and grinned. She was about to say something else when he opened the lid on the plastic container. Her eyes widened as she looked in.

"Triple chocolate cheesecake with a mint chocolate ganache topping. For my lady," Joe said, handing her a plastic fork with a flourish.

"Oh my gosh," Tori gushed. "Where in the world did you find

something like this?" She scooped a bite onto her fork. "Oh, it's really cold! Mmm, but *awesome*."

Joe laughed. "I hope it didn't freeze in here while we were at dinner." He took a bite. Wow, delicious. "At least the mint flavor goes well with the cold."

The cars ahead of them moved slowly enough that Joe could drive with his knee while he shared the cheesecake with Tori. This neighborhood had some of the best Christmas decorations in Double Bay. The house they were now passing had a Santa Claus scene with the sleigh and reindeer on the roof, Santa's rear end sticking out of the chimney, and an air-filled snowman directing a choir of singing children on the lawn.

The next house had a nativity scene with animatronic characters. Baby Jesus was waving his hands at Mary who was stroking his head while Joseph nodded. A young boy played a drum in time to "The Little Drummer Boy" music while an animatronic ox and lamb kept time with their nodding heads. The three wise men turned their heads to each other and then raised their arms to point at the star on the roof. The star was magnificent — at least five feet tall and glowing with a pulsing rainbow of pale colors.

"I'd say these people know about Bronner's in Frankenmuth." Tori laughed. "Have you been there?"

"Not yet. Been meaning to check it out sometime."

Tori gasped. "You haven't been to the world's largest Christmas store, and it's only a few hours away?"

Joe pretended his own shock with a gasp. "I can't believe I haven't taken time off work to go Christmas shopping." He opened his mouth wide and covered it with his fingertips.

Tori laughed and pushed at his shoulder. "If we had time, I'd take you there this year. Trust me, we *are* going next year."

"Fine." He really had been meaning to visit Bronner's. Just hadn't gotten around to it. It would be fun to let Tori show him around. She'd probably light up like a Christmas tree herself.

Sometimes she was very quiet, like she was trying to burrow into herself and hide. But when something caught her attention that she felt was important or that she had a strong opinion about, this vibrant woman appeared. That's what she was like when he met her on Halloween night. She was strong, tough, beautiful, and funny. He was smitten from the start.

If only she didn't have such strong feelings against super-heroes. He wanted to find a way to change her mind tonight without spoiling the mood. How could he explain to her that she already knew and loved a superhero? More than one, in fact, though he couldn't tell other peoples' secrets.

They drove past a couple more houses decorated with enough lights and decorations for most entire neighborhoods. "I don't even want to think about their electric bill," Joe said, shaking his head. "Just so you know, I'm not ever planning on doing this to our house. We'll just drive over here every year to look."

Tori chuckled and patted his hand. "We'll see."

The next house had a giant air-filled purple menorah in the center of the front lawn. A polar bear dressed in a sweater and knit cap played with a dreidel. Two more bears held a sign that read "Happy Hanukkah." More menorahs shone inside the windows. A wreath shaped like the Star of David decorated the front door.

Next came Joe's favorite house, and the reason for all of the slow-moving traffic. A light show flashed across the lawn, the garage door, and the roof with a loud upbeat mix of holiday songs playing along. The trees flashed on and off in time to the music, and different holiday greetings lit up on the roof and garage, flashing in a lively beat.

Tori laughed and watched the display for a couple minutes until they moved on. "I can't imagine how much work that must be, but I love it!"

She unfastened her seat belt and scooted into the middle of

the truck's bench seat, snuggling up next to Joe. Putting one hand on his chin, she leaned over and kissed his cheek with a loud squeaking sound.

"You are the best, Joe Clarke. Thank you for all of this." She cuddled into his side as he put his arm around her shoulders. "This is the best last date I can imagine."

Joe chuckled and kissed the top of her head. "I'm glad you like it. But just because we're getting married doesn't mean we aren't going to do stuff like this anymore."

"Good to know," Tori said, eating the last bite of cheesecake. "If being married to you is at all like dating you, I'm going to be a very happy girl." She licked her fork. "Fat, but happy."

Joe laughed and kissed her. He wanted to kiss her more, but he couldn't while he was driving. Home. They should go home soon. While he was considering the relative merits of cutting short their night out, he noticed a furtive movement. A dark-clad figure stood in the shadows outside the house on the right. Joe braked as he'd done in front of other houses they'd admired.

No. Not now. What would he tell Tori? *I need to run out for a minute. Will you get behind the wheel and keep following this line of cars? I'll catch up to you as soon as I can.*

Right. And then when she pressed for an explanation? *I've been meaning to tell you, I'm a superhero. Kind of heir to the leadership, too. Even though you don't believe in superheroes, you're still going to marry me, right?*

Joe watched the punk, willing him not to do anything stupid. How did these guys think they could get away with breaking into houses with people around?

He squeezed Tori tighter. The bigger question might be, how did he think he could continue to keep his secret from her when they were married and living in the same house? He'd promised his parents he would tell Tori before the wedding. Surely she would believe he was one of the good guys, not a poser.

In Joe's superhero vernacular, those people were called

Pretenders, and there were plenty of them. The colloquial "super-hero" came from comic books, but people with powers had been called Paladins for thousands of years. Unless, of course, they used their powers for anything other than the protection of the human race.

While Joe didn't believe "villain" was a fair descriptor of many of those people, he was a product of his generation and tended to use the word too freely. Especially since he knew there were some truly nasty villains around, most notably The Nine. Thankfully, the one member of The Nine who had lived in Double Bay died a couple years back. The city became a much better place after his passing.

But this was the problem: as he tried to explain himself and his abilities, Tori would likely have more and more questions, and he'd have to explain about the history of the Paladins, try to explain why so many people didn't know they existed, reassure her that their life would be pretty normal. She'd just have to accept that his job might be similar to that of a police officer or a government agent with him coming and going at all hours, in and out of danger, mostly working undercover.

And then she would ask about their children.

Joe shook his head slightly and kissed the top of her head. He couldn't tell her before the wedding. As determined as he'd been only a few months ago not to settle down too quickly, now all he wanted was a permanent tie to the woman in his arms. When they were married, he'd figure out a way to explain everything so that she would understand. He hoped, in fact, that she would embrace the challenges like his mother had, that she would partner with him as part of his support system. His mom could help show Tori what to do.

If he were so certain it would all work out — Joe could hear his dad's voice in his head — then he would tell her now. In fact, he would have told her before he proposed.

Another figure crept out of the darkness from behind the

house Joe was watching. Great. What should he do? He couldn't run out as Joe and confront them. As he watched in indecision, the pair clasped hands and ran hunched over under the cover of trees, then walked sedately out to the sidewalk in front of the house next door. The first one opened the passenger door of a parked car, kissed the second one, and went around to the other side.

Teenagers. He should've known.

Joe decided to put his dilemma out of his head and enjoy his last date night with his bride-to-be. They spent another hour wandering around looking at Christmas lights. Then Tori made him laugh as she took a few selfies of them both and posted them to Facebook and Instagram. Eventually he turned his truck for home.

Their own neighborhood certainly looked different from the ones they'd been driving around. The asphalt on the street was buckled and cracked. Half of the streetlights didn't work. There were Christmas lights along the roof eaves on many houses, but no expensive decorations on the lawns. Too easily stolen. The windows of many of the older houses were covered in heavy plastic to keep out the cold.

Joe had spent the money to put double-paned windows in his house before his first winter there, but he still needed to put better insulation in the walls. The city gave him the abandoned house two years ago on the condition that he live there under-cover, patrolling the neighborhood as Superhero X. City officials wanted to test the theory that crime would drop in areas with more adjunct patrols. Of course, "undercover" meant not standing out, which meant not spending lots of money, so Joe still had a long list of home improvements he wanted to tackle.

Coming from a long line of superheroes who had saved and invested so that family members who wanted to work full-time had something to live on, Joe could afford a nicer house. But he and his team wanted the new Superhero Liaison Unit of the

Double Bay Police Department to thrive and produce results so that the temporary unit would become permanent. They were willing to accept the city's terms, hoping that as they proved themselves, superheroes would be allowed to work more and more with the police. Including undercover work with the SLU.

He pulled into his driveway and shut off the truck. He'd turned on his porch light and Christmas lights before he left to pick up Tori so that they wouldn't return to a dark house. Looking at the place now, after touring those other areas, he decided he'd let Tori convince him to buy a few more decorations next year. They sat quietly for a moment, enjoying the lights of home.

"I like these icicle lights the best," she said. "It's funny how similar our tastes are. I don't think that's ever happened to me before." She chuckled. "Not that I've dated that much. Before I met you, I had grand plans for a full life as a single woman."

Joe grunted in agreement. "You and me both." Then he looked down at her. "Well, not the woman part."

Tori laughed up at him.

God, I love her so much. Please don't let me mess it up.

Joe leaned down slowly and placed a kiss on her lips, filled with all the promises he wanted to make. What if it wasn't enough to *want* to be a good husband, a good friend? What if he should have — but hadn't — learned an essential relational principle vital for building a great life?

He was beginning to see what his dad was getting at during the very little pre-marriage counseling Joe had agreed to. He and Tori had a lot to learn about being husband and wife, and not knowing each other very well would make the whole process more difficult.

But the loving part would be easy. He pulled back from the kiss, feeling himself get carried away. Five more days. It was only five more days, and Tori said she wanted to wait. Good thing it was already getting cold in the truck.

"We should probably go inside," he said. At the look on her face, he added, "To move things around and make room for your stuff."

"Soon," she said in answer to what they left unspoken.

Joe kissed her forehead and opened his door, welcoming the icy blast against his face. This was going to be the longest five days of his life.

Tori awoke slowly the next morning. She couldn't remember what she'd been dreaming about, but she remembered being happy. She stretched a little and then opened her eyes with a start. This wasn't her bed.

She looked around her former bedroom in Lexie's apartment. Oh, right. She grinned into her pillow. When she and Joe got to his house last night, they needed something to keep their minds off what they wanted to do to each other. Joe's newly-adopted cat, Snickers, a former stray he had been feeding for months, wandered in from the living room demanding attention, food, and more attention.

Tori had teased Joe about the smell of cleaning products in his house, something she'd never noticed before. He stuttered for a moment before admitting he'd hired a cleaning service. He wanted the house to be as perfect as possible before she moved in. That had seemed a good segue into their task for the evening — moving furniture around and rearranging the closets to make space for Tori's belongings. Since she didn't have much — she'd only moved into her tiny studio apartment a few days before she met Joe — they were able to complete their task relatively quickly.

With nothing else that had to be done, she and Joe had cuddled in front of the fire to watch "A Charlie Brown Christmas" and "Dr. Seuss' How the Grinch Stole Christmas." But the stolen kisses during commercial breaks had morphed into stolen moments to watch favorite scenes from the shows in between kisses. And more than kisses.

Tori had called a halt to the progression, but Joe was already moving away before she finished her sentence so it must've been on his mind as well. When he took her home, the kissing goodbye part had become never-ending. Finally, she'd told Joe to give her a minute, she put together an overnight bag, and she'd directed him to take her to Lexie's. Nothing could happen there, not with her sister and nephew around. If it wasn't for the fact that their wedding was mere days away, Tori didn't think she or Joe would've been able to stop.

She grinned again. The anticipation was about killing her, but she knew it would be worth it. Only four more days and four more nights. She giggled. Yes, it was definitely a good thing she'd be sleeping at Lexie's for the next four nights. Then it would be her and Joe and a big bed at Disney's Grand Floridian Resort in Orlando.

Her musings were cut short by the sound of the door opening. A high-pitched shriek barely preceded the sound of tiny running feet. Tori looked over to see Lexie grinning at her three-year-old son. Ben launched himself into Tori's waiting arms. She kissed him all over his face and head, the only parts besides his hands not covered in yellow fleece footy pajamas.

When he'd had enough, he sat up and began to tell her all about the last couple days of his life, everything she'd missed since she'd last seen him. Tori nodded and agreed that it all sounded very exciting. She only caught a few actual details — something about a dog and a soccer ball, and she was pretty sure he'd had pizza last night for dinner.

Lexie finally interrupted. "Let Aunt Tori get up, Ben. Come on, time for breakfast."

Ben jumped off the bed with a thud. "Pop Tarts, please?" he asked, running to his mother.

"Oh, so now you use your sentences." Lexie rolled her eyes at Tori. "Mom and Dad will be here at 9:30. Dad's taking Ben, and Mom's driving with us. Yay," she said with forced enthusiasm.

"We're going to have a fun day," Tori said. "What's not to love about trying on wedding dresses?"

Despite the fact that their mother Dixie loved them and did a lot for all three of them, she also could be a pain in the patootie. Nonetheless, Tori was determined not to fight with her mother this week, not a big fight anyway. Dixie had made it clear that she didn't approve of Tori's "hasty" wedding, but she was at least trying to come to terms with it.

They were almost ready when their parents knocked at 9:25. Lexie had Ben's shirt halfway on when he slipped away and ran to the front door as Tori opened it. Her dad Danny scooped up the toddler and motioned for his wife to precede him inside.

"There's my boy!" Danny said, jiggling a half-naked Ben in his arms. "Guess who gets to spend the day with Pop-pop?"

"Ben and Pop-pop," Ben squealed, clapping his hands.

"Give Grandma a kiss," Danny told him, handing the boy over.

Dixie cooed over him while she walked over to Lexie and the rest of Ben's clothes. "You need to be an octopus to dress them at this age," she said to Lexie. "Can I help?"

Tori saw Lexie smile as she kissed Dixie hello. Whew. Looked like the day would go smoother than most.

Danny met her gaze and winked at her. "We're all going to play nice today," he whispered in her ear as he gave her a bear hug.

"Thanks, Dad," Tori whispered back. "I knew I could count on you."

"Now I'm not trying to start anything myself," he said quietly so that only Tori could hear him, "but just because you're doing the final fitting on your dress today doesn't mean you can't get off the train. I've got a shotgun in the car. I can whisk you away anytime you want."

Tori laughed. "You don't own a shotgun. And I'm not getting off the train, but thanks for asking."

"I rented one for your wedding. And you've got until the final 'I do' to change your mind." He held up his hand as Tori started to interrupt. "I'm not trying to stop the wedding, but these things can take on a life of their own and make you feel like you don't have any choices left. I just want to be sure you know that you *do* still have a choice. Humor me and say, 'Yes, Dad.'"

Tori grinned and hugged him again. "Yes, Daddy. Thank you. I'll let you know if you need the gun, okay?"

Danny kissed her forehead and shook his head. "Where's my little girl gone?"

"She hasn't gone anywhere," she said with an affectionate smile. "She's just adding someone new to the family."

"He seems nice enough, I guess. I'm not sure if he's good enough for you, but—"

"Okay, time to go," Tori interrupted, pushing away from her dad. She grabbed her purse, a duffle with the clothes she would change into for tonight's bachelorette party, and her wedding shoes to wear at the dress fitting. She pointed to a box of little gifts and prizes Lexie had wrapped for the bridal shower games, and Danny took it out to Lexie's car.

A fresh dusting of new snow covered the ground and cars. Just enough to be beautiful and make it feel like Christmas. Perfect.

Dixie carried Ben outside, kissing his cheeks and making him giggle. "Honey, don't go to the mall with Ben, okay?" She handed Ben to her husband to buckle into the child seat.

"Why not?" Tori asked. "They have a S-A-N-T-A playground there that will keep him happy for an hour, at least."

"Haven't you heard about the ring of thieves targeting mall

shoppers? It's just horrible. Breaking into cars, holding people up at gunpoint."

"I'm not sure there were any guns, honey," Danny said in a reassuring voice.

Dixie gave him "the look" and Tori watched her dad back down.

"But I promise, we won't go to the mall today," he said. He kissed her and turned her around toward Lexie's car. "Now go have fun. The men can take care of themselves."

Tori smiled at the exchange and opened the car door for her mom. Soon everyone was in the correct vehicle with the things they needed — Lexie almost forgot to give Danny the diaper bag — and off they went. Tori suddenly felt that surreal feeling come over her, like you wondered if you were dreaming or inside a movie or something. A movie dream where you got to be the bride.

Thank you, God, she said in her head. *Please let the rest of this week be filled with love and laughter and no arguing.*

An hour later, Tori stood on a dais looking at herself from half a dozen mirrored angles. Her breath caught in her throat. Today she saw herself in a way she never had before — beautiful. She caught her mother's eye. Dixie's chin trembled as she tried to restrain her tears. Then she gave it up.

"It's my blood right to cry when my babies get married," she said as she wiped at her cheeks. She sniffled and thanked the shop attendant when she handed Dixie a box of tissues.

Lexie walked out in her bridesmaid's dress. She stopped suddenly when she saw Tori. "Oh, Tori, you're stunning!"

Tori smiled at her sister and glanced back in the mirrors. The white satin dress had clean, simple lines, cap sleeves, and a sweetheart neckline. Delicate lace fell from her waist partway down the skirt. The train trailed just a foot or two behind her.

She looked like a princess.

Joe was going to love this.

Tori's best friend, Hayley Addison, walked out in her brides-maid's dress and stopped in her tracks. "Oh my gosh! Tori!"

Tori giggled. "This dress is a show-stopper, isn't it?"

"No." Hayley, generally full of something to say, paused as if looking for the right words. "*You* are the show-stopper."

Tori felt her eyes well up.

"She's right," Dixie said. And her face and tone conveyed that motherly love and pride that Tori so often longed for more of.

She stared at her mother in the mirror, smiling at her. This was one of those moments she needed to remember and cherish forever, especially when times were tough. "I love you, Mom." Tears rolled down her cheeks.

Suddenly all of the women jumped toward the dais.

"Don't let the tears fall on the dress!"

"The satin will stain!"

"Hand her the tissues!"

The box was shoved into her hands, but the woman doing the alterations had already pressed a linen handkerchief against Tori's cheeks. Tori took it and wiped her eyes, laughing at the attention. She glanced at the hanky. *Congratulations from everyone at Princess Bridal.*

"We had them made up for moments like this," the woman said.

Tori laughed. "Can my mom have one?" Dixie loved to collect little mementos from her children's milestones.

Dixie stepped onto the dais and took the hanky from Tori's hand, giving her the fresh one. She hugged her daughter tight. "I want to keep the one with my baby girl's happy tears on it, okay?"

"Oh, Mom," Tori said. Then they both laughed and cried at the same time, and everyone went crazy to protect her dress.

Hayley came to the rescue as she always had over the years. She called out orders and made jokes and helped push yet another emotional crisis behind them. Tori appreciated it. But this was one emotional crisis she would treasure.

3

"Even though a certain Grandma is being silly," Danny said to the toddler in the back seat, "we'll keep our word and avoid the mall. However, we're still going Christmas shopping. I bet you've done about as much shopping as I have, right buddy?"

Ben stared at Danny in the mirror, then turned away to look out the window.

"Just as I thought," Danny said, hitting his turn signal. "It's only the twentieth. We have five whole days before Christmas. I bet we can get everything we need today. Men are good like that." He turned into the bank parking lot and pulled into a space on the side near the ATM. "You stay here, I'll be right back."

Even though he didn't worry about being robbed at the mall — he wasn't a small man and felt confident he could take care of himself — he was always extra careful with his grandson. He took his keys and locked the car. At the ATM, he turned to wave at Ben. No tantrums, good. That's one of the things he liked about his grandson.

Danny opened his wallet and pulled out his ATM card.

Before he could slide it into the machine, he heard someone else walk up. He turned to see a young man in a dark coat, dark knit cap, and gloves walking toward him. It wasn't cold enough outside for anyone to need their collar pulled up around their face.

He smiled and nodded at the man, and turned back to his car. "Wrong card," he said.

From behind him, another voice said, "Why don't you try it anyway?" Someone pushed him roughly toward the ATM.

Danny turned to look at the new guy and weighed his options. This fella looked like he was up for a fight. While Danny considered how to best land his punches, the new guy opened up a switchblade knife. The odds shifted further out of his favor.

Danny forced himself not to look toward Ben. They might get his money, but he wouldn't give them his keys, not even at knifepoint.

He decided to play the scared older guy. He let his hands shake and dropped his card. "You take it," he said, "I don't want any trouble."

He backed up a step toward the first man, purposely landing hard on the guy's instep. The man cursed and shoved him. Danny let himself be propelled farther away from the ATM. Now how could he reach for his keys and get into his car before they overpowered him?

The second man lunged for Danny and shoved him hard toward the cash machine. "Withdraw four hundred dollars. Now." He held the knife near Danny's face and pushed the card into the machine.

Unfortunately, this guy seemed to know exactly what he was doing. Fine, maybe they'd leave with the money, and he and Ben could go safely home. Where he'd pour himself a stiff drink perhaps.

Danny looked around for cameras, police cars, other people,

any distraction. Seeing only the dark glass that likely covered the bank's hidden camera, he made a point of looking fully into the glass for a moment. If the worst happened, at least the police would be able to identify him.

"Enter your PIN."

Danny typed it in wrong, buying time. Surely the bank parking lot had some kind of security service doing rounds. He remembered to make his hands shake, which wasn't too hard. "You've got me all flustered."

"You don't look like the easily flustered type," the leader said harshly. "Do it right, or you'll have a scar to remember and I'll take your car."

Danny's heart froze.

"Yeah, I saw the kid. Now enter your PIN!"

His hands shaking for real, Danny carefully entered the correct number. He pushed the button for Withdrawal and then the one for Checking Account. He was about to reassure the leader that he would withdraw the maximum amount when a third voice spoke up.

"Didn't your mother ever tell you not to play with knives?"

Danny looked up in surprise. A massive hulk of a man stood calmly to one side, his arms folded over his chest. He wore an outfit that could've come out of one of the *X-Men* movies. Something disguised his voice so that it had a metallic sound.

The man's expression flickered for a moment as he glanced at Danny, as if he were surprised. Then his focus returned to the man with the knife.

Danny heard the other robber stutter and turn to run. A cheerful man's voice said, "Not so fast." Danny turned to see another strangely costumed man stretch out his leg and trip the robber.

Danny blinked hard. What...?

The robber got up to run again, but the costumed man stretched out his arm — yes, he was seeing what he thought he was seeing — the man stretched his arm at least four feet and grabbed the robber's collar. Then he stretched his leg out — several feet longer than should've been possible — and tripped the fella again. All without moving from where he stood.

Like Danny, the knife-wielding robber just stood and stared.

The big man moved forward to grab the leader. The leader turned quickly, bringing the knife in low and fast.

"Watch it!" Danny called.

But the big man didn't move. The knife hit him squarely in the stomach...and didn't sink in. Did the man have Kevlar in his outfit?

Before Danny could understand what was happening, the two costumed men had shoved the two robbers against a post, back-to-back, and zip-tied their hands together. The big guy took the switchblade knife and hit the button to send the knife back into the handle with a click. Then he grabbed both ends of the knife and twisted his hands down.

Danny gaped. The man had bent the knife at a thirty-degree angle. With his bare hands.

"Who *are* you?" Danny heard his voice crack.

"Stretch and Superhero X, at your service." The wiry man who could move in unnatural ways bowed and grinned. He extended his hand and Danny numbly reached forward to shake it. It felt like a normal hand.

"Show off," muttered the big guy. "Your card is still in the ATM, sir. Did they get anything from you? Hurt you in any way? The police will be here soon. You'll need to stay and make a report. You can wait in your car with the doors locked, if you like. We'll wait here until the officers arrive."

Danny nodded and hit the buttons on the machine to get his card back. When he turned, he saw the big man leaning over and looking in the window of his car. The man's fingers squeezed together twice, imitating Ben's childish wave from inside. Danny saw the man smile, and Ben shrieked with laughter, kicking his legs against his car seat and reaching toward the window.

The man stood up, saw Danny watching, and cleared his throat, wiping any expression from his face.

"I-I don't understand," he said to the big man. He turned to the other guy. "Who are you again?"

Both men's costumes covered a good deal of their faces. All he could see was a strong white chin on the big guy, and an angular black chin on the wiry fella. The man who called himself Stretch didn't disguise his voice. Maybe Danny could pick it out again later if he needed to. Despite the fact that he practiced real estate law and had never dealt with criminal cases, his attorney instincts were running high. But he had very little to go on if he ever wanted to describe these two to the authorities.

"We work with the police, sir," said the big one. He turned aside slightly and didn't meet Danny's intent gaze. "Ah, here they are now."

Did the man sound relieved? Why would that be? *How* did they work with the police? And where had they come from? Who were these men?

The lawyer-like questions ran through his mind, but inside Danny had known the truth minutes ago. Despite all Dixie's insistence over the years that there was no way, these men were... well, he didn't know another word.

Superheroes.

It was true.

He'd held onto disbelief all these years because it would upset his wife if he allowed himself to wonder aloud. If he didn't believe in superheroes — or super villains — then his daughters had never been in danger, would never be in that kind of danger.

But now...

Danny shook his head as he tried to focus on the policeman now standing in front of him. "What?"

The officer pointed to Danny's car. "Why don't you turn on

the engine before your son gets too cold," he suggested. "I can question you over there."

Danny did as he was asked, turning the heat to high, and reaching into the back seat to reassure himself that Ben was fine. He turned back to the policeman and looked around for the...superheroes.

But they'd disappeared.

4

With all of the dress alterations approved, the women piled into their cars and drove to the church. Tori used to think of it as Joe's church, or Pastor Owen's, but she had recently started attending with Joe, so she supposed it was her church now, too. Hannah, Joe's mom, had asked to host the bridal shower there since so many people were expected.

The "so many people" part kind of freaked Tori out, but she wasn't allowed much of a voice. Both mothers, her sister, and her best friend had worked together planning the party, and Tori had been told in no uncertain terms that the guest of honor didn't get a say. In fact, there would be even more people than might otherwise be expected due to family from both sides visiting from out of town for the holidays.

Tori led the way downstairs to the fellowship hall in the basement. When she came around the corner, her younger sister Sam yelled, "Surprise!" and flung her arms out to show Tori the decorated room. It looked amazing.

Pale green and white streamers dipped and curled from one end of the ceiling to the other. Twinkling white Christmas lights added a magical feel. Red silk roses decorated the tables in glass vases filled with green beads. The tables were covered with an alternating pattern of red and green Christmas tablecloths, and white tablecloths with silver doves and wedding bells.

An enormous amount of food covered several tables — pans over burning Sternos for hot dishes, bowls of salads and pastas, a full table of desserts. Tori could see half a dozen women bustling about the church kitchen preparing more food.

"Wow," was all she could say.

"Do you like it?" Sam asked, giving her a hug.

"Sam headed the decorating committee," Lexie said, giving their little sister an affectionate squeeze.

"I love it," Tori said, still staring around the room. She looked closer at the nearest table — yes, little bowls of red and green M&M'S sat on each table. She grinned. Her sisters knew her well.

She noticed little Christmas trees on some of the tables, each topped with a pair of tiny white doves.

"The Christmas trees are from Hayley's nursery," Sam told her. "She decorated all of them herself."

"Hayley," Tori exclaimed, giving her best friend a hug, "they're beautiful."

"And they double as game prizes," Hayley said. "Lex thought people might like them."

"What I *said*," Lexie interrupted, "was that people would *love* them."

Tori let Sam take her coat while people pulled her farther into the room. There were dozens of people there, many of whom Tori was pretty sure she didn't know.

Hannah rushed over and hugged everyone, giving Tori a teary-eyed squeeze. "I can hardly believe you're going to be my new daughter in a few days." Then she hugged Dixie, took them both by the arm, and promised to introduce them to all of the women on Joe's side of the family. "Don't worry, there won't be a quiz."

A few of them, Tori had already met. Joe's twin sisters, Gwen and Daphne, and his youngest sister Melissa, who was a year younger than Sam, had been at Thanksgiving dinner and had gushed over Joe's unexpected proposal.

Then there were Joe's sisters-in-law, Brenda and Amy, and their young daughters, Katie and Ashley. There were several aunts and a boatload of cousins. Wow, and these were just the female relatives! How many people was Joe related to?

"These two darlings," Hannah hugged Katie and Ashley to her sides, "volunteered to play with the children in the Sunday School room after we eat. That way whatever happens in here, stays amongst us adults." Hannah winked at Tori.

Before Tori could decide if she should be worried about what exactly was going to happen, what could only be described as a small white whirlwind rushed over from the kitchen. An older woman, who could have been a stand-in for Olympia Dukakis, embraced Tori with exuberance. She stood back, hands gripping Tori's shoulders, and appraised her from head to toe.

"This must be my new granddaughter, Victoria!" the woman declared. She gave Tori another bear hug.

Tori tried to keep a friendly smile on her face, but she'd already been feeling a bit overwhelmed from the onslaught of familial attention. This new attack threatened to push her over the edge. In her own family, she was the quiet one. People were generally friendly, but mostly they thought she and Lexie were a bit odd, so they didn't engage them in long conversations.

Or long hugs. The white-haired woman appeared to be coming at her again.

"Millie, stop." Hannah laughed. "You're scaring the poor girl. Tori, Dixie, I'd like to introduce Millie Clarke, Owen's mom and Joe's grandmother. And the most fun mother-in-law in the world."

Millie grabbed Dixie for a quick hug, eliciting an "Oh! Hello!" from Dixie, then she turned back to Tori. "You can call me Nana," she said firmly. "All the grandkids do. I think it's destiny that

Jonas is marrying a girl named for victory." She leaned in closer and continued in a conspiratorial stage whisper. "Since he's—"

"You're favorite," Hannah interrupted with a laugh. "Yes, yes, we know."

Millie glanced up at Hannah and Tori saw something pass between them. "Yes, my favorite." She turned back to Tori. "I know I shouldn't pick favorites, but..." She shrugged.

"Is everything ready?" Hannah asked.

The whirlwind rushed around the room, Lexie was given a microphone and she and Hayley welcomed everyone, then people lined up to eat lunch before the games began.

Tori was pulled to the front of the line. She looked for someone safe to grab onto. Her friends Liz and Gabrielle stood nearby. "Liz! Gabe!" she gushed as she hugged them hello. "I'm so glad you came." In an undertone, she said, "Stand with me. I'm freaking out at all the attention."

They laughed and the three of them grabbed plates, oohing and ahhing over the delicious-smelling dishes.

Liz leaned close and said in a low, excited voice, "So tell us, what's the fuss with the rushed wedding? Are we planning a baby shower soon, too?" She giggled.

Gabe spoke up before Tori could reply. "I saw the pictures you posted on Facebook last night. Dang, girl, he's *hot*. No one would be blaming you for saying yes to that."

Tori felt herself blush. It was one thing to be teased by your friends, but another thing entirely when family might be listening. "No! I'm not — I haven't — we're getting married because we *want* to."

"Well, who wouldn't want to marry that hunk," Liz said, putting a couple of hot wings on her plate. "But you just met him, didn't you?"

"Oh!" exclaimed Gabe. "Unless you have been secretly dating him for months and didn't want anyone to know. That would be so romantic." She sighed theatrically.

Tori laughed, and moved to the desserts table, out of earshot of family. "No, no secrets." Well, not the kind they were talking about anyway. She hadn't told Joe about the shrink and the meds and the years of being thought of as a bit of a freak. But she had put all that behind her, so there was no reason to tell him. Not until they were old and gray and he was so far beyond in love with her that it wouldn't matter.

She took a big breath. She wanted to tell someone and have them understand. Her family wasn't really listening. "You know those stories about love at first sight?" She looked at both of her romance-minded friends, willing them to believe her and understand and be happy for her. "It was kind of like that, but it took a few hours rather than a few moments." She giggled. "It was love at first date, I guess, since we eventually ate dinner together."

Gabe got a mushy look on her face. "Aww. That's so adorable."

"It is adorable," agreed Liz. She looked over her shoulder. "So why do I feel like it's a secret?"

"You know my family. They're very practical and..." She searched for a word. "Careful. Mom says if I'm so sure I'm in love with him, I'll still be in love with him next summer and I should get married then." She worked hard not to let any bitterness creep into her voice.

"Parents." Liz shook her head. "They seriously need to relax."

"And remember what it was like to be young and in love," Gabe added. "They must've been young and in love once."

The girls giggled together and started to sit down to eat. But Hayley came over and apologized and said the bride had to sit at the middle table where everyone could see her.

Tori looked out over the crowded room.

Hayley squeezed her shoulder and picked up her plate. "You'll be fine," she said, understanding. "I'm sitting on one side of you and Lexie will be on the other. Come on."

"This is why we're having a small wedding," she said. "So I don't have to stand up in front of crowds of people."

"Well, you still aren't," Gabe said, chuckling. "You'll be sitting. Not so bad. We'll cheer you on from here."

Tori smiled at her friends and let Hayley pull her away. She began to relax a little as everyone sat down to eat and talk amongst themselves. "You all really outdid yourselves," she said to her sisters, both mothers, and Hayley, all seated with her. "Thank you so much."

Sam giggled. "Just wait until the games begin." She had an impish look Tori hadn't seen in awhile. Sam's first semester at college had brought out old insecurities and anxiety. It was good to see her laughing.

The games were the fairly typical ones for bridal showers. Timed lists, word searches, purse raid. It was more fun than Tori thought it would be. And she was getting to know her in-laws-to-be as well as seeing her own cousins and aunts in a new light. Even the relatives she thought of as the conservative ones had relaxed in the spirit of the games.

When the purse raid game finished, Sam rose and set up an easel, then pulled a covered board from behind a table. Tori watched her suspiciously, a half smile on her face, because Sam kept glancing at her and giggling.

Lexie retrieved something from a bag next to her and stood up. "Okay, everyone, this next game is the most important one so it has the *biggest* prize." She held up a huge box of condoms for everyone to see. The crowd laughed.

Tori gasped and covered her mouth, choking on a laugh. She looked over at her mom and Hannah. Both women laughed easily, not looking embarrassed. If they weren't, she'd try not to be either.

"To play," Lexie continued, "we have this box of condoms, this blindfold—"

People laughed and hooted. A few whistles and boisterous yells pierced the air.

Tori shook her head and covered her eyes. Oh my gosh. She could feel her cheeks getting hotter.

"This box of colored pushpins," said Sam from in front of the easel, "and..." She pulled the cover off the board with a flourish.

A huge poster of The Avengers taped to foam core generated more laughter.

Tori noticed Joe's family laughing harder than anyone else. Maybe they'd played this game before.

Hayley elbowed Tori and nodded to the poster with a big grin. "You'll never win at this," she whispered. "You don't know what to do, right?"

Tori stuck her tongue out. Hayley laughed and hugged her shoulders.

"What you'll do," said Lexie to the room, "is open a condom, unroll it," she did so as she walked over to where Sam stood, "put a push-pin in the top here, spin around three times, and pin it on the poster as close to the correct piece of anatomy as possible. Blind-folded."

"Oh. My. Gosh." Tori looked at Hayley and shook her head. "What were you two drinking?"

Hayley laughed, but before she could say anything, Dixie leaned over and patted Tori's hand.

"Don't worry, sweetheart, you'll get the hang of it after a while."

"Mom!" Tori gasped and laughed and covered her mouth. She was sure she'd never in her life heard her mother say something like that. It was both disturbing and hysterical.

"She's right, Tori," Hayley whispered in her ear. "Getting it on is the hard part. Getting it off is easy."

"Hayley Addison! I'm never going to be able to get that out of my head," Tori whispered back, wiping the tears from her eyes as she laughed.

"Okay, everybody," Lexie called to the room. "Come on up.

The bride will go last. She'll have to beat all the other — um, *scores* — on the board."

The next few minutes were side-splitting fun. The condoms were attached to the most unusual places on The Avengers poster. Some people got so disoriented after being spun around three times that they walked off to the side of the poster, blindly flailing their arms around to the vast amusement of the onlookers. Lexie would give them a little nudge in the right direction, and the condom would land someplace ridiculous. One was currently hanging off the end of The Hulk's nose.

A little old woman stood next in line. She handed her cane to Lexie and snapped her fingers for a condom. Joe's relatives grinned and called out encouragement.

"That's Millie's mom, Esther," Hannah said to Tori and their table. "Owen's grandma, Joe's great-grandma."

At the easel, Lexie gently tied the blindfold over Grandma Esther's eyes but didn't spin her around. Grandma Esther took her cane firmly in one hand, stood quietly for a moment, then shuffled up to the poster with her other arm outstretched. As soon as her hand hit the poster, she pushed the pin in.

Everyone laughed. The condom was pinned directly to the appropriate part of Thor.

"What? Didn't I do it right?" Grandma Esther asked, trying to get the blindfold off.

Lexie helped her, laughing. "No, you were great. Look, you've done the best so far!"

Grandma Esther moved forward to take a closer look. Then she turned to the room and said in a matter-of-fact voice, "Well, I do have the most experience."

The entire room exploded. All the women were holding their sides and wiping their eyes, they laughed so hard.

Tori couldn't talk, she could hardly breathe. But she wanted to say, this is the most fun party I've ever had!

"Tori! Get Tori!" someone called.

"It's the bride's turn!"

"Bring down the bride!"

Tori got up and stood next to Lexie and Sam. "I don't think I can follow that," she said to Joe's great-grandma. She leaned down and gave her a gentle hug and a kiss on the cheek.

"I can show you if you want," Grandma Esther said in a voice loud enough to carry.

Everyone laughed and Tori blushed some more. "No, thank you, I'll manage."

Lexie turned her to face the room, then tied the blindfold around her eyes. "Wait, you have to give me a condom first," she told her sister.

"Oh no," Lexie replied. "You need to learn to do this in the dark."

More laughter.

Tori opened the condom wrapper, but when she pulled the condom out, it slipped through her fingers onto the floor. Oh boy, was this an embarrassing game. She started to bend her knees, but Lexie pulled her arm, giggling.

"Here, just take a new one."

This time, Tori was careful not to drop it. She laughed as people called out directions on how to unroll it. When she finally got it to its full length, she played along with the crowd, holding it up and asking, "Is it long enough now?"

"You'll find out in four days!" someone called out.

Tori felt Sam's hand on hers, and she put a pushpin in the top of the latex. Then she felt both sisters spinning her around. When they stopped, Tori put her arm out, but Lexie must've been gesturing to the crowd because everyone laughed again.

"Nope, not yet," Sam giggled.

Then they spun her around the other way. Tori nearly fell over, she was so dizzy. Her sisters let go of her and when she took a step forward, they took turns saying "warm" and "cold" and "warmer" until Tori could reach out and feel the poster.

She started to push the pin in, then moved her hand to another area. Someone called out "Ice cold!" and Tori moved her hand again. More people called out advice, some of it quite risqué, until Tori finally pushed the pin into the foam core.

By the time she was done, the room echoed with hilarity.

Tori pulled off her blindfold. Her condom was pinned to Captain America's shield. "Well, it's sort of close to the right part of Iron Man," she said with a grin.

"Close, but not close enough," Lexie said. "The winner of Pin the Condom on the Avengers Poster is Grandma Esther!"

Sam pulled out a big basket wrapped in cellophane. Tori saw it was filled with scented products from Bath & Body Works. Sam handed it to Tori, and Tori walked it over to Grandma Esther.

"Why, thank you, lovey," said her about-to-be-great-grandma. She reached up for Tori to hug her. "Don't worry," she whispered in Tori's ear, "his powers are nothing to be afraid of. You'll be fine."

Tori was so glad no one else heard that. How embarrassing! His "powers"? Was that how people used to talk about sex? She pulled away before Grandma Esther gave her a lecture on the birds and the bees.

When she walked back to her sisters, face burning, she was so relieved to find the games were over. Hayley motioned her over to the gifts table. Okay, good, that would be easier on her nerves.

Lexie handed her presents, Hayley wrote down who they were from in a little white book, and Sam took all the ribbons, doing something with them out of Tori's view.

The gifts overwhelmed Tori with the generosity and creativity of the givers. There were kitchen items, including a Crock-Pot and matching cookbook, silver picture frames, baskets of soaps and bath salts and lotions, and pre-made "date night" packages with gift cards for restaurants and the local movie theater chain.

While Lexie took a moment to figure out which gift went with a card, Tori leaned over and whispered to her mother. "This is wonderful, but it seems like too much. I'm stunned and..." She shook her head a little.

Dixie hugged Tori's shoulders and kissed her cheek. "I know you don't like to be the center of attention, but this is your *one* day, sweetheart. Relax and enjoy it." She smiled warmly. "It's only going to happen one more time in your life, and then it won't be about you as much as it'll be about your unborn baby. Today, all these people are here to congratulate you and welcome you into their family. They need to believe you're enjoying this. It's your gift back to them."

Tori thought about the times she'd been on the other side of this table. She absolutely loved to watch people unwrap the presents she gave them. It was fun to see their faces light up, no matter whose gift they opened. She took a deep, calming breath.

Okay, God, help me to give them a gift, too.

Lexie figured which gift bag a card went with and handed both to Tori.

"This one is from Liz," Tori said and waved her fingers at her friend. She read the card, laughing at the message, then opened the gift bag. She pulled out a small box and opened it. It was a beautiful silver necklace with two hearts joined together.

"'First comes love'," she read aloud from the tag inside. "This is beautiful, Liz."

She pulled a large box wrapped in tissue paper out of the gift bag. "'Then comes marriage'," she read from another tag taped to the outside. She pulled off the tissue paper and sucked in her breath. The box was decoupaged in all kinds of pictures and little decorations.

There were pictures of Tori and Joe that she remembered posting on her Facebook page. Pictures from a bridal magazine, pictures from a home and garden magazine, and words like "love" and "forever." Four black picture corners in the center of the top of the box waited for a new photo.

Tori opened the box to find the inside decorated as beautifully as the outside. Lying on the bottom of the box was a picture of Liz and Tori in front of one of the big roller coasters at Cedar Point in Ohio. It was taken in junior high when the church youth group went down for a weekend. Liz had decorated the picture to make it look like a Polaroid. On the bottom, she'd written "Best day ever — until now."

Tori teared up. She couldn't read it aloud. "Tissues, please!" she barely got out.

Sam ran for tissues while Hayley leaned over Tori's shoulder and described the gift to the crowd. "Aww, that's so sweet, Liz."

Several people joined in with "Aww."

Tori held the picture to her heart and smiled at her friend. "I'm framing this," she told her.

Liz picked up her napkin and dabbed at her eyes. She waved her hand at the bag. "Keep going. There's one more."

Tori reached inside and drew out another tissue-wrapped bundle with one more note. "'Then comes a baby in a baby carriage!'" Tori rolled her eyes and grinned. So much for trying to convince Liz there was no baby coming soon. She unrolled a piece of cloth to find a cute baby rattle. Unfolding the cloth, she found a hand painted baby bib. Amid the colorful pictures it read, "I love Aunt Liz."

Tori laughed and held it up for people to see. "Thank you, but don't be offended if I don't use it for a couple of years," she said to Liz.

Her friend shrugged. "The best laid plans..."

Sam took Liz's gifts and carefully fit everything back in the bag. Then Lexie handed her more presents. Tori remembered what her mom said and made sure everyone could tell how much she loved everything.

There were handmade Christmas ornaments with their names and wedding date, a set of four hand-tatted lace doilies shaped like snowflakes, a satin bathrobe that was definitely not for staying warm, and so much more.

Or less, depending on how you looked at it. Hayley gave her a barely-there teddy from Victoria's Secret. "Really, Hayley," Tori said loudly so everyone could hear. "You couldn't give me something like this in private?" Then she leaned over and hugged her. "It's beautiful, thank you."

"Just don't tell me anything more than 'he liked it,' okay?" Hayley laughed.

After Tori opened the last gift, Sam presented her with her bridal shower ribbon bouquet. Tori didn't know how she'd done it, but Sam had twisted some of the ribbons into flowers, braided others to make an edging, and left trailing tendrils to hang from Tori's hands when she held the bouquet. She'd also braided the silver and white ribbons together to create a headpiece that looked like something out of a Disney movie.

"Sam," Tori breathed as Sam arranged the ribbons on her hair. "This is beautiful." She hugged her little sister tight. Since they hadn't lived in the same house for several years, Tori hadn't realized how much she didn't know about Sam, like how artistic she was. "Wow."

All the ladies ooh'd and ahh'd and suddenly everyone had a phone or a camera in hand, taking pictures. Tori smiled and grinned and hugged and laughed and smiled some more. By the time the last of the guests had left, her cheeks ached. But her heart was overflowing.

"Lex, Hayley, Sam, that was wonderful. Really beautiful." She hugged them each in turn. "Thank you so much. That was the loveliest shower I could have imagined."

She turned to Joe's mom. "Hannah, thank you so much for this. I hope your family thinks I'm..." She fluttered her hand, trying to think of a word better than "okay."

Hannah hugged her tight. "They think you're wonderful," she said. "You and your whole family."

Tori smiled and felt her usual quieter self return. She ducked her head to hide the blush she feared was blooming. "Oh...well, good. Um, do you need help cleaning up?"

"You girls go on, I've got it covered." Hannah pointed behind Tori to four women coming down the stairs. "The troops have arrived." At Tori's questioning glance, she clarified, "My Bible study offered to do the cleanup today."

The ladies waved and called out greetings to each other. Tori recognized one woman, but didn't know her name. These strangers had come to help make her day perfect. Wow.

Tori turned to her mother. "Mom," she started to speak as she hugged her, but her throat closed up. Dixie held her close, rocking her slightly in her arms. Neither of them said anything, just sniffled and held on.

Eventually Dixie pulled back. She placed her hands gently on the sides of Tori's face. "I love you."

Neither one of them mentioned any of their struggles to get along over the years, the fights, the misunderstandings, the times Danny had to step in and negotiate peace. They just stood *together* for a moment.

"I love you." Tori poured her heart into the words, willing her mom to believe she meant it, no matter what.

"It's been a beautiful day," Dixie said. "Everything a young bride could want. You could treasure up these moments," her words began to trip over each other as she hurried to get them out, "and have a lovely June wedding. June is a beautiful—"

"Mom," Tori interrupted. She tried to stay calm. "A Christmas wedding is beautiful, too."

"Spring then," Dixie pressed. "I'm not asking you not to get married. Just let us get to know him better, make *sure* this will..."

Tori knew her mom was going to say, *make sure this will work.* She gave her credit for not finishing the sentence, at least. Danny had said more than once that it wasn't that they didn't trust Tori's ability to make sound decisions, but that a few weeks wasn't long enough to know if you could make a fifty-year life together.

Tori couldn't explain how, but she *did* know. "Mom, I appreciate your concern for me, but I'm marrying Joe on Wednesday." She was trying to decide if she should say more, press her case, but they'd been over this a dozen times.

Dixie took a deep breath and stepped back a step. "Okay," she said, wiping a finger below each eye, "go get dressed. Fix your makeup. Have fun and *be safe*. And keep Sammie safe," she added.

"I will, Mom. Don't spoil Ben too much." Tori wiped her eyes and turned to grab her bag and head for the ladies' room with the other girls. For all that her mom had been trying to get her to reconsider her rush to the altar, except for the last two minutes, today she was the epitome of support. Tori closed her eyes for a moment and willed herself to commit this day to memory. Hard to say how long this truce would last.

5

J oe straightened his cuffs as he looked in the mirror. The alterations were perfect, no small feat for a man of his size. The last time he'd worn a tuxedo must've been the twins' weddings about four years ago. He was pleasantly surprised. Tori would probably like this look.

The tailor at the tuxedo shop made a few adjustments and stepped back again, eyeing Joe critically from every angle. He finally nodded his head. "Good."

Joe nodded back. "I'm sure my friends will be here any minute. Work must've kept them."

The man nodded and returned to his station behind the curtain.

All of the Paladins in the various sectors of the city were taking shifts to patrol their own neighborhoods as well as to provide backup when one of them had a holiday event, or to give added protection to the worst areas of the city. Stretch's team agreed to cover Joe's team's area during Joe's wedding, and an older team offered to cover tonight when many of Joe's friends would be at his bachelor party.

That didn't explain where his non-superhero brother Carl

was, though. Joe looked at his watch. Right as someone punched him hard in the arm. Joe turned to see his big brother coming in for another swing. They traded a few punches and fell into a backslapping hug that would've felled smaller men.

The sharp sound of a clearing throat cut short their greeting.

The tailor stood nearly a foot shorter than Joe, and must be easily sixty pounds lighter. But he had the same commanding presence as Joe's old high school principal, Mr. Granger. Carl must've sensed it as well because he, too, stood up straight, hands to himself.

Joe whispered to his brother, "You're late."

"Kids," Carl whispered back. "You can't make them listen and you can't trade them in."

Joe snickered. When the tailor raised his eyebrow, Joe put on a more serious expression. Apparently, grooms were supposed to act more mature. He stood waiting for the tailor to tell him what to do.

The tailor appeared to be waiting for Joe to do something. He finally swished his hand at Joe. "You may take that off now. *Carefully.*"

The rest of the men in the bridal party — Bull Kincaid, Mickey Valient, and Darian Johnson — all walked in together a few minutes later as the tailor adjusted Carl's trousers.

"Hey, guys!" Joe called. "Where ya been?" He pointed to his watch. "Another time zone?"

Joe saw the tailor give Carl a menacing glare for waving. He stepped back. Safer to stand over here with his friends. "Hey, you guys better hurry," he said quietly, shaking hands and doing fist bumps. "The little guy is getting perturbed."

The men started toward the back room to find their tuxedos. Another loud throat-clearing stopped them in their tracks. That tailor could say more without saying anything. Joe tried not to smile.

While Carl's tuxedo was tweaked—"What have you been

eating?" Joe heard the tailor ask his brother—Joe asked the others about work.

"Aw, man," said Darian, "there were *five* muggings in Memorial Park last night. And those are just the ones that got away."

"What happened?" Joe asked.

"Christmas party," said Mickey with a scowl.

Joe frowned.

"Sector Eight had a team Christmas party," Bull explained, "and J-Mac forgot to tell his Sector One team that they were to cover for them."

"Irresponsible." Mickey shook his head. "Someone could've been hurt."

"But they weren't," Darian said soothingly. "We can't be everywhere, neither can the police. One starfish at a time, buddy." Darian slapped Mickey's shoulder. "Who's covering for us tonight?"

"Sector Eight," Mickey grumbled.

Joe and Bull grinned at Mickey's fresh scowl. The man was a perfectionist in the worst way, and a tough team leader as Tick Tock. But the three of them and Hayley Addison worked well together keeping Sector Seven safe from the worst of Double Bay's crooks and criminals.

Darian slapped Mickey's back and gave him a reassuring smile. He was a glass-mostly-full kind of guy and loved to compare their superhero work with the story about a guy saving starfish on a beach — we can't save them all, but we can help as many as we can. Joe liked his attitude. Too bad he served with Sector Four. It would be fun to work together more often than just the high-crime Christmas season.

The tailor, finished with Carl, brought over three garment bags, handing them to each man without asking for names. Joe didn't know how he could remember so many people's names and faces. Must be a gift.

The man stared up at Darian. "I know your face, but the

name isn't right. You are related to Cesar Johnson, yes? Michigan Wolverines basketball?"

Darian grinned. "He's my little brother."

The tailor actually smiled. "Excellent player. How is his knee?"

"He's walking again. Beat the odds. Got hired a few months ago by a high school south of Ann Arbor to teach English and coach basketball."

The tailor beamed at Darian and clasped his arm briefly. "That is wonderful news. Blessings on your family." Then the stern expression returned. "Now dress, all of you." He swished his hand toward the curtained area.

In between the trying on, the final adjustments, and the tailor letting out a button on Carl's tuxedo jacket—"No more cookies until *after* the wedding," scolded the tailor—Joe told the guys about the morning's terrifying events.

"There I was, staring Tori's dad, Danny Lewis, in the eye — *as Superhero X!*" Joe wiped his hand across his eyes. "What if he recognized me?"

"Did he?" asked Carl.

Joe shrugged. "I don't know. But if he says something to Tori…"

"I was there, man," said Darian, "and the guy had the same shell-shocked expression everybody does when they're being robbed. He didn't recognize you."

"I can't let any of her family know until she knows," Joe said. "I'm just saying, we've got to be careful."

"So tell her, already," said Mickey.

"I'm going to," Joe heard his voice rising with a defensive ring. "As soon as I'm sure she…that she…" He rubbed his chest, unsure how to put it in words.

"You want to be sure she loves you for you, *Joe*, before she has to decide what she thinks about X," Carl stated, as if it were obvious.

Joe glanced at him in surprise.

"I get it, brother," Carl said. "You want to make sure the glue has hardened before you have to test it."

Joe nodded. "But Dad's not..."

"He may be a superhero, but he's also a pastor with a whole other agenda of things he thinks are important. And he's our dad. You know he's gotta be feeling protective."

Joe raised his eyebrows. "No, actually, I hadn't thought of that. I thought he was acting tough as the head of the Paladin's Guild."

"That, too," Mickey said with a firm nod.

Carl clapped Joe on the back. "When you have kids, you'll understand. I'm beginning to get it now after thirteen years of being someone's dad. I think parents are always a little messed up in the head. There's more second-guessing going on up here," Carl tapped his temple, "than a squirrel trying to cross a four-lane road."

Carl was the only married one of the group. Even though he didn't have powers, Joe's oldest brother had always been a fount of wisdom in just about everything Joe had ever needed to learn. If Carl understood why Joe was feeling nervous about explaining his family to his fiancé, then Joe must not be completely out of line.

"Or you could not get married," Mickey said.

Joe glared at him.

"What? I'm just stating the obvious. I'm sure I'm not the only one thinking it." Mickey looked around at the others but no one would meet his eye.

"You love her, marry her," Bull said, folding his arms over his chest. "Everything else will work out."

Joe took a deep breath. "Okay, so tonight, we need to make sure no one gets too drunk and forgets that they're in public — or forgets that Tori's brother will be with us. Agreed?"

"Relax, man," Darian slapped his back. "It's just a bachelor party."

JOE'S FRIENDS had arranged for a private room at the back of a local sports bar. Most everyone had already arrived. Driving over had taken longer than usual because the long-awaited snow had finally started to fall. People were driving as if they couldn't remember what to do when the white stuff came down.

As Joe walked in, a loud chorus of yells and whistles and raucous cheering filled the air. The dark wood tables were already covered with pizzas, hot wings, chips and salsa, mozzarella sticks, and pitchers of beer. His younger brother Stuart and Tori's brother Kevin stood at the door collecting car keys in empty French fry baskets.

Joe's friends came over, slapping him on the back, ribbing him about his rush to get married, and talking animatedly about the Notre Dame football game on one of the televisions. Joe saw basketball on another television, and his brother Eddie was up on a chair trying to change a golf channel on a third TV. A waitress in a short skirt laughingly told him to get down.

Yup, it was gonna be a good night.

Joe shucked his coat, took the beer his brother Eddie handed him, and grabbed a slice of pizza with everything. As soon as the Notre Dame game hit half-time, his friends crowded around the entrance to the room. Joe started to walk over to see what was going on, but Bull pulled him back.

"Hold on there, buddy." Bull grinned at him and folded his arms over his chest. "Just watch."

Music beat heavily from the direction of one of the food tables. A moment later, the crowd of men parted in a riot of whistles and calls. A beautiful young woman dressed in what appeared to be only a Norte Dame football jersey sauntered in toward Joe.

Darian pulled up a chair in the center of the room and several hands forced Joe to sit. He groaned and laughed and didn't put up too much of a protest.

The girl danced around him for a minute, then began pulling off her jersey. Joe assumed she must have something on underneath since it was a public place, but he wasn't prepared for the University of Michigan cheerleader uniform. The hooting and hollering got louder. He hoped the Wolverine fans wouldn't start knocking around the rival Fighting Irish fans.

The girl had fantastic abs. The thought had barely formed when she did a backwards flip in front of him. She broke into a suggestive cheer that fit the occasion and proceeded to shimmy and shake in a most delightful way.

Suddenly some guy Joe didn't know reached out and grabbed at her. She was in the middle of a cheerleading move so he didn't get a good hold before she jumped away.

Joe was out of his chair a second later, but two of his friends had already gotten between the newcomer and the dancer.

The guy called out something crass. Obviously drunk, if the slurring and smell were any indication.

"This is a private party," Carl said, reaching his hand out to turn the guy toward the door.

"Get your hands off me," the guy's voice got ugly and he pushed Carl.

Joe stepped up just as a few more unknowns broke through the crowded doorway. "Now that's enough," he said firmly.

Eddie stepped to Carl's other side. The three brothers were lumberjack-huge, Hannah always said. Joe knew they made an imposing barrier.

Apparently not imposing enough for the heavily inebriated. One of drunk #1's cohorts swung at Eddie who easily ducked. Darian, behind him, didn't see the swing coming until it almost landed. He moved enough to take it on the shoulder. As he spun, Darian swung his leg out wide to trip the guy.

As in, swung his leg *way* out. Not all of his friends were super-heroes, and Joe didn't want anyone — especially Tori's brother — asking questions about strange things they thought they saw. He needed to stop this *now*.

"No, guys, let's just—" That was all he got out.

He ducked a punch and looked around for the girl. She was safely surrounded by the younger brothers and Mickey. Though Mickey was rolling up his sleeves.

He saw Bull pick up one of the drunks and haul him out of the room in a fireman's carry. If there had been a snowbank, he was sure his friend would've happily dropped the guy into it. For all that Bull was huge and stronger than any normal man, he was a bit of a pacifist.

Not so for most of the rest of Joe's friends, if prevailing activity counted for anything. One of his friends grinned as he ducked a punch and threw his own.

Joe turned to ask Carl to help him carry the drunkards outside. He walked right into a punch in the jaw. Ow. His strength came from absorbing the tensile strength of any metal he touched. Unfortunately, he wasn't wearing any metal right now. So much for off-duty.

The moment of pain destroyed his good intentions. Joe grabbed the guy in a chokehold and pulled one of his arms behind his back till he cried out. Then he walked the guy out of the bar.

Well, Joe walked. Drunk #3 couldn't quite keep his legs under him. The bar's security man met Joe outside, giving Joe a brusque nod as he let the drunk fall to the ground.

By the time he walked back into the private room, the ruckus was mostly over. The unwanted company had been cleared out, and half of the guys were already eating again.

"Not even a spilled beer," exclaimed one of Joe's normal friends with a grin. "Happy bachelor party, old man!"

Joe couldn't help but chuckle. He slapped his friend's back

and walked over to where the dancer stood. Stuart and Kevin were obviously enjoying assuring her of her safety. They looked a little googly-eyed, in fact.

"I'm sorry about that," Joe said to her. "Are you okay?"

"I'm fine, thanks," she said. "A little more exciting than I thought it would get, though. I heard you're a preacher's kid. I figured this would be tame."

"You and your friends certainly know how to fight," added Kevin.

Joe ran one hand through his hair, feeling a little embarrassed and not sure how to respond.

"Even preacher's kids grow up to be strapping young men," Stuart said to the girl.

He must've realized how ridiculous that sounded right after the words came out of his mouth. He turned red and struggled to say something else, anything else. "Pizza?"

The girl bit her lip, smiled, and shook her head.

"Really," Joe said, thinking that sounded like a gentlemanly thing to offer, "can we buy you dinner? Get you something to drink?"

"Um," she paused, looking around at the roomful of men yelling at TVs and eating and drinking with both hands. "Did you want me to finish?"

Joe smiled at her like he would have at one of his sisters' friends. "That's okay, you were great. Nice bit with the football rivalry."

She nodded toward Joe's friend, Tom, currently cheering on a play by the Irish. "Tom thought it would be funny."

Before Joe could respond, Kevin spoke up. "You want to hang out and watch the game? There's plenty of food."

She paused, considering, and Joe was certain Kevin would be shut down. Then she shrugged and nodded. "Sure."

She followed Kevin over to a pile of plates. Joe and Stuart

watched for a moment as the two laughed at something, then looked up at the game and whooped.

Stuart shook his head. "During the fight, he told her he was pre-med."

Joe laughed. "Didn't I tell you? You need a sexier major than computer science. Hey, he didn't see anything, did he?"

"I thought you were supposed to tell her already?"

"I'm going to. But that doesn't mean her family is ever going to know. I'm pretty sure our secrets will have to keep forever where they're concerned."

Stuart shook his head. "I don't think he saw anything more than a bar brawl with some guys who know how to fight."

Joe nodded. "Thanks for taking care of things over here."

Stuart shrugged. Then he looked up at Joe and grinned. "You gonna tell Mom if I have a beer tonight?" he asked. "We've got a line of cabs coming at eleven. We already arranged with the bar owner that everyone would pay twenty bucks for overnight parking."

"If I don't see anything, I won't have to lie." Joe hit his fist gently against his brother's arm. "Three more months and we'll give you a twenty-first birthday party to beat the band."

"Yeah?" They walked over to get some food. "There gonna be girls?"

6

Tori and Lexie held tightly to Ben's wrists so his hands didn't slide out of his mittens. "One, two, three," they sang out, pulling him up high in the air and dropping him to his feet.

Close to four inches of snow had fallen last night, and all three of them wanted to walk to church this morning. Their breath puffed out into the cold air and their boots crunched on the snow. They swung Ben up in the air again. This time he didn't put his feet down so that he landed on his knees.

The equivalent of "Make a snow angel, Mommy," came out in his broken toddler English.

"No, Benji," Lexie scolded. "Stand up." She brushed the snow off his dark blue corduroys. "We can play in the snow at Grandma and Grandpa's. I don't want you to get wet before Sunday School."

After a minute, Ben complied, stomping his feet through the snow so it puffed up.

Tori kept thinking, I'm going to miss this. Then she had to remind herself, she would only live a few blocks farther away than she had before.

She smiled in the crisp morning air. What kind of magic was this — she wouldn't have to give up anything when she got married, and she was gaining the whole world.

Lexie looked over at her. "What are you smiling at?"

Tori grinned. "Isn't the world a beautiful place?"

Lexie shook her head and chuckled. "You're drunk on love."

Tori laughed out loud. "I know!"

"You're so lame." But her sister smiled when she said it.

"You know, you and Hayley and I made that no-men pact, but you two are the only people who aren't telling me what a terrible mistake I'm making." Tori had been waiting for one of them to say something. The suspense was killing her.

Lexie walked in silence for a moment or two. "It's possible, I suppose, that out of the three or four billion men on this planet, not all of them are irredeemable jerks."

Tori smiled. She knew Lexie tempered her language in front of Ben. What she meant was much worse.

"The older he gets," Lexie nodded to her son, "the more I see how I can help him learn to be a good man. Kind, honest, compassionate, responsible."

"Like Dad," Tori said.

Lexie glanced over and gave her a quick smile. "Yeah, like Dad. But hopefully with a little more backbone."

Tori didn't want to argue with her. She vacillated between thinking Dixie was a control-freak or Danny was a push-over. She didn't understand her parents' marriage.

But she sure appreciated Lexie's high praise — Joe fell into the category of "not an irredeemable jerk."

When they got to church, he was waiting for her by the front door. He pulled her in for a quick kiss, making her giggle. Then he crouched down and held up his hand to Ben.

Ben high-fived him and laughed.

"Morning, Joe. Come on, Ben, let's get your coat off," Lexie said.

"No!" Ben turned his back to his mom and held up his hands to Joe. "Off."

Joe laughed and pulled off the boy's mittens. "Ooo, you've got mittens on a string. You're so lucky."

Ben smiled at Joe and swung his arm, making his mitten fly around on the end of the cord it was attached to.

Joe made a game out of getting Ben's outerwear off, handing the pieces to Lexie. Then he tossed Ben up in the air a couple times and airplaned him over to his mom.

Tori promised Lexie they'd save her a seat as her sister took Ben to Sunday School. She turned back to Joe. "You are so good with kids."

He shrugged. "'Cause I still am one." He leaned down and whispered in her ear, "Wanna go make out in my dad's office?"

Tori gasped and slapped his shoulder. "Joe!" she hissed. "We're in *church*."

He laughed. "I just wanted to see your expression. I can't tell if you're blushing since your cheeks are still red from the cold."

Probably. Everything he did made her blush. She wondered how long that would last. Hopefully, a long, long time.

Joe took her hand and led her from the cloakroom at the side of the narthex toward the sanctuary. But crossing a lobby never took longer. Tori figured *every single person* they tried to walk past stopped their conversation to congratulate them. She hugged at least a dozen people she didn't know.

By the eighth or ninth exuberant embrace from a stranger, her enthusiasm became forced. Her stomach started to feel a little hot and nervous. She hadn't felt this way in months. Apparently, she'd gotten all the hugs she could take at the bridal shower yesterday. She needed to stop soon before she did something embarrassing. Like tell everyone to back off.

Tori wondered if Princess Kate felt this way at her wedding.

Having successfully navigated the narthex, they stopped at almost every row inside the sanctuary. Good thing they had gotten here a little early. Tori saw Lexie walk by and wink, mouthing, "I'll save *you* a seat."

Tori smiled, then turned to hug another couple. At least these people she knew. "Thank you," she said yet again.

Tori and Joe joined Lexie a few rows from the front. While a guest pianist played some Christmas music off to the right, Joe whispered to her, "Have a good time last night?"

"Yes," Tori whispered back. "You?"

"Yeah. What'd you do?"

The pianist started playing *Greensleeves*.

"Oh, I love this song. We went to dinner, and we all wore little plastic tiaras. Mine said Bride." She flashed him a grin. "Then we went line dancing at a place on the UNM campus. Country music," she teased, and he made a face. "Very fun. We laughed so much my cheeks hurt."

"Dancing, huh?" Joe squeezed her hand. "Did you dance with anyone?"

Tori looked him in the eye and made a soft sound that she meant as, *I know what you're really asking and you're being silly*. But she said, "It's line dancing, Joe. You dance with everybody."

He raised his eyebrows. "Were the people you danced with good-looking?"

Tori giggled softly, trying not to draw attention. "Was the cheerleader at your party good-looking?" She raised her eyebrows in return.

"How did you know there was a cheerleader?"

"Because your very sweet brother who planned the party asked me if it would bother me."

"And you said?"

"No, as long as she kept her clothes on. So was she pretty?"

Joe grinned. "She was easy on the eyes." He raised her hand to his lips and kissed her knuckles. "Nothing like my girl, though."

Tori grinned and ducked her head. He said the sweetest things. She just loved that about him.

"Anyway, it was your brother who got her number, I think."

Tori glanced up in surprise. She was about to ask more questions, but the service began. More ammunition to tease Kevin with at lunch today.

A young family with three small children lit the Advent candles and read a passage about the birth of Jesus. The congregation sang "Angels We Have Heard on High," and Owen gave a lovely sermon about holding the joy and peace of Christmas in your heart all year. The service ended with a rousing rendition of "Joy to the World."

Tori sighed happily. "I love Christmas."

She pulled Lexie along as she and Joe faced another wave of well-wishers. If she had to meet every single person who went to this church, so did Lexie. Both of them were too used to keeping to themselves. It would probably do them good to get a little more connected here.

Even with all the chatting, they still had some time before they had to be at Mom and Dad's for Sunday brunch, so Joe and Tori walked Lexie and Ben home. That is, the adults walked. Ben rode piggy-back, played horsey, and pretended to be an airplane all the way home.

"Thank you for ruining him for me for the next month," Lexie complained. "I don't know why guys have all the strength and endurance when moms are the ones who really need it."

Joe chuckled as he swung Ben from his shoulders. "I love kids." Then he bent down and whispered in the boy's ear.

Lexie shot Tori an expectant look. Tori grinned and shook her head, sticking out her tongue at her sister. It was far, *far* too soon to think about having kids. They needed time on their own first. Though it was nice to see that Joe would almost certainly make a great dad. One day.

Tori gave her sister a hug, congratulated Ben on his snow

angel, and waved goodbye. Lexie wanted to drive her own car to Mom and Dad's today since Tori and Joe would be going to Owen and Hannah's later. Back-to-back family get-togethers. She should probably get used to this.

Tori took Joe's hand as they walked back to the church. Joe had left his truck there this morning after he picked it up from the bar parking lot. As they walked back and then drove to her parents' house, they discussed wedding details.

Tuxedos — check.

Bridal gown and dresses — check.

Cake — Joe's Aunt Trudy said "check."

Luncheon — Hannah said "check."

Rehearsal dinner — check.

The church had a Christmas caroling event scheduled for 4:30 on Tuesday, and the bridal party had been invited to join them. The rehearsal dinner and rehearsal would follow. Tori was excited that so many family and friends had agreed to go caroling beforehand.

"This is going to be so fun," she gushed. "Much better than a June wedding. You can't go Christmas caroling in June."

Joe gave her a questioning look, then made a turn toward Tori's old neighborhood where her parents lived.

She rolled her eyes and sighed dramatically. "My mother once again pointed out the virtues of a summer wedding yesterday."

"Yeah, I'm still getting some of that from my side, too." Joe reached over and took her hand.

She squeezed it, and looked out at the neighborhood they were driving through. Her family had moved here when Mom was pregnant with Samantha. Dad had made partner at his law firm and they wanted to move to a better neighborhood. Tori had a vague recollection of their old neighborhood, and she'd thought it was nice, too. But Mom wanted to make Dad a proper lawyer's wife, and this house was better for entertaining. How many times had Tori heard that over the years?

She knew Mom and Dad loved each other, but sometimes she wondered if her mom was trying to prove something by being the perfect wife. And recently, Tori had been worried her mom thought Tori *wouldn't* make the perfect wife, and that's why she kept urging her to push back the date.

"Do you think I'll make a good wife?" she asked Joe now, still staring out the window at the big, beautiful houses in this well-to-do neighborhood. A neighborhood so unlike the one where she and Joe and Lexie lived.

Joe pulled over and put the truck in park. Tori glanced over in surprise.

"Neither one of us has any idea what our marriage is going to be like," Joe said, lacing their fingers together. "We both have ideas based on what we've seen in our parents' lives and our friends' lives, but we don't know how *you and I* will do it. I'd guess we'll have the fewest disappointments if we're willing to go with the flow a little.

"But I believe you and I will have a great marriage. You're honest and generous and loving, and you bring out the best in me. I hope I bring out the best in you. What other people think will only matter if we let it."

Tori felt her chin quiver. She undid her seat belt and slid over to him. He pulled her into his arms and held her tight.

"I think you're going to make a great wife, Tori." He pulled away. "I'd marry you today, if I could, but I'm willing to wait until Wednesday."

Tori laughed and felt the tears roll down her cheeks.

He wiped them away with his thumbs. "But I'll wait till June if it would make you happy."

Tori shook her head and wrapped her arms around him again. "No, I don't want to wait. You make me so happy." She pulled back enough to meet his gaze. "Not just happy, but..." She searched for a word to describe what she felt. "I feel strong when I'm with you. Strong and happy and peaceful and safe. But also, like I could do anything I set my mind to."

She tucked her chin down, feeling slightly foolish. She wasn't in the habit of sharing her deepest feelings with anyone, not even Lexie or Hayley. At least not like this.

Joe tilted her chin up and kissed her. At first, it was warm and reassuring. As it continued, it became a kiss of promise, and Tori reveled in it. Then it became a longing to end the waiting.

"Just in case I wasn't clear," Tori said when they pulled away, her eyes closed against Joe's cheek, feeling his heavy breathing in her ear, "I want to marry you *now*." She opened her eyes and said with a teasing grin, "But I'm willing to wait till Wednesday, if you are."

Joe grinned back at her. "I guess we could do that. Since we all have these nice clothes and everything."

Another laugh, another hug, another kiss cut short, and Joe pulled back onto the street.

Tori sat close to him, absorbing his strength. Together, they could do anything.

Even stand up to her mother.

JOE TRIED NOT to act nervous as he and Tori walked into her parents' house. He'd never been particularly uneasy about a girlfriend's parents in the past. But this was different. He hadn't met Danny and Dixie Lewis until the day he proposed to their daughter. Now, less than four weeks later, they were about to become a permanent part of his life.

His mother-in-law-to-be was intimidating, even if she was half his size. She may not have extraordinary powers, but she certainly wasn't powerless. When she looked at him, Joe felt like she was cataloging all of his strengths and weaknesses, and he wasn't sure which attributes were which around her. She brought out his best manners, his best posture, and more second-guessing than he'd experienced since he was a teenager.

Then there was the whole superhero thing. Dixie had made it plain at the first Sunday dinner he'd attended that she didn't believe in superheroes, thought everyone who professed to be one was mentally unbalanced, and that it was not acceptable subject matter in the Lewis household. Ever. Joe felt pretty confident she'd ban him from their house should the topic come up again.

Testing the waters, in this case, showed that they were indeed infested with crocodiles.

Tori's father, Danny, was much more easy-going. He was friendly and welcoming from the first, discussed Lions football and Red Wings hockey with Joe with enthusiasm, and acted like he genuinely liked Joe. But he'd also displayed that "I've been cleaning my shotgun in case I need it" look several times since Joe and Tori announced their engagement.

Joe had vented about all this to Mickey and Bull a couple weeks ago. Bad idea. Mickey told him he was a fool for getting involved with a girl whose family was so opposed to the idea of superheroes. Some people have unusual gifts — were they opposed to chess prodigies as well? Mickey had been trying harder than anyone, including Tori's parents, to shut down this wedding. Joe didn't want to ask why. He might not want to know the answer.

Bull, ever the supportive friend and a true romantic, leaned heavily in the other direction. He eagerly performed the duties of best man, reminding Joe about expected gifts to the bride and bridal party, urging him to spend the extra money on the honeymoon package, and helping him get his house ready for his new bride. "Love changes everything," he insisted. It made Joe wonder why Bull and Hayley couldn't make things work.

But today was going to be even more difficult than usual. Today Joe had to pretend he hadn't seen Danny yesterday morning, hadn't saved him from a pair of armed muggers, and in fact didn't know anything about it. Would Danny bring it up? Did the family know? Tori hadn't said anything and he was sure she would have if she had known.

So probably Danny hadn't told anyone. Which was good. Joe wouldn't say anything and the whole situation would be a nonissue.

Unless Danny started thinking that Joe looked like the guy who helped him. And, darn it, Stretch had given their superhero names. No way to take that back. Granted, only the Paladins and the SLU knew Joe was Superhero X. But Joe already felt under the microscope with this family. And Danny was a lawyer. Didn't lawyers go around digging up facts? The SLU wouldn't tell him anything, if he found out about the SLU at all. It wasn't a secret, but they didn't advertise their presence.

Joe took a deep breath as he took off his coat and hung it up. He just had to act normal and no one would be the wiser.

Everyone called out their greetings, and Joe sank with relief onto the couch beside Kevin. A football game was on — the Lions versus the Bears — and all the men were in the living room. Football was safe. That's all they'd be talking about today.

"So, how was your bachelor party last night?" Danny asked.

Joe stuttered as he tried to decide what to say. What was appropriate to share with the protective father of the bride? Some of his friends had allowed their powers to show a little, but Kevin had been pretty focused on the cheerleader, oblivious to everything else. "It-it was good. Very low-key. Football and food, mostly." He tried to make it sound like nothing untoward had happened, nothing that would make him look like a bad choice for this man's daughter.

Danny raised his eyebrows. "No girls?"

"Uh, just one and she..." Joe looked to Kevin for help. What had he told his dad?

Kevin apparently didn't mind talking about her. "She's a cheerleader at UNM, Dad. We think we might've been in a chemistry lecture together."

He told his dad that Teresa was a junior like him, but she was in the Honors College, majoring in international finance.

Danny turned his focus to his son, listening to him go on and on about the girl, asking him questions and ribbing Kevin about his new crush. Joe all but groaned in relief.

Then the Lions scored and everyone's focus returned to the TV. Joe cheered a little too loudly, an outlet for his nervous energy. He had to get hold of himself. Act like it's a job, an undercover job. Darned if it wasn't.

Even after he told Tori, her family would probably never find out. Carl's in-laws didn't know. Of course, Carl himself had never gotten a power, and he was quite happy about that. Joe's next oldest brother Eddie wouldn't acknowledge his power, and Joe assumed his in-laws didn't know either.

Lexie and Ben arrived, and the little boy gave Joe something else to think about. Ben high-fived all the men, then climbed on Joe and used him as a jungle gym. A few more relatives showed up that Joe hadn't met yet. He was beginning to think he couldn't wait until Wednesday. The "why are you getting married so quickly?" looks were getting harder to ignore. He wanted to tell everyone, I did *not* get her pregnant.

When Dixie called everyone in to dinner, Joe could hardly believe what happened — all the men got up and filed into the dining room. The Lions were on a third down, two yards from the goal line. In the next sixty seconds, they could score and get ahead for the first time this game. Joe knew Danny and Kevin cared. They'd all been cheering together a moment ago. Wow, Dixie sure held the power in this house.

Danny left the TV on, but muted the sound. In the dining

room, Joe noticed the TV wasn't visible to anyone from the table. He knew because he walked around the table looking for a seat with a view. This family was so unlike his own.

Tori took his hand and they sat down next to each other, a cousin on Tori's side and Grandma Lewis next to Joe.

Okay, you can do this.

Danny said grace, and various bowls and platters were passed around. Always to the right, Joe remembered this time. Maybe everyone would talk around him and he could get through the next hour or two by smiling and nodding.

"So explain to me, dear," said Grandma Lewis as she patted his hand, "why you feel like you need to get married so quickly."

Smiling and nodding probably wasn't going to work this time.

Joe's gaze darted around the table to find everyone listening, waiting for his answer. How could he get out of this quickly and politely? "Chastity," he finally said. They knew he was a preacher's kid. It was a good answer.

Tori choked on a sip of water. Her siblings and cousins all started to laugh, then quickly tried to hide it. Joe wasn't sure why that answer was funny, but by the strange reactions around the table, he wished he could take it back.

"We all know how you feel about virgin brides, Grandma," Lexie said with a cheeky grin. "At least one of your grandchildren is going to follow in your footsteps."

Grandma Lewis pursed her lips slightly at the laughter from the young people. Then she leaned around Joe. "Is that right, Tori? You'll be a virgin bride?"

Joe glanced down at Tori. He tried to send her a message — sorry, and could they please go home now? Under the table she squeezed his hand, but she didn't look at him. She leaned over to tell her grandmother, "Only until we get to the hotel, Grandma."

"Victoria Joy!" exclaimed Dixie.

"What?" Tori asked with an innocent smile. "I only have to

wait until after the wedding, right? I'm waiting another seven hours after that."

"That's going above and beyond," one of her cousins said seriously. "Good for you."

Dixie sputtered at one end of the table. Joe noticed Danny chewing and trying not to smile at the other end.

"At least we don't live in one of those cultures," Kevin piped up, "where they consummate their vows during the reception with someone watching to make sure they do it right."

Dixie spiked her son with a quelling look.

Joe didn't look at anyone else, just stabbed a forkful of beans from his plate and chewed, trying to stay out of the line of fire. He wanted to laugh with the younger people, but the older adults weren't laughing. They mostly seemed irritated.

In his family, teasing was as natural as breathing, and everyone laughed. But the Lewis family was so serious when they were together. They seemed to be big fans of privacy, apparently thinking you shouldn't talk about or joke about anything remotely personal. If anyone had a reason to be careful and secretive, it was his superhero family. Didn't Tori's family trust each other enough to be relaxed and open when they were together?

Grandma Lewis patted Joe's hand again. "Well, then I give you my blessing, young man."

Joe desperately wanted to laugh, or at least grin, but he forked a bite of meat into his mouth and nodded to the woman. If he could keep his mouth shut for the rest of the meal, maybe he could keep from adding ammunition to the hundred and one reasons Tori's family cited for postponing the wedding.

A few minutes later, when Dixie was engaged in another conversation at her end of the long table, Danny said, "So Joe, you work in security, right?"

Joe nodded. "Yes, sir."

"You're a security guard?" asked an aunt. "That can't pay very well." She sent a pointed look to Tori.

It wasn't that far from the truth, Joe supposed. "So to speak, yes, ma'am." Let her think what she wanted.

"Does your company do residential work or commercial work?" Danny asked.

"We do both, though we have more residential customers right now. It depends on the needs of the client."

"I see." Danny nodded. "So do you protect retail stores, strip malls, banks, that sort of thing?"

Joe stiffened. Did Danny recognize him? Or was he asking strictly from the security angle? "There is another company who nailed down most of the banks a few years ago. I think we might have a strip mall or two, and yes, we do individual retail stores. A little of everything."

"Security at the mall is atrocious," inserted the aunt with a contemptuous sniff. "I hope you're not a mall security guard."

"Joe isn't a security guard," Tori said firmly to her aunt. "He works with clients to create a security plan tailored for their needs. He has a dual degree in engineering and computer science. He's excellent at what he does and makes a fine living. He even owns his own house."

Joe stared at his girl with surprise. Apparently, she was a good listener. He barely remembered telling her some of that. He lifted her hand and kissed it.

She gazed up at him with that gorgeous smile of hers, then she leaned over and kissed his cheek. From what Joe had been able to tell, this was a huge and embarrassing display of public affection in the Lewis house. He felt his heart swell.

Danny cleared his throat.

Tori winked at Joe, dropped his hand, and went back to eating. Joe was still staring at her when her father spoke up.

"So banks have good security?" he asked. He looked a bit skeptical.

Joe could understand why. "I don't like to comment on other firms' work," he said. "It can be a difficult business, especially this time of year. Every time you upgrade your system, there's a criminal working on a way to get around it."

Danny nodded. "Makes sense."

Joe cut a piece of meat and chewed. Should he say any more? If he asked a direct question about the bank, or commented on muggings, it might push Danny to wonder why Joe asked just the right question. On the other hand, it was his job — his calling — to protect people, make them feel safer.

"If you're interested, I could take a look at your security system here, see if I have any suggestions for improvements."

Danny's expression cleared a little. "That'd be great. Let's talk later."

Joe nodded. Tori's family may not have warmed to him any more as a "security guard" than they had to conversations about superheroes. But maybe he could win them over one person at a time.

7

Tori tried not to be disappointed. Yesterday was the perfect mother-daughter day. Dixie was everything a girl could want — supportive, loving, laughing and smiling with everyone at both the dress fitting and the shower.

Today, well, it almost seemed as if her mother needed to make up for yesterday. As if, for one day, she had forgotten how much she didn't want Tori to get married and be happy. Might she be so worried about appearances that she would pretend to be supportive in front of Joe's family? That didn't even make sense since his family would be happier if they moved back the date, too.

"Flo is right, you know," Dixie said in the kitchen after dinner. "We need to know if he makes enough money to support you. I don't know why I never asked before."

"Probably because it's none of your business," Tori said, scraping bits of food off plates into the trash. She wished she were a boy child so she could go hide in the living room and pretend to be excited about football. She couldn't remember Kevin ever having to help in the kitchen when they had company.

"It is their business," Aunt Flo interjected, taking the plates from Tori and loading the dishwasher. "They don't want to be supporting you years from now like George and I are with Jessie and her husband."

Tori prayed for patience. She would not play this game with them, especially with Joe right here in the house. And at Christmas! She ground her teeth to keep her mouth closed.

"That's so true," Dixie agreed with her sister. "And you don't want to turn out like Lexie, either," she added.

"Mom!" Tori looked through the kitchen door to make sure Lexie wasn't within earshot. "That's mean."

"But true," Aunt Flo said, shaking her head. "Two babies, one taken away, no husband." She made a tsk-tsk sound. "Your mother says that you said you aren't pregnant, but if you are, you definitely *should* get married this week. You can always get divorced after the baby is born. That way you won't shame your parents."

Tori wondered why Christmas was advertised as this beautiful, loving time of year when everyone put their issues on hold for a day. That had never been her experience. Since Aunt Flo and her family only visited at Christmas and during the summer festival season, those seemed to be the times when all the gossiping and nastiness came to the center.

Now that she was getting married, Tori decided she would be away on vacation during Aunt Flo's visits.

"There are too many things you don't know about him, Tori," said Aunt Flo. "And I'm not talking about does he snore, though that will definitely impact your future happiness. I'm talking about things like does he have a retirement plan, how does he vote, does he buy expensive man-toys without asking. A couple of weeks is not enough time to know if you'll be compatible, let alone if he can support you in the manner you deserve."

Be quiet. Don't speak. Think about something pleasant...like the plane that will take you away from this family in three days.

"See? You don't know, do you?" Aunt Flo nodded. "And what

about his relatives? What do you know about them? When you marry a man, you marry his whole crazy family as well. You're going to have problems. Mark my words."

Tori shot her mother a glare — *make her stop or else*. Dixie didn't seem so bad when compared to her sister. Tori should be grateful for that small favor.

"You can never fully know another human being," Dixie said, "no matter how long you know them. And part of the fun of a good relationship is getting to know them and all their idiosyncrasies. But you can do that while you're dating. That's what dating is for."

"Okay, I think the table is clear," Tori said, changing the subject. "Shall I find out who wants coffee?" She left before anyone answered.

In the living room, everyone was watching the Lions with varying degrees of excitement. Sam was only half-watching as she texted someone. One of their cousins read a book on her tablet.

"Who wants coffee?" Tori called out, then counted hands.

Her little brother grabbed her in a gentle headlock and kissed her temple. "Gonna miss you, sis."

She pretended to try to wrestle out of his grip in their usual play. "I'll only be gone a week. Then you can come over and we'll watch an NCIS marathon some weekend and eat until we can't move."

"You're on," Kevin said and pushed her away. Something happened on the TV, and he was off on a rant, yelling and jumping around.

Tori glanced at the screen, but she only saw a bunch of uniformed men wandering around hitting each other on the head or the back or the butt. She shook her head. She had never understood the draw of this game. She couldn't wait till spring. Baseball, that was a sport she enjoyed.

Back in the kitchen, she helped cut and serve pie while Lexie passed out coffee and other drinks to the family in the living room. When everyone had a plate of dessert, Dixie urged her sister to go relax. Tori took her slice of chocolate cream pie in an Oreo crust and headed for the living room.

"Tori, just a minute," Dixie said.

Aunt Flo raised her eyebrows at Tori and sauntered from the room.

Great.

Tori waited for her mom to speak. She tried as hard as she could not to have a combative look on her face, but she suspected she looked defensive, at best.

"I apologize for some of the things I said earlier." Dixie's gaze dropped to the kitchen towel in her hands, one finger tracing over the holly berries. "It's hard not to get carried away agreeing with everything your older sister says. Sometimes you say things or let her say things that you later regret."

Dixie looked up from the towel, and Tori could see she meant it.

"You have an older sister, and you are an older sister. You must know what I mean."

Tori nodded. Though personally, she didn't think she agreed with everything that came out of Lexie's mouth the way Dixie seemed to always agree with Flo. Something to be aware of in the future.

Dixie took a deep breath. "I'm trying to protect you. I love you, and I don't want to see you get hurt. You don't—"

"Mom, I don't need protecting anymore," Tori interrupted as gently as she could. "I've seen a lot more of life's dark side than almost any other 27-year-old I know. I can—"

"You *don't* know how bad it can be," Dixie insisted. She tried to keep her voice down. "You've seen a lot, but you have no idea what I've protected you from. You don't know what's out there in the world, how quickly things can go horribly wrong, *especially* with a new husband and—"

"But that's true for anyone, anywhere." Tori waved her arm

toward the street. "Any of our neighbors could have their house burn down from a few sparks on their Christmas tree. Any of our friends could go to the doctor tomorrow and find out they have cancer. I appreciate that you want to take care of me, but you must know you can't keep me safe from every bad thing that can happen."

Dixie shook her head. "That's not what I mean."

"Then what *do* you mean?" Tori asked in exasperation, her stomach feeling queasy from arguing. "Tell me!"

Her mother's expression froze for a moment. Then she said, "Your father was a very bad man." Her voice had a dead quality to it, almost without emotion.

"You've said that before. But just because you had a bad marriage the first time doesn't mean—"

Dixie frowned, pulling her arms around herself and rubbing one shoulder. "Tori!" she snapped. "Are you still taking your medicine? Dr. Huntington's office told me you've missed two appointments this month. I know you've been busy planning the wedding, but you can't stop going to the doctor just because you're busy."

Tori closed her eyes and took a deep breath. Should she lie or tell the truth and have an even bigger fight?

"Everything is fine," she said. That was true. She felt great. Maybe a little weird sometimes, but that was no doubt what happened as drugs left your system.

"I want you to call the receptionist tomorrow and get an emergency appointment—"

"Mom—"

"—for tomorrow or Tuesday, before you leave town."

Tori opened her mouth but her mother interrupted.

"Promise me," she insisted. She moved her hand as though to touch Tori's shoulder, then she pulled back. "Promise me you'll take care of this."

Tori sighed. She would take care of herself, but in her own

way. She was an intelligent adult. She'd researched the pros and cons of the medicines Dr. Huntington had prescribed. She'd researched the various disorders the shrink insisted she had. And she had been writing how she felt in her diary every day to track the changes.

One thing she could promise her mother was that she would take care of herself. "I promise," she said. It wasn't really a lie so much as it was sidestepping the specifics of Dixie's demand.

"When you have children of your own..." Dixie paused and shook her head. "Go eat your pie."

Dixie turned back to where she'd left a plate for herself. Tori watched her for a moment. When her mother picked up her fork, her hand shook so badly Tori could see it from across the room.

Feeling like she'd once again not only let down her mother but somehow done something worse that she didn't understand, Tori picked up her plate and looked for a quiet corner.

She ended up in the window seat in her old room, now Sam's room. She pulled her feet up and stared out the window at the falling snow. She'd always fallen short of her mother's expectations and she'd never understood why.

Would she end up being a disappointment to Joe as well?

Maybe the rules she and Lexie had drawn up when Lex was pregnant with Ben were something to reconsider. No men. Keep everyone out. Protect themselves at all costs.

Fourteen years ago, when Lexie got pregnant at fifteen, their parents had insisted she give the baby up for adoption. It had nearly destroyed her. She'd been arrested several times for stalking the adoptive parents, and eventually she ended up living on the streets using who-knows-what to try to choke off her emotions. It had taken years for her to get her life together again. And it had scared Tori and Kevin and Samantha into trying to be perfectly well-behaved overachievers.

Well, Kevin and Sam were overachievers. Tori had been trying to help Lexie save herself since Tori was barely thirteen.

She hadn't had much of a life outside of that mission. When Lexie got pregnant with Ben, Tori moved in. Add to that their pact not to date, and Tori had been focused on her sister and nephew most of her adult life.

But then she'd met Joe. He was practically a fairy tale hero. Tall and strong and good-looking with a big heart and an easy smile. The only "weird" thing about him, and she wished she could think of a different word, was how strong and courageous she felt around him. She not only felt safe, which is what she'd yearned for her whole life, but she felt like she was strong enough to keep other people safe, too.

She ate a bite of the chocolate pie. Her eyes closed for a moment. Her mom made the best pies.

Maybe that's part of why she wanted to be with him, to use that strength for the good of others. Tori had enjoyed helping Lexie build a new life. She liked taking care of Ben. She simply liked helping people. Period. Maybe that's why she enjoyed her temp jobs — she knew she was helping people who needed it. Maybe how she felt with Joe made her want more of the same.

She sighed. Or maybe she didn't know the *why* of anything in her life.

She savored her pie while she watched the snow fall. She'd think about it later. She wanted to be in a good mood today. Her dad would call everyone in after the football game and they'd exchange presents since Tori and Joe would be in Florida on Christmas Day.

Tori smiled. That was a thought to put her back in a good mood. Disney World at Christmas as a bride.

Wow.

She finished her pie and watched the snow for another minute. Finally. She was beginning to wonder if they weren't going to have a white Christmas after all. The way it was piling up this afternoon, the kids might even have a snowman built in Joe's parents' yard by the time Joe and Tori arrived later.

Before Tori knew Joe or any of his family, she'd admired the various snowman scenes in Owen and Hannah's front yard each winter. She always wondered if the family who lived there was as fun as the silly snow statues suggested.

God, help me not to compare my family to someone else's, but to love them for who they are. And please let Joe and his family be truly as wonderful as they seem.

Tori took a big breath and left the room, determined to love each one of her family members the best she could.

At least for Christmas.

RUNNING AND RUNNING. Monsters in the darkness. Chasing her. Running.

Mom screaming. Monsters in the dark.

A dark corner with a mirror. Hiding from the monsters. Looking in the mirror.

Monsters in the mirror.

She was the monster.

Tori fought against the monsters in the dream, fought to wake up, fought the darkness and the fear. She kicked and kicked, finally realizing only blankets trapped her legs.

She fumbled for the bedside lamp. Breathing heavily and blinking against the light, she told herself it was just a dream. There were no monsters in her room. No monster under the bed.

She began to cry and rolled into a ball on her side. She hadn't had that dream in years. What brought it back? Shivers ran down her spine.

Still crying, she reached for her phone and texted Hayley.

You awake?

Beginning to shiver, she pulled the covers back up and wrapped them tightly around her. She hated feeling so alone after a nightmare. She wanted to go get in bed with Lexie like they used to in bad times past, but Lexie had to go to work today. She shouldn't wake her.

God, help me not to feel so alone.

She opened the texting feature on her phone again. No reply from Hayley. Probably asleep at 3:49 a.m.

She stared at the list of names on the list of recent texts. She shouldn't wake him. Did he turn his phone to vibrate at night? Everyone did, right?

This is what Aunt Flo meant — she didn't know Joe well enough to know if he slept with his phone nearby, if he turned the ringer off at night or not, if he was a light enough sleeper to wake up at the ding of an incoming text.

Tori buried her new sobs in her pillow. She didn't want to wake her sister. Though she also hoped Lexie would miraculously hear her and come in and hold her until the fear left and the tears stopped.

She stopped crying enough to type a text to Joe.

> You awake?

Please be awake, she begged him from three-quarters of a mile away.

But no one answered. No one came. And she lay alone in her bed until she cried herself back to sleep.

When Tori awoke again, it was 8:52 a.m. She couldn't believe she'd slept so long. Thankfully, the last few hours held weird dreams, but not nightmares.

Her eyes felt gritty and her mouth was dry. She reached for the glass of water she always kept by the bed. As she drank, she heard the light whirring sound of her phone vibrating on a soft surface. It took a minute to figure out where it was coming from — under the covers. She'd fallen asleep with it in her hand.

She pressed the middle button and saw that she'd received texts from Hayley, Lexie, and Joe. She flopped against her pillow and read them, rubbing her sore eyes gently.

Lexie teased her for still being asleep, and wanted to know if Tori would be eating there tonight.

Joe apologized for being asleep when she texted him, asked if she was all right, and said he missed her and loved her.

Tori ran her finger over the words. She loved him, too. So much.

Another text from Hayley flashed in and Tori read four from her. The last one said,

Wake up sleepyhead, I'm walking to your door.

A knock on the front door made her jump and then chuckle a little. She got up, pulled on her warm fluffy robe and sheepskin slippers, and let Hayley in.

"Aren't you supposed to be at work?"

"I called and asked Brie to hold down the fort. She is turning out to be the best employee I've ever hired."

Hayley stomped fresh snow from her boots, took off her outerwear and followed Tori into the kitchen.

"Hot chocolate?" Tori asked.

"Sure, or we could go out to breakfast, my treat," Hayley said.

Tori thought about it for a moment. It was the sort of fun, carefree activity she should be enjoying two days before her wedding. "If you don't mind," she started to say, and then she started crying.

"Oh, Tori," Hayley said in the exact right tone of voice. She came over and wrapped Tori in a big hug. "What's wrong, sweetie?"

Tori tried to talk, but she couldn't. Images from her nightmare scuttered through her head. She shivered and hugged Hayley harder.

It took a minute for her to get hold of herself enough to tell Hayley about her nightmare. She couldn't say any more. She didn't want to tell her *why* she sometimes dreamed she was a monster. There were some secrets she kept close, even from Hayley, her best friend since elementary school.

It was only Dixie's lies and shaming that kept the truth of the shrink and meds from Hayley when she lived with Tori's family during their senior year of high school. The last thing Tori needed now was for Hayley to decide she was a freak and no longer worthy of friendship.

Hayley looked around and pulled a paper towel off the roll. She handed it to Tori and pushed her into a kitchen chair. Then she got another paper towel, wet it with warm water, and handed that to Tori as well.

"I'm sure this is perfectly normal nerves," Hayley assured her. "Remember how Sarah cried before she got married? And Margie told us that funny story of how she cried so hard the night before, she still had hiccups the next day at the wedding?"

Tori nodded and tried to chuckle. It came out more like a grunt. She gently wiped her face with the wet paper towel. That felt better.

"It was just a bad dream," Hayley continued. "Let me guess. You had a fight with your mom yesterday, and you ate way, *way* too much at both parents' houses."

Tori nodded.

Hayley got up and put some water in the electric kettle. "I told Bull to get you one of these for a wedding present," she said with a smile. She turned it on and rummaged through the tea canister. "Then I told him if they were on sale, he could get me one for Christmas. I love this thing."

Tori smiled at her friend and patted her face with the dry paper towel. Hayley always made things seem not so bad. Of course, Tori's troubles weren't nearly as awful as the things Hayley had gone through, but Hayley hardly ever talked about her past and rarely complained.

Usually Tori did the same, but it seemed like everyone was stressing her out. "No hot chocolate?" she asked. It occurred to her that Hayley was heating water not milk.

Hayley turned, hand on hip, and raised her eyebrows. "You really think you need more sugar in your system right now?"

Tori giggled for real this time. Ah, that felt better.

"Aunt Flo said some terrible things yesterday and Mom didn't stop her."

Hayley shook her head and muttered something under her breath.

"Not just about me, but Lexie, too. Even about my cousin, Jessie."

The kettle button popped and Hayley poured hot water into both mugs. Then she covered each mug with a small plate.

"If I'd been there, I'm sure she wouldn't have left me out." Hayley pulled two eggs from the fridge, and got out a frying pan.

Tori raised an eyebrow wryly and nodded. Hayley became one of the family in more ways than one when she came to live with them. Aunt Flo had decided she was fair game, too.

Hayley cut holes in the middle of two pieces of bread, buttered both sides, and lay them in the frying pan. She cracked an egg into each hole, then checked the tea.

"I'm not really hungry," Tori said. All the bad dreams and crying had made her feel a little sick to her stomach. That reminded her of the queasy feeling she had arguing with her mom. She got up and took the mug of English Breakfast tea, and doctored it with milk and honey before sitting back down at the table.

"Your long silence is making me uncomfortable," she told Hayley.

"Sorry." Hayley sent her a quick smile. "Just trying to figure out what to say that doesn't make things worse."

"Worse as in trying not to call my family members a-holes," Tori half-laughed, "or worse as in trying not to agree with everyone that I shouldn't get married right now?"

Hayley flipped the eggs and toast, and pulled two plates from the cabinet. She didn't smile.

Tori felt her stomach drop. Hayley didn't think she should get married either?

"Eggy in a basket for two," Hayley said, setting the plates down. She got two forks out of the drawer behind her and sat next to Tori. She took a bite of her breakfast, chewed, smiled, and swallowed. "I was so hungry. You know I can say the wrong thing when I'm cranky, and I was getting close to cranky-hungry."

Tori just stared at her, waiting for the bad news.

Hayley gestured. "Eat."

Tori sighed. "Talk."

Hayley looked down at her plate. "Okay, if you eat. You'll feel better."

Tori took a bite and closed her eyes for a moment. No one made eggy in a basket like Hayley. She took another bite. Maybe she did feel a little better.

"Pinky-swear honesty?"

Tori nodded. If her best friend couldn't be honest with her, how could she figure things out?

"Ever since you introduced me to Joe, I haven't stopped being shocked. I mean *shocked*, Tori," Hayley said. "How in the world did you two find each other? To only live a few blocks apart for years and then suddenly run into each other? And then, *bam*, you fall in love just like that. And then you decide to get married a few weeks later?"

Hayley shook her head and chewed another bite. "You two are like a romantic comedy. I kept waiting for the other shoe to fall, but it hasn't. And I'm beginning to think it won't."

Tori looked up, feeling hope wash away the sick feeling. "But Mom is positive things will be easier if we wait to get married. Do you think so?"

Hayley shrugged. "You know how we used to laugh at those old re-runs of *The Love Boat*, about how people would fall in love in seven days? Did you know Kelly's boyfriend's dad did that? Apparently, he and the woman he married two weeks after they met have been married for something like four years. So who's to say what's the right or wrong way to do this?"

Tori cut a corner of the toast and a piece of the middle of the egg and put them in her mouth together. It was true, no two courtship stories were the same.

"A couple weeks ago," she told Hayley, "Stacy who runs the youth group at church told me that when she and her husband Gary were dating, they broke up and got together again seven times in five years. Now they've been married for eleven years." She looked at Hayley and they both shrugged.

"So who's to say?" Hayley asked.

"But not everyone who gets together, stays together. What if my mom is right and things would be easier if we waited?"

"Not to put too fine a point on it, Tori," Hayley said, pointing her fork at Tori, "but I've seen you two together. You really think you can make it until next summer without giving in? And how are you going to feel about this magical love you have if you *do* end up moving the wedding date up because you're pregnant?"

Tori thought about Friday night. No matter how strongly she believed in her choice to wait, she wasn't sure she could make it six more months. "Not being able to keep our hands off each other isn't much of a good reason to get married."

Hayley tilted her head. "Is that why you're getting married?"

Tori shook her head firmly.

"So what's really bothering you?"

She thought about it for a moment. Thought about yesterday's conversations with various family members on both sides.

Thought about her nightmare and the other bad dreams and what they might mean.

She chose her words carefully, not wanting Hayley to know about the shrink and the meds any more than she wanted Joe to know. "What if there is something wrong with me? Something that would be bad for our relationship? What if our previous pinky-swear to never get married was wiser than we realized?"

Hayley finished her last bite of breakfast, staring at a space on the far wall. "I worry all the time that we're broken, permanently broken, you and me and Lexie."

Tori nodded, running her fork lightly over the designs on the plate. That's why they'd made those promises years ago, and she and Lexie had renewed their vow to remain single when Lexie's boyfriend Rodney left her.

"So why do I feel this overwhelming certainty," she asked quietly, "that I can be whole again with Joe? It's not that I think I need him in order to be okay." She tried to find the right words. "It's more that when I'm around him, I feel like I can conquer the world. He's big and strong and he makes me feel safe, but *I* feel stronger around him. Even when I'm not around him, really. I feel like...I don't know how to say it...like I'm the *real me* when we're together. The "me" God had in mind when he made me. I feel beautiful and strong and confident."

Tori looked up to see if Hayley was terribly confused. But she was nodding. Still staring at the wall, Hayley said, "Funny, Joe said something almost just like that."

"What?" Tori gasped. "When? Where?"

Hayley turned to her and seemed to come out of her thoughts. She shrugged. "A couple weeks ago. I was with Bull, and Bull was with Joe, and...I don't know. It came up."

Hope soared. She and Joe both knew that their sudden, explosive love for each other was outside the norm. They'd talked about it enough to know that loving each other wasn't a problem.

Liking each other wasn't a problem. Combining their two disparate lives and families seemed to be the real hurdle.

And he didn't even know about her mental health history. Maybe that would prove to be the high bar on the hurdle that knocked them back.

"You know I haven't told him much about our past, me and Lexie's." As teenagers, Hayley had sometimes gone out into the city with Tori to look for Lexie after she'd given up baby Charlie and run away. "You think I should? Is it the kind of secret that needs to be told? Because I just don't see how anything good can come from the telling, or anything bad from not telling."

Hayley took their plates to the sink. "You know how I feel about secrets."

Tori nodded. "Don't tell if you don't have to." She thought about it some more. "But if I'm going to share my life with someone, am I being selfish by bringing secrets into the marriage? Am I being selfish by wanting to get married now instead of waiting?"

Hayley picked up her mug of peppermint tea. She liked it best when it was warm, not hot, having steeped for at least twenty minutes. She tested it, then took a few swallows, leaning against the counter.

"I think to be human in this broken world is to be selfish in many areas of your life," she said. "And I think there's a difference between selfishness and self-preservation."

Tori nodded, agreeing while also realizing she still didn't have an answer. Maybe subconsciously she thought that getting married now would help seal the success of Operation Freedom, her challenge to find her real self. Maybe that was selfish of her.

Or maybe all this pushback was the world's way of forcing her to really think about what she wanted, and to work for it, fight for it.

She thought about Joe. He was so wonderful. She would fight for him any day. She just didn't want to fight so hard that she hurt him, allowing him to marry someone who was so broken that he would be cut on the harsh edges.

Was keeping her secrets an act of selfishness or self-preservation?

And what she had worked for years to disprove, did she need to reconsider — was there really something wrong with her that could hurt other people? If she was wrong and she did need to remain on medication and continue seeing a psychiatrist every week, there was no way she could keep that from a husband. And if she told him, she'd have to tell him that it had been going on for over twenty years.

What would he think of her then? Worse, if she found that she was right, and she didn't need the doctor and his drugs, but she'd told Joe about twenty years of medical "issues," would he ever look at her the same again?

A mistake like that could break the one thing in her life that was undamaged.

8

Being on vacation from MGV Security was not the same as being on vacation from work. Christmastime in Double Bay meant double-time for the superheroes who were willing. And because some weren't willing to work extra hard when they, too, wanted to be with their families, it meant you never knew when you were going to get another call for help.

Joe had barely woken up Monday morning when Mickey phoned. Of course, Joe told his friend he'd meet him at the clubhouse in forty minutes. He took a minute to reply to Tori's text from last night — wished, in fact, that he'd heard it come in so he could chat with her — then he threw on his super suit, put some cat food in Snickers' dish, and rushed out.

At the clubhouse, Mickey was waiting in the black SUV with dark tinted windows that they used when working. It was just the two of them this morning. Bull, a history teacher at Washington High School as his day job, wanted to visit one of his students at the juvenile detention center. Hayley, the fourth member of their team, had taken the week off so she could help Tori with wedding preparations.

Joe still couldn't believe Hayley and Tori had been best

friends since elementary school. How odd it had been when Tori "introduced" them last month. Hayley had responded by saying he looked familiar, wasn't he one of Bull's friends, and Joe had gone along with it. From her reaction, Tori hadn't known Hayley was dating Bull either, which goes to show how scrupulously Hayley protected her privacy.

Still, she had obviously kept Tori in the dark all this time about her secret identity as Green Thumb. Joe had only kept his secrets for a few weeks. That wasn't so bad.

"What's up?" Joe asked Mickey, buckling his seat belt.

Mickey pulled onto the street in the industrial neighborhood where their office, MGV Security — with the clubhouse in the basement — was located. "A church over on Wesley Avenue had just loaded a rental truck with over one hundred boxes of Christmas meals. Driver went inside to refill his coffee and the truck was gone when he came out."

"And the police are…"

Mickey slanted him a look. "Spread too thin. Still trying to work through the four car break-ins and two carjackings at the mall yesterday."

Joe nodded. Double Bay never had enough law enforcement to cover the city. That's why superheroes congregated here, plenty to do. Didn't hurt, of course, that despite the crime, the weather, and the unemployment, it was a beautiful place to live.

"Any ideas?"

Mickey didn't answer right away. He had some kind of crazy genius gift with technology, and he invented all kinds of gizmos that came in handy for their team, and for other superheroes as well. Over time, they'd also discovered that Mickey could often drive around, with no specific route in mind, and locate a vehicle he wanted to find.

It had happened accidentally several times when they were still in college. One day, Bull decided they would test Mickey and see what happened. Joe and Bull hid their cars in various parts of the city and asked Mickey to find them. Then they borrowed Joe's parents' cars and his sibling's cars, and then they rented a couple of big trucks. Still Mickey could discover the location of the vehicle in question.

So Joe didn't ask where they were going, just waited quietly in the passenger seat. He thought about Tori's text. Why was she awake at three in the morning? She'd never texted him in the middle of the night before. He wished he had an excuse to see her before tonight, but she and Hayley were working on wedding stuff. He was vague on the details.

Joe noticed that the snowfall from yesterday and last night had accumulated about six inches on the ground, nearly a foot total. Not enough for Michigan people to be concerned with. Though as he was thinking about it, he noticed a few flakes coming down. He wondered how weird it would be to have a sunny and warm Christmas. This year would be his first, assuming the forecast for Orlando proved accurate.

That thought led to thoughts of Tori again. And her parents' conviction that the wedding should be postponed. His parents wouldn't be against that decision, either. His dad had gotten on his case again last night, asking if Joe had explained to Tori about their family.

Joe told him that he'd brought it up a couple times, but she didn't understand that he wasn't joking. He was working on it.

Owen hadn't been particularly happy with that answer. He'd lectured Joe about keeping secrets from one's spouse, the physical difficulty in running off to work at a moment's notice with believable excuses to one's spouse, the impossibility of explaining late nights, bruises, and missing or ripped clothes to one's spouse.

"If you don't want a spouse," Owen had said grimly, "now is the time to decide."

Joe told him he *did* want a wife and he *would* tell her when the timing was right. He was feeling kind of proud of himself for standing up to his dad without letting anger overrule reason.

Then his dad said, "If you don't tell her, I'm not marrying you."

Joe had stood there in the garage where Owen had ambushed him, staring at his dad and trying to decide if it was a bluff. He'd finally nodded his head and walked back into the kitchen.

He wondered now, as he watched the snow fall, how serious his dad was. Would he really stand there in front of the church and Tori's family, holding up the wedding until Tori nodded her head and said she understood that Joe wasn't joking around?

Mickey mumbled under his breath.

Joe turned to look at him. "Close?"

"Maybe," he muttered.

They were in a residential neighborhood in the Park City area. The name implied a lovely little community, but it had long ago lost its luster. Today's Park City streets had as many thugs and boastful bandits as it had working class people trying to hold onto their integrity.

It was the "boastful" part that made it easy to find the bad guys here. Sure enough, Joe saw what must be the truck they were looking for a block away. People were pulling boxes out of the back and taking them to nearby homes and cars.

Mickey growled when he saw it. He braked for a moment and both men pulled their masked headpieces over their faces, adjusting the voice-disguising units at their throats and doing a sound check.

"Testing one-two-three," said Joe, now Superhero X.

"Dirtbags, scumbags, and thieves, oh my," said Mickey, now Tick Tock.

Tick Tock pulled the SUV to the other side of the street, grill to grill with the stolen truck, and tapped the other vehicle's bumper just enough to make the truck shake. Then he turned off the engine and jumped out.

Superhero X was already on the street, glaring at people carrying the stolen boxes of food. Most of them ran. Two lanky young men in flannel-lined coats and knit caps peered around from inside the back of the truck just as X and Tick Tock came around the sides.

One of the two started cursing up a storm, kicking and punching boxes in the truck. Apparently, he didn't think he'd get caught so quickly. Tick Tock bounded up into the back and pulled one of the guy's arms behind his back.

X followed the movement of the second guy. He stuffed a wad of cash in his jeans pocket and jumped out of the truck onto the street, his legs already making a running motion as he hit the ground. X let him jump, afraid the guy would fall and hurt himself if X grabbed his leg.

But the guy forgot how slippery the street was now with the packed snow. He didn't get two steps before he fell on his face. X put a foot on the small of his back, using just enough pressure to keep him down.

He pressed a button on his wrist and called the police. Then he folded his arms and glared at the neighbors taking advantage of the situation.

A boy of maybe fourteen crept back slowly with his box. He made a wide circle, never taking his eyes off X. He stopped about twenty feet away and put the box on the snow-covered sidewalk.

"I didn't steal it," he said quietly. "I gave him all the money we had."

X let his glare soften a degree of two. "You understand that *they* stole it?"

The boy hung his head and nodded.

"I can see that you know it was wrong," X said sternly. He paused and then said, "So why'd you do it?"

The thief under his boot started spouting a string of curses and threats. X pressed his boot down harder until the man was gasping for breath.

"Well?" he asked the kid.

The boy shrugged. "We was hungry."

Well, crap. X sighed. The worst part about his job was that he couldn't help everybody. He couldn't solve all the problems. And he couldn't give this hungry child something that didn't belong to either of them.

All right, Lord, what can we do? We've got some hungry orphans and widows down here needing your provision.

The boy started to walk away, his head still hanging.

"Wait," X called. He remembered what Stretch spent his time doing when he was just Darian Johnson. "You know the East Side Youth Center? Near Overland Boulevard and Sixth?"

The kid looked up, hesitated, and nodded.

"Go over and ask for Darian. Tell him Superhero X sent you. He'll fix you up."

The kid furrowed his eyebrows, trying to find the catch. Then he nodded again.

"How much you give this thief?" X asked.

"Twenty bucks."

X bent down, dug the wad of cash out of the scumbag's front pocket, and started to peel off a twenty. The guy started fighting him so X pulled a zip tie out of a pocket and tied his hands. Then he picked up the money roll, pulled off the twenty, and stuffed the roll back in the guy's pocket.

He held the twenty-dollar bill out to the kid on the sidewalk. The kid took a step toward him, then stopped.

"Everybody makes mistakes," X said. "It's whether we learn from them that determines the kind of people we become. What are you going to do if this opportunity presents itself again?"

The boy looked at the scene around him — a stolen truck filled with boxes of Christmas food meant for other people; two superheroes standing on the thieves while waiting for the cops; neighbors watching from behind their curtains, hiding the boxes they'd bought so the superheroes wouldn't take them.

The boy turned back to X and said with all seriousness, "Cut the bologna into turkey shapes."

X burst out laughing. He almost fell over with his foot on the thief's back. He looked over at the truck and saw Tick Tock laughing, too, a rare sight indeed.

Darian's words came back to him suddenly. X couldn't help all the people in this neighborhood, or all the people on this street, but he could help one starfish.

"What's your name?" X asked.

"Jackson."

"How many people are going to be at your house on Christmas, Jackson?"

"Ten."

"All right, you're going to have all the makings for Christmas dinner for ten delivered to your house by tomorrow night. You know why?"

Jackson shrugged. "Because you're a superhero?"

X smiled at him. "Because I think you're a good kid trying to take care of your family, and I think you've learned something here today."

Jackson shrugged again. "Yeah, stealing's wrong, no matter who stole it."

"Exactly. And sometimes you get rewarded for being honest."

Jackson nodded. He scuffed the toe of his shoe against the snow on the sidewalk. "Can I shake your hand?"

X walked over to the boy and shook hands, giving him the twenty-dollar bill the kid had been too nervous to retrieve. Jackson pointed to his house and let X record him giving his address into the tiny microphone in the wrist of his suit.

When the thief on the ground struggled up as far as his knees, X told the boy he had to get back to work.

Eventually a patrol car arrived and the thieves were carted off. By then, someone from the church had arrived and, by some miracle, they were allowed to take the truck and deliver the remaining Christmas meals. One of the cops told the driver he'd call him later, see if the precinct could round up some more meals to make up for the missing ones.

By the time Tick Tock and X were back in their SUV and pulling away, X was feeling particularly good.

"I'm starving," he told Mickey after they stopped to pull their masks and headpieces off. "Where do you want to eat? My treat."

"Norm's burritos?"

"Done." Joe let out a contented sigh. "I love this job. That kid Jackson was a surprise, wasn't he?"

"I'll never think of bologna the same again."

"Too bad Bull wasn't here. He would've loved that kid."

"Good thing he wasn't. He would've taken him home with him."

Joe figured a lot of people had the Monday Morning Blues right now. They didn't like their job, wished they could be some-place else. But he wasn't one of them. He knew Mickey wasn't either. They couldn't be happier with the direction their lives were taking.

"If you go through with this wedding, how are you going to explain to her why you jumped out of bed so fast this morning?" Mickey was back at his new favorite subject.

Okay, so Mickey could be happier with the direction Joe's life was taking.

"Tori knows I work in security," Joe said patiently. "Some jobs have weird hours. She understands. And when she understands better, I'll explain everything to her and there won't be any more secrets."

"And you think hiding all your stuff at the clubhouse is a long-term solution?"

Joe was determined not to take offense at Mickey's grousing. He knew Mickey didn't care where Joe's super suit was, just that Joe could get to it when he needed it. And starting tomorrow, he needed to keep it at the clubhouse. No, Mickey's problem was with Tori's family.

"I won't need a long-term solution, Mick. I'm going to tell her. In my own time."

"So marry her after you tell her. If she thinks you're mentally unbalanced, you can still call it off."

"Why do I bother telling you anything if you're going to use it against me?" He never should have told Mickey what Tori's mother had said.

Mickey braked harder than he needed to at a yellow light turning red. He glared over at Joe. "Because I'm one of your best friends and my job is to protect you."

Joe sighed but it came out as more of a frustrated growl. With his elbow resting on the door, he rubbed his chin. How could he explain?

"You're afraid she won't love you if she knows who you are." Mickey stared at him as the idea dawned on him.

Joe started to protest. "She loves me, Mick."

A horn beeped behind them and Mickey accelerated. He sighed. "Joe, you've got a future already mapped out. The team can be without you for a week, but not forever. You gonna quit if she tells you to? What about your plan to work your way through the Paladins Guild and take over for your dad? You're the heir apparent, man! The Guild needs stability in leadership now more than ever. Are you sure you can offer that?"

Joe looked over at Mickey and frowned. "That is harsh, man."

Mickey shook his head. "Someone has to be harsh with you. You're not thinking. Guild leaders need to be able to see the big picture as well as all the tiny parts that make it up. They need to know their weaknesses so they can defend against them. This girl is your weakness."

"Her name is Tori. Not *she*, not *this girl*." Joe's plan not to get angry with his friend was reaching the breaking point.

"Maybe you two should hold on a little less tightly to each other and see what happens," Mickey said as he pulled into the drive-thru lane at Norm's. "Maybe you're both stronger than you think."

Both men put on their coats to cover their suits. No need for the cashier to guess who they were. Joe was trying to compose a reply when Mickey pulled up and placed their order for breakfast burritos.

Protect her.

The words didn't so much make themselves heard in Joe's head as they impressed themselves upon his mind. He'd been hearing them on and off since he met Tori, and he was convinced they referred to her.

Protect her.

Joe looked at his watch. It was barely ten in the morning. She couldn't be in danger. She was at home as far as he knew. Still, he couldn't shake the feeling that the voice came to him when she needed him.

He pulled his cell phone out of his coat pocket and dialed Tori's cell.

"Tori's phone, Hayley speaking."

"Hayley, it's Joe. Where is Tori? Is she all right?"

"Hey, Joe. She's in the shower. Is something wrong?"

Joe didn't want to try to explain. He hadn't told anyone about the voice, afraid what it would sound like. On the other hand, he didn't want to ignore it either.

"Would you go check on her, please?"

"Um, sure, hold on."

Joe could hear in Hayley's voice what she thought of his request. But she was a professional Paladin and didn't argue.

She came back on the line a minute later. "She's fine," she said.

Was Hayley's voice strained? Was she hiding something from him? "Hayley, I'm serious. Is she absolutely okay?"

He heard Hayley take a deep breath. Then she said, "It's just pre-wedding jitters, Joe. She had a nightmare last night and it freaked her out. That's all."

Joe rubbed his forehead. She'd needed him last night and he hadn't been there for her. They weren't even married yet and he wasn't taking good enough care of her. Even as the thought crossed his mind, he suspected it was a little over the top. But he didn't care right now.

"Would you do me a favor? Would you go tell her I'm on the phone?"

"Joe, this phone isn't waterproof," Hayley half-laughed.

"Just tell her I called to see how she was doing, and..." He bit back his embarrassment. "Tell her I love her. Tell her, and then let me know if she said anything. I'll hang on."

Hayley laughed. Joe could hear a knock on a door, then Hayley's muffled voice. A minute later she was back on the line. "I never knew you were such a romantic, Mr. Clarke. I told her what you said, and I think you made her cry. She said to tell you 'I love you back.' Satisfied?"

Joe wanted to drive over and see her, hold her, make sure she really was fine. But he thought of Mickey's words — try holding on less tightly. He'd give it a shot.

"Thanks, Hayley. Listen...be careful today, okay?"

She heard the worry in his voice and got serious. "You got it, boss. We'll see you tonight."

Joe started to say, I'm not your boss, but Hayley had already hung up. He took his burrito from Mickey and ate in silence.

He wished he knew what it meant, where the danger was, if there *was* any danger. Why else would he hear such a message? The first time he heard it was the night he met Tori, just after she was mugged on Halloween. That must mean that he heard it when there was some kind of danger, right?

"Everything okay?" Mickey asked.

"Just trying not to hold on so tight," Joe said, staring out the window at the falling snow.

His good mood had taken a beating. What if he was wrong

and Tori wouldn't understand? What if the voice in his head meant that he was to protect Tori from *him*, from his life and calling? Or maybe he was to protect her by marrying her and keeping her close and safe. Now he wasn't sure.

He and Tori had decided to get married on Christmas Eve, not just because it was coming up quickly and they didn't want to wait, but because of what Christmas meant to them. It was a celebration of the moment God poured himself into human form to bring life and hope to the world.

To join their two lives into one on the eve of that celebration would be a symbol of the hope and love they shared as they started a new life together.

But maybe starting a new life with secrets, no matter the reason, would undermine everything they were trying to build.

9

Tuesday morning, Tori felt a little edgy as she drove Bill, her blue Honda, over to Joe's house. They had decided she would leave her car there, and tomorrow they would drive Joe's truck to the airport.

Assuming they got married tomorrow.

She did some deep breathing exercises as she drove so she wouldn't get a stress stomachache. One good thing about seeing Dr. Huntington for so many years, she'd learned a lot about staying calm. If she allowed herself to get too upset, her insides got all hot and tense.

They planned to meet Bull and Hayley at the mall for last minute Christmas shopping, but they would have a few minutes on the drive to talk in private. She still wasn't sure if she wanted to tell him about her supposed mental health problems, especially since she'd never felt better, but she needed to have the courage to at least have a conversation about secrets. After all, he'd sort of started a discussion on that topic at dinner Friday.

At Joe's, she saw his truck parked on the street as expected. She pulled into the recently shoveled driveway, up to the garage door. There would just barely be enough room for both vehicles when they lived there together.

Joe opened the front door before Tori could knock. He pulled her inside, kissing her before the door closed.

Tori felt the heat rise between them as he leaned her against the wall. Their lips and tongues and hands joined in a dance of exquisite torment. She *did* want to marry him. How could she not?

He pressed against her and whispered in her ear, "I missed you."

She giggled breathlessly. "You just saw me last night." He kissed her deeply again, requiring a better answer. "I missed you, too," she admitted.

"Are you sure we have to go shopping?" he asked a minute later.

"It was your idea," she said with a laugh. "You're the one who asked Hayley and Bull to meet us at the mall."

Joe groaned and made a funny face. She'd begun to realize not long after they met that he did it on purpose so she would laugh.

"Besides," she teased, "you promised my grandma I'd be a virgin bride. We just have to make it one more day."

He kissed her one more time, this one gentle and loving rather than hot and lusty. "Then let's get outside in the cold."

Tori laughed. A meow sounded from above her head. Snickers sat curled up on top of the coat rack, blinking down at her. Tori reached up and stroked his head. He arched his neck and back and purred.

"We'll be back, Snicks," Joe said and gave the cat a good scratch. Then he opened the door for Tori and locked it behind them.

As she sat in the truck with the engine running, Joe brushing off a dusting of snow, she tried to order her thoughts. The Bible said not to let the sun go down on your anger, but she couldn't think of any advice about keeping secrets from your spouse. She wondered where secrets fell on the heavenly list of suggestions for better living.

Joe climbed in and off they went. The truck had better traction than her smaller car, but it slid a little on a patch of ice as Joe pulled into the street.

"Can I ask you something?" she began a few moments later. "I was thinking...everyone has things they don't want other people to know. Some of them aren't important, just embarrassing, like a boy who wet the bed until he was seven. No one needs to know that. It doesn't help to know that about someone, and it certainly doesn't hurt anything to keep it to yourself, right?"

Joe nodded. "Agreed."

"So how do we know as a married couple what is a 'bad' secret"—she made air quotes with her gloved fingers—"and what is just private?"

Joe made that grunting noise he always made when he was thinking. Tori thought it was rather adorable. See? She did know things about him.

"Funny," he said, "I've been thinking about that, too."

Tori looked over at him in surprise. "Really? Thoughts?"

"I don't know. Lately, I've been wondering..."

"Yeah?" Tori hoped they would find themselves in agreement on this topic. Then she would have nothing to feel guilty about.

"Some people think we're being selfish by, you know..."

"Getting married so quickly. Yeah, that's a word that came up in a conversation with me recently, too."

Joe reached over and squeezed her hand, then put both hands back on the wheel. Tori knew the roads were still slippery in spots, especially since the sun hadn't yet warmed the icier areas shaded by trees.

"So I'm wondering..." Tori knew she had to continue or she wouldn't be able to relax and enjoy their wedding. "For instance, do you think I have to tell you that in the second grade I got mad at a boy and gave him a bloody nose?"

Joe snorted a laugh. "Did you really?"

"Well, I wouldn't want to tell you if I thought it could change your opinion of me, so you answer first." She smiled when she said it, but she had thought half the night about what example she would use to test the waters.

"Honey, kids do that sort of stuff. It's part of being a kid."

"What if I told you that afterward I was told I had an anger management problem, and went to counseling?"

Joe raised his eyebrows and looked over at her. "I'd say that this is probably the kind of thing you were asking about — something that would be embarrassing for you to tell me, and not at all important to our relationship."

Tori released a deep sigh in her head. Relief rushed through her and she felt her shoulders relax. *Thank you, God. Thank you, thank you. I don't want to do the wrong thing, but even Joe doesn't think we need to tell each other every awful detail of our lives before we met. Since I've been asking you for advice, I'm taking this as a sign.*

The street opened into more of a business area with fewer trees. The sun and traffic had melted most of the snow on the street so the asphalt was only wet, not icy. Joe took her hand again.

"What about other things," Joe asked, "things that aren't embarrassing childhood incidents? What do you think we need to tell each other before tomorrow?"

"The way everyone has been pushing us," Tori said, letting some of her frustration through, "it seems like *they* think we should tell each other everything. But I know a girl who went speed dating once, and she didn't like it. She said she learned more than she'd ever want to know on a first date. But later, she said, she realized some of that stuff wouldn't have bothered her if she was already into the guy."

Tori let Joe digest that before continuing.

"I can see that," he said, nodding.

"I've been best friends with Hayley since we were in second grade. We know *a lot* of each other's secrets, but we learned them over time, as the need came up to share, or as we trusted each other more. I'm sure we still don't know everything about each other."

Though that was something Tori really wanted to have the courage to change. Hayley often seemed shut off from the world, perpetually lonely even when she was laughing with girlfriends. Tori wanted to help her relax and enjoy life more. She just didn't know how.

"Part of me," Joe said slowly, "wants to tell everyone who has a problem with us that it's none of their business."

Tori nodded. Boy, did she feel the same way.

"But then I think about Solomon, the wisest man who ever lived, and his many advisors. He felt so strongly about it, he wrote several proverbs suggesting we all seek the advice of others. I don't want to be hard-headed and make things more difficult than they need to be."

"Yeah," Tori sighed. "That's crossed my mind, too."

Joe pulled into the mall parking lot and drove toward the entrance near Target where they were to meet Hayley and Bull.

Because of the way the snowplows cleaned the parking lot earlier, there were bigger spaces farther back from the doors.

"Mind walking a bit?" Joe asked. "My truck needs a bigger space."

"I don't mind. It's gorgeous out."

Joe pulled into a spot and killed the engine. Like Tori, he sat staring out the windshield.

"I don't want to be selfish—" they both said at the same time.

Then they laughed and unclipped their seat belts. Tori scooted over and Joe pulled her closer. That fabulous and overwhelming feeling of safety and strength encompassed Tori. They could get through anything together, she knew it.

"I love you—" they said together.

They both laughed again and Joe pulled her into a tight hug. "I don't want to do anything to hurt you," he said, the tone of his voice betraying the depth of his feelings.

"Ditto," Tori said, her throat too tight with emotion to say more.

They sat like that for a moment. Tori hoped these feelings lasted longer than the honeymoon phase like some people predicted. But it was more than infatuation or lust. It felt like friendship, partnership, the kind of thing that lasts.

Joe's cell phone went off. He saw it was Bull and answered it on speaker. "Yeah?"

"Get a room!" yelled Bull and Hayley. Laughter filtered through the phone.

"We saw you pull into a parking space two minutes ago," Bull said. "There'll be plenty of time for hanky-panky in Disney World. Get in here."

Tori felt her face heat as she laughed. Being part of a couple was new and wonderful, but being part of a group of couples was more fun than she would've thought.

Joe hung up, then kissed her nose. "Finish this conversation later?"

"Sounds good," Tori agreed.

Joe pulled her out his side of the truck and held her dangling above the snow. Tori wrapped her arms around his neck, giggling at the strange feeling of hanging in the air. She still couldn't believe how strong he was. He kissed her soundly once more before he set her down and took her hand.

They met Hayley and Bull at the entrance, and the four of them made their first stop at Starbucks. Joe ordered Tori's hot chocolate exactly as she liked it, right down to the size she always chose. She smiled and wondered why people were so convinced they didn't know enough about each other to get married.

"Wipe that goofy look off your face before you embarrass us all," Hayley whispered in her ear.

Tori turned to her and grinned. They linked arms and walked over to where others were waiting for their drinks. "I'm so in love!" The words came out in a singsong whisper.

Hayley chuckled with her. "You're such a goofball. Listen, I have an idea. You know how we're going to split up after lunch, and you and I will get mani-pedi's while they do heaven knows what?"

Tori nodded.

"I saw a sign when we walked in that Victoria's Secret is having a sale. Let's go there after, okay?"

"Ooo," Tori clapped her hands twice, "yes, let's!" Hayley would probably buy something red or black like she always did. Those colors complemented her thick dark hair and creamy skin. Tori would have to walk past the cute flannel loungewear and buy something — gasp! — with lace. She could hardly wait.

The four of them spent the next couple hours shopping and laughing. Joe asked her and Hayley's opinions on gifts for his sisters and nieces. Bull bought Hayley a red scarf with a green ivy pattern. Tori noticed a soft look pass between them. So sweet.

She couldn't remember the last time she had so much fun. The mall looked so beautiful draped in green and gold garlands with white candles and red bows. Lively Christmas music filled the air along with the smell of pretzels, cookies, chocolate — when they walked past the chocolatier — and scented candles. Tori wanted to look and taste and smell and buy a little of everything.

They shopped and talked and walked and laughed until they were hungry. Bull and Joe offered to take all the bags to their trucks while Tori and Hayley waited for a table to open up in the food court. The delicious aromas of pizza and Chinese food made Tori's stomach rumble.

They'd been waiting about ten minutes when her cell phone

rang — Joe. Tori smiled and hit the talk button, noticing that Hayley's phone rang at the same time.

"You guys having a snowball fight or something?" she said. "The womenfolk are getting hungry."

"Tori, honey," Joe's voice was serious, "listen to me. The gang of thieves is back. I want you to stay in the mall, all right?"

"What? Well, wait, what are you going to do?" Tori stumbled over her words. Joe was outside with the gang of thieves? They were dangerous. He shouldn't be out there.

"Bull and I are going to try to help catch them," Joe said. "The police will be here any minute. Mall security is already—"

"Joe, no, you could get hurt! Come back inside and let the police take care of—"

"Listen," Joe interrupted. "Honey, listen, this is my job. You know that."

She bit her lip. Sure, but not the day before their wedding. What if he got hurt? He was big and strong, but it's not like he could stop a bullet. "But you don't work here," she protested. What if those men had guns? The reports all said they didn't, but what if they were getting bolder since they hadn't been caught?

"Do you want me to let other people get hurt?" Joe waited for her to answer.

"No," she finally said. If anyone could take down one or two of these thieves, it was Joe. And Bull was even bigger. So long as they stayed together, they could watch each other's backs.

"Do you trust me?"

"Yes." She didn't have to think about it. "I trust you."

"Then I'm going to help out here, and you finish up in there. Bull and I know what we're doing, we'll be fine." His voice was quick, tense, confident, and — for some strange reason — it gave her strength.

"Stay with Hayley," he continued. "She has keys to Bull's truck. We may be awhile if we have to make a police report. I'll see you tonight at church, okay?"

She took a deep breath. This was the first time she'd been with him when there'd been a situation he had to rush off to help with. It felt strange.

But she believed him when he said he could handle it. "Be safe," she said. "I love you."

After she hung up, she looked over at Hayley. Her friend spoke quietly into her phone, glanced up at Tori and nodded, and a moment later hung up.

"Soo..." Tori said. "This is a new experience for me. Happen often?"

Hayley shrugged. "Yeah." She put her arm around Tori and gave her a hug. "Don't worry, Tori. They know what they're doing. No one has ever hurt them. If you're going to worry about someone, worry about the punks who are about to get their butts kicked." She grinned.

Tori gave a little laugh. "Okay, I guess I'm following your lead."

What an unusual twist her life had taken. On the one hand, the current situation was a shock and she didn't know how to respond. On the other hand, it didn't surprise her one bit that if she were going to fall in love, it would be with a man who was a protector.

What did he say he was — six-five? Joe was huge, and the strongest man she'd ever met. She doubted he'd get into it with anyone near his size.

Nonetheless, she prayed, *God, please keep him safe*.

Joe hung up the phone with Tori, then spoke to Hayley for a moment on Bull's phone. "Stay inside. Don't let her out of your sight. No, Mickey will be here soon. We'll be okay without you. Enjoy your foot massage." He laughed at Hayley's response and hung up.

Bull flexed his shoulders. "I was tired of shopping anyway."

Joe grinned. "Same here. So how do you want to handle this?" He pulled his warm knit cap out of a pocket and pulled it on.

"Thorn in the side until backup arrives?" Bull pulled his hat on as well.

"Love it."

The two men split up, keeping their eyes on the men and vehicles that had caught their attention a few minutes earlier. The SLU had briefed the teams with what information the police had been able to gather from past victims and witnesses.

The two- and three-man teams included a point man who would walk the parking lot looking like he was heading to his car or like he'd forgotten where he parked. He'd try to cross paths with someone with a lot of bags opening their car door or trunk. If the catch looked good, he'd grab all the bags while the second man pulled up in the getaway car. They'd load the car and take off, sometimes picking up the haul from a second point man.

Descriptions of the vehicles varied, so police figured they drove off-site to unload and came back with a different car. It seemed that each team tried to make two to three runs before they quit for the day.

Joe had spotted the first man while taking his and Tori's bags to his truck. The man's gaze darted around, always coming back to face forward as he walked toward the far end of the lot. But the man was noticing people, not cars, and not people going *in* the mall.

Joe walked back up to where Bull had found a parking space closer to the mall entrance, told him what he'd seen, and Bull pointed to a car two aisles away. Dirty nondescript sedan, dark windows, looking like it was waiting for a space to open up.

Now the two of them started walking, Joe toward the man he'd seen, Bull toward the idling car.

Joe didn't want to scare the guys off, not with backup on the way. He wanted to surround and catch them, take down the whole team. But he also wanted to keep the locals from getting hurt or robbed.

A woman with more bags than she could easily carry exited the mall and walked down the aisle to Joe's left. Joe looked for the man he'd seen earlier. There. And on a collision course with the woman.

Joe walked toward them, trying to guess where the woman was headed. The green Explorer? No. The red Honda? Maybe. No. Just as she slowed near a white Mercedes, the handle of one of the bags ripped. The other man started jogging toward her.

Closer by a couple car lengths, Joe arrived first. Trying not to scare her, he said quietly, "Ma'am, get in your car."

She looked up, still struggling with her packages. "I don't need any help, thank you." She tried to get everything back in her hands.

The other man jogged up. "Let me help you with those," he said in a smooth, honeyed voice.

Joe stepped between them. "I don't think so. Ma'am, get in your car, please."

"OMG! OMG! You're the robbers!" She struggled frantically with her bags causing another one to rip open. "Leave me alone!"

While Joe was processing the fact that the young woman actually spoke in acronyms, the other man stepped around him. In a reassuring voice, he said, "Don't worry, I'm part of the community watch. We're patrolling the parking lots to make sure no one gets hurt. Is this man bothering you?"

"Yes!" The woman shouted. "Help me!"

The man reached for her bags and grabbed one before Joe lifted him off his feet.

"Give it back to her," Joe commanded.

The man's eyes widened in alarm as Joe lifted him over his head. Joe gave him a shake, but the guy didn't drop the bag. He turned at the sound of a car's engine.

The car Bull was tracking pulled up, but Bull wasn't in sight. The driver slid out and grabbed several of the young woman's bags. She screamed and pulled. The bags ripped open, littering the snow with gaily wrapped gifts. The driver started grabbing and tossing.

Just as Joe reached for the driver, the first man kicked at his groin. Joe groaned and twisted, grateful it hadn't been a direct hit. He let the guy drop, hoping he'd get the breath knocked out of him. He reached for the driver, but the young woman started hitting him with her purse.

"Lady, *get in your car!*" He was tempted to let her get robbed. He hadn't experienced this kind of abuse in months.

The driver threw another bag in the front seat. As he reached for another, Joe clotheslined him. Wham! And down. He grabbed the keys from the ignition and tossed them a few car lengths away.

The other man began to stir, crawling toward the car. Joe picked him up, opened the rear door and tossed him in. Then he tossed the driver into the front seat and slammed the door.

Keeping his back to the screamer still whacking him with her purse — what did she have in there? — Joe placed his hands on the doorframes and focused. Then he squeezed. The metal crumpled in his hands like aluminum foil. With one hand firmly on the metal of the car, he hit his other fist into the door handles, then went around and did the same on the other side.

The perps weren't going anywhere. Neither the doors nor the windows were going to open now.

He turned to the woman who followed him around to the other side of the car, still screaming and trying to hit him with her purse. "Call the police," he told her. "Tell them exactly where you're located and wait for them here. They'll get your packages back."

Not waiting for a thank-you he knew would never come, Joe took off across the parking lot. Without his costume, the police wouldn't know who he was. And he wanted to protect his real identity as much as he could from any officers not in the SLU.

He jogged to another section of the huge parking lot, his lungs burning a little in the cold air. He looked around for Bull, or anyone who looked like they were getting robbed.

A minute later he thought he saw Bull several aisles away. Joe jogged closer. Then he laughed. Bull was helping a little old lady into her ancient Cadillac. Joe watched him wait until she was buckled in, then he closed the door gently. He used his gloved hand to wipe the snow from all the windows and taillights. Then he stood out in the aisle, held up one hand to an oncoming car, and used his other hand to motion the woman to back up.

When she was safely out, she pulled up so the other car could have her space, then she rolled down her window. She spoke to Bull for a moment, he laughed, and she pulled away.

Joe walked up as Bull was waving goodbye. "What is it with you and kids and old people?" he asked, shaking his head. "A young woman in a Mercedes was beating me with her purse while the thief kicked me in the jewels."

A laugh burst out of Bull's throat. "Oh man, you all right?"

"I would've been better if I'd been holding onto the metal car," Joe said wryly.

"Aw, buddy, you and Mickey gotta keep working on those titanium-lined gloves."

Joe grunted and nodded. They walked down the aisle, looking for more thugs. "How do you keep yourself safe? Don't tell me no one's ever kicked you there?"

"Cup," Bull said.

Joe raised his eyebrows. "Every day? Even when we're not officially working?"

Bull snorted. "At Christmas, we're always working, aren't we? And it's not so bad, you get used to it."

"Better than the alternative, I guess," Joe said, stepping sideways and trying to rub his thigh unobtrusively.

It only took them a few minutes to find the next team. By the time they ran over and tried to stop them, both thieves had already gotten in the car. The sedan slipped and slid as the driver hit the gas.

"Light pole," Bull called and pointed.

Joe nodded and they both ran as fast as they could, angling to intersect with the car near the end of the aisle. Both men slammed into the sedan as the driver tried to turn onto the outer drive.

The car slid sideways. Joe and Bull hung on as it spun from the force of the collision. Near the light pole, they both sank their feet into the packed snow and pushed. The angle was perfect — the car smashed into the light pole nose first. The engine clunked and clicked and died.

The two men made short work of sealing the two thugs inside. They high-fived. Joe enjoyed his work most of the time, but it was particularly fun when they were winning. The adrenaline rush wasn't bad either.

In the distance, a police car headed their way around the outer drive. Both men pulled their hats down and walked nonchalantly toward the closest mall entrance.

"That's two," Bull said. "How many more do you think there are?"

Joe shrugged. "At least one more, I'd say. Let's call Tick Tock, see if he's here." He pulled out his cell phone and hit the speed dial for "Pizza Delivery," which was really the communication system in their super suits.

"Tick Tock, it's X and Powerhouse. You at the mall yet?" Joe nodded and shut the phone. "The entrance where the carousel is," he told Bull. "What's the closest way to get there?"

"Behind us, where the cops are," said Bull. Then he looked around to orient himself. "But if we go through the department store here, we can cut through the mall."

The men rushed in, taking off their coats and hats as if they were regular shoppers. They took ground-eating but unhurried-looking strides through the women's wear and cosmetics sections, across the mall to the carousel going round and round with its music and horses, and back out to the parking lot.

Upon exiting, both men once again donned their winter outerwear to walk unnoticed amongst the mall's patrons. It only took a moment for them to find Tick Tock. He stood in his suit in front of another dirty older sedan, fighting with another man. As Joe and Bull jogged up, Joe noticed the engine making an awful noise. Tick Tock could use his gift to destroy machinery as easily as to create or repair it.

Bull picked up the man taking a swing at Tick Tock. Joe ran toward another man sneaking up behind the superhero. He tackled him, punched him once in the jaw, and left him knocked cold in the snow.

Joe dusted the snow off his knees and grinned at his friends. "What a day, huh?"

"Behind you!" Bull ran forward as Joe turned.

Another sedan sped toward them down the aisle. The three men worked together to stop the car before it ran over people, including themselves.

Joe and Bull ran toward the car, giving themselves space to slow it down before it hit the barely idling car directly behind them. Off to the side, Tick Tock threw his arm out toward the moving vehicle and focused.

The engine began rattling before the car got to Joe and Bull. The acceleration had dropped off, but it still hit the men with force.

Not as much force as Bull hit the car, though. Joe threw both hands onto the metal hood, felt the cold, hard energy rush through his body, and let his feet slide on the snow for a few yards. Then he and Bull both pressed their feet more solidly against the snow-packed asphalt.

The ragged sound coming from the engine gave Joe confidence they'd stop the car without any problem. Then he looked behind him. They were still closing in too fast on the car Tick Tock had disabled.

He reached one hand behind him, turning his body sideways. Bull saw him and imitated his movements. Tick Tock shouted to the shoppers walking down the aisle toward them. One teenage girl was talking on her phone and not paying any attention.

Joe and Bull braced for impact. Tick Tock ran toward the girl.

Bam!

Joe felt his teeth clatter together as the bone-jarring impact rippled through his body. But his power protected him, and he didn't get pinned between the vehicles. The cars slid several yards on the snowpack before he and Bull stopped them.

Joe looked up to make sure all the pedestrians were safe. He saw Tick Tock with the shocked teenager between two parked cars. He turned to trap the passenger into the car the way he had the others.

Thwack!

Joe heard a loud crack and felt a blazing pain burst from his hip down his leg.

He hit the ground hard, remembering at the last moment how to land without hurting himself more. He realized his eyes were closed against the pain. Training and instinct pushed him to open them, looking for his attacker to strike again.

A lug wrench swung inches from his face when Joe reached out with both hands and gripped it hard.

A battle cry burst forth as his body reacted to the steel against his hands. He felt his muscles instantly gain strength equal to the metal, felt his skin tighten, and the pain in his leg lessen.

Joe jerked the lug wrench to the left, pulling his attacker off his feet. He rolled on top of him and pressed the X-shaped bar against the other man's chest. With the intense pain in his hip and leg, it was all he could do to remember not to press down so hard that he might break the man's ribs.

The man kicked and punched at Joe, but to no avail. Joe knew hitting him now was like hitting a metal statue. The man probably broke a couple knuckles before he realized he couldn't fight back.

Joe heard sirens, shouting, and in a minute — it felt like ten — a police officer pulled Joe off the other guy. Joe fell onto his back again, squeezing the lug wrench in his fists.

This did not sit well with the police officer who put his hand on his holstered gun and yelled for Joe to drop the weapon.

But Joe couldn't drop it. The power coursing through him from the metal tool was the only thing keeping him from screaming in agony.

A moment later, Tick Tock knelt next to him. Joe heard him tell the officer to cuff the other man, that he'd take care of this one.

"Joe, talk to me, brother."

Joe gritted his teeth, trying to squeeze the metal harder. He focused on the steel. His body's reaction to metal was instant and all-encompassing. The incredible healing power of his body accelerated dramatically when combined with the metal's strength.

He just had to wait it out.

He groaned, squeezing his eyes tight. Vaguely, he noticed the cold snow beneath him, smelled the acrid exhaust from running cars, sensed moisture on his face. But mostly, he felt searing pain throughout his right leg like he'd never felt before. He clenched his jaw tighter, trying to hold in a scream.

"Focus, dude," Bull said quietly from nearby.

Joe heard his friend praying for his healing. Pray faster, he wanted to say.

But he couldn't speak.

Instead, he held on tight.

Tori sat in the passenger seat of Bull's truck as Hayley drove them to the church. The men hadn't come back inside the mall or answered their phones. The parking lot, at least the area where they'd parked that morning, looked normal. No screaming or running people, no police, but no Joe or Bull either. Tori kept telling herself not to worry. Joe had promised her that he knew what he was doing.

Hayley had reminded her a few times as well, but Tori could see she was concerned. They hadn't heard from either of the guys since that initial phone call in the food court.

That was the unspoken reason why they arrived at the church a little earlier than necessary. Just in case the guys were already there. But they weren't. And the girls were too early to meet up with everyone for the Christmas caroling party. So they busied themselves with unnecessary tasks.

They checked the bride's room to be sure there were enough chairs and tissue boxes. They peeked into the sanctuary to see if the decorating had begun. Then they walked downstairs to the fellowship hall to see if anyone had started bringing in food for tonight's rehearsal dinner.

They found a big pan covered with aluminum foil in the kitchen. They wiggled their eyebrows at each other like schoolgirls.

"Should we peek?" Tori asked. Anything to keep her mind off Joe.

"It's probably for your wedding rehearsal," Hayley said. "Or even the wedding lunch. Nothing else requires food, right?"

Tori pulled up the edge of the aluminum foil. "Oh my gosh, I think these are Hannah's oatmeal raisin cookies," she exclaimed. "I swear, I recognize them." She inhaled deeply, the scents of cinnamon, oatmeal, and raisins making her mouth water.

Hayley giggled. "Should we have one? They must be for you."

"Split one?"

Tori waited for a nod from Hayley, and took a cookie out. It was soft and thick. She broke it in half and gave Hayley the bigger piece.

They bit into the dessert, closing their eyes in pleasure, then were startled by a man's voice.

"Gotcha!"

Tori spun toward the kitchen door and froze mid-chew. Joe's dad, Pastor Owen, walked toward them. She didn't know what else to do so she giggled, covered her mouth, finished chewing, and said, "Hello, Owen."

He grinned at them both, kissed Tori on the head, and reached for the pan. Before he lifted the foil, he looked over his shoulder toward the door. "I think she's still at the house. Have one more. I don't want to get in trouble by myself."

Hayley laughed and reached for another cookie. "I knew I liked you for a reason."

Tori hesitated. "I've got to fit into my wedding dress tomorrow, you guys."

"We walked around the mall for like," Hayley shook her head, "five hours or something. I think you've exercised enough for another cookie."

Tori grinned and took one before Owen sealed the foil around the edge again. "Hannah makes the best cookies."

"Hannah makes the best everything," Owen agreed.

"I hear my name," Hannah called from the kitchen door. She walked toward them, then stopped, hands on her hips. "Do I have to lock up all the food to keep it from being eaten?"

"Speak of an angel and she appears," Owen said.

"Don't try changing the subject, mister," Hannah scolded. She kissed him. "Just as I suspected, you taste like cinnamon and oatmeal."

Tori looked at Hayley and grinned. Owen and Hannah were so cute. She hoped that she and Joe would be like that.

"So where are the boys?" Hannah asked. "I thought they were with you today."

"They're working," said Hayley. "The mall thieves came back while we were there."

Owen and Hannah looked from Hayley to Tori and back.

"It's okay," Tori said. "Joe told me this is his job, and not to worry. I'm not worried." Okay, maybe a little, but he said to trust him, and she did.

Joe's parents look relieved, more so than Tori would have expected under the circumstances. They knew Joe worked in security. Where they always this worried about him? They looked to Hayley, who shook her head slightly.

Tori appreciated the way they all tried not to worry her or speculate about what might have happened.

"They'll probably be here anytime," Hayley said. "They know what time the caroling starts."

Both parents frowned. Hannah put her arm around Tori and pulled her toward the kitchen door. "Well then, girls, let's go get ready to sing. I hope you brought warm enough clothes."

"Aw, man!" Tori smacked her forehead. "I left my duffle with my long underwear in Joe's truck."

"Not to worry, my dear," Hannah assured her. As Hayley came

up to the door from the other side of the long stainless steel table, Hannah wrapped her other arm around her shoulders, too. "This is Northern Michigan. Melissa and I have enough to go around."

By 4:45, Joe and Bull still hadn't called or shown up at the church. Tori hung back as the caroling group, including quite a few people in the wedding party, started outside.

"Go on, Tori," Owen urged her. "Sometimes in the security business things take longer than you expect."

Tori made a face. "He did say that it would be awhile if he had to file a police report."

Owen grunted in agreement. So that's where Joe got it from. "That's certainly the truth," he said.

She did want to go Christmas caroling, but she really wanted to do it with Joe.

Hayley came back inside, looking for her. "They're waiting for you."

Owen patted her back and gave her a little push. "I'm sure he'll be here by the time you're back. Have fun. Stay warm!"

Tori gave him a little wave as Hayley pulled her outside. Did Owen's expression change to worry as she stepped through the door?

It only took a few minutes for the infectious good cheer to buoy Tori's spirits. Everyone had a little book of song lyrics for the songs they would sing. Some people held fat candles, other people had flashlights. Tori decided a candle would be the most fun, and potentially warmer. She just had to remember not to get it too close to the songbook.

They walked through the neighborhood singing "Hark, the Herald Angels Sing," "Joy to the World," "Silent Night," and so many more. The darker it got, the more beautiful the scene looked with all the candles and lights. Tori was glad she'd come.

Except that Joe still hadn't arrived. She kept looking back over her shoulder, searching the darkness for him. Keeping people safe was more important than caroling, true. But he was supposed to have this week off. They'd planned for this whole day to be special, ending with their wedding rehearsal. She knew he wanted to get married, but...

Tori forced herself to ignore her doubts and believe in Joe, believe he'd be here as soon as he could. Meanwhile, she would focus on singing. That always made her feel better.

They stopped at every third or fourth house, waving to anyone who watched and waved from the windows. It was bitter cold out, and the snow that had been spitting on and off all day began to fall in heavy fat flakes.

It was beautiful.

About twenty minutes in, as they stopped to sing in front of another house, the song leader announced that they would sing "Mary, Did You Know?" together at the marked parts, with a soloist singing the other verses. The first notes that he sang alone were rich and sweet. Tori looked around to see who was singing. He was an older black man she recognized from the choir.

As he sang, wondering aloud to Jesus' mother Mary if she knew that her baby would walk on water and give sight to a blind man, Tori felt her heart swell with the emotion of the season. There was something haunting and beautiful about the words and the tune together. Tori always felt like crying when she heard this song. With tonight's temperatures, she would have to control herself if she didn't want frostbite on her cheeks for her wedding day.

If only Joe were here. Then it would be a perfect, beautiful night.

Another twenty minutes of singing and walking, then the leader asked if people wanted to return early. Normally they would stay out for an hour or more, but most people's hats and scarves had a coating of snow on them, icy where their breath froze against the material.

Soon they were back at church. By then, even the dissenters were glad they'd returned to the warmth of the building. Hot chocolate, coffee, and cookies awaited them in the fellowship hall.

When people noticed a few of Tori and Joe's friends and relatives decorating the hall, they came over to tell her congratulations and ask where Joe was.

"He had to work," she told everyone, "he'll be here any minute."

But she was beginning to wonder. Maybe their conversation this morning had given him pause. Maybe it wasn't just that he'd gotten tied up with something. Maybe he hadn't called because he was trying to decide if he was sure now was the right time.

That seemed to be the gist of their problem. Not should they get married — they were both convinced of their love for each other — but when. Maybe he was rethinking it and didn't know how to tell her.

Looking for ways to stay busy, Tori and Hayley helped set out paper plates and cups and plasticware for the rehearsal dinner. When Hayley took a call, Hannah called Tori into the kitchen.

"Do you think your parents will like this?" she asked, holding a fork for Tori to taste some kind of casserole.

Tori blew on it and took a bite. "Oh my *gosh*," she exclaimed. "What is that? It's amazing!"

Hannah sighed in relief. "Oh, good, I wasn't sure." She told Tori that it was an old family recipe, passed down from her grandmother on her mother's side. She explained how it was made and promised Tori she would teach her to make it, if she wanted.

"That would be wonderful, thanks, Hannah," Tori said.

Hannah looked over Tori's shoulder. "Oh, look! Joe and Bull are here. Why don't you go sit with him and we'll finish up in here."

Tori spun around. There he was, seated in the groom's chair at the front table in the hall. He looked a little tired, but he waved and smiled as he caught her eye. Tori smiled in relief and rushed over to him.

"Hey," she said as she gave him a hug, "I was beginning to wonder if you weren't coming." She'd meant it to sound teasing, but even she could hear the insecurity in her voice.

"Oh honey, I'm sorry." Joe pulled her down to sit next to him, and gave her a longer hug. "I know I should've called." He leaned back. "Check this out."

He opened his shirt pocket and pulled out several pieces of electronics that looked like they might have once been a phone. "I believe this is what is referred to as smithereens."

Tori's eyes popped open. "Holy cow! How did that happen?"

"It got run over by a car," Joe said. "Bull's phone broke, too. He tried calling Hayley several times, but it just made a bunch of weird sounds and wouldn't put the call through. But we helped catch that ring of thieves at the mall. Proud of me?"

Tori grinned and hugged him again. "Of course, I am." She looked at him more closely. "Did you get in a fight?" she asked in a quiet voice.

He shrugged one shoulder. "A little one. I'll be fine. A slight limp that will be gone by tomorrow."

Her heart gave a little stutter. How hurt was he really? Men never came clean about that kind of thing. She knew her dad and brother always tried to make injuries sound like nothing at all.

He leaned closer. "Do me a favor, wife-to-be?" He smiled at her.

Tori's heart thumped harder. All it took was his smile. Add in the loving words in that husky voice and she would do anything he asked. She nodded.

"Act like nothing's wrong, okay? I don't want to worry anyone. Do you mind? We'll sit here tonight and let them"—he nodded his head toward the roomful of guests—"come to us."

"On one condition," she said. "Promise you'll never lie to *me* about whether you're okay. I mean it. If you tell me the truth about that, I'll always trust you. And I'll back you up."

Joe raised his hand to her cheek, and gazed into her eyes. Solemnly, he said, "I'll never lie to you about whether I'm okay."

A funny picture of The Grinch crossed her mind, and her heart swelled three sizes more. Joe trusted her with his secrets. He trusted her to protect him from nosy, if well-meaning, friends. He trusted her enough to marry her. He hadn't decided to call it off.

"To prove it, I'll admit to you and you only..." He leaned over and whispered into her ear, *"Ow."* He chuckled a little. "I'd like to give what-for to the guy who hit me, I'll tell you what. But I controlled myself."

"Tell me where it hurts so I don't touch you there," Tori said. "Then tell me where to find the guy and I'll beat him up for you."

Joe laughed and hugged her. "Want to know a little secret?" he asked. He pulled her chair closer, and spoke low in her ear. "I asked Bull not to tell anyone, but I wanted to share it with you. In fact, I wished you were there."

He told her about a boy he'd met recently, how he had an opportunity to buy stolen food for his family for Christmas, and how Joe had promised to bring Christmas dinner for them as a reward, of sorts, for the boy doing the right thing.

Tori felt tears near the surface. *Wonderful* and *amazing* weren't adequate descriptors of this man. How did she get so lucky?

"It was hard to explain that I wanted to do this to help him, but that he wouldn't always be rewarded for doing the right thing. Sometimes, in fact, it seems like you get punished for making the right choice."

Tori nodded. "That's a hard lesson. Hopefully, you made it a little easier for him to learn."

"Bull was there, helping me deliver the food, and he's great with kids. He did a better job of encouraging Jackson and his little brothers and sister than I ever would've. I'm glad he was there."

Tori and Joe talked quietly for a few minutes, catching up on their time apart. Tori told him about sneaking cookies with Hayley and Owen. Joe wished he'd been there for that. And he wasn't surprised the carolers came back early. It wasn't fun weather to drive in, let alone walk in.

Soon, the dinner started. Joe limped as they headed to the food tables, but Tori walked slowly, saying hi to people, so no one would notice his limp. Both sets of parents gave heartfelt toasts, making Tori cry both times.

Everyone ate and talked and laughed until Owen finally called them upstairs to rehearse in the sanctuary. Joe and Tori grabbed two more oatmeal cookies, giggling together like children. Then Hayley and Bull joined them, and the few cookies left, vanished.

"Hey, let's take the elevator," Bull said, "so no one sees us eating the rest of the cookies."

Tori squeezed his arm and smiled at him. She'd been trying to think of a way to get Joe on the elevator without undermining his manliness. Bull patted her hand and winked.

Partway through the rehearsal, which would've gone much faster if there was less horseplay, one of Joe's brothers came in and announced that the snow was getting worse.

Most everyone went to the windows and doors to look out. Owen spoke quietly to his other son, then Hannah joined them. Danny walked over, followed closely by Dixie.

"You get the feeling they're planning our demise?" Joe asked.

He started to get up and Bull put a hand on his shoulder. "Down boy," he said, "let that leg heal for tomorrow."

It sure looked like Joe had nailed it. Tori saw both mothers look over at her and Joe a time or two. It didn't look good.

Owen walked back to the front of the church. "Can everyone

come up here, please?" He waited for people to get close enough to hear him.

"Eddie has an updated weather report and it's not good. We're supposed to get at least a foot of snow tonight, and it may not stop there. I know most of you are pretty local, but bad weather can be nerve-wracking whether you're driving for an hour or a few blocks."

Owen looked at Tori and Joe, and Tori knew what was coming next. The way Joe squeezed her hand, he did, too.

"We think you should consider postponing long enough for the weather to clear. For safety's sake."

Tori wanted to shout at them all for trying once again to stop their wedding. But who was she going to blame this time — God? She sighed and looked at Joe. She wouldn't cry. But she wasn't going to roll over and let other people dictate her life. She and Joe would decide their fate.

He put his arm around her and pulled her tight against him. Hayley took Tori's free hand and squeezed it. Bull leaned in close from Joe's other side. Tori felt like a fortress of friendship surrounded and supported her. Despite the situation, it almost made her smile.

"What do you think?" Joe asked her quietly so no one but the four of them could hear.

She studied his expression. They hadn't had time to finish their conversation this morning, but both of them were here. Neither one of them had backed out when the excuses were vague warnings about the future. She didn't think either of them wanted to back out now, even with this clear and compelling reason to postpone.

"I think," she said slowly, "that we need a minister and two witnesses." She looked around the room. "Which we have."

Joe's eyes widened a bit when he caught her meaning. "Do it now?"

"It would be a shame for so many people to miss it if the weather clears," Hayley said. "Mickey's not here."

"We don't have any of our wedding clothes," Bull said. "But we don't live far. We could run and get them. Still, if we were to go out in the weather now, why not go out in the morning? Even if it ends up being just the four of us."

Despite the fighting over the wedding, Tori still wanted all of her family there. She only planned to do it once.

"What about the people who might get snowed in tonight?" Hayley asked.

Bull shrugged. "I'm an early riser." He looked over his shoulder at the waiting sets of parents and turned back to Joe. "Give me addresses of who you absolutely want to be here tomorrow, and I'll call some of our friends. We'll dig everyone out in the morning in time to get here by eleven." He looked at Hayley and said, "We can split up a list of the guests and start making calls letting them know the wedding is still on, but only to come out if they feel comfortable driving in the weather."

Hayley smiled at Bull, then said to Tori, "We'll be sure everyone knows you guys understand if they don't want to drive. We'll remind your relatives of the reception your moms are throwing when you get back from your honeymoon."

Tori looked at Joe and smiled. The generosity of their friends amazed her. "Well?"

Joe kissed her soundly. "Looks like we're still going to have our Christmas Eve wedding."

J oe woke up slowly. Such weird dreams last night. In the one he remembered best, he was helping Iron Man save New York from aliens. One alien attacked him from behind and Joe went down. He woke up in Tony Stark's lab, connected by wires to the inside of the Iron Man suit, healing faster than ever.

That was a fun dream. Joe wished he didn't have to wake up. He felt Snickers move beside him, and he reached over to scratch his cat.

"Hey, buddy. What day is it anyhow? I feel wrecked."

Snickers purred and stretched under his hand.

Joe rolled onto his back and felt something hard. He reached behind him and retrieved an iron pipe. As the metal touched his hand, a gentle whoosh of energy rippled through his body. All the memories of the day before rushed to the surface.

Today was his wedding day!

Joe sat up and pulled back the covers, much to Snickers' annoyance. All kinds of metalworks were taped to most of his body. Only a couple of pieces had come off in the night. He checked out his right thigh.

Last night, Bull had helped him into his dad's office while Tori and his mom were out with the carolers. They made sure no one saw them because he could hardly walk. Owen had acted like a father first, then a field medic, then the Guild leader — he'd hugged his son, then made Joe undress to his boxers so he could examine his wounds, then reprimanded him for getting in a fight without his super suit.

"That's why Mickey put the body armor in it!" he yelled.

That's when Joe knew his leg was as damaged as it felt. "Pastor" Owen rarely yelled.

His dad and Bull had argued with him about going to the hospital. Joe reminded them that every time he'd gone in the past, his body was mostly healed by the time he ever got to see a doctor.

So they decided to tape as much iron and steel to his body as they could, and see how he felt at the end of the wedding rehearsal. Bull and Owen raided Owen's garage and came back with an impressive collection of wrenches and pipes, and a roll of duct tape.

Joe saw the tape and demanded Bull get a roll of paper towels. The metal needed to be in contact with his skin for him to gain power from it, but he wanted a layer of paper towels before they taped everything down.

"I don't want to explain to my wife on our honeymoon why it looks like I wax my legs," he said.

"Plus it would hurt like Hades," Bull chuckled.

Last night, when Joe had seen his leg for the first time — and that was after two hours of healing — his entire right hip and thigh was a huge black bruise.

Looking at it this morning, Joe was amazed to see much of the bruising had already faded to yellow. Still sitting on the bed, he flexed his knee, bringing his heel to his buttocks, listening for any crunching sounds. He hadn't wanted to admit it to his dad, but Joe felt pretty confident he'd broken a bone.

The flexing didn't hurt, so Joe did it again. Still no crunching noise.

"Thank you, God," he breathed. He sagged with relief, letting his face fall into his hands. His wedding day could have gone very differently, very *badly*.

He moved Snickers and swung his legs over the side of his bed. No vertigo or nausea. No pain in his leg, hip, knee, back. He was about ready to stand up when something caught his attention. He sniffed the air.

Bacon.

Joe stood, giving himself another minute to test his leg. Everything seemed to work fine. It didn't hurt, just felt like he'd knocked his leg against something.

Yeah, something like *a lug wrench.*

The door opened and his little brother, Stuart, walked in. "Hey, morning, I'm supposed to — aw, for Pete's sake, put some shorts on, will ya? I'm supposed to check your leg, see if we need to leave the hardware taped on or not. Then feed you all the protein and vitamin C you can inhale."

As he spoke, Stuart waited for Joe to pull his boxers on, then he checked out Joe's leg, prodding it and looking at the bruises on the back that Joe couldn't see.

"How's it look?" Joe asked, trying to twist around.

Stuart stood up. "You scared the crap out of us last night, man." He gave Joe a hard backslapping hug. "I can't believe how much better it looks. Can you walk on it?"

Joe cocked an eyebrow at him. "I walked on it last night." He moved to the closet, to the bathroom door, to the dresser, and back without limping.

Stuart snorted. "I mean, does it hurt?"

Joe grinned. "Wanna dance?"

"You're such a blockhead. Why would you get in a fight without—"

Joe held up his hand. "Save it. I heard it from Mom and Dad

last night, and Mickey before that. I'm sure I'll hear more today. When's that bacon gonna be ready?"

"Shoot!" Stuart shot out the door and took the steps two at a time. A moment later, he shouted, "Saved! Come and get it."

Joe chuckled and pulled on some sweats. He picked up Snickers and started gingerly down the stairs. Nothing hurt, nothing creaked, nothing acted any differently.

Except that he still had every wrench his dad owned taped to his legs and arms. That felt pretty weird.

Downstairs, Stuart put a mound of scrambled eggs covered in another mound of bacon in front of him. Joe raised his eyebrows at his brother and chuckled in disbelief.

"Mom said." Stuart planted two tall glasses of orange juice in front of him. "By the way, you're out of eggs now." He brought another plate of bacon and eggs to the kitchen table for himself. "Thank you, God, for keeping Dopey here from getting killed, and please bless him and Tori with an awesome day."

Joe grinned. "Amen." They both dug into their breakfasts. Joe was pleasantly surprised. "Since when can you cook?"

Stuart chewed and swallowed. "Since I'm in college and don't eat at normal times." He ate a huge forkful of eggs. "Mom's been bribing me. She's only been teaching me how to make my favorite foods. So far, I can do bacon and eggs, hamburgers and frozen French fries, and chocolate chip cookies."

"A balanced diet." Joe heard a sound from the front of the house and turned. "Was that a snowplow?"

"Bull dug out your truck already. It's still snowing, but pretty lightly. If that was a plow, I'll go shovel out what the plow threw in the drive after you get out of the shower."

Joe gave his brother a questioning look.

Stuart rolled his eyes. "Mom said to talk to you while you shower so I can help you if you pass out or fall or something."

The two of them looked at each other for a moment, then burst out laughing.

"Yeah, yeah, well, she was wiping at her eyes and pretending she wasn't crying, so I'm going to do as she asked. We can talk about my list of souvenirs I want you to look for at Disney World."

After breakfast, Stuart cut all the duct tape off Joe and lay the metal tools aside. Joe sat on his bed in his boxers again, trying to decide how he felt. Definitely weaker.

"So now I know for sure where my strength comes from," he said.

"Psalm 121, man," said his brother. "Anyone else would be laid up for weeks. You wanna lie down?"

Joe shook his head. He did, but it was already 8:30 a.m. "I want to get to the church."

Stuart chuckled. "I guess it's a good sign for your marriage that you're an eager groom."

Joe showered without incident, so Stuart went to clear the end of the driveway while Joe shaved. As he ran the blade down his cheeks, he thought about Tori's reactions last night. He'd asked his friends and family to keep her occupied until he could sit down so she wouldn't see him stumble in.

He rinsed the blade under the water and glanced at his bruised leg. He'd been badly hurt yesterday. It was stupid to keep going like he did. And the way Tori treated the situation calmly, helping him without making it noticeable, he was more convinced than ever that they were going to make a great team.

Joe promised himself now that if he ever got hurt like that again, he'd allow himself to be taken to the hospital. Testing his limits was hardly worth finding out the hard way what his body couldn't heal by itself.

His home phone rang. He glanced up in surprise. He rarely got calls on his home number. Then he remembered that his cell phone looked worse than he did. He walked over and answered the extension by his bed.

"Hey, Joe." Detective Arturo Paredes of the SLU was on the

other end. His voice came through with a cheerful ring. "I wanted to give you a little Christmas gift. Those guys you and your team caught for us at the mall yesterday, confirmation just came in that we got them all. Thanks to your friend, Tick Tock, we were able to find the vans the thieves were filling, *and* the warehouse they used to store and sell the merchandise."

"That's great news, Art," Joe said, a sense of pride and accomplishment washing over him. "Thanks for letting me know."

"I heard you got hurt helping us take them down, and I wanted you to know it was worth it. We found guns in two of the cars. We think they might've been looking to upgrade their efforts."

"Wow." Joe hated to think what would've happened to the young woman in the Mercedes who fought the thieves for her packages. And he definitely didn't want to think of what would've happened if his attacker had used a gun instead of a lug wrench.

"Yeah," Art said, "bad news. But the good news is they're off the street, thanks to you. Listen, I know you're getting married today — congratulations — so I'll let you get back to it. Merry Christmas!"

"Merry Christmas, Art," Joe said. "Thanks for the call."

When he clicked off, he stared at his phone for a moment. Then he smiled into the mirror. He had a hard job, but he made a difference in people's lives. That was worth it.

He finished shaving, dressed in his tuxedo sans bow tie, and patted on some cologne. If his wet hair didn't freeze into icicles between here and church, he was about ready.

Stuart helped him load his suitcase and duffle into the truck, then Joe put Snickers in his carrier and grabbed the bag of cat stuff Stuart and Melissa would need for the week.

"Got everything?" Stuart asked from the door.

"Just need me a bride," Joe said with a grin, and locked up his house.

At the church, the parking lot was plowed and there were a

lot of cars already there. Inside, there were *a lot* more people, most walking around with cups of coffee and baked goods.

Joe turned to Stuart and found his brother grinning widely.

"Bull and Mickey and your other friends starting picking people up an hour ago and bringing them in, then going out for more. Mom's Bible study came in to make coffee and muffins for everyone while they waited. And three deacons came over to plow the parking lot and shovel the sidewalks. I think they're shoveling them a second time already."

Joe stood there with his mouth open, stunned.

"After you two leave for the airport, we'll start ferrying everyone back to their homes," Stuart said. "I wanted to hang with you this morning, so I'm on duty later."

"When did everyone decide to do all this?" Joe asked. "I just saw all you guys last night."

Stuart shrugged. "You know how it is at church, kind of an avalanche effect." He swung his head toward the weather outside. "No pun intended."

Joe was still feeling a little punch-drunk when his mother came around the corner. "There you are!" She hugged him tight, then kissed his cheek. "How's my boy?" she asked in a quieter voice.

"I'm fine, Mom," he said, returning her hug.

"Stuart, how is he?" she asked.

"He's in better shape than I was when he tackled me playing touch football at Thanksgiving," he said. "And he ate everything you wanted him to, washed behind his ears, and packed his teddy bear for his honeymoon."

Hannah pressed her lips together and smacked her youngest son in the shoulder. Then she hugged him, too. "Thank you for being there," she said, her feelings running close to the surface, making her voice quiver.

"I'm glad he came over," Joe said. "We watched old movies and braided each other's hair."

Both men laughed when Hannah smacked Joe's shoulder, too.

"Come with me." She took Joe's hand. "Let's go see your father. Stuart, get something to eat."

Hannah led Joe to his dad's office. He could guess what they wanted to discuss with him, but at least with the obvious wedding activity going on, canceling the wedding was finally off the list of potential topics. He figured it would be about seeing a doctor or telling Tori about the family's legacy of powers.

"Joe, how are you?" Owen got up from his desk and hugged his son hard, then slapped him on the back. He pulled back only enough to leave his hands on Joe's shoulders. "How's the leg?"

Bingo. First guess. "It's good," Joe said. "The bruises are already yellow, and I'm not limping. No pain."

"Let's see," said his mother. Joe walked to the door and back. "No, let's see your leg," she insisted.

"Mom, I'm twenty-nine years old. I'm not taking my pants off in front of you. It's fine. If you don't believe me, ask Stuart." Joe loved his parents, but they never seemed to stop...parenting.

"Your mother wants you to get an x-ray," Owen said, hands on his hips.

Hannah cleared her throat.

"We both do," his dad amended.

Joe took a deep breath. He normally believed in the wisdom of "pick your battles." But there was quite literally no time to get an x-ray, get married, and get on a plane by three o'clock today.

It was possible his dad would let up on his "tell Tori" campaign if Joe gave in on this item. But then they'd be a day or two late for their honeymoon. He'd rather be relaxing with Tori than hanging out with his family, wishing he were alone with his new wife.

He thought of where in particular he'd like to be relaxing with her. Hey, right. Bed rest.

"If there were time, I would do it just to set your minds at ease," he said. "But without saying too much to my *parents*"—he eyed them both sternly—"I'm going to spend much of the next week in bed. If the leg starts hurting again, I'll get an x-ray right away. I promise."

His mom and dad looked at each other and did that silent communication thing they did. He wondered when he and Tori would start doing that. No doubt it would irritate their children. That would be fun.

"All right," Owen finally said. "We're trusting you on this. But as Guild leader, I'm giving you a verbal warning about getting involved in hand-to-hand combat without proper equipment."

Joe opened his mouth to object. A verbal warning would be passed on to his team leader, Mickey. Written warnings about a Paladin could affect his whole team, keeping them from coveted assignments. A verbal warning, on the other hand, wouldn't be a mark against Joe in the same way, but he'd never done anything to warrant anything but praise from his father in the past. This seemed unfair.

And yet, there was the "pick your battles" bit of wisdom. The warning wouldn't hurt him as he worked his way up the ranks. He just needed to nod and take it.

Nod and take it. He gritted his teeth.

Then he nodded. "Okay."

Owen gave a slight nod, then lowered his eyes. Joe wondered if his dad didn't want to give the warning. He could have easily let it go. But good leaders couldn't let things slide, not even with — especially not with — their own family. Joe suspected this was a lesson he needed to learn as he worked his way into his father's position. He gave his father a nod of respect.

"So what's the update on Tori and her family?" Owen asked. "What do they know?"

Joe turned his face away for a moment, working on controlling his temper. Just hit all the soft spots at once, Dad. Geez. And on his wedding day.

"Dad, no matter what Tori knows or when, nothing is going to change with her family," he said firmly. "I *literally* saved her dad's life on Saturday, and they still refuse to believe superheroes are real. We're going to have to keep everyone from letting their powers show when her family is around. I'm sorry, but I don't know what more I can do."

Owen rubbed the back of his neck. Hannah sighed and folded her arms.

"Honey, we can't make them believe," she said gently.

"I know, but..." Owen shook his head. "Joe, I've counseled hundreds of people over the years who are head over heels in love, but have some difficult hurdles they'll have to jump to make their marriages last. A secret like this is going to make every part of your marriage harder. Every. Part."

"It's going to be fine, Dad." Joe said the words as sincerely as he could mange considering he wasn't sure he believed them himself.

But what more could he say? He didn't want to share his private conversations with his fiancée, but maybe it would help to tell his parents a little.

"We've talked about secrets, about finding out unexpected things about each other over time. She was wonderful last night, didn't freak out, didn't even let on she knew I was hurt."

"You told her?" Hannah asked.

"Yeah, I told her almost everything, and she took it like a pro." Joe felt himself feeling proud of her. She was going to make a great wife, period, but eventually she would be a fantastic Paladin's wife.

"Well, that's good, right?" Hannah asked his dad.

Owen shuffled his feet around and stared at the ceiling for a moment. "I just don't know. I don't know if I should marry you, knowing what I do."

"Dad..." Joe tried to hide his frustration. "This is my wedding day."

"It's not you, son," Owen said, but he couldn't meet Joe's eyes. "This is about me, about *my* integrity."

Joe sighed deeply. There was no argument for that. After a moment he said, "So I tell her, try to make her understand something she's been led her whole life to believe is a lie, try to explain that I'm not nuts, *the hour before we're to get married*, and hope she still marries me, or you might decide in the next hour not to go through with this."

Owen didn't say anything, just stared at his shoes.

"Be fair, Joe," his mom said quietly. "Your father has been asking this of you since the day you got engaged. The timing here is on you, son."

Joe stared hard at her for a moment, arranging his argument in his head. Then he dropped his eyes, turned, and walked out of the room.

His mom was right.

Tori stood in front of the full-length mirror in the bride's room at church. She smoothed down the folds of her wedding dress as Lexie zipped and buttoned. Hayley stood by the edge of the mirror putting on her makeup. Dixie stood to the side, directing.

Tori smiled at herself in the mirror.

Look at you. *A bride.* She almost couldn't believe it.

And she looked so beautiful. Hayley had done her hair, swept up on the top of her head with lovely little curls trailing down. Her mother had added sprigs of real holly and baby's breath as she attached the veil.

Joe had given her a pair of pale blue sapphire earrings last night before they left the church. They sparkled in the light when she moved her head. She loved them. She loved that Joe gave them to her and didn't care if they were paste or real. But the way they sparkled, she wondered.

This morning, her mother had surprised her by opening a very old velvet jewelry box and pulling out a dainty chain with a single pearl. As she attached the clasp around Tori's neck, she said, "My father gave this to my mother when they got married. It was her 'something new.' Then she gave it to me when I married"—she cleared her throat—"your father. My 'something old.'"

She stood back and adjusted the pearl against Tori's throat. "Now I'm giving it to you as your 'something old.' I'd love it if you loaned it to your sisters when they get married as their 'something borrowed.'" She smiled at Lexie. "If they'd like that."

Tori hugged her mom tight. She didn't want to let go. When she sniffled, Lexie and Hayley jumped in with tissues and washcloths dipped in cold water. The cloths were pressed against her face to keep her eyes from getting red and puffy. Tori laughed at the commotion and blew her nose.

"*This*," Hayley said, "is why I said I'd do everyone's makeup at the last minute. Come on, Lex, get in here and get the crying over with."

Lexie pulled something from her pocket. Tori recognized it immediately.

"Your dress is 'something new' so I wanted to loan you my count-your-blessings bracelet for 'something borrowed.' It's one of my most treasured possessions."

Tori tried to saw, "Aw, thank you," but it came out as "Aw, sob, sob."

She remembered the day she bought it. Lexie's boyfriend-about-to-be-fiancé had declared he wasn't interested in being a father and had left the week before. Lexie was close to inconsolable.

Tori was at Target, the most expensive store she could afford, buying toilet paper and dish soap and wondering how to make her sister feel better. She walked by the jewelry counter and saw this pretty little charm bracelet for twenty dollars. The thought popped into her head that this could be a way for Lexie to count her blessings, focus on the positive things in her life — which seemed few and far between the last few years.

A few charms lay on a small tray. Two caught her eye — one of two little girls holding hands, one of a baby carriage. They were ten dollars each. Tori stood staring at them, unable to shake the feeling that this simple gift might bring Lexie back from the brink.

Though she hated to ask her parents for help, she didn't have enough money for the gift *and* the toilet paper and soap. She put the other things back, told herself it would be better to let go of her pride if it might help her sister, and bought the jewelry.

Lexie had loved the gift. She heard Tori's unspoken warning that she could lose herself in grief like she had as a teenager, and she forced herself to let go of her heartache and focus on the blessing of her unborn baby. And, Lexie had told her, the blessing of her sister.

With that memory between them, Tori and Lexie held on to each other for a long minute. Tori cried and Lexie tried to keep it in, as was her habit.

Then Lexie fastened the bracelet on Tori's right wrist, and said, "We've both got more blessings than this bracelet can hold, but I'm glad you're getting another one."

Her sister couldn't have said anything more eloquent. For all that they'd tried to protect each other from the havoc and heartache in the world, Lexie wasn't upset that Tori had found love. Tori felt a few more tears slip out as she hugged her sister again. When she pulled back, she saw Hayley and her mom wiping their eyes, too.

"Okay, are we done now?" Hayley asked. "I've got to do our makeup soon."

Tori laughed and wiped the cool cloth across her face.

"Done." Hayley was as good as Lexie at hiding her emotions. But an entire day of emotional displays was about going to kill them.

Standing in front of the mirror now, Tori could see all three of them fussing over her, trying to help make her day perfect. She felt a sudden sense of peace wash over her. Not just a feeling of being "okay." But a supernatural strength of purpose that permeated every cell.

It was a feeling she always associated with God's presence. She took a deep breath and smiled into the mirror. She knew the tears were behind her now, even the happy ones. The strength and peace in her heart were a sign that life was going exactly as it should.

Just like the rhyme, she now had something old and something new, something borrowed and something blue. If there was a "something holy" brides should have on their wedding day, it was this peace.

A knock sounded at the door. Her mom went to answer it.

"Must be a man," Lexie said as she put finishing touches to Tori's lip gloss.

All the women could come and go as they pleased, but no men were allowed in the bride's room. Mostly because all the women dressed in there together, although Tori figured the original idea was to preserve the sense of mystery and surprise.

"Joe, you can't see her now," Tori heard her mom saying.

"What does he need?" Tori asked.

"I just need a minute," Joe called from the hallway.

"Be right back," she told the girls.

"Tori, he can't see you before the wedding," they complained.

As Tori approached the door, Dixie closed it to a crack and said, "Here she comes. Turn your back, at least."

Tori waved her mother away and Dixie left reluctantly, shaking her head. Tori stood hidden behind the door and spoke into the crack. "Hey, Joe," she said, keeping her voice quiet enough for his ears only. "How are you?"

Joe sighed. "It's good to hear your voice."

He didn't say anything more. Tori closed her eyes and breathed in the scent of him. "You're wearing my favorite cologne."

"I bet you'll think I look as good as I smell."

Tori could hear the smile in his voice. "I can't wait to see you," she said softly. "But I always think you look good."

They were both quiet for a moment. "You okay?" she asked.

There was a long pause. "Do you want to know all my secrets? Right now? I'll tell you every detail about me right now so you can be sure you want to marry me."

Tori heard the almost desperate worry in his voice. She looked over at the clock on the wall. Ten minutes to eleven. She closed her eyes and felt that enormous blanket of peace inside.

Please, God, help Joe feel your peace.

"Joe?" she said softly. "Are you listening to me?"

"Yes."

"I am so sure I want to marry you, I'm willing to learn all your secrets over the next sixty years. That's the way everyone else does it. But if you absolutely have to tell me something, you can tell me tonight, in our hotel room, in bed." She couldn't believe she'd just said that! She felt a grin stretch her lips. As much as she looked forward to consummating their marriage, she'd never spoken about it out loud. "I'll listen to whatever you want to say then. Okay?"

After a pause, Joe chuckled softly. "It's a deal, almost-wife."

"All right then," she said. "Isn't there somewhere you need to be, almost-husband?"

"Yes, ma'am," he said. "I'll see you in a few minutes."

Tori felt a huge grin on her face as she shut the door. She leaned there for a moment thinking, *he's almost my husband! I'm almost his wife!*

The women finished their final preparations, then Tori's dad came to escort her mom to the front of the church.

Dixie gently pulled the long gossamer-thin veil over Tori's face. "You're a most beautiful bride," she said.

Tori smiled widely. "Thank you."

A minute later, there was another knock on the door. "Everyone decent?" Owen called.

"Come in," she said. "Are you ready for us?" She was so excited now that the moment was upon her, she almost couldn't contain herself.

"Bridesmaids and flower girls to the front," Owen confirmed. "I'll chat with the bride for a moment."

Hayley and Lexie blew kisses to her and left. Tori felt her smile widen as she turned back to Joe's dad.

"I'm so excited," she said. "My stomach is doing a little dance."

Owen chuckled with her. Then he asked, "Joe came to talk to you?"

She nodded. "Yes, poor nervous man."

Owen looked around the empty room. "And he told you...his secret?"

There were moments when Tori equally loved both sets of parents, and also wanted to move far away from them. They all wanted to be just a little too involved.

But the strength of the peace she felt muted her frustrations. She wanted to be generous and loving with them, especially on her wedding day. She took his hand in hers. "We are going to be fine, Owen. Joe and I are going to get through this together."

Owen half-nodded and half shook his head. "This...meaning...?"

He was making her nervous. Her stomach twitched. Whatever Joe wanted to tell her, he could tell her tonight. Alone. With all the weeks of people trying to stop the wedding, she just wanted to get on with it before her stomach took flight on its own. She smiled up at him and squeezed his hand.

"We are going to be fine. You don't have to worry about us." It felt

like the energy building in her abdomen escaped with her words. She felt better.

Owen tilted his head at her, frowning. Then he smiled faintly back. "You're going to be fine. I won't worry about you two."

His words sounded stilted, but Tori smiled and squeezed his hand again. "Good. Here's my dad. Are we ready?"

Owen nodded, looking a little strange with a half-smile, half-frown. Danny led Tori down to the doors at the entrance to the sanctuary while Owen went a back way to come out in front next to Joe and the groomsmen.

Tori heard singing inside the sanctuary. It was beautiful, haunting, and full of emotion. "Who's that?" she asked her dad.

"Joe's friend, Mickey," he said. "Amazing voice, huh?"

The song ended. At the brief silence, Tori knew the pianist had moved to the organ. She smiled up at her dad.

"My little girl is getting married," he said, a catch in his voice. "You look like sunshine." He looked down at her and Tori felt enveloped in over two decades of his love.

"I don't deserve you, Daddy," she said, "but I'm glad I have you."

He started to say something, then cleared his throat and wiped at his eyes. He faced forward, patting and rubbing her hand on his arm.

Tori smiled and faced forward. This amazing joyful peace filled her in such a way that she didn't feel the usual push of tears that strong emotions always brought out. She was such a heart-on-her-sleeve kind of girl. But today she felt stronger and more confident than she'd ever felt in her life.

As the organ music played, Bull led Lexie down the aisle, little Ben the ring-bearer walking in front of them. Then Joe's oldest brother Carl walked Hayley down the aisle. Two of Joe's younger nieces followed throwing out flower petals.

And then it was her turn.

Danny led her to the door. The crowd stood. A much bigger

crowd than she expected on this snowy December day. At the front, Owen nodded to the man standing next to him.

Joe turned around.

Her Joe.

She smiled at him, feeling like she was indeed a sun burning brightly just for him.

The music played and Danny led her forward. When he put her hand in Joe's, Tori felt like she was going to burst, her body hardly able to contain all the joy she felt.

She tried to focus on every detail of the service, to memorize it all, to enjoy every moment. But she felt like they moved on a helium cloud, a beautiful gravity-free dance that culminated in the words —

"I now pronounce you husband and wife."

Tori barely registered that Joe's dad sounded happy. She watched as Joe lifted her veil over her head, his hands shaking. She leaned forward.

He cupped her face in his hands and kissed her tenderly, sweetly. She raised her face to enjoy all the promises in that kiss, one hand lifted to cover his, the blessings bracelet tinkling near her ear.

Joe pulled back a little and they grinned at each other. He leaned his forehead against hers and whispered, "We did it."

The joy inside tumbled out in Tori's laughter. Then Joe leaned back his head and gave a loud, "Whoop!"

Their friends and family burst into laughing applause.

Joe wrapped his arms around her, and kissed her with passion and abandon, leaning her back over his arm. Tori kissed him until she thought she was going to lose her balance. She began to laugh.

He pulled her up tight to his chest, put one hand on her cheek again, and said, "I'm never gonna let you go."

The next hour was a whirlwind of hugs and congratulations, a quick parade of pictures with the photographer — in attendance only because Bull had driven across the city to pick him up — and a fairly quick, light lunch that Tori could barely eat.

Joe rarely let go of her hand, and she couldn't stop grinning at him.

Soon, her bridesmaids were helping her change into her going-away dress. Hannah and Dixie pressed a bag of wrapped sandwiches and other snacks into Joe's hand for the plane ride. Hugs and kisses and not a few tears later, the two of them pulled on their coats and ran to Joe's truck.

Someone had already started the engine and turned on the heat. Bless them.

Joe pulled Tori close and fastened the middle seat belt around her waist. "I don't want you too far away," he said.

Tori grinned up at him with a mile-wide smile. "I'm not going anywhere."

He rolled down the windows so they could wave at everyone willing to brave the cold. Then he put the truck in gear. "You ready to start our new adventure together?"

"Yes!" Tori laughed.

Nothing could make her happier.

TWO THINGS always surprised Joe Clarke at Christmas: the weather and the people of Double Bay.

Barely a week ago, there had been no snow to add a Christmas-y touch to the festive season. Today, without the help of friends and family, that freshly fallen snow would have kept him from getting married.

Ah, yes, the wonderful citizens of Double Bay constantly surprised him. They organized calling parties to let the wedding guests know that the wedding was still on. They organized driving parties to pick up those too afraid to brave the snow-covered streets. They even organized a baking party to feed the guests as they arrived at the celebration hours early.

As Joe drove to the airport with his bride, he counted his blessings, overwhelmed with the avalanche that had been tumbling down around them for days. He turned on the radio to the station that played all Christmas music this time of year. One of his favorite bands, Pentatonix, was singing.

Hark the herald angels sing, glory to the newborn King!

A Double Bay police car pulled up next to Joe and flashed its lights. Detective Arturo Paredes of the Superhero Liaison Unit waved and grinned and pulled ahead.

A police escort. Joe grinned. Time to hightail it out of town with his girl.

A NOTE FROM KITTY

I hope you enjoyed reading *A Very Merry Superhero Wedding* as much as I enjoyed writing it! I never intended to write this story when I started the Adventures of Lewis and Clarke series, but the idea is fascinating to me. How can two people meet and immediately know that they want to spend the rest of their lives together — and then do it successfully?

If you enjoyed this book, keep reading — *Unexpected Superhero* is next!

My books are available as ebooks and in print at most online retailers. *Unexpected Superhero* and *Little Miss Lovesick* are also available as audiobooks. All the ebooks, print books, and audiobooks will be added to my own web store over the course of 2024. Purchases there support me and my work in a significantly greater way so I'd love it if you'd like to buy from me directly (kittybucholtz.com/books)!

You can also join my free or paid membership community over on Patreon (links at the end of About the Author). Read chapters early before the books even come out, discuss the stories with other readers, see fun art about the settings of the books, and more!

Would you like to read *Cherry on Top* for free? It's set in the same town as *Little Miss Lovesick* during the famous National Cherry Festival. It's my gift to you when you join my reader newsletter at kittybucholtz.com/freebook. Have fun!

If you really want to make my day, I'd love for you to post your thoughts about the book in a review. Thanks so much!

And just so you know, I rebranded all my books in 2024 to be "sweet" — so no swear words or overt sex scenes. I hope you enjoy the change.

Happy Reading!

UNEXPECTED SUPERHERO

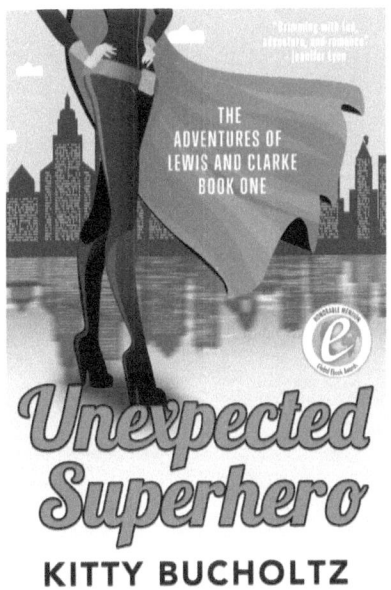

For John,
This one's all for you, baby!

Unexpected Superhero

KITTY BUCHOLTZ

1

Tori Lewis was out of M&Ms. None in her purse, none in the glove box. Even the emergency packet in her brief-case had been consumed during her pre-wedding jitters. After the job interview she'd just endured for Half TV, a local cable TV station, she needed a chocolate fix. Now.

"I know I'm supposed to go to you for comfort," she muttered to God as she pulled into a parking spot, "but if you wouldn't mind, a package of M&Ms would jumpstart the process."

The bell tinkled over her head as the door of Ed & Eddie's Corner Market closed behind her. Tori stamped the snow off her boots as her eyes adjusted from the deepening twilight outside to the bright fluorescent lights of the store. It took her a moment to notice everyone in the store staring at her. Including the guy with the gun.

Tori froze. She always assumed her love of the colorful chocolate candy might one day destroy her figure, but she never expected her addiction to end in gunfire.

The gunman swung toward her. His bulky open coat couldn't hide the fact that the skinny boy was no man. A Detroit Tigers baseball cap covered most of his brown hair, but not his panicky eyes. "What do you want?" His voice came out higher at the end and he cleared his throat. "Well?" he asked, forcing the word out at a lower pitch.

"Uhh...M&Ms," Tori said. It sounded like a question. Her brain was having a hard time getting up to speed in this unexpected situation. *God, help me.*

Her eyes darted around the small store. An older woman cried and held a nearly hysterical younger woman, shushing her to no avail. One of the men held a baby ensconced in a little pink snowsuit. Another nodded quietly at her as if to convey caution.

Situation confirmed. She was hip-deep in doo-doo. Where was her big, strong new husband when she needed him?

The armed boy-man cocked his head toward the candy aisle. Tori didn't know if he meant for her to move out of the way or if he was just being unusually helpful by pointing her in the right direction. Erring on the side of caution, she forced a fleeting smile and mumbled "thanks" as she walked past him and down the middle aisle to stand in front of the M&Ms. Now what?

The gunman turned back to Eddie, the cashier and half-owner of Ed & Eddie's. "Hurry up before someone else comes in!"

"Easy, dude, easy," Eddie said, moving his hands slowly toward the cash register. Eddie wasn't very old either, early 20s or so, but he was sadly experienced in the holdup category. Tori couldn't remember the details, but she'd heard bits and pieces of stories. Come to think of it, why did she shop at a store with a record anyway? She remembered Eddie had played sports in high school. Something like baseball or wrestling or karate could come in handy right now. Hopefully his sport hadn't been cross-country running.

Tori glanced at the M&Ms next to her. More than ever she needed to stress eat. Could she open a package now and pay Eddie later? Maybe two packages. Her hands started to shake. She shoved them in her pockets.

Today was only day ten of her new and fabulous married life.

She hadn't wanted to go out today anyway and now this. Only two days ago she and Joe had checked out of their Disney World hotel, blue skies and temperatures in the 70s, nothing on their minds but a long and blissful life together. Tori prayed now that she'd make it to day eleven of that life. They hadn't been married long enough to do anything except make love—which was *awesome*—but she'd hoped for more. After all, they figured they'd have the rest of their lives together. Neither of them thought the "death" part of "till death do us part" would happen until there was a lot more gray hair involved.

The sound of a crying baby registered. Tori glanced over at the well-dressed man in the expensive trench coat. He kept his back between the gunman and his child. A gesture Tori would normally find heartwarming. But today it was the action of a man who wasn't going to get involved. Great. He wouldn't be of any use. So this is where equal opportunity gets us. Tori considered offering to hold the baby so he could help the other men save the day. Her self-esteem would be fine with that. Maybe if she were comforting someone, she wouldn't feel like crying herself.

Enough! Tori wiped at her eyes. She was not letting some stupid, scared boy dictate her life and death. She'd spent too much energy changing her life into just what she wanted to lose it now. She chewed on her lip. What could she do?

A movement from the corner of her eye. She saw one of the men—the one who'd nodded calmly at her—edging closer to the gunman. Yikes. Should she duck or help?

A POLICE CAR raced past the entrance to Harborview Mall. Lights and sirens cleared a path among the post-Christmas shoppers. But mostly people moved to avoid the speeding white Toyota hurtling through the night like a rusty snowball.

The cars sped through two more lights. Divine intervention surely prevented a crash as the Toyota skidded on a patch of ice, nearly sideswiping another car. The police cruiser missed that particular bit of ice, but a close call at the next light had the cop in the passenger seat crossing himself with one hand while hanging on with the other.

Another police car parked in the next intersection forced the chase to take a hard right and brought them into a quieter industrial area. Quieter except for the jarring sirens. Large warehouse-style office buildings magnified the piercing sound and reflected the red and blue lights onto the snow. The Toyota picked up speed, blowing through three stop signs amidst honking horns and flying middle fingers.

The police cars slowed down enough to ensure that the chase continued to be accident-free. The Toyota made a left down an alley to avoid yet another police car, and raced out of sight.

SUPERHERO X LOOKED up at the roof of the nearby three-story office building and spoke into a microphone concealed in his mask. "What do you see, Tick Tock?"

Team leader Tick Tock, Mickey Valient to the rest of the world, coordinated the car chase with the police. "It's our lucky day, boys. They're herding him right toward us."

In the growing winter darkness, the men stood nearly invisible in their midnight blue outfits, masks covering the upper half of their faces. When they spoke, their voices came out with a metallic distortion courtesy of Tick Tock's voice-disguising device.

Adrenaline rushed through his system as X waited on the ground. He missed being out with the guys. Had it only been two weeks? The rushed wedding and honeymoon had been exhilarating, but he was glad to be home and back at the work he loved.

Standing half-hidden in the alley, X grinned at his other friend and partner in crime-fighting. "Ready to play, big guy?"

Powerhouse, otherwise known as Bull Kincaid, smiled back, his pale skin and white teeth a sharp contrast against the dark mask. At least six and a half feet tall and built like a linebacker, Powerhouse usually played the "immovable object" against the unstoppable forces they came up against. He cracked his knuckles, then his neck. "Bring it," he said.

Police sirens wailed in the night, getting louder.

"How close?" X asked Tick Tock.

"Just turned down the alley," Tick Tock replied. "Get ready."

Powerhouse peeked around the fence that separated the alley from the parking lot where they waited. Gauging the distance to the approaching Toyota, he stepped back and moved behind an overflowing metal garbage bin. He placed his hands and one shoulder against it, waiting, shifting his weight from one foot to the other in anticipation.

X waited behind him, anxious for the fracas to begin. Sometimes he got to be the front man, but tonight they needed Powerhouse's muscle to end the chase. X tossed a short steel pipe from one hand to the other, feeling the rush of energy flow through his body. The gloves he wore were palm-less rather than fingerless. They protected him from leaving fingerprints, but allowed his skin to absorb the strength of the metal. He had been working on plans for flexible titanium-lined gloves before he met Tori, but the craziness of falling in love and getting married over the last two months had disrupted a lot of things. The gloves fell to the bottom of his to do list. Tonight he'd have to make do with the pipe.

X squeezed his right palm around the steel. Hot energy tightened his skin all over his body. The rush felt good. He put his new bride out of his mind and focused on the job at hand.

"Ready, set..." Tick Tock's voice came through their earpieces.

X shifted onto the balls of his feet in anticipation.

"Now!"

Powerhouse shoved the garbage bin into the alley. The squeal of brakes, the crash of metal on metal as the car hit the heavy steel container full-on. Powerhouse jumped behind the garbage bin and locked his elbows. He kept the car from skidding toward the surrounding buildings by digging his heels into the snow-covered asphalt. X watched the pavement buckle behind his friend's feet.

The car stopped with a final screech of damaged metal. X watched the doors for exiting passengers. His turn at bat.

The garbage bin began to roll toward the opposite building. Powerhouse pushed it to a flatter area. Less paperwork if there wasn't any damage to surrounding private property. X didn't like to waste time with paper when there were always more people to protect, more criminals to catch.

"Driver side," came Tick Tock's voice in their ears.

The driver side door flew open and X took his position. A young man stumbled out—maybe old enough to vote, not old enough to drink, but dumb enough to run. He looked over his shoulder toward the approaching police car, his feet already double-timing in the opposite direction.

Right into the path of Superhero X.

Wham!

The young man slammed into him and fell.

X grinned down, tapping the pipe against his thigh. He had only an inkling of what it felt like for someone to run into him. His brothers said it was like running into a steel wall. X put his palm out and raised his fingers twice. The universal sign for "come and get it."

The driver gaped up at him from the pavement. One hand held his head. Must've cracked it on X's chest.

"He's not a mouse, X. Hold him for the officers." Tick Tock

sounded either exasperated or amused. X couldn't tell through the voice-disguiser. "Powerhouse, another one on the passenger side."

X shook his head slightly. There was no challenge in it when things went according to plan. He reached down to grab the driver. Not quick enough.

The man rolled away. Standing, he now held a 9mm pistol. Jogging backwards with the gun aimed at X, he ducked between two buildings.

X muttered under his breath. Careful what you wish for. More squealing brakes signaled the arrival of the police. X gave chase. A cop pounded a few yards behind him.

"He's got a gun," X yelled over his shoulder.

More sirens sounded from the front of the building. Police shouted to each other. X struggled to hear Tick Tock in his earpiece.

"Say again?" he shouted as he ran.

"Turn right. Bushes in front."

The buildings gave way to the parking lot and X turned right. Three more police officers came running from their cars at the front of the building. X paused, searching the snow for footprints. He saw movement, halogen security lights reflected a flash of red fabric. He bounded into the bushes just as the driver jumped up with his gun.

X pulled up short. A shootout was not the kind of excitement he was looking for. Too many ways for it to end badly. Putting out his hand in a conciliatory gesture, he turned his body to shield the police officers behind him. Slow movements and quiet words would win the day. "Now just—"

"Drop your weapon!" a cop behind him shouted.

The cop moved into X's peripheral vision on the left. Idiot. Didn't he know X was here to protect him? He was supposed to stay back. If the driver started shooting now, he could hit any of them.

The young man flinched at the cop's shout and raised his gun. To his left, X saw all the officers bring up their guns, everyone shouting at the guy to drop his weapon. X groaned. So much for slow movements and quiet words. The situation had spiraled out of control. Which left only one option.

Before anyone could start shooting, X leapt at the guy, holding tightly to the steel pipe. In a flash, an image of Tori appeared in his mind, a picture of his lovely little wife with a gun pointed at her. Another flash, and Tori was advancing on the gunman.

Protect her.

The same imperative voice that shouted in his mind when he first met Tori was stronger than ever. Along with the vision, it shook him, and X realized as he launched himself at the gun-wielding drug dealer that his timing was a half-second too late.

Bang! The gun went off.

TORI PULLED her fisted hands from her coat pockets, looking around, trying to decide what to do. *Please help me, God.* Her eyes darted to Eddie behind the counter. He saw the quiet man moving toward the gunman, too. Eddie opened the cash register and started counting the bills out loud.

"Twenty, forty, sixty—"

"Just put it in the bag, man!" the kid shouted.

Eddie shot him an angry look. "I have to tell my dad how much got stolen for the insurance paperwork, you idiot! Eighty, one hundred..." Eddie kept counting, picking up the tens and then the fives.

Tori felt her lips twitch in a tiny smile. Brilliant! The kid was so focused on the money, he didn't see the other guy sneaking up behind him. Tori tensed, praying this would work.

Crash!

Behind her, near the women, a glass jar fell and broke. The young woman screamed.

The gunman swung around. "Everybody freeze!"

More screams tore the air. Tori ducked as the kid waved the gun. The idiot looked like he was in a gangster movie. He probably didn't even know how to use the thing.

The gunman turned back to the cashier. "Give me the money and no one gets hurt!"

Eddie stopped counting and started putting the money into a paper bag. Tori thought he nodded to the other man, only four or five feet away now and gliding forward soundlessly.

When Eddie started to put all the change into the bag, the gunman interrupted him. "Forget the change! I don't want no change! What, you never been held up before? Get me the money from the safe, and I'm gone, and you live."

Eddie shook his head. "I-I can't—the safe—"

"Give him the money!" one of the women screamed.

The kid cocked his gun (okay, maybe he did know how to use it), looking back and forth between the customers and the cashier. As Tori watched from the cover of the candy aisle, the man behind the robber darted with amazing stealth first one way then the other, always keeping out of the gunman's line of sight. How did he do that? He was over there, and then he was there, and then—

The robber didn't see it coming—the other man closed the distance, thrusting the kid's gun arm into the air, and shoving him into the counter. Eddie reached for the customary convenience store baseball bat, but he wasn't fast enough. The robber twisted under the other guy. The two men tussled. The women screamed. Eddie ducked, and—

A shot rang out!

Tori flinched and ducked again. Could she do something to help? But what? She pressed a fist into her stomach, trying to keep the roiling fear down so she could think. The hot feeling in her stomach grew as she struggled between self-preservation and the overwhelming urge to help keep everyone safe.

The robber jumped away as the other man fell to the floor.

Another crash of glass. The gunman whirled again. He pointed the gun at the man with the crying baby.

Not the baby! Not if she could stop him. Tori grabbed handfuls of yellow M&Ms packages and started throwing them at the gunman. "Don't shoot!" Tori screamed at him, hot anger bursting out. "Stop it! Put that gun down!"

The kid ducked her shots, candy hitting him in the face and shoulder, unable to keep the gun aimed any more. Tori marched toward him, too riled up to think. Out of ammunition, she pointed her finger at him like a kindergarten teacher. *"Put it down now, mister!"*

The kid looked at her like she was crazy. Then with little hesitation, he put the gun on the counter.

A split second later, Eddie had the baseball bat against the robber's throat. As the guy clawed for air, the front door burst open and police officers crashed in, flowing through the room like a dam had burst.

Tori jumped out of their way, her hand pressed to her queasy stomach. Police threw the robber to the ground and cuffed him. One officer checked the man who had been shot while another asked Eddie if he was okay. Tori noticed Eddie's bleeding head. When had that happened? The police waved in EMTs who worked on the guy with the bullet wound.

The hero of the day. Tori hoped he was okay. That was amazing the way he just—just stepped in and saved everyone. The guy was a real hero. And so was Eddie.

"Are you all right, ma'am?" Tori felt a policeman shake her shoulder.

"The guy that was shot..." she said, still watching the EMTs.

She couldn't see the man himself. *God, please let him be okay.* She tried to focus on breathing, in and out, don't look at the blood.

"They're taking care of him. I'm sure he'll be fine. Are you hurt?"

"No, I—no." Tori tried to swallow but her mouth was bone dry. She noticed her hand hurt and looked down. Her fist had wrapped her purse strap in a death grip. She looked up at the policeman. "I thought he was going to shoot the baby." There was no way she could ever, *ever* let someone hurt a child.

The policeman smiled and said, "The baby is fine. See?"

Tori followed his pointing finger to see the man rocking his little girl, talking to another officer. They both looked fine. Then the man looked at Tori and pointed at her as he spoke.

It only took Tori a moment to realize why. She looked down at the floor littered with peanut M&Ms—yellow, green, blue, red, brown.

The policeman laughed. "I've never seen anyone take down a gunman in quite that way before."

"I'm sorry." Tori didn't know what to say. What had she been thinking? She never would have interfered like this a few months ago. The policeman questioned her about what had just happened, but Tori's mind darted around like a chickadee. Since she'd stopped seeing her psychiatrist and stopped taking her medications, she felt better than ever. Freer and more alive. But maybe she shouldn't allow herself to be quite so free. Walking up to a man with a gun!

The meds kept her from any kind of spontaneous action or uncontrolled emotional response. Maybe that was better than, than...whatever just happened.

"Are you okay?" The policeman looked at her closely.

Tori wasn't sure of the correct response. She was alive—thank God—and she was going to see Joe again, and day eleven of married life. But...she wasn't exactly feeling well. Her stomach was calming down, but she felt herself beginning to shake from the inside out.

"Let's sit you down for a minute, shall we?" The policeman took her arm and escorted her outside toward his car.

The bitter cold night air helped clear her head. As they walked past the stretcher where the wounded man lay, Tori paused. Had everyone thanked him? He certainly deserved their gratitude. She bent down. But she didn't know what to say. What words were enough?

"You're very brave," she murmured, touching his uninjured shoulder briefly. "Thank you so much."

He glared back at her. "What? Your suit at the cleaners?" he whispered fiercely, "Or is this your day off?"

Tori pulled back a little. "What?" Why was he attacking her?

"I'd think a guy with a gun would be enough that you could use your powers before someone gets shot," he spat at her. "But no, had to be the hero, huh? Had to wait till you were the only superhero who could save the day. That's why I work alone. Superheroes like you are just super*egos*. You don't care about anything but your media image!"

The EMT moved Tori out of the way. She heard the man moan as they hustled him into the ambulance.

What was he talking about? When she called out to the gunman she was just...worried, scared. That's all. It was probably a stupid thing to do, but it distracted him enough so that Eddie could grab him.

The policeman put his arm around Tori as she swayed on her feet. He tucked her into the back seat of his police car. "Why don't you put your head down?" he suggested.

Tori shook her head. She just needed to get her bearings. The car was warm, and she closed her eyes, leaning back into the seat. She let her mind wander as she tried to relax. She tried not to think about what kinds of people had been sitting in the back of this police car lately. Could lice survive the winter? Ugh, best not to think about it.

Her thoughts returned to the conversation with the man who'd been shot. It hit her then—was he saying he was a superhero? Tori's eyes flew open and she turned in time to see the ambulance pull away. She'd met a superhero?

She flopped back against the seat. No. Impossible! Her parents had always insisted the "superhero" stories in the news were publicity stunts. Crime was on the rise and the city government would say anything to look like they had it under control.

She'd heard her mother's voice saying a hundred times over the years, "There's no such thing as superheroes. A few freaks out there who want to be more than they are, but no one has any kind of supernatural power."

Tori accepted this version of the world. It made sense. It was logical, orderly. To believe that people might have supernatural abilities opened the door to possibilities Tori didn't want to consider. She and her sister Lexie had enough freak factor with the strange things that sometimes happened around them.

This guy accusing her of being a superhero did seem a little freaky, that's true. Of course, he'd been shot, lost blood, was probably out of his mind with pain. But that other guy...

Tori's mind drifted back for a moment to Halloween. Some kid had grabbed her purse and taken off. Tori chased him, but she tripped and fell. Moments later a man dressed as Zorro appeared, gorgeous and thrilling. He helped her get her purse back, and picked her up like she weighed no more than a doll. Then he kissed her like—

Tori shook her head and opened her eyes. Sure it was a great kiss, but she never saw him again. She met Joe a couple days later, fell madly in love with him, and married him on Christmas Eve.

She straightened her shoulders. She had no intention of thinking about another man now that she was married. But she wondered if her parents were wrong. Maybe superheroes did exist. If so, they weren't all freaks. Not Zorro anyway.

Still, why would this possible "superhero" accuse *her* of being a superhero? Maybe in the pain of getting shot, he...got confused. In her mind's eye, Tori saw the look on the robber's face as he put the gun down. There was something about it, something familiar. Her mind tripped and twisted with roiling emotions and panic-infused imagination. She needed to stop this crazy thinking.

But her brain wouldn't stop working on it. Now she remembered. Last night when she and Joe had stopped over at her sister Lexie's and little Ben wouldn't go to bed, she'd used her Aunt Tori voice and forcefully insisted he go to bed. He'd looked at her with that same funny look on his face. Then he did. The barely-three-year-old turned and went to his room without another word.

And a few months ago. When Lexie told her that it wasn't just that Tori could convince people of things, but that she could force people to *do* things. And Lexie had only said that because—oh my gosh, that's right—Tori had *insisted* that Lexie tell her what she was thinking.

Tori felt her breath coming quicker but she couldn't catch it, she couldn't breathe. She kept trying to breathe, but the air just kept going in and out of her mouth without hitting her lungs and she couldn't get a breath and—

The door opened and the policeman said something but Tori couldn't catch his words and then he was pushing her head onto her knees and still talking and she thought she heard, "That's it. Breathe."

Tori gulped in air, then tried to slow down and get the blood to stop pounding in her head. It's not possible. It simply wasn't possible to live for twenty-seven years and not know...not make the connection.

She'd test it. Then she'd know. It wouldn't work, and then she'd know her mother was right. There was no such thing as superheroes. No such thing as super powers.

Tori looked up at the cop. "I need some M&Ms. I went in for M&Ms and I need them, please." She knew she was jabbering, but she had to know. "Please get me some."

"Just take a deep breath and—"

She glared into his eyes, hoping and terrified and feeling very, very alone. Her gut burned with heat. *"I need M&Ms! Please!"*

The cop stopped in the middle of his sentence. He looked at her for a moment, then stood up and turned back toward the store. When he came back with every kind of M&Ms flavor the store sold, Tori fainted.

2

S LAM!

The bullet hit Superhero X in the shoulder just before he tackled the younger man. X had jumped at an angle that would allow him to bring the man down without a full-on tackle. But the bullet hit him hard enough to change his trajectory. He tried to break his fall so he wouldn't hurt the guy. But the vision of Tori and another gunman caused X to lose his focus. For a moment, he was just Joe Clarke, a regular guy with a new wife and strange new fears.

He felt the snow on his face. Wow, his shoulder hurt. He changed his mind about not crushing the shooter and let his weight fall a little heavier on the guy until he heard him groan.

Someone shook his aching shoulder.

"He's been shot! Call an ambulance!"

Work. He was at work. He forced himself to focus. Superhero X, helping to keep the streets safe. Finish this job and get home. Hold Tori safely in his arms and rest in the assurance that the vision wasn't real.

"Powerhouse, get down there!" Tick Tock's voice barked in X's ear. "He's not responding."

X pushed himself off the gunman. The man coughed and gasped for breath. Having the equivalent of a 260-pound steel beam fall on him had probably cracked a few of his ribs. *That's what you get for shooting a superhero who absorbs the power of metal, you imbecile.*

Half a dozen police surrounded them. The officer who started it—a new guy obviously—kicked the gun away, then cuffed one of the kid's wrists. Two more officers grabbed his other arm. Three more crowded around X, firing questions at him. He waved them off and got up, dusting the snow from his super suit.

"I'm fine," he said. "Just had a—" A what? A vision? A hallucination? A premonition? "A moment," he finished lamely.

His shoulder was killing him. He forced himself not to groan as he inspected the hole in his suit. It was important that the men in blue trusted him to protect them. If they worried that they needed to keep him safe along with the rest of society, they wouldn't be as effective a team.

"Okay, we got him," one of them said.

"You okay down there, X?" Tick Tock asked in his ear.

X gave half a wave toward the roof. "Yup."

Powerhouse jogged up then. His body language played it cool, but his eyes drilled into X's. He walked over and casually pulled X a few feet away from the bustle. He didn't say anything, just raked X over with his eyes. For a moment, X felt like he was a kid in school with the teacher reading his face and knowing what he'd done. By day, Bull had super-teacher powers as well. High school history teacher and wrestling coach, beloved by all.

"I'm fine!" X wished Powerhouse would turn off the teacher look. He didn't want to talk about whatever had just happened. He looked down at his shoulder and probed the area with his fingers. "Ow! Hurts like a son of a gun!" This was not part of the night's plan.

Tick Tock chuckled in his ear. "I told you not to play with him."

"Want me to beat him up for you?" X turned to see Power-house grinning at him. The teacher look was gone. In its place was the brothers-in-arms let's-get-em look familiar since grade school.

X forced himself to grin back. "Tempting," he said, watching the police shove the glowering young man toward one of their patrol cars. Looking back at his friend, he said, "You didn't even break a sweat, did you?"

"The passenger just about peed his pants," Powerhouse said. "You shoulda seen him."

"You should see the car," Tick Tock said. "He ripped the door right off it."

Powerhouse shrugged. "Car was totaled anyway."

X laughed and clapped Powerhouse on the back. "I gotta see this." They walked back to the alley, letting the police finish doing their job out front. X focused on the work at hand and tried not to think about the disturbing image he saw when the gun went off. His beautiful new wife standing in front of a shooter. He couldn't decide what scared him more—the idea of Tori in danger, or the fact that she didn't look that frightened.

"Thanks, X, Powerhouse," one of the cops called from the parking lot.

"Tell Tick Tock 'hey' for us," yelled another.

"Tell them I said 'hey' back," Tick Tock said in their earpieces.

"He says get your sorry excuse down here sooner next time," Powerhouse shouted to them.

The officers laughed and waved. One of them waved toward the roof.

"And explain to the new guy how this works, will you?" X called, reproach in his voice.

"Will do, sorry about that X."

Tick Tock met them in the back parking lot. "Cop got in the way, huh?"

X pressed his lips together to keep from saying something rude. He shook his head. "You think?"

Tick Tock and Powerhouse both chuckled. "Baby," Tick Tock said.

"Just because it didn't break the skin doesn't mean it didn't hurt at *point-blank range*," X growled. He'd be fine. He knew he sounded like a whiner. After all, he'd been shot plenty of times.

But Tori—there was nothing to keep *her* from getting killed. His spine tingled and he stretched his shoulders to try to get rid of the feeling. The concern he felt for Tori wasn't the kind that moved him to use his powers to protect the community. It was more like...an imperative.

Whatever it was, all he wanted was to hear her voice. Better yet, hold her in his arms. Then he could breathe easy again. He'd been itching to get out and back to work tonight. But now he was itching to get home.

He walked out into the alley with the others to see the wreck of a car. The hood had folded up and in on itself, and the front engine mounts had snapped when the force of the collision shoved the engine back several inches. The windshield, while technically still intact, looked like a spider web. The front wheels had turned in at an odd angle. X bet the front axle had snapped. Warm engine fluids dripped into the snow, hissing and steaming.

An unexpected laugh burst from his throat. "Geez, Powerhouse!"

"It's a beauty, eh?" One of the officers going through the car and cataloguing its contents looked up at the superheroes and back at the car.

X recognized him as someone they'd worked with before. This cop would've stayed out of the way, let X protect him and do his job. X shook his head. He needed to snap out of it. But it was making him cranky, wondering if Tori was okay.

Of course she was okay.

He forced himself to join in the laughter and conversation as the men looked over the car and its contents. The passenger door appeared to be missing. No, there it was, a couple yards away.

"When he ripped the door off," the officer said to Tick Tock and X, "we had a clear view of the baggies under the seats. Regular pharmacy on wheels crystal meth, coke, roofies." He pointed to the other officer, inventorying the drugs at their squad car. The other cop nodded and went back to what he was doing.

"Excellent!" Powerhouse beamed. "My favorite kind of bust, making the streets safer for my boys."

While the cops probably thought Powerhouse meant that he had sons, X and Tick Tock knew he meant his boys at school. He was intense when it came to those kids. He had no problem using his stature to scare them when he lectured them about staying out of trouble. But X knew more than a few of them had called Bull instead of their parents from the police station. Most of the cops had no clue, though, that Bull and Powerhouse were the same man.

Powerhouse looked longingly at the damaged vehicle. "I don't suppose you'd let me play with it some more," he asked the cop.

"No," he said with a laugh, "I gotta have it hauled down to the yard. Maybe you could move it outta the way a little, though. Put the door on the roof or something?"

"Sure thing." Powerhouse walked over and picked up the door with one hand and laid it on top of the roof.

"Show off," Tick Tock called out.

Powerhouse waved as he moved the garbage bin back to its usual spot, whistling as he went.

"I tried moving that Dumpster," the cop said in a stage whisper. "I couldn't even budge it and I'm a big guy! Holy smokes, he's strong!"

X chuckled with him. He pointed at two six-inch impressions in the asphalt. "Did you see the holes where he dug in his heels?" The cop's jaw dropped.

Tick Tock took that moment to examine the bullet wound.

"Hey! That hurts!" X pulled back, curbing his urge to push the smaller man away. At about six feet, give or take, Tick Tock was several inches shorter than X and he didn't have any physical powers. X tried to be conscious of that at all times so he wouldn't accidentally hurt him. Or anybody else for that matter.

Powerhouse, bigger than both of them at probably six-seven and 275 pounds, was even more careful. X thought of him as the sleeping gentle giant. He'd never seen Powerhouse riled up, and wasn't sure he'd want to.

Tick Tock chuckled as Powerhouse walked up, wiping his hands on his suit. "You gotta see this. The bullet *dented* his skin."

That sounded kinda cool. X checked it out with the others until the pain reminded him it was *his* shoulder that got shot. "Okay, enough. If we're done here..." X let the sentence hang. Sometimes they'd work for hours, one situation after another. Sometimes they'd power down and have a beer somewhere. Tonight, X hoped the guys would accept that he just wanted to go home to his wife.

He looked at the bullet dent again. He hoped she wouldn't notice. He hadn't quite gotten around to explaining...things.

"You gonna be all right?" the cop asked.

"I'll be fine," X assured him with a smile he wasn't quite feeling.

"He won't even have a bruise in the morning," Tick Tock said, slapping him on the back, close to his sore shoulder.

X slapped him on the back in return. Hard. Tick Tock stumbled and laughed.

"Maybe next time," Powerhouse said under his breath as they started to walk away, "we'll get to do something *hard*."

"Good luck, officer," Tick Tock said over Powerhouse's grumbling.

"No matter how often I work with you guys, I still—geez, it's amazing." The cop shook hands with each of them, and went back to work.

As Superhero X and the others faded into the shadows, he heard the cop say, "Hey, could my son get your autographs...sometime?"

TORI WAS STILL SHAKING when she walked in the front door. The wind off the bay made the January temperatures feel colder than ever, but it wasn't the weather that made her shiver. It was the idea that she might be a super freak.

She kicked off her boots at the door, hung up her coat, and dropped her purse on the couch. She headed for the fireplace, swaying a bit on her feet. Which shock was greater—being part of an armed robbery or learning you might be a... Don't think about it. Just get warm. Taking kindling and old newspapers from a metal bin on the hearth, she built a fire in short order.

Soothing warmth danced in front of her eyes, taking the chill off. Dropping onto the couch as close to the fireplace as she could get, Tori cuddled down deep into the cushions, pulling the nearby afghan tightly around her. Joe's tan-colored half-Siamese cat Snickers wandered in and jumped up on her lap. Tori pulled him under the afghan and held him close, trying to soak up his warmth.

The last nine days combined her favorite time of year—Christmas and New Year's—with the best time of her life—getting married to a fabulous, gorgeous guy and spending a week with him in a Disney World hotel. Joe's willingness to be silly, his romantic gestures, and his gallant nature made a heady mixture. Add in the sense of comfort and safety she always felt when he was around, and she was a goner, head over heels.

Then she'd come home to...this. Images of the robbery taunted her. The gun, the blood, the wounded man's words. She squeezed her eyes shut. It couldn't be true.

But the policeman. Could it be true?

Could it be that she forced people to do things just by telling them to? Or was she just a girl who had an uncanny ability to get people to follow her? Dad always said she was a natural leader. Mom said she was too pushy, that she went too far when she wanted something.

She sucked in a choking breath—could she be a freak? Tori saw that superhero's face—maybe he really was a superhero, how else could he have moved almost faster than the eye could follow?—and heard his harsh words again. Then her mother's face appeared, and she saw Dixie turn her back on her daughter. They may not always get along well, but she loved her mother. She didn't want her to think Tori was something...unnatural.

God, help me figure this out. I'm not a freak. I have to stop listening to the voices in my past. But who am I? Am I different in some way? Could you really have created superheroes?

Sure, the Bible was filled with stories of heroes, but *superheroes?* When Lexie got upset, she could get so out of control that everyone around her would get upset, too. But that just meant they had a dysfunctional family like everybody else. If Tori was accused of being too pushy, well, maybe she was. But she was working on it. That guy, whoever he was, couldn't be a superhero. And he definitely didn't know anything about *her.*

She threw off the afghan and jumped up. Snickers meowed his protest. Marching into the kitchen, Tori took pots and pans and kitchen appliances out of the cupboards. She'd cook; that would clear her head. She'd cook a lovely dinner for her wonderful new husband, and she would think. She'd figure this out.

She pulled food items out of cupboards, out of the refrigerator, out of the pantry until it looked like she meant to prepare a gourmet Thanksgiving dinner for twelve. Her hand shook as she plugged in the food processor. As she pulled off the cover, it fell to the floor.

Her tears fell, too. This couldn't be true. She wasn't a freak! She didn't want her family to hate her!

Tori felt panic grow within her. They would. They would hate her, think she was trying to be something she wasn't, something important. That's what Dixie always said when a "superhero" story came on the news. Another freak trying to be famous and important. Her face would curl into a mask of disgust. Then she would forbid anyone to talk about it.

No! Tori shook her head. That wasn't her. She didn't want to be famous or important. She just wanted to live a nice quiet life, watch her nephew grow up, raise some kids of her own, volunteer at church and at school. Same as every other normal suburban housewife. She didn't have any powers. She wasn't a freak.

Now stop thinking about it. She gripped the counter hard with both hands, eyes squeezed shut. Forget it. Just forget all about it. *You're not a superhero. Forget it. It's not true! Forget it! Forget it!*

She repeated it over and over until she felt herself relax. Her hands lost their death grip on the counter. She took a deep breath and tried to relax the muscles in her face, her neck, her back. She breathed in again. And out. Calming breaths. All was well.

Tori finally opened her eyes and took one last long breath. Better. She felt better. She looked at all the food and pans on the counter. What had she been making? She couldn't remember. Was company coming over tonight? Why else had she pulled out so much food?

Shaking her head, she chuckled a little. Maybe this is what happens to all new brides. She got so excited about making Joe his first home-cooked meal as a married man, she'd forgotten what she was going to make. She decided on baked chicken with pasta and put everything else away.

Snapping and crackling from the living room caught her attention. Had she made a fire when she came home? She didn't even remember. She shook her head and smiled to herself. She had to find a way to get more sleep before she forgot her own name.

"Hey, honey," Joe called when he walked in later.

Butterflies danced inside as they always did when she heard his voice. Tori heard him taking off his coat and boots and went to greet him. Dinner had been ready for ten minutes, and Joe hadn't answered his cell phone for the last half hour. She couldn't decide whether she should be worried or angry. She opted for neither now that he was safely home, but made a mental note to talk to him about improving his communication skills. Right now, she only wanted to work on non-verbal skills.

"Hey there, gorgeous," she said with a smile, wrapping her arms around him. "How was your day?"

"It was fine," he said, holding her tight and giving her a long warm kiss, "but I missed you, decided to cut short my night with the guys and come home."

"D'oh!" Tori slapped her forehead. Any pique she'd felt, banished. She gave him another kiss. "I'm such an idiot, I totally forgot. Well, I made dinner. Are you hungry?"

Joe grinned. "I'm a man, I'm always hungry."

Tori's feet left the floor as Joe pulled her closer, his lips doing wonderful things to hers, then trailing over her cheek, around her ear, down her throat.

"Joe!" she squealed, her toes curling from his kisses, her feet kicking to get down. "Dinner! Chicken, not me."

He laughed and put her down. "Why didn't you say so?" He picked up his briefcase and headed for his room.

Their room, Tori reminded herself. She felt like giggling every time she thought about it. Tonight would be only the third night they'd sleep together in *their* bed. She never thought she'd have this life—love and marriage and living in a house with a fireplace and a cat. She loved it. Definitely different from her and Lexie's plan to grow old together, safely alone in their little apartment, hidden from the world.

As she watched Joe walk away, Tori remembered what he looked like under his clothes. Maybe they'd go to bed early again tonight. She sighed and smiled, her fingers touching her still-moist lips. Yup, this life was way better than the one she'd planned.

"Let me wash my hands and I'll be right there," Joe called from the hall.

Tori pulled her thoughts from the bedroom and straightened the pile of boots and shoes by the door so none of the wet ones got on the carpet. She frowned and picked up one of her boots. Had she stepped in dog poop? Gross. No, she looked closer at it, not dog poop. Something kind of brown had dried onto it though.

She picked up the other boot. Oh, much worse. Whatever it was covered the bottom of that one. Sighing, she took both of them to the laundry room and stood them in the sink. She ran the water, waiting for it to turn warm. Joe had an old toothbrush lying there, presumably for scrubbing things, so Tori used it on the first boot. Sure enough, the stain began to wash away.

"Whatcha doing?" Joe asked, coming up behind her and wrapping his arms around her waist, nuzzling her neck.

Tori smiled, loving the feel of him so close. Marrying Joe was the best decision she'd ever made, regardless of what other people said.

"I got something on my boots today." She let warm water wash over the bottom of the boot in her hand. "I wanted to get it off just in case it stains."

Joe leaned closer to look at the other boot. Tori followed his gaze and saw a red puddle around the sole.

"What in the heck?" Tori frowned and picked up the boot.

Joe tensed behind her, then pushed her aside to examine both boots. "Tori, this is blood! Are you okay? What happened?" He dropped the boots and turned to her.

"No, I'm—I'm fine." Tori tried to think of anywhere she'd

walked today where there had been—"Paint. It must be paint. It's not blood." Eew! That went beyond gross.

Joe touched the puddle and rubbed his fingers, then sniffed them. Wiping his hand on a towel, he turned back to her. "What happened? Where are you hurt?" he demanded. His voice sounded angry, but his eyes looked scared.

Tori took a step back. Her head felt fuzzy, like she'd just awakened from a dream but couldn't quite remember it. Joe ran his hands over her body—something she normally liked quite a lot, but now it felt impersonal and intrusive. He lifted her shirt, turned her around to check both her front and her back, ran his hands down her legs.

"Joe! Stop it!" Tori pulled away from him, but he grabbed her and hauled her close. "What are you doing? What's wrong with you?" Tori's annoyance held an edge of fear. Why did he look so frightened?

Joe stopped manhandling her and stared her down. "You're sure you're not hurt? Were you around someone else who was hurt?"

This conversation was giving her a headache. And it wasn't the kind of thing she wanted to talk about before dinner. But she wanted to reassure him that she was fine. Boy, and she thought *she* watched too much TV.

"Joe," she said, forcing herself to speak calmly. She could see him trying to relax, taking a deep breath and pulling her closer. "Listen to me, baby." She took his face in her hands, eye to eye. She focused on calming him down. *"There is no blood. I am not hurt and there is no blood. Understand?"*

He stared at her for a moment, and Tori wondered what he was thinking. But he finally relaxed, rubbing a hand over his forehead.

"Are you okay?" she asked him.

"Yeah, yeah," he said. "I'm fine, I'm just tired. A little headache, that's all."

Tori took a deep breath and tried to relax. Joe held her close and she closed her eyes, that wonderful warm feeling permeating her soul. Never in her life had she felt as absolutely safe as she had since she'd met Joe. She didn't like to examine the thought because it implied that she hadn't felt safe before. Life had been hard, almost unbearable sometimes, but that didn't mean anything. Everyone had hard times. She pushed the disturbing thoughts away. Whatever the reason, when she was with him, she felt like she could do anything.

"We need to eat, Mr. Clarke, before the chicken turns to rubber," she said, patting his behind and pulling away toward the door. Her boots could wait. She didn't want him thinking about them anymore.

"Lead the way, Mrs. Clarke," he said.

He sounded as tired as Tori felt. They definitely should go to bed early. She smiled as she put dinner on the table. Time to find out if her husband's willingness to cuddle extended past the honeymoon.

here was his son?

W Evan Ruffalo sighed heavily and rubbed his eyes. Replacing his glasses, he tried to concentrate on the spreadsheets in front of him. He hoped the new temp was an Excel whiz. He'd arrived at six this morning to work on the reports for today's meeting, but he wasn't sure the information made sense. He couldn't concentrate.

Getting to a meeting on time lately was a minor miracle, and not a little stressful. Evan was afraid he'd get the ax soon if he didn't get his work back up to an acceptable level. Management had been understanding at first, but people were beginning to grumble. If he could find a temp worth his time, he could train her to get the work done while he continued his search for Jason.

Where was he? Where was his son?

He slammed his fist on his desk. The sound reverberated in his empty office. He'd begun to look at the police as part of the problem, not part of the solution. Since he and Sharon hadn't yet taken custody of Jason, and the adoption paperwork hadn't been completed, they had little grounds to push the authorities to find a child everyone believed dead.

Even Sharon believed Jason was dead. How could she not see?

Seventeen children under the age of ten had gone missing in the last two years—in a ten-block radius of the orphanage. There were two elementary schools and six preschools in the area, so perhaps percentage-wise seventeen missing children weren't worth anyone's time...even if twelve of them had lived at St. Silvia's Home for Orphaned Children. How could no one see the pattern, the significance? Sure, it was a bad area of town and the authorities blamed it on runaways and custody problems, but what six-year-old runs away from the place where he eats and sleeps? The place where he waits for his new mommy and daddy with uncontrollable excitement?

Evan had interviewed every member of the orphanage staff, most of its volunteers, and parents of other children missing in Double Bay. He'd even interviewed the street people living nearby. One drunk told him all the kiddies had been abducted by tall red aliens. Another that they'd been eaten by the alligators in the sewers. Lot of help they'd been.

Evan dug in his desk drawer for more aspirin. The guilt was eating away at his head and his stomach. He didn't want to lose Sharon. She was his life. But he couldn't join her in her grief, not yet. Not until he held his dead son in his arms. But Sharon couldn't take the strain anymore. Evan wondered if she believed Jason was dead only so she could grieve him and move on with her life.

But would she move on without *him*?

Not yet, honey. Don't give up yet. I may have found something.

Last night Evan had returned from a weekend trip to Vegas. The trip had been a gamble that paid off—he had a name. The Nine. He didn't know if The Nine represented nine companies or nine people, but they were involved in illegal genetic research, at least some of which was happening here in Double Bay. And Evan's tipster was sure The Nine were experimenting on children.

It wasn't enough to go to the police yet, but Evan was determined to find something or someone who could lead him to his son. He opened his bottom desk drawer and pulled a folder from beneath a jumble of office supplies. Inside, a smiling little six-year-old beamed out at him. Evan couldn't help himself. He smiled back, touching the boy's cheek, remembering the day he and Sharon had asked Jason if he'd like to join their family.

Evan's computer beeped at him. The pop-up on the screen reminded him about his meeting in fifteen minutes. Evan shut the file on Jason, then tucked him safely into the bottom drawer. With a sigh, he forced himself to get the lead out as he rushed from his office and down the hall to the copy room. A minute later, he hurried past some coworkers chatting and sipping coffee in the hall outside the kitchen. Just a few minutes after nine, most people were barely at their desks, but Evan was five minutes away from being late.

"Oh, there he is. Evan!"

Evan turned his head while still heading toward his office. Pam Higgins from Human Resources waved a hand at him, another woman in her wake. "I can't right now. Late for a meeting across the street."

"But this is your new temp," said Pam.

"Temp. Right." Evan swore under his breath. He forgot he'd interviewed someone yesterday. He should've asked for her to show up at noon. The last temp had been a nightmare—always late, didn't know what "cross-foot" meant, swore Excel was her spreadsheet software of choice but couldn't create a macro to save her life. Pam had been great about trying to get him the right person. He'd lost count of how many people he'd tried. And since he needed her help, he didn't want to make her mad.

"Follow me," he told the women, and kept walking.

In his office, Evan put the pages he'd copied in his briefcase, grabbed his wallet and cell phone from his desk drawer, then looked over his desk to see if he'd forgotten anything. He grabbed his coffee cup. "Can you get her situated, show her around?" he asked Pam. "Craig in IT can give her the computer and voicemail passwords."

He grabbed a pen and sticky note pad from his mess of a desk and shoved it at the new girl. "There's a how-to file under F, studio, financial—write it down!" The lights seemed to suddenly come on and the girl started scribbling. This one wasn't going to work out either, but he didn't have time to tell Pam now. "F, studio, financial, Ruffalo—no wait, you can't get to that copy. Look under financial, and if it's not there, try development."

He started past them, glancing at his watch.

"What's it called?" the girl asked.

He frowned at her over his shoulder. "What's what called?"

She shook her head and made a note on the pad. "Never mind, I'll find it."

Evan rolled his eyes and waved his arm as he rushed out the door. "I should be back around eleven," he called.

He heard Pam say as he exited, "Well, Tori, that's your new boss."

THE FIRST DAY is always the hardest, Tori reminded herself as she drove to lunch. The first couple hours had gone well enough, but her boss was in an even worse mood—if that were possible— when he came back from his meeting. She tried to help him as best she could until she realized he wasn't going to stop for lunch. At 1:30, she finally asked if she could go get something. Her stomach growled again as she headed toward a restaurant with a drive-through. She'd bring a lunch from home from now on.

Her cell phone rang. She sighed and punched the button on her hands-free device.

"Tori Lewis, uh, Clarke." She and Joe needed to discuss

whether she would change her name. They'd gotten married so quickly, she hadn't thought about it until she started answering her phone a couple days ago.

"It's me. Sorry to bother you during work, I just have a few questions about the party."

"Hi, Mom. Go ahead, I'm driving. I can talk." Talking to someone made the time in traffic pass quicker. Or at least it seemed to. Even though it was lunch hour in the city, the streets were currently free of snow, so traffic was moving. And with the wedding and the honeymoon behind her, the wedding reception was the last bit of fun to plan before she settled into married life.

As Dixie proceeded to give her a mini-lecture about the hazards of talking on the phone while driving (then why was she calling?), then asked if the honeymoon had gone well (no way was she talking about *that* with her mother), Tori wondered if a silent traffic jam would've been better. She relaxed when the topic turned to the pros and cons of a dozen different foods Dixie could make for the wedding reception on Saturday.

Because of all the Christmas plans and parties on both sides of the family, and the wedding on Christmas Eve, having a small family-and-close-friends reception when they returned seemed like a great idea. Dixie had been less than thrilled about the whirlwind romance (what an understatement), but two extra weeks for her and Joe's mom Hannah to plan the reception mollified her somewhat. Dixie was much calmer about the unexpected if there was something she could do.

Call waiting beeped in Tori's ear. She glanced down at the display. "Mom, I gotta go, that's the temp agency."

"Well, what about the potato salad?" Dixie asked.

"Hannah said you guys are planning a potluck. Just bring the strawberry salad," Tori wanted to make sure her mom made *that*, her total favorite, "and the ham. That's enough."

Dixie started to ask whether Tori preferred ham with a

pineapple glaze or cloves, but Tori cut her off. "I gotta take this call, Mom. I'll talk to you later, okay?"

She growled in consternation as she ended one call and picked up the other. Her mother could be...her mother. "Tori Lewis."

"I thought you were Tori Clarke now."

Gloria. The receptionist at Totally Temps, and one of the few people Tori had ever met whom she disliked on sight. "What's up, Gloria?"

"Janice wanted to know how your first day is going, but she had an emergency dental appointment so she asked me to call." She sounded annoyed. But then Gloria always sounded annoyed.

"Tell her it's going fine, thanks." Tori frowned as she stopped at a red light. Not because of Gloria's tone, but because something didn't seem right. She looked over at Ed & Eddie's across the street. Was she supposed to pick up something there for the reception? Drop off a forgotten Christmas card? Something.

"Hey, Gloria?"

Tori heard her groan into the phone. "Yes?"

"Did I have an interview with Ed Carlisle to do accounting work?" Maybe she'd made an appointment and not put it in her calendar program. Something about the store was picking at the back of her brain. And not just because she frequented the place so often. Though sitting here at the light staring at it reminded her that they made a killer pastrami sandwich in the deli area. If only they had a drive-through.

After a pause, Gloria said, "No, not through our agency."

"Uh, okay, thanks." Tori hung up. She jumped when the car behind her honked. The light was green. Tori drove slowly as she passed the convenience store. Why did she think she was forgetting something? It wasn't a big enough place that she would have ordered anything there for the party. She didn't know what else it could be.

Her phone rang and Tori jumped again. She wanted to

answer it, "Grand Central Station," but went with the more professional, "Tori Clarke" instead.

"I'm sorry, I'm looking for Tori Lewis," said a woman's voice. "Do I have the right number?"

Tori brought her attention back to the road and the phone. "Yes, this is Tori Lewis." She really needed to answer her phone one way or the other before she developed a split personality.

"Ms. Lewis, this is Detective Casey Knox with the Double Bay Police Department. Do you have a moment?"

"Uh, sure. What can I do for you?" Tori's heart raced a little. Why would the police be calling her?

"Can we meet someplace to talk? It won't take very long."

What is it about school principals and police officers that make people so nervous? Tori fought to stay calm. Nothing to be nervous about. She'd never even had a speeding ticket. And she paid that parking ticket last year the day after she got it.

"Where are you now?" Casey prompted.

Tori spoke without thinking. "McConnell and Crocker, near Memorial Park." Should she have told the police where she was? Why did they want to talk to her? She felt a little queasy. She really, *really* didn't want to talk to Casey Knox or anyone else from the police. Theoretically, police were the good guys. She knew that. But Tori's feelings about them had soured during her teen years when Lexie had been in so much trouble.

"We're nearby. We'll meet you at the park then," Casey said.

Tori gave in to her good girl, do-the-right-thing impulses and gave the police the requested details of her vehicle model, then hung up and sighed. She turned into the park at the next light and tried to ignore her growling stomach a little longer. She pulled into a parking spot and let her head sag against the headrest. Nothing to worry about. A few questions.

But about *what*? Her stomach flipped again. She hoped she wasn't coming down with the flu.

She reached into her purse for M&Ms. Nothing. "Ah," she

mumbled. That must be why Ed & Eddie's was on her mind. She'd meant to stop and get some more. She watched chickadees play in a nearby tree. Today's weather was gorgeous for early January, the sun making diamonds on the snow. Tori felt her spirits lift in spite of herself.

Five minutes later, a gray Ford sedan pulled up next to her with a man and a woman inside. The woman rolled down her window and smiled and waved. Must be the police. Or a friendly and well-dressed ax murderer. Not sure which might be worse.

Tori rolled down her window as well.

"Tori Lewis? I'm Casey Knox," the woman said in a friendly way.

She didn't seem like a *Law & Order* kind of cop. Tori felt her guard drop a little.

"Would you like to talk in our car, or would you prefer to walk?"

Tori tensed at the thought of getting into a police car, unmarked or not. "Walk," she said. "Please."

She got out and shook hands with Detective Knox, who immediately insisted Tori call her by her first name. Casey was cheerful, pretty, and immediately likable. She wore a dark gray hooded wool coat with a creamy wool scarf around her neck. Her long, dark hair spilled over her coat and down her shoulders. Tori would love hair that long, but her curls were hard enough to manage at shoulder length.

Casey introduced her partner, Detective Arturo "Call me Art" Paredes, and Tori shook his hand as well. She stared for a second as he smiled at her, their handshake lasting a moment longer. He was, well, *gorgeous* for lack of a better word. Tori smiled back, unable to help herself. There was something about Latino men. He had dark hair, deep brown eyes, and olive skin that contrasted nicely with his white button-down shirt and tan trousers visible under his open tan overcoat. He looked like a man who knocked women off their feet with a whisper.

Exactly the kind of man who'd always spelled trouble for Lewis women. And pretty boy here looked like he could spell it in several languages. Good thing she was safely married now.

Tori pulled her hand and her eyes away—did she see Casey smirk at Art?—and started to walk down the path. Even in the winter, the city kept the outer paths clear for joggers and walkers. Tori wanted to walk now, walk and think, but Casey gestured to a nearby bench.

"Why don't we sit?"

Art leaned casually against a tree next to the bench as the women sat down. His coat stayed open despite the crisp air.

Tori looked around the park, then back at Art, who looked like he was standing guard. "Is there a problem?"

Reassurance poured off him like sunshine. "I just want to make sure our conversation is private."

Tori nodded but looked questioningly at Casey. "Then why aren't we down at your office?" Tori didn't want to go to the police station, but it seemed like a better place for a private conversation than a public park.

"Well," Casey said, "we thought this would be less intimidating after all you've been through."

All she'd been through? What had she been through? Tori frowned. She got married, she went on her honeymoon, she went back to work—

—got robbed—

What? She didn't get—

Strange images danced through her mind. Ed & Eddie's. A kid with a gun. A fight. A man on a stretcher. Blood on her boots.

She'd had a horrible nightmare last night.

"I had to wash blood off my boots." The words burst out without thought or warning. Stop it! She did not. "No, wait." She pressed one hand against her eyes. "It was a nightmare. I dreamed it."

Why had she said that? She told Joe it was paint. In the dream or real life?

Tori's hand fell away as she stared at Casey.

Casey shook her head sympathetically. "I'm sorry."

Tori swallowed, trying to keep the sick feeling in her stomach from coming up. Maybe she was dreaming *now*, still asleep, having nightmares about—

"Do you know a superhero named Spook?" Casey asked.

Tori blinked. Definitely still dreaming. Did she *know* a superhero? Hardly. She shook her head a little. "No. Why?"

"He was at the robbery yesterday." Casey waited, as if this were important news.

When she didn't go on, Tori said, "Okay."

"He was the man who was shot." Art spoke up from his tree. He smiled at Tori as if encouraging her to relax and tell them all she knew about Spook.

Which was absolutely nothing.

"What are you talking about?" she asked, shaking her head at Art. This conversation sounded uncomfortably like her nightmare.

The two detectives shared a look, frowning at each other and shifting like they were uncomfortable. What the heck was going on?

"Tori, can you tell us your version of what happened yesterday?" Casey asked.

Tori's confused gaze bounced back and forth between the officers. "I ran some errands, went to a job interview, and went home and made dinner for my husband." She shrugged. "Will you please tell me what's going on?"

Casey folded her hands, looking very serious. "We want to know about the robbery."

The images in Tori's brain were coming together now. It wasn't a pretty picture. Then—flick!—like a light switch coming on, the memory was back in its entirety. Tori remembered the whole thing. Stomping the snow off her boots, the gunman, the M&Ms—oh, geez, she may never see M&Ms the same way again. She closed her eyes when she remembered her fear that the kid would hurt the baby, the gun going off, the police rushing in.

"Oh my gosh..." she moaned, covering her face with her hands and letting her elbows catch her weight on her knees. "It really happened."

She was in Ed & Eddie's when it was robbed! That's not the kind of thing a person forgets. Maybe it's some kind of post-traumatic stress thing? Is this what happens? You just block out the whole thing? Holy cow.

"Are you okay?" Casey touched her shoulder.

Breathe, just breathe deeply and you'll be okay. Don't throw up on the nice police officers.

Tori felt Art's hand lifting her face—man, he smelled good—and she opened her eyes, tried to focus on him squatting in front of her. Her jumbled brain registered that Art was considerably shorter than Joe. And really, Joe was better looking.

Art lifted one of Tori's eyes open a bit more as he stared at her with concern. "Why don't you put your head down for a minute?" he suggested as he gently pushed her head between her knees. Normally, Tori didn't like to appear weak or sick, especially in front of strangers, but right this minute putting her head between her knees seemed like a very good idea.

Casey patted her back as they silently waited for her to regain her wits. Very kind of them, actually. But as the blood flowed back into Tori's head, she wasn't pleased with the memories that followed. Eddie had a gash on his head. Another man had gotten shot and then was mean to her. Tori thought she might've walked through his blood on the way out. Her stomach clenched. Good thing she hadn't gotten her lunch yet.

"Is he okay?" she asked. She lifted herself up to rest on her elbows again. Art still squatted in front of her, so she asked him, "That guy who was shot, is he okay?"

Art nodded and leaned back on his heels, giving Tori some space. "His name is Spook. He's a superhero. He tried to keep the kid from firing his gun, but this time he got shot. It happens. He'll be fine in a few weeks."

Tori nodded and looked down at her hands. She'd left her gloves in the car; her hands were freezing. She clasped them between her knees. Taking a deep breath, she sat up straighter, hunching her shoulders against the sudden cold. She wanted Joe. She wanted Joe to come take her home and assure her there was no such thing as superheroes. She wanted Joe to tell her she wasn't a freak.

Tori looked at Casey, unaccountably embarrassed. "I'm sorry. I guess I blocked it out."

Casey smiled and patted her arm. "It happens."

"So did he tell you..." Tori wasn't sure what she could have done to make the guy so mad he'd sic the police on her. "That I did something? Got in his way or...? I don't know what I could have done. He'd already been shot by the time I got involved."

"No, it wasn't your fault he got shot," Casey assured her. "He said..." She hesitated. Tori wondered what she wasn't saying.

"He said you saved the day," Art interjected.

Tori frowned. That didn't mesh with what she would assume about superheroes—if she believed in them. Didn't they either swoop in and save the day (she thought of Halloween night and felt a little thrill) or, according to her mother, they were fakers who blamed their failures on someone else. And isn't that what this guy had done?

Tori knew her mother had a bad experience with someone who'd claimed to be a superhero once, but Dixie refused to talk about it. Tori had no idea what had happened or when. But superheroes were taboo conversation at home so she knew little to nothing about them.

Now that she thought about it, though, why was her mother so adamant in her views of superheroes? Maybe she was hiding something. Tori wished she were alone with a computer so she could do a Google search and find out what *exactly* had been written about superheroes in Double Bay.

"You're telling me," she said to Art, "that a superhero named Spook tried to stop an armed robbery, got shot, and told you *I* saved the day?" She laughed at the end. "Yeah, right." That *definitely* didn't make any sense.

Art and Casey exchanged another glance. It was beginning to wig Tori out the way they kept looking at each other like they had some kind of unspoken communication. What if they weren't really police?

"Can I see your badges?" she asked, feeling her fight or flight instincts kick in. She'd never checked their ID. What if they were...what? Honestly, what could they be? Alien hunters named Mulder and Scully?

Art straightened and pulled out his badge. Casey held up hers. Tori looked at them and nodded, trying to relax. They sure looked like police badges. As if she'd know a real badge from a fake one anyway.

"We're with the Superhero Liaison Unit," Art said, moving back against the tree. His manner returned to "policeman at work" and Tori felt a little shiver of unease. "We work with superheroes who help us solve crimes, catch criminals, go undercover, that sort of thing. It's new," he added at her skeptical look.

Superheroes. Cops who work with superheroes. Tori wondered if she should put her head down again. Maybe she shouldn't have stopped taking her meds. She'd never felt better, but life had gotten a lot weirder since she'd gone cold turkey.

"What did Spook say to you?" Casey asked.

Tori let her gaze rest on a crow cawing loudly in a distant tree. She didn't want to remember. *I'd think a guy with a gun would be enough that you could use your powers before someone gets shot.* Nice, thank you, brain. She wished she could forget it again.

"I don't really remember," she lied. "It all happened so fast."

Tori wouldn't look at them. They were the police. They could probably tell she was lying. She focused on breathing, on not throwing up, on not saying anything crazy.

"He's a lunatic!" Tori jumped up from the bench. "He-he was shot and lost blood and doesn't know what he's saying!"

So much for not acting crazy. Her heart raced like it was going to spring from her chest. What was wrong with her? She really, *really* didn't want to go back to Dr. Huntington. That part of her life was over.

She paced in front of the bench. "Honestly, I was in the wrong place at the wrong time and—"

"Actually, you were in the right place at the right time," Art interrupted. "If you hadn't used your...*skills* to stop that guy, he would've shot more people. The police were waiting outside for an opportunity and you provided them with one. If it wasn't for you, someone might have died."

Tori stared at Art, weighing what he'd said. He obviously believed it. Was it possible? Did she have a...*skill* that saved the day?

No.

Casey shifted on the bench, leaning forward like one girl-friend talking to another. Tori braced herself for a story, a sales job.

"Let me tell you about what we do. Art and I established the Superhero Liaison Unit—or SLU—to make contact with both licensed and private superheroes, gathering information that we can use to catch criminals and reduce crime in the city." Casey's expression showed her excitement and passion for her job.

Exactly the sort of thing Tori found hard to resist. Great.

Art pushed away from the tree and moved in closer again. "More and more superheroes are willing to help here in Double Bay because we protect their identities if they want us to. We're even trying to get the city to pass statutes that protect super-heroes against lawsuits."

Lawsuits? For heaven's sake, why would you sue someone for trying to help you?

"The city's overall crime rate has stopped climbing the last couple of months," Art continued, "and Casey and I are convinced it's because more superheroes are coming forward and helping us out."

Tori listened and tried to figure out how this affected *her*, how it all fit into the events of yesterday. Sure, it was great to hear about a drop in crime rates, especially if it was in her neighborhood. But...

"I didn't sleep well last night," she said. "I understand what you're saying—I think—but I'm not really following you. You work with Spook and other superheroes. I get it. But what do you want from me?"

Casey smiled at her, a really big smile. Tori got the feeling she was supposed to be making a connection here. She looked at Art. He grinned, too.

She jumped away from them. "No no no no—"

Absolutely not. Ridiculous! Outrageous!

Tori kept backing up, sliding on the snow, tripping as she backed into a snow bank. Art rushed to her side. His arm around her waist kept her from toppling over into the snow. He worked his charm, obviously trying to do the reassuring bit again, moving her back to the bench. Tori wrenched herself away from him.

A superhero? They thought she was a *superhero*?

Tori's knees buckled. Art grabbed her again, guiding her so that she plopped onto the bench and not onto the ground.

He pressed her head between her knees, and she let him, paranoid she'd pass out again. She remembered *that* from yesterday, too. Twice in two days, in front of police, not something she could take. One of them patted her back again. Someone told her to breathe. *Again.*

She had to think.

Think.

Is that really what they were saying? Because neither detective had said the words, had they? What did it mean?

No, they were wrong. If she were a superhero—

The gears in her brain smoked with the effort to make sense of this.

How could she be a superhero and not know it?

She tried to sit up. "How?" she asked. Her voice sounded more like a croak.

Casey cleared her throat. "We don't really know. You haven't experienced anything like this before?"

Tori hesitated and shook her head. The last few weeks had been a blur of activity—getting engaged, getting married, moving into Joe's house, the honeymoon. She'd been so excited, so *happy* that nothing else really stood out.

Something tugged at the edges of her memory. She struggled to dig it out. Last night...in the kitchen...she was crying...and talking to herself—

"*Holy crap.*" She looked up at Casey in astonishment. "I can even do it to *myself?*"

4

"Phase four testing is complete. I've done it."

Kane Curtis stared at the intercom phone on his mahogany desk. He'd been waiting for this call for almost five years. He inhaled deeply and held it, trying to calm his racing heart.

"Which one?" he said into the intercom.

"Teddy, Lab Two." Jade Mantis' voice came through high-pitched, breathless. She was the senior research scientist at Curtis Enterprises and head of the Genesis Project. Kane had high hopes for what she could help him do, and today she might prove his faith well-founded.

Kane pressed a button and a live feed from Lab Two appeared on one of the six monitors built into the paneled walls of his office. He walked over to watch the screen closely. In the middle of the sterile white room stood a stainless steel table and two chairs. An assortment of toys covered the table, and a cherubic blonde boy, maybe four or five years old, sat on a chair. He played with a stuffed tiger and an army action figure.

A door opened and Jade walked into the lab. Her rich red hair glowed in the florescent lights. Though she arranged it on top of her head when she worked, Kane liked it better down, in long red curls to the middle of her back. Sometimes he forced her to wear it down, whether it got in her way or not. He watched as Jade made notes on a clipboard then walked over to the child.

"Hello, Teddy," she said. "Are you having fun with your toys?"

The little boy gave her a shy smile and kept playing.

Jade sat down in the other chair, positioned so it was not in the way of the camera. "Can I play?" She waited but the little boy said nothing.

Picking up a yellow dump truck, Jade pretended to drive it around the table in front of her. Teddy ignored her. Jade picked up a stuffed bear and walked it over to the tiger Teddy held. Teddy pretended to have the tiger talk to the bear. Jade played along.

Just as Kane became impatient, Jade looked into the camera. Her lips curled up in a terrible smile and she winked into the camera. Kane leaned forward, his shoulders hunched toward the monitor.

Jade turned back to Teddy, dropped the bear, and grabbed the stuffed tiger from the child's hand. "This looks like a fun toy. I'd like to play with this one." She danced the tiger on the far edge of the table, out of Teddy's reach.

Kane watched the child. Surprise, then anger, contorted his cherubic features. "Mine," he yelled.

Jade ignored him and kept the tiger out of reach.

"Mine!" Teddy screamed. "Mine! *Mine!*" As he screamed, he reached out his hand and the tiger shot into it.

Kane blinked and squinted at the monitor. Jade looked into the camera again and raised her eyebrows. Kane stared at Teddy. He looked like any other child who had just thrown a fit, breathing heavily, watching Jade suspiciously, clutching the tiger to his chest.

Jade wrote something on her clipboard and left the lab.

Kane leaned back on his heels and blew out a breath. He

continued to watch the monitor, but the child played quietly alone. Nothing else happened. Kane hit a button on the console, and the recording—everything was recorded—played again. He played it at regular speed and in slow motion, studying the boy and the tiger. The tiger flew to the boy's hand like a paper clip to a magnet.

Kane folded his arms, his right hand stroking his chin, and paced the large room. Excited energy pumped through his body. His plans were finally coming to fruition. The Nine would have to accept him now. Accept him? He'd be *leading* them before long. Teddy was the first child to have survived the genetic engineering intact and come out with a controllable power. But he was only the beginning.

Kane would create dozens of powerful children. His father's bitter accusations would be proved false. Just because his two daughters had no powers didn't mean Kane couldn't father an impressive force of sons. Jade used Kane's blood in her experiments—he'd call them The Sons of Kane. They would help him gain control over The Nine. After that, he could control anything, anywhere.

He stood at his office window, his breathing sounding like he'd run up a flight of stairs. He chuckled to himself. When was the last time he'd been this excited? Outside, the wind moved through the leafless branches of maples and oaks and pine trees. A pristine white blanket covered the lawn and garden below. By the time the grounds were green and in bloom, his Sons would be ready.

Kane loved this view. Just outside Double Bay, the Curtis family enjoyed a genteel country estate, beautiful in every season. He could see the roof of his house from this window. The other two buildings in the research segment of the family business stood at nine o'clock and twelve o'clock with a cobblestone circular drive in the middle. A forest of trees stood sentry around the property.

It occurred to him suddenly that no one had bothered to put up Christmas lights. His mother loved Christmas more than any other time of year, and made sure that their home as well as the businesses were lavishly decorated. But she died last spring—had it been so long already?—and Kane hadn't bothered with Christmas this year. Perhaps next year he'd order the decorations again, for the children.

Kane smiled as he felt the energy spill out around him. The late afternoon shadows in his office shifted and blended. Outside, a worker shoveling snow paused and looked up toward Kane's third floor office window. Just for fun, Kane let his excitement build until his body merged with the shadows. In this amorphous form, he moved along the wall in front of the window. Below, the man's eyes grew round. He crossed himself and hurried away.

The darkness shook when Kane laughed. He'd enjoyed scaring people ever since he was a boy. The tales told around the estate, tales of ghosts and the devil, heightened his delight in his power.

But enough fun for now. He went through the mental exercise that quickly coalesced his form and he sat down at his desk. Now it was time to implement the next part of his plan.

Time to meet his grandson.

How could this happen?

Tori sat in her car staring sightlessly out the windshield into the dark. The engine rattled as it warmed up and Tori tucked her mittened hands under her arms.

The afternoon had been difficult bordering on impossible. She'd wanted to go home and think about the sudden craziness in her life. But her new boss Evan insisted she work overtime, even though he didn't seem impressed with her work so far.

Hardly surprising since she couldn't remember half of what she'd done since her meeting with the police. But she remembered every word of *that* conversation.

She sighed. She couldn't go home now either, because she'd promised to meet Lexie and Hayley for dinner. How much thinking could she do without them noticing the worried look on her face? And how could she explain the conversation she had with the SLU to Joe? She hadn't known him long enough yet to guess how he would take the news. Would his manly-man feelings be hurt? Would he think less of himself because his wife was a superhero and he wasn't? Worse, would he think less of *her*?

If only she could understand exactly why Dixie hated superheroes, why she'd always insisted they weren't real, Tori would have a better way to gauge her own feelings. If her mother had a good reason, Tori wanted to learn from her mother's mistakes, not the hard way. But if her mother's reason was personal... Maybe that meant superheroes weren't the awful people Dixie believed them to be. Trying to sort it all out alone, Tori didn't know what to think. Even right this second, was she excited? Scared? Disbelieving?

Yes, yes, and yes! All those and more!

She smiled a little and shook her head. Okay, let's just say for one tiny minute that God said to himself, "Let's make, oh, a hairless cat, a duck-billed platypus, and give Tori Lewis a super power. That'll be fun." Okay, so... Her smile gained width even as she tried to reign in a growing sense of excitement. That meant she had a *purpose* in life. Something she'd always wanted but had never really found.

But did that mean she *had* to be a superhero? How would she know what to do? What would she wear? Did she keep her day job? She didn't even know *how* she did whatever it was she did. Somehow, people listened to her, did what she asked. Could that be some kind of "super power"?

Images of Tobey Maguire flashed through Tori's mind. *He*

didn't know what he was doing, but *he* figured it out. And Hugh Jackman, too. He didn't even know who the X-Men were and then he met them and everything worked out great. Well, not great, but better than being alone.

Tori put the car in gear and pulled out of the parking lot. She'd watch the movies again later tonight and see what she could glean from them. There, she had a plan.

Turning right onto Michigan Avenue, Tori's glance fell onto a brightly papered window beckoning from a strip mall. Of course! A comic book store! Perhaps the answers to some of her questions could be found there. She swung into the parking lot, tires sliding a bit in the slush, and pulled into a tight spot near the store. Her heart beat erratically as she got out of her car.

A bell tinkled overhead as she walked in. A young man with a scraggly goatee and a wrinkled black T-shirt nodded absently at her. "'S'up," he said, turning from the books he was shelving. Tori nodded to him and read his shirt, *Jesus Saves*. Cool. He turned to help someone and Tori noticed there was more on the back: *And Only Takes Half Damage*.

Uh, okay, don't know what that means.

She tried not to look conspicuous as she wandered. Another world. That's where she'd landed. Not just the comic book store, though that was certainly the outward manifestation of the changes she couldn't see. It was like she went on her honeymoon and when she came back, the plane flew down the rabbit hole. Only things looked pretty much the same. Was that scary or comforting?

Tori walked around, looking at comics and books. Comic book stores had books? And toys. And T-shirts. Who knew? Well, maybe something here would help her find her footing, give her some kind of foundation from which to begin to understand what was happening.

Where to start? She felt a bit like a foreigner without a guidebook. Walking down the aisles, she stopped and stared at the shelves on both sides. What exactly was she looking at? Turning her head sideways, she perused the titles. Ah, Manga. She didn't know what it was, but she knew it was Japanese and popular. Maybe she should buy one. They were thicker than the other comic books, so maybe she'd learn more.

Tori continued to read the titles, sort of, while she surreptitiously checked out the other customers. A couple of teenage boys, a large man with a full beard and a fuller waistline, a couple about her age—the woman looked bored to tears. The front bell chimed as the door opened to a tall man in a suit, tie loosened around his neck. He wandered to the wall behind Tori where she noticed dozens of comic books were arranged. He looked fairly normal. Maybe she should follow him and see what he looked at.

About to turn away, Tori spied the title *Read or Die*. Curious, she picked it up and opened it, getting it right on the second try. She forgot the Japanese read from back to front. For a few minutes, Tori got lost in the story. The big bearded man bumped into her as he passed down her aisle and Tori looked up. She felt her cheeks flush with embarrassment. Wasn't she too old to be enjoying comic books?

She took the book with her and tried to amble as if she didn't care where she was going. Near the businessman, she read the titles on the wall—*Fantastic Four, Wolverine, Supergirl, Captain America, Batman, Wonder Woman*.

Some, like *Hellblazer*, looked too gruesome when she flipped through the comic. Some—*Sin City*, for instance—were too violent or sexual. Tori shoved *Preacher* back on the shelf with some embarrassment. Definitely not what she thought it'd be.

She spied an *Amazing Spider-Man* with relief. She'd seen the movies. She liked Spider-Man. In fact, the more she thought about it, *Spider-Man* was probably the perfect comic for her. A young person suddenly gets powers he didn't ask for and does his best to save the world while staying true to good old-fashioned values.

Tori bit her lip as she thumbed through the comic book. She wondered if Peter Parker was still trying to hang onto Aunt May's values. Or did being a superhero mean you had to kill people, even if they were the bad guys? She glanced at the businessman out of the corner of her eye. If she asked him what comics he liked, would he take it as a come-on? When he reached for another book, she saw his ring finger was empty. No point in taking a chance. Before Joe, she'd never been good with men. No reason to think it'd be easier now that she was married.

She looked around for Geek-boy. He was putting books away near the front of the store now. She rehearsed how to ask her question in an intelligent manner as she walked toward him.

"Hi," she said when she approached. Nice. Good opening. Intelligent.

This was so embarrassing.

"Hey," he said. The word came out very long. The boy's shoulders were slumped, his eyes heavy as if he could barely keep them open. Tori wondered if he was high.

She cleared her throat, her eyes falling on a T-shirt nearby. *Your village called. Their idiot is missing.* She grinned—yeah, that's what I was thinking, too—then tried to school her features into a pleasant mask.

"I was wondering if, uh,"—gosh, this was going to sound stupid—"you could recommend any comic books to me. I've, uh, I've never read any."

Geek-boy's expression didn't change. "Whaddaya looking for?"

Duh. That's what I'm asking *you.* "I-I'm not sure. Something —" Tori fumbled wildly in her mind, searching for anything she knew about comic book movies. "Maybe something on the beginnings? How they become superheroes?"

Same expression, same tone of voice. "Origin stories. Sure. You want something in particular? DC? Marvel? Darkhorse? You don't look like the Vertigo type."

His eyes flicked over Tori's Banana Republic wool coat and pantsuit, clearance bargains from last spring. She remembered the book she'd shoved back on the shelf was a Vertigo title. So she interpreted the look as "You're a classy chick and probably wouldn't like that dark stuff."

"Well," he prompted as Tori continued to stare at him blankly.

Grabbing at straws, Tori stuttered, "I-I don't know. What w-would you recommend? I could really use your advice."

As if a light beamed down from heaven, Geek-boy's face brightened. His eyes cleared, his posture straightened. "Well..."

For the next thirty minutes, Chad—Geek-boy's real name—showered Tori with information on the comic industry. He tutored her in comic books, graphic novels, Manga, collectibles, and more. He asked her questions and piled books into her arms —*Ultimate Spider-Man, Danger Girl, Powers, Kingdom Come.* Looking at the prices, Tori finally called a halt to his enthusiasm.

"This is great, thanks, Chad," she said, "but I better stop until I know if I even like them." And before I run out of grocery money.

Joe had warned her that money was tight. She didn't want him to think he'd married a spendthrift. Come to think of it, that was yet another topic they hadn't discussed. No joint checking account yet. So really, she didn't even have to tell him she spent *over a hundred dollars* on comic books. Yeah, that's a conversation she didn't want to have.

"Read *Kingdom Come* first," Chad said with a knowing nod. "You'll be totally hooked." He plucked a business card from a pile and wrote his name on the front. He looked up at her and smiled, then he wrote his home and cell numbers on the back and handed it to her.

Assuring Chad that she would come back soon, thanking him for offering to answer any question, any time, Tori finally left with her bag full of comics. Uh, that is, *graphic novels.* She hoped her education into the ways of superheroes would prove to be helpful in real life. Maybe she'd even figure out how to tell Joe. Peter Parker *did* tell Mary Jane, didn't he?

Tori opened Bill's back door and started to put the bag on the back seat. On second thought, she closed the door and opened the trunk. Not that she was hiding them. She just wanted to explain when she was ready, not in a surprise ambush.

As soon as the car started, she turned the heat on high. Waiting for it to warm up, she remembered the look on Joe's face when she told him she'd named her Honda Accord "Bill." That car payment was the biggest bill she'd ever had—still was—so it made perfect sense to her. And it was funny. She couldn't believe he'd never named any of his vehicles. Wasn't that what guys did?

Tori smiled to herself. She'd have to think of a name for Joe's black Dodge pickup, see if she could make Joe laugh. She loved his laugh.

Her smile faded as she wondered what his reaction would be when she figured out how to tell him about the super power and the visit from the SLU. How exactly did one go about revealing such a thing? And how would she explain why it only came up now? She didn't know the answer to that herself.

The heater finally blasted warm air through the car. Tori glanced at the dash clock. Time to go to Lexie's for dinner. If she were really, *really* lucky, maybe Lexie and Hayley wouldn't completely freak out at her news. Maybe they'd even help her figure out how to tell Joe.

Tori tried to swallow the growing lump in her throat. She gripped the wheel tighter as she drove. *God, you did this to me, so you better help me.*

"Please," she whispered.

"If you don't tell her soon, she's going to figure it out." Mickey Valient, one of Joe's two best friends, relaxed on an oversized black sofa in the basement of his office building.

Joe slouched across from him, inhaling the luxurious scent of leather. His other best friend, Bull Kincaid, stretched out to his left, the four matching sofas making a big square around an area rug with a low marble-topped table in the middle. A table currently covered with chips, dips, cookies, pop cans, and a huge plate of piping hot burritos.

At the other end of the long room, a small kitchen sported every appliance a man could want—fridge, microwave, coffee machine, toaster oven, dishwasher. A couple arcade games and a pinball machine lined another wall. Mickey didn't bring work home, he brought home to work. Best secret office ever. Joe wondered what Tori would think if he bought a pinball machine for the living room at home.

"He's got a point," Bull said. "She's a smart girl."

Joe sighed and slipped deeper into the cushions.

He'd known Mickey since college and Bull since grade school. Joe trusted them with his secrets and his life, and they trusted him. He wanted to feel the same way about his wife. He did. He just had to figure out how to tell her. Preferably in a way that didn't send her screaming.

"I'm going to tell her," Joe said, pulling the tab on a Coke. He sounded a little defensive even to his own ears. "I'm just waiting for the right time. I told her we play poker every Thursday night, that we always have and we always will. She's fine with it."

"He's got a point," Bull said to Mickey. "We've been doing this for years. Getting married's not going to change that."

"Today's Tuesday," Mickey said, reaching for the plate of homemade cookies Tori had sent over.

Bull nodded. "He's got a point," he said to Joe.

Joe ignored him. Bull could see seventeen sides to a six-sided die. "I'll tell her I'm working overtime. That's pretty much true anyway. She made the cookies when I told her you didn't have any family around here," he said to Mickey, "and that you needed us because you'd spent the holidays alone." He laughed at Mickey's scowl.

Joe leaned forward to grab a handful of corn chips. The leather squeaked under him. He loved these couches, so much better than what he had at home. He might have to buy one. But he'd kind of implied to Tori that they couldn't afford much. He'd have to think about how to handle that. "Broke bachelor" had been his cover story for the last five years or so, even though his tax man knew differently.

"Besides," he said, getting back to the conversation at hand, "Tori trusts me. She loves me." Joe tried not to grin, thinking about how much she'd *loved* him on their honeymoon. "I'm just waiting for the right moment."

"Been and gone," Mickey grumbled around the food in his mouth.

"I don't know," Bull said. "Remember the way she looked at him when they got married? You pointed it out." Bull turned to Joe. "I didn't even notice till then, but Mick noticed it right away. She adores you. It's all over her face. You're probably fine not telling her."

Joe looked at his team leader in surprise. He didn't think Mickey was the type to notice the softer side of life. Mickey scowled back.

"You're asking for trouble," Mickey warned, eating another cookie. "When she finds out on her own, you're going to wish you'd told her yourself. Control the situation, control the response." Mickey owned a security and protection firm, a real company with employees and clients, and a solid cover for their superhero team. He was all about crisis management.

Joe frowned. "I *tried* to tell her. She didn't want to know."

"You tried to tell her because your dad threatened to not marry you guys if you didn't." Bull scratched his head. "I don't know much about brides and stuff, but I don't think there's much on their minds besides lace and flowers on their wedding day. Of course she didn't care about anything else—what was it? *Ten minutes* before the wedding?"

Mickey smirked, brushing away cookie crumbs. "He's got a point."

Joe closed his eyes and pillowed his head into the leather. "I'll take care of it. We just got home, for crying out loud."

He wasn't worried. Not much. He was only keeping one secret from her (well, two if you counted the money), and only because her family had made their stand quite clear. There was no such thing as superheroes and anyone who believed otherwise was a moron. But now he and Tori were their own family. They'd make their own stand. As soon as they discussed it.

"Where is she now?" Mickey asked.

Joe reached for a burrito. "With Hayley and Lexie, I think."

"Why doesn't Hayley like to hang out with us anyway?" Bull grabbed two burritos and a paper plate. "I mean, we're talking about what we're going to do. Doesn't she want to have a say?"

"For someone who's sleeping with her, you don't know her very well, do you?" said Mickey, finally taking a break from the homemade cookies and taking a burrito.

"I'd know her better if she talked to me," Bull grumbled. "I don't think she sees me as boyfriend material. I think I'm her fall-back guy."

There was nothing to say to that. It was true. But still Joe tried to think of something encouraging. "I don't think she talks much to anybody except Tori." Joe thought of Hayley's secret life as Green Thumb. "And obviously, *she's* never told Tori everything either. They've been friends since they were kids, right?"

Bull nodded, his mouth full. None of them knew much about Hayley except that she'd had an exceptionally bad home life and she'd been on her own since she was seventeen. When she found out Joe had met and was dating Tori, Hayley had laid into him.

Joe hadn't been able to figure out if she was protective of Tori, or just trying to protect her own private life.

Turns out it had been both. She'd threatened to tie off Joe's private parts with the many vines growing out of her pockets if he did anything to hurt Tori. Including telling Tori anything about Green Thumb. The threat had endeared her to Joe. None of the team knew Hayley even had a best friend. To find out it was Tori, a woman with a heart as big as Lake Michigan, made Joe see Hayley in a new light.

Yet another reason not to worry. If Hayley could stay friends with Tori for all these years and keep her secret, so could Joe. Not that he would, of course. He'd tell her. But it didn't have to be today, or even this week. Even though Hayley played it close to the vest, she didn't approve of Joe keeping secrets from Tori. She'd been hounding him since she found out they were dating. But she understood. Women were like that.

A moment later, it hit him. What was he *thinking*? Of all the women he knew—his mom, his sisters, his sisters-in-law, friends, and old girlfriends—women certainly were more understanding than men, but when they didn't approve of something…

He sat up abruptly, dinner momentarily forgotten. Mickey raised his eyebrows.

"You think Hayley's gonna tell her?" Joe rubbed one hand over his forehead, thinking. There wasn't any reason for Tori to suspect anything. He'd been *so* careful. Never left anything at home anymore, or in his truck.

"She is, isn't she?" She wouldn't! She was part of the team, sworn to secrecy. He glanced at his watch. If he called Hayley now, he could pretend he had to talk to her about a surprise for the party. No reason Tori would suspect anything. *If* she even realized who Hayley was talking to. Safer to wait and talk to Hayley tomorrow though. After all, Tori thought he and Hayley had only just met each other when she introduced them two months ago.

He groaned into his hand. Then he had a thought. "You call Hayley," he told Mickey. "Tell her it's important for the safety of the team that she not mention anything to Tori."

Mickey looked like he was going to argue, but Joe knew Mickey counted nothing above the safety of the team. Mickey pressed a button, spoke quietly, his eyes on Joe, and hung up.

"For the safety of the team," he said, still pinning Joe with his gaze, "fix this."

"I will," Joe said into his plate. He bit into his burrito. His dad, Owen Clarke, may be the head of the Guild, but Mickey was the head of this team. He had the right to be pushy. "Give me a week, will you? Just let her enjoy the wedding reception before we have our first fight, okay?"

Mickey looked at the homemade cookies and softened. "A week. No more."

Joe made a mental note to have Tori bake Mickey more cookies. "Okay, we're making too much of this. Let's move on." He leaned back on the sofa again and pulled out his smart phone, checking his notes.

Mickey pulled out his iPad, and Bull opened the leather bound diary he used for meetings.

"Spook was released from the hospital today," Mickey announced. "He'll be recuperating for a while, but he's okay."

Joe frowned. "Thank God. Poor guy." They all willingly put themselves at risk to protect the citizens of Double Bay, but it was unnerving that two superheroes got shot on the same night.

"That's the same holdup Tori was in, right? How's she doing?" Mickey asked.

Joe shook his head. "She was pretty shaken up Monday night after it happened. Heck, *I* was pretty shaken up. I thought I saw blood on her clothes or something, but I guess it was just my imagination working overtime." Joe didn't want to share, even with his closest friends, that he'd had a vision of Tori with a gunman. It scared him. He didn't want to think about it. "She's a real trooper, though. She went to work this morning and seemed to just forget about the whole thing."

Joe watched Bull toss a couch pillow in the air as they talked, a burrito in his other hand. The man found it difficult to sit still. Even when they were on a job, he was constantly moving.

"Hayley's been hyper ever since she heard about it," Bull said. "She says we should look into it. I called Art and he said the dude was on drugs. Hayley won't let it go, though." Bull looked at Mickey expectantly. "Have you heard anything?"

"Nothing more than you have," Mickey said. "I'll stay in touch with Art and Casey, but they seem to think it's a closed case. Art did say they've got a Pop-Up on the radar. I assume it's related to the robbery, but he wouldn't say anymore."

"A real Pop-Up?" Joe asked. "They know he's not a Pretender?"

"That's what he says."

Interesting. A new superhero in Double Bay—what they referred to as a Pop-Up—was fairly unusual. Now, someone who *says* they're a superhero and makes sure the media hears about it, they're as common as snowmen in winter. And as likely to last.

"It's kind of weird, isn't it," Bull said, "that Tori gets involved in a superhero mess as soon as you guys get married?" He turned to Joe, chewing the last of his burrito.

Joe hadn't thought of it that way before. Should he be more worried? Even without the visions and voices, his wife's safety was his prime concern. Maybe he should talk to his dad about these things, find out if and how they related to his super powers.

Another thought struck him—what if it was a spiritual thing? Some kind of warning? Not everyone with powers believed in their origin story, but Joe sure did. Experience had taught him God was right in the middle of it all.

Mickey shook his head, interrupting Joe's train of thought. "It's an unusual situation, but I don't see how there's anything more to it than bizarre coincidence."

"That what you want me to tell Hayley?" Bull asked.

Mickey nodded. "If something else comes up, we'll check it out, but right now let's follow SLU's lead and move on."

Joe shrugged off his unease. If Mickey and the SLU didn't believe there was anything to worry about, Joe wouldn't let himself get riled up. But he would treat these weird "feelings" about Tori with a little more respect until he could figure them out.

Bull's expression darkened. "Fine. You're the security man. I'm just the sweaty wrestling coach." He tossed the pillow higher. "All brawn, no brains."

"Aw, don't start with that!" Mickey rolled his eyes.

Joe blinked and tried to get back in the conversation. "Hey, relax, guys. Both of you."

He didn't know what they were arguing about, but Bull had always been sensitive to people thinking he was stupid just because he was big. That notion came courtesy of Bull's dad, the moron. While Mickey never ascribed to that mindset, he wasn't the kind of guy to tiptoe around someone else's feelings either.

The two men backed off as quickly as they'd gotten into it. The three of them talked about the recent muggings in Memorial Park. Stretch, from another team, stopped one of them. Sonic had stopped another. No one had been hurt, thank God, all snatch-and-grabs. They agreed to watch the park more.

No new missing children reported. Unfortunately, nothing new in terms of leads for those already missing either. The police hoped the extra vigilance on the part of Double Bay's super-heroes would continue to scare off the kidnappers.

The hospital reported some unexplained deaths to the police. Younger men dying from heart attacks, autopsies showing healthy hearts. One looked like he might've been poisoned, but no poisons were found in his system. They'd keep their ears open for any word on the street.

Mickey had heard about some gardening on the east side, and Bull agreed to take Hayley over to kill all the plants. One of his boys got kicked off the wrestling team last semester for smoking pot, and it ticked Bull off. He'd been determined ever since to reduce the availability of any illegal substance to minors. Joe was afraid Bull would offer to be the superhero poster boy for the anti-drugs war. But he couldn't. The team was still trying to get more undercover work from the SLU. Poster boy status would definitely hinder that.

Mickey finished making some notes. "Okay, that's all I've got. What about you guys?" He looked up expectantly.

"Nothing."

"Nope."

"What do you mean nothing? How can you have nothing? What's wrong with you two?" Mickey's glower appeared to be decreasing tonight in direct proportion to his consumption of baked goods. Right now it was at Level Orange.

"Eat a cookie, Mick," Joe said. "We've all been on Christmas vacation, right?"

Joe figured Bull couldn't sit still physically, but he could relax. Mickey couldn't relax if his life depended on it.

"Wrestling season just began, too," Bull reminded them, "so I'm not going to have a lot of time till spring break."

Joe worked full-time as a superhero, undercover with Mickey's firm as well as with the team. Bull, on the other hand, had always wanted to be a teacher. He loved expounding on history almost as much as he loved working with his boys as the high school wrestling coach. That's where his heart was. He moonlighted at saving the world.

"Yeah, yeah, I remember," Mickey said, sighing. "Joe? Nothing?"

Joe shrugged. "What's with you today? You're wound up tighter than a clock."

"Nothing that a new secretary couldn't solve," he grumbled. "I'm losing prospects left and right. Then I talk to you schmucks and we can't even find anything interesting to do after hours."

Joe put away his phone and stood. "Come on, let's hit the bag. It'll make you guys feel better."

The other two stood and followed him through a door to the left.

"Bull, you can hold the bag for one of us, but no more workouts with it!" Mickey and Joe unbuttoned their shirts as they walked into Mickey's personal gym. Bull still had his sweats on from wrestling practice. "I bought a new bag for now," Mickey continued to Bull, "but I need to modify it before you can use it."

Bull dropped his eyes to the side and grinned like a ten-year-old. "Really sorry about that, Mick. Good thing you didn't have one of the water-filled bags, huh?" He spotted a machine on the other side of the room. "Hey, is that working?"

Bull walked over to examine a computerized weight machine Mickey had developed, while Joe and Mickey went into the changing room.

The spacious room was like a bedroom without a bed. Cedar dressers and cedar-lined closets held clothes and super suits, designed by Mickey, for all three of them. Big chairs accommodated the big men comfortably. Another door led to a large and well-furnished bathroom with two shower stalls and two sinks. Off that room was a laundry room that opened up behind the kitchen.

Joe loved this part of the basement, too. If only he'd had an inkling he'd be getting married so quickly, he would've redone the house much like Mickey's space before Tori ever saw it. Maybe when he told her about his secret identity, he'd tell her about the money, too. Suggest finishing the basement. 'Course, if he did that she'd probably want to put up flowered wallpaper or something. Hmm, he'd have to think about it. So many adjustments to make as a married man.

Changed into workout clothes, Joe and Mickey joined Bull in the gym. Mickey adjusted the machine Bull was fiddling with. "You okay working it by yourself?"

"*No problemo,*" Bull said with a grin. "I love this thing. When you gonna start selling them? Make a fortune."

He lay down on the bench under what appeared to be a free weight bar. The computerized controls were just above eye level and easy to reach.

"I can't sell the stupid things," Mickey grumbled. "They're too expensive. Who's going to pay twenty-five thousand dollars for a weight machine?" He walked over to a rack of boxing gloves and started pulling a pair on.

"Yeah, right. Well, I can't tell you how much I appreciate you sizing it up for me," Bull said as he pushed buttons. "Best workout I've ever had."

"Start off slow, two hundred pounds," Mickey warned. "Make sure there's no kinks in the system before you go over five hundred."

"Gotcha, boss." He entered his personal code and heard a husky female voice say, "Hello, Bull." He turned to the others and grinned. "I love that part."

"Don't tell Hayley," Joe said with a laugh. He watched Bull adjust himself so his shoulders were under the bar.

Mickey held out his hands for Joe to tie on his boxing gloves. "Don't worry, he'll be fine. I've got so many safeties built into that machine, I don't think there's any possible way to hurt yourself."

They looked over to see Bull bench pressing two hundred pounds. Not free weights, though. The bar was connected to a hydraulics system connected to the computer. The system emulated free weights exactly, evidenced by Bull's right arm extending higher than his left.

"Right's too high," Joe called out.

"Yup, thanks. It's harder to keep it even with so little weight."

Mickey laughed and punched his gloves together. "Show off."

"Whiner," Joe called out before he walked over to the punching bag and held it steady.

"Losers," came Bull's voice, without even a hint of exertion.

Mickey hit the bag with a couple of test punches, then settled down into a serious workout. It seemed to Joe like he was particularly aggressive tonight. When Joe's turn came to work the bag, he started off slow. He wasn't as tense as Mickey.

Punch!

Life was good. Punch, punch!

He really had no complaints. Punch, punch! Punch!

"Hold up," Mickey stopped him. Joe was surprised to see his friend panting. "You wearing any metal?"

Joe looked down and shook his head. Then he and Mickey said at the same time, "Wedding ring."

"Bull, can you come hold the bag for Joe?"

"Forget your ring?" Bull chuckled. "Thought that's why you got the soft gold, so it wouldn't make you too strong."

"Thought that'd be enough." Joe shrugged. "Guess I'll have to be more careful than I thought."

Bull braced the bag against his body. "Go for it, man."

Joe let Mickey coach him through a grueling workout. Tori wouldn't find out. Not until he told her. Which he'd have to do right after the party since he'd promised Mick.

Punch! Punch!

She might take it hard at first, but she believed in him. She loved him. She'd come around.

Punch!

As Joe hit the bag, images from last night weaved with other pictures behind his eyes. The drug dealer with the gun. Tori's face. Another kid with a gun. Blood. He shook his head, trying to clear it. He couldn't allow marriage to reduce his effectiveness at work. No reason to fear for Tori's safety.

Protect her.

Except for that voice he'd been hearing since the day they'd met. He slammed his fists into the punching bag. Every day they were together, Tori would do something or say something or just smile at him and it twisted him up inside. He didn't know if it was a good feeling or a bad one. But every day was a little brighter, a little warmer, and he couldn't say he didn't like it. He had the power to absorb the strength of metal, but he'd never felt stronger than the last two weeks. The way she looked at him, like he could do anything...

He shook his head and hit the bag hard. No, nothing to be afraid of. Of course he could protect her, but nothing was going to happen.

He stood panting, hands on his knees when he was done. Mickey examined his new bag, obviously concerned he'd have to buy yet another one. Or maybe start making custom bags. Like he didn't have enough cool gadgets on his to do list.

Joe stood up and let Bull unlace his gloves. No worries. He'd protect Tori the way any man protects the woman he loves. But she wasn't in danger. What could happen?

5

Tori knocked and opened the front door to Lexie's apartment. It felt weird—she'd lived here with her sister and nephew until two months ago, but now it was no longer her home. Neither was the cute little apartment she'd rented down the street. She'd given notice less than two months after she signed her lease. Now she just had to learn to make Joe's house feel like home and life would be perfect.

Well, perfect except for her new secret.

"Hey, Lex!" she called out as she walked in. She was about to close the door when she saw Hayley heading up the sidewalk. Hayley jogged a little while Tori held the door open.

"Hey, sweetie!" Tori hugged her best friend. "How are you?"

A high-pitched screech and tiny pounding feet came from behind her. "Ree! Ree!" screamed Ben as he raced around the corner in his yellow footie pajamas. The little boy stood with his mouth wide open like he couldn't believe his luck—both Tori *and* Hayley had come to visit.

Tori laughed. "Hey, buddy!"

Ben screamed his laughter and stomped his feet. Then he looked at Hayley and said something that sounded like "hurry"—

his version of her name. Hayley held up her hand and he raced up and high-fived her. Then he waited for Tori to finish taking off her coat and boots and high-five him, too, jabbering away the whole time.

Tori scooped him up and cuddled him close. She missed him. His tiny arms wrapped around her neck and she felt calmer than she had in hours. Some things in life hadn't changed.

She looked up to find her sister staring at her with a mix of panic and fear in her expression. Tori sighed into Ben's hair, smoothing her hand up and down his back, never breaking eye contact with her sister.

Lexie knew something was wrong. She always knew. But Tori didn't want to talk about it until Ben was safely in bed. She'd learned that toddlers pick up on an awful lot more than you give them credit for, and she didn't want him hearing their conversation.

Hayley broke the silence. "What's wrong?"

Tori didn't know if she wanted to talk about it in front of Hayley either. Her one good friend. She didn't want to lose her. But Hayley had been through a lot in her own life, and had seen all the trouble and chaos in Tori and Lexie's lives. Tori didn't know if Hayley would handle it well at first, but in the end Hayley would always be there for her. Tori would bet her life on it.

Tori said to Ben, "Give your Aunt Hayley a big hug, Benji!" The boy jumped into Hayley's arms with a giggle, and Tori picked up the grocery bags she'd brought in. "Let me just say that tonight's conversation will require at least two bottles of wine and a whole lotta chocolate."

Lexie watched Tori, her forehead wrinkled with worry, then finally spoke to Hayley. "Hi, Hayley. Happy New Year."

The three women talked, and cooked, and talked, and played with Ben, and talked. By unspoken agreement, the conversation stayed light and fun while three-year-old ears were listening. Tori was wrong. This was still home, even if she didn't live here anymore. Joe's house didn't feel like home yet, but she hoped it would grow into what she felt in this little apartment.

Lexie soon put Ben to bed, and they sat down to eat. Tori's honeymoon was the topic of choice. She tried to keep the details to herself, but the less she said, the more Hayley teased her.

"What happened?" Hayley asked. "Come on, give us something! You guys have only known each other for two months. Are you happy? Have you fought yet? Do you find the way he brushes his teeth bizarre? Does he fold his underwear? What? Tell us!" Hayley laughed.

Tori tried to hide her smile by looking at her plate, pushing around the carrots. Everyone thought she was nuts, but meeting Joe two days after Halloween when she was outside taking down the decorations, seeing him every day after that and falling in love, marrying him on Christmas Eve... She felt her heart swell up inside. It was the most perfect, romantic thing she'd ever done, and she'd never regret it. But she wasn't sure how to talk about it.

"So there's nothing to tell because you never saw Disney World? You're just tired from," Hayley waggled her eyebrows, "you know."

Tori raised her head at that and giggled. "You didn't tell me how often guys want to do it!"

"It's easier to name the times they *don't* want to do it," Hayley said, patting Tori's arm.

Lexie raised her hand. "Much as I'd love to hear all about how my baby sister finally lost her virginity," she said, her voice verging on sarcastic.

Tori sobered. She felt Lexie's fear pulsing in the air. Tori knew that the sarcasm came from Lexie feeling Tori's worries and not knowing what the problem was. She put her hand over Lexie's. "Everything's going to be okay, Lex. Trust me." She hoped she wasn't lying.

A moment later, Hayley exclaimed, "Are you pregnant? Oh my gosh, you are, aren't you?"

Tori laughed and Lexie rolled her eyes. "Hayley, is that the only thing you ever think about?" Lex asked. "Look at her. Something's wrong."

Lexie met her eyes, looking for an explanation. Tori broke eye contact and said to Hayley, "I'm not pregnant. I'm on the pill."

Lexie frowned. "Why are you on the pill? It's not reliable with your other meds."

Tori played with the carrots again.

"Oh, right." Lexie leaned her forehead on her hand. "You stopped taking them." She shook her head and stared at Tori.

"Nothing will happen." Tori stabbed her veggies with her fork. "I told you before, I've never felt better in my life! I'm happy, Lex. I don't need that stuff anymore. And like you said, it doesn't work with the pill, so..."

"What are you guys talking about?" Hayley asked. "You're on medication?"

Tori shook her head. "No. Not anymore." She sighed. She was doing a heck of a lot of that lately.

"But something's bothering you tonight," Lexie pressed. "Tell us and we'll help you fix whatever it is."

Hayley looked confused. "Yeah, what's the problem? Come on, Tori, like a Band-Aid. Be quick and it'll be over." She smiled her encouragement.

Tori took a deep breath. Hayley was right. The quicker, the better. "The police think I have a super power and want to know if I want to work for them as a superhero."

Hayley choked on her wine.

Tori thumped her back while Lexie gaped.

"Sorry," Tori murmured. "You said be quick." She gave Hayley an apologetic shrug and tried to analyze her expression. Surprised, but not repulsed. Not yet anyway.

Looking at Lexie, Tori thought her sister seemed more

cautiously curious. Which made sense because she and Lex, well, they had a history of strange things happening in their lives. To find out that the underlying cause might have an explanation, however bizarre it might be, was sort of a relief.

Hayley, on the other hand, had really turned her life around since she'd left her mess of a home as a teenager. Despite years of emotional abuse, neglect, and a lack of almost every material item a child should expect, she'd built her own nursery business.

Tori had never asked, but she assumed Hayley must make a pretty good living at it because she lived in a bigger apartment in a nicer neighborhood than Tori and Lexie could afford. An apartment filled with more kinds of plants than Tori knew existed.

Hayley was definitely the most normal of the three. Very private to the point of having few friends, but normal. Maybe Tori's worries that Hayley wouldn't want to be friends with a freak—no, a *person* with unusual abilities, maybe that worry would prove unfounded.

"Honestly," Hayley said after she'd caught her breath, "this is a good thing. We should all support each other, like Lex said. It'll be better for everyone. In fact—" Her cell phone rang. She looked irritated when she looked at the caller ID. "One second, I'm sorry, Tor. I gotta take this." She moved away from the table.

Lexie drank deeply from her glass of wine. Then she looked a bit sheepish. "Do not rely on alcohol to get you through this, Sis." Then she grinned. "Maybe just tonight, though."

Tori and Lex both looked over at Hayley who was having a heated conversation in whispers. She stabbed her phone with her finger and came back to the table.

"Everything okay?" Tori asked.

"Nothing that won't be cleared up in a week or so," Hayley replied. Her voice sounded tight and she looked upset.

"Do you want to talk about it?"

"Yes!" Hayley grabbed her wine glass and gulped some of it

down. "But later. You first. So..." She shook her head. "How in the world did all this happen?"

Tori did her best to explain about yesterday's robbery, last night's argument with Joe about blood on her shoes, and today's interview with the police. "It looks like what Dad called 'leadership traits' and Mom called 'bossiness' is more like..." Tori paused, not sure how to describe her ability. "I guess I can tell people what to do. And they do it."

"Huh," Hayley said when Tori was done.

She didn't continue, but it was clear from the look on her face that she had more to say. Tori prompted her. "Huh, what?"

"Well," Hayley hesitated as if she were choosing her words carefully. "I thought these sorts of things began to show themselves in childhood or adolescence. Why now?"

Tori looked at Lexie. Lex smiled grimly back at her, encouraging her without words to tell as much of the story as she wanted. Or as little.

"I haven't, uh, told you some stuff. From, like, our past." They didn't talk about this, not out loud. Their mom would have a heart attack if she were here. This "airing the family laundry" was exactly the sort of situation Dixie had been trying to avoid for as long as the girls could remember. Secrets and hush-hush and keep your head down and don't stand out in a crowd. That's how their parents had raised them.

"Mom used to make me see a psychiatrist every week," Tori said. "He had me on a prescription—several different prescriptions over the years—but I don't need them anymore." She sent a pointed look toward her sister. Lexie shrugged and nodded.

Tori turned to Hayley. "I was too embarrassed to tell you any of this before. I didn't want you to think I was... Dr. Huntington said I have an anger management problem and/or a self-serving personality disorder and/or impulse control issues. His diagnosis seemed to change every time I'd learn enough to argue with him about it."

Hayley frowned. "What kind of witch doctor were you going to?"

Tori wanted to hug her. Always loyal, that was Hayley, always on her side. "Dr. Huntington most recently said that I'm an egomaniac, that my problem is that I always want my own way and that I force people to do what I want." Tori stabbed the carrots so hard the sharp ping of metal on stoneware echoed. She took a calming breath. "I haven't taken those drugs since Thanksgiving. I haven't seen Dr. Huntington since the week after. And I'm never going back to either of them because *there's nothing wrong with me!*"

Tori felt Hayley staring. Lex was probably gaping at her, too. She kept her head down. This was the sort of outburst she had to control. She breathed in deeply three times, exhaling three times, imagining the stress leaving her body, leaving her life.

Lexie leaned over and kissed Tori on the temple. "I've *never* thought there was anything wrong with you." Her voice was quiet but firm.

Tori reached for her sister's hand and squeezed.

Hayley looked from one sister to the other. "You don't have to convince me. I don't think there's anything wrong with either of you." She laughed and said in a teasing tone, "But I've always known you two were a little off. That's why I like you." She toasted them with her wine glass.

Tori laughed in relief. She felt much of Lexie's tension dissipate as well. Wait, what did Hayley just say? They were *both* a little off. Suddenly, the pieces began to form a bigger picture. Lexie had been constantly searching for the perfect boyfriend in junior high and high school. Her rebelliousness had led to a teenage pregnancy. Mom and Dad had said it was Lexie's hormones that made her emotional tantrums worse, but now Tori wondered if her big sister had also been on meds until she got pregnant. And everything had gone downhill from there.

Holy smoke! If Tori had a power, Lexie's "problem" might be a super power, too. But why hadn't she ever said anything?

Hayley nudged Tori to get her attention. "So the drugs have worn off and your powers are showing. Are you going to say yes?"

Tori blinked, confused. "To what?"

"The police. Are you going to be a superhero now? Save us from the bad guys?"

Tori looked from Lexie to Hayley and down at her plate. She had no idea what in the world was happening, but the people she loved most in the world supported her in doing...whatever it was she was going to do. She raised her glass and smiled. "I think I'm going to at least try. That's all I can say right now."

"Here's to Team Tori," Hayley said with a laugh. She clinked her glass against Tori's.

Lexie raised hers in a toast, too. "To Team Tori!"

"Now you guys have to help me figure out how to tell Joe." Tori hoped it would go as smoothly as tonight's confession. Maybe she had nothing to worry about after all.

TORI TOOK a long pull from her hot caramel apple cider with whipped cream. It may not have caffeine but the sugar should give her a jump-start. And she needed the heat on such a cold morning. She was so freakin' tired from working overtime the very first two days at her new job.

She and Joe had fallen into bed Tuesday night after they both got home from time with their friends. Tori figured the bedroom was not the right place to rock Joe's world with a crazy confession. And last night when she'd come home late from work, Joe met her at the door with re-warmed pizza, then massaged her shoulders in front of the fireplace. She needed to tell him, but the timing just hadn't been right.

That's my story and I'm sticking to it.

Meanwhile, she wasn't sure about this new job either. Working at Half TV had seemed exciting when Janice at Totally Temps called her about it. But Tori needed to know if all this overtime was the norm. If so, she may have to call Janice and get a new assignment. It was kind of fun to be involved in making TV shows, but not if you worked like a dog every day.

On the other hand, she seemed to be impressing her new boss. That was something. He'd been shocked to return from his meeting Tuesday and find that she'd found the how-to file, taken a few phone messages, and started work on a spreadsheet. Tori didn't think it was that big a deal. The last temp hadn't deleted any of the email messages, and the spreadsheet and the directions were all there. On the other hand—Tori needed a third hand to think this through—once Evan realized she was halfway competent, he'd started working her half to death.

Tori flashed her ID badge and smiled at the security guard. He nodded without returning her smile, watching IDs as the morning rush continued. Before going upstairs to her desk, she stopped in the Human Resources office to talk to Pam. Tori found it interesting that the lobby and most of the ground floor had fresh paint, lots of potted plants, and lovely furniture. Upstairs, where the worker bees made things happen, the walls were a dim version of once-white, the carpet looked like something you might find in government housing *after* you'd had several tenants, and the smell—well, Tori didn't want to think too much about what the smell was up there.

Her hand shook a little as she opened the door to HR. She hated, *hated* complaining. But why waste time on a job you know isn't going to be a good fit? She didn't see how working ten or twelve hours a day was a good life-choice. And she didn't know if there was a way to keep the job if she only wanted to work forty hours.

"Good morning, Tori," Pam said from near the coffee machine. "How's it going up there?"

Pam was either permanently peppy, or Tori needed to start drinking coffee.

"Um, it's great, nice people. Looks like they have a lot of work," she hedged. "I just had a quick question. If I'm asked to work overtime, am I required to say yes? Is there a minimum amount I have to agree to?"

Pam frowned. "How long are you working?"

"Till 6:30 Tuesday and 8:00 last night." Tori tried not to sound as tired as she felt.

Pam's eyebrows rose. "Really? No, as a temp you don't have to work overtime." Her expression changed to reflect her job—encouraging people to do their work with a smile and without complaint. "But I will say it would get you brownie points if you'd like to be considered for a full-time position later."

"Right." Tori nodded and smiled back. "Of course." She'd have to see if she even wanted the job before she started campaigning for it. She thanked Pam and hiked up the stairs to her cubicle. There was an elevator, but it was slow as molasses. Besides, the wide staircase was decorated with posters from the shows the station had produced over the years. Tori liked to look at them all, liked to think that she might have a hand in making something lasting someday.

It's not that she had aspirations in the film or television industries, she just wanted to *do* something with her life sometime. Preferably, before she died.

On the other hand, Tori glanced at her watch—9:07 a.m. and half the office wasn't even at their desks yet. Maybe working in TV had its perks. She almost ran into Joanie as she came around the corner.

"Morning, Tori," Joanie said, and motioned toward the kitchen. "Did anyone tell you Thursdays are Bagel Day? We have extra security handling crowd control."

Tori laughed. "I wondered where everyone was."

"Drop your bag at your desk," Joanie said. "I'll wait for you. Otherwise, you're doomed to the onion bagels and no cream cheese."

Leaving her purse and lunch bag on her chair, Tori followed Joanie to the kitchen. Her coworker had been awesome from day one, filling Tori in on office procedures, politics, and gossip, as well as making sure Tori knew about all the extras. First Tuesday screenings of various shows or movies once a month was the one she looked forward to most, and now Bagel Thursdays. The job did have its perks. Maybe she shouldn't have said anything to HR quite so quickly.

Toasted blueberry bagel with a schmear of cream cheese in hand, Tori met a ton of new people in the kitchen. She'd never remember all of their names. But she wouldn't forget the tiny little lawyer named Candy with the bubbly laugh. Sweet, Candy, she could remember that. And José in residuals was charming, showing everyone pictures of his newborn son.

Twenty minutes later, after Joanie walked her around the second floor showing her what departments were where, Tori felt a little more settled. She liked knowing where things were, what goes where, where to find what you need, and Joanie was a much bigger help than Evan had been so far. Maybe it's just that women relate better, understand what other women need to feel at ease.

Back at their desks, the ladies were putting their purses away when a man Tori didn't know walked up. "Either of you see Evan yet?"

"Good morning to you, too," Joanie admonished him. Joanie didn't look that old, maybe mid-forties, but she must have kids. You could hear it in her tone.

He glanced at her, and Tori wondered if he looked a bit sheepish. "Good morning, Joanie." He looked at Tori. "Hi. Have you seen Evan?"

Tori shook her head.

"We'll tell him you're looking for him when he comes in," Joanie said.

"Thanks," the man said as he turned back toward his office.

Joanie turned to Tori and said under her breath, "You'd never know he was a temp, would you?"

Tori pulled out her chair and turned on her computer. "Who is he?"

"His name is Chuck." Joanie laughed. "Can you believe it? *Chuck*. Anyway, he's been here for months, right hand man of Evan's boss, Richard. The station just hasn't gotten around to hiring him yet."

Tori sat down and scooted her chair closer to her computer. Her foot hit something and she repositioned herself. Half a dozen file boxes were stored under her desk. "Months, huh?" Did she want to hang around for months without benefits?

Joanie started to say something else, but her phone rang, so Tori opened her email. Three messages from Evan from last night. Did the man ever go home? She opened the first one, her foot knocking against something under her desk again. Evan had sent her another spreadsheet that needed to be updated with current numbers.

Tori opened the next email—more directions on the kinds of formulas he wanted to use, the spreadsheets he wanted linked, and a reminder to cross-foot the totals. The third email was time-stamped around midnight and seemed more like a P.S. It read, "If I'm not around tomorrow, remember the Nine."

Tori frowned and tried to think of what he meant. Her face cleared suddenly—of course. When totals don't cross-foot, you divide the difference by nine to see if you'd transposed any numbers. Tori deleted the email; she already knew that. Evan certainly didn't have high expectations for temps, did he?

She turned to the file cabinet next to her to pull the file she needed. Swiveling back, her feet again bumped into something under her desk. What in the world was under there? It felt softer than a box. Using the extra space under desks for storage seemed to be a common practice around here.

She rolled the chair back a foot and leaned over to check it out. The desk was deep, and the lighting here was awful, so it was dark under there. But that looked like...

"Oh, I'm sorry, are you working on my computer?" Tori felt herself turning red to think she was kicking some poor IT guy without even noticing it. Why hadn't he said something, for heaven's sake? She paused and waited for the man to answer, but he didn't move. That was a man, wasn't it? "Excuse me?"

Tori squinted to get a better look in the poor light, then bounced up, her mouth open in surprise. She turned to Joanie, but she was still on the phone. The way the cubes were set up, she couldn't easily see the other cube-dwellers. She put her hand over her mouth and took a deep breath. She'd definitely noticed that Evan's eyes were red last night, and on other occasions in the last two days. Was he a drunk?

She tentatively lowered her head under her desk again.

"Um," she cleared her throat. "Evan?" she whispered. That was him, wasn't it? Lying on the floor under her desk, looking for all the world like he'd passed out there last night. Crap.

"Mr. Ruffalo?"

Tori looked up again, but no one was nearby. She bit her lower lip. Should she call Pam? She hated to get Evan in trouble. Maybe he had a reason for... Yeah, right. Still... She peeked at him again. She'd already hit him with her foot a few times, so he needed more than a little prodding to wake up.

Chuck. Joanie just said he worked for Evan's boss. Tori got up and pushed her chair back in, hiding Evan from sight. She walked nervously around the corner, looking for Chuck's office. Finding him, she knocked on the doorframe.

"Chuck, can I talk to you?"

He looked up but didn't say anything. Tori didn't like making snap judgments about people, but Chuck seemed rude and she didn't particularly like him. She wondered if she should call Pam anyway. But if Chuck was a temp, too, certainly getting his help couldn't hurt Evan.

Tori walked in and leaned over his desk so her voice wouldn't carry. "I found Evan. I think he's passed out under my desk."

Chuck frowned at her, his forehead creasing as he processed this information in the same disbelieving way that Tori had.

"Yeah, I know, weird," she said. "I accidentally hit him with my foot a couple times before I realized he was down there. Then...I didn't know what to do so...I thought maybe you could wake him up, get him back to his office or something."

Chuck stood and ushered Tori back to her desk. He still hadn't said a word. He glanced around the office then leaned down to look under her desk. "Aw man...Evan?" He got down on his knees and reached in to shake Evan's shoulder. "Evan? Wake up!"

"What's going on?" Joanie said from her desk. She got up to see what they were doing. When she saw the men under Tori's desk, she burst out laughing then clapped her hand over her mouth. "Oh, this is good. This is going to go round the office for *months*."

Tori let slip a nervous laugh. It *was* ridiculous. Coming in to work and finding her boss passed out under her desk. Watching another man try to shake him awake. Chuck was going to rattle Evan's teeth loose if he wasn't a little gentler.

Finally, Chuck crawled back out and turned to them, his face white.

"Is he drunk?" Joanie asked.

"No," Chuck said, his eyes unfocused, "he's dead."

Tori giggled again. "Dead to the world?"

Joanie just stood there, not laughing anymore.

"No," Chuck looked at Tori. "Well, yeah, dead to the world, dead to everything. He's dead."

Tori stopped laughing and felt her mouth fall open. *Oh, God, please don't let him be dead. Not really. Please wake him up!*

She put her hand over her mouth and looked from Chuck to Joanie to the dark shadow under her desk. *Her* desk. Where *her* feet had been kicking him all morning. Well, not kicking exactly, but she watched those forensic shows. They'd find her shoe marks on his back and—

"I didn't do anything!" She shook her head back and forth as she watched her coworkers for a sign that they believed her. "I didn't do anything! He was just *there*—" she pointed and then looked away, holding her stomach. Her bagel wasn't handling this new development very well.

She gulped at the air. "I'm calling HR," she said and rushed to Joanie's phone.

"Tori, don't—" but Tori didn't hear the rest of what Chuck said.

"Pam, he's dead! Evan's dead!"

"Calm down, Tori." Pam turned on her soothing voice. "Is this about the overtime? If he needs more personnel, we—"

"No, he's dead!" Tori could feel the bagel working its way up out of her stomach.

"You can't threaten your boss just because—"

How many different ways could she say it? No more, not with breakfast on its way. She grabbed Joanie's garbage can and made a mad dash for the ladies' room. She made it about ten feet before she lost her breakfast.

6

Tori no longer considered Bagel Thursday a job perk.

She endured thousands of questions from her coworkers, Pam and everyone else in Human Resources, half of management, and a dozen police officers. She even met the owner of the TV station. By lunchtime, Tori and half a dozen others had gone home, too upset to work. Pam suggested she take Friday off, too, since they had to figure out who Tori would report to now.

She didn't care so long as it wasn't a dead man.

Joe's reaction when she called him was to rush home, wrap her in his arms, and let her cry, promising over and over that he'd keep her safe, always. It was probably the nicest way to end such a horrible day. That wonderful odd feeling of absolute safety encompassed Tori, and she slept fairly well.

Friday morning, she and Joe agreed not to mention Evan's death to their families—after Tori convinced him *not* to cancel their wedding reception the next day. Instead, he called a cleaning company (clever, wonderful man!) and, after a brief foray into work, stayed home with Tori for the rest of the day. He helped her prepare food, put up decorations for the party, and field phone calls from both of their mothers and three aunts who all had questions about the party. Best of all, he made her laugh until her cheeks hurt.

She loved him more than ever. Nothing could ever make her feel differently.

By eight o'clock Saturday morning, they were both up and making final preparations. Joe was outside shoveling and salting and sanding the sidewalk. Tori tried to get a turkey in the oven while answering three phone calls on two phones. Chances were good she'd be glad when this spectacle was over and she and Joe could settle into a quiet life together.

Hopefully, a long and happy life. Tori was getting more nervous about what Joe's reaction would be to her recent, uh, *condition* the longer she put off telling him. No way could she tell him now, though, hours before his entire family arrived. But the longer she waited, the more she wished she'd just told him as soon as she found out. This whole keeping a secret thing was beginning to fester inside her.

Joe stuck his head in the kitchen door. "Honey, will you hand me a garbage bag? I don't want to track snow all over the floor."

"You are a wise, wise man," Tori said, handing him a bag in the doorway, and kissing his cold cheek.

He grabbed her around the waist and kissed her soundly on the lips. "I know. That's why you love me." He copped a feel, then went back outside.

Tori giggled and started her home version of *Egg McMuffins* while she pondered the craziness that permeated her life. Lexie and Hayley agreed that Tori needed to protect her identity if she was going to find herself in the "saving people" business. Hayley wanted to draw up some costume ideas. Tori tried to convince her that she didn't know yet when she'd be out doing whatever it was she was supposed to do. But Hayley said she wanted to be ready when Tori decided to commit full-time. It was easier not to argue.

Tori flipped the eggs. Lexie had calmed down and seemed

less against the idea of Tori as a superhero—so long as she promised to tell Joe by the end of the weekend. Hayley seconded that idea. Tori was nervous. The conversation with Joe might go smoothly and it might not, but it wasn't going to break up their marriage, was it? Maybe this was one of those things, she thought philosophically, that you just have to get through and deal with. Part of the "for better or for worse." Only they wouldn't be able to deal with it if she didn't tell him.

Tori called Joe in and they ate at the kitchen counter to keep the paper tablecloths on the various tables clean. Lexie, Ben, and Hayley came over around ten to help, but Tori and Joe pretty much had everything done. The girls fiddled in the kitchen while Joe chased Ben around the house. Both sets of parents arrived about eleven, and by noon the house was bursting with friends, siblings, aunts, uncles, nieces, and nephews.

Tori looked over the crowd as she refilled the punch bowl. The hard work was worth it. She loved having Joe's big, boisterous family around. They were like the Borg on *Star Trek* in some ways. They were going to pull you in and love you, period. Resistance was futile. Even Tori's family was becoming part of the Clarke clan. Her mom, Dixie, had tried to resist when she first met Owen and Hannah, Joe's parents. But Tori saw her sitting on the couch now—pumps and pearls on a wintery Saturday—reading to three-year-old Lily as if the little girl were her own granddaughter.

"About ready for me to say grace?" Owen appeared at Tori's shoulder. "The meat's ready." Joe and his dad had insisted on cooking another turkey on the grill outside, despite the snow.

"Yeah, I think so." She smiled up at him. If she'd made a list of everything she could hope for in a father-in-law, the end result still couldn't be better than Owen. Today, more than ever, she needed to count her blessings. If she could count that high. "I'll try to round up people from the front and herd them in here."

After Owen prayed and people were lining up to serve themselves, Dixie came over and stood near Tori. "I hear you've had some excitement in your life, young lady."

Uh-oh. Forgot to tell her about the robbery. How'd she find out? Good thing she hadn't heard about the murder. Yet.

Tori smiled and shrugged. Act nonchalant, make it sound less scary than it was. "It was interesting, I'll say that. One minute you're buying a drink, the next the police are asking you what happened and you don't even know what to tell them—it all happened so fast."

Ooo, good! Got through it without even lying. Nice wording. Where's Dad to save me 'cause I know it's not over.

"Uh-*huh*." Dixie sounded like a lawyer cross-examining a witness. "And it was such a non-event that Joe told his mother about it, but you didn't think to tell yours?"

"Mom, I wasn't purposely hiding it from you"—*liar!*—"but there's been a lot going on with work and stuff"—emphasis on *stuff*—"and the last dozen times we've talked, it's been about the party." She shrugged. "Are you hungry?"

Dixie gave Tori an exasperated look. "I'm fifty-three years old, which makes me old enough to know when my daughter isn't telling me everything, and young enough to be offended if she thinks I'm going to have a heart attack every time something bad happens."

Tori sighed and looked contrite. "I don't think you're going to have a heart attack. I just...sometimes I just want to deal with things my own way. I don't always want my mother trying to make everything better."

Dixie put her hand on Tori's shoulder and gave her a rueful smile. "That's a mother's *job*, dear, and the only reason I'm forgiving you so easily is that you don't know that yet. When you have children, we'll talk."

"There's my two girls," broke in Danny. He gave Tori a big squeeze. "I have to get in my overdue hugs today. Don't you let me leave before I'm done."

Tori grinned. "Oh, Dad, you're so silly," she said, but she squeezed him back. In some ways, he still acted like she was a little girl. On the other hand, he seemed to understand what she needed and wanted a minute—or ten—before Mom did.

"I was just telling her that I heard about the robbery from Hannah," Dixie said. "It seems like a good daughter wouldn't let me hear such a thing through the grapevine."

Danny squeezed Dixie's hand. "You're only complaining because you've raised such a good daughter, she doesn't give you much room for complaints. Now let's eat."

Tori sighed in relief. She could always count on Dad. A moment later, with Dixie engaged in a conversation with Aunt Trudy, Danny whispered in her ear.

"Honestly, I thought I might have a heart attack when I heard. Are you sure you're all right?"

"Don't say that," Tori said, swatting at his arm. "*That's* why I don't want to tell you guys anything. I'm fine. Nothing happened." She met his gaze for a moment and dropped her eyes. Dad could always read her expressions, even when she tried to have no expression at all. He was worried. And she didn't know how to reassure him.

Danny studied her for a moment. "I believe you that you're okay, but I don't believe nothing happened."

Tori reached for two paper plates and handed him one. "Da-ad."

He sighed. "You're an adult, and you don't have to tell your parents everything anymore, regardless of what your mother says. But tell me this—will you trust me to treat you like an adult, give you adult advice, if you find you need it?"

Tori's eyes filled up for a moment and she blinked back tears. "I love you, Daddy," she said, giving him a kiss on the cheek.

He put his arm around her shoulders. "All right, which one is the barbecued turkey? That sounds like my kind of meat."

When Tori refilled the potato chip bowls an hour later, Owen came over and took the bag, filling the bowls himself. "Nice party, new daughter of mine," he said. "Let me help you with that."

"Thanks," Tori said with a smile. "Did you get enough to eat?"

"Oohhh," he patted his stomach. "Too much. And I'm sure I'm not done for the day."

They both laughed. Tori had liked Joe's dad from the moment she met him. He was solid, hard to fluster, seemed to have an answer for everything—and told you if he didn't. Good qualities in a pastor *and* a father-in-law.

A pastor. Maybe she could confide in him, ask him for advice. But she had no idea what his position was on whether or not superheroes were real or fakers. Maybe she could just casually bring it up.

But if he turned out to have a negative view of them, like her mother, what was to stop him from telling Joe? No, maybe she could talk to him about it after she told Joe. Owen might be able to shed some light on how she should proceed.

"Hannah and I were worried about you when Joe told us about the robbery."

Tori groaned. "How could he have told so many people? I don't think I've told anyone besides him and Lexie and Hayley."

Owen ate a potato chip and looked at her. "Seems like the kind of story a person would tell. Very exciting."

Tori looked into the bowl and ate a potato chip, too. Owen had a look like her dad's, like he could see all of her secrets. "Well, not everything's as it seems." She forced a laugh.

Owen made an understanding sound. He reached for another chip.

Tori knew he was waiting for her to break and spill. The longer he waited, the more she wanted to. How much better she would feel if she could get some advice, an answer to the question *why*. Surely a pastor would have an idea.

"I'm a good listener," he said.

She looked up at him. She was tall for a woman, but she liked being around the Clarke men—they towered over her. "As a pastor or a father-in-law?"

"Both." He winked and ate another chip.

"Hmm, I like the pastor part better, that whole confidentiality thing." She watched him out of the corner of her eye, gauging his reaction.

He grunted again. "Something Joe doesn't know that you don't want him to know? Take it from a man who's been married for nearly forty years. It's better to get things out in the open. I've been telling Joe that since he met you."

Tori's head snapped to look Owen in the eye. "Really?" Did Joe have a secret, too? What could it be?

Owen shrugged his shoulders and started to move away.

"Owen." Tori waited for him to come closer and lowered her voice. "What if you want to tell someone something but...you're afraid of the consequences?"

"The bigger the problem, the bigger the prayer," he said. "Pray your heart out and let God take care of it. He's good at his job." He smiled at her and tapped the tip of her nose. "You should enjoy the party. Everyone knows where the kitchen is, they can find the food by themselves."

Tori smiled. Only a man would say that. She finished refilling everything, then relaxed as only a hostess can—working her way through the house, making sure everyone was happy.

She'd been hiding her whole life. She'd just have to continue a little longer.

JOE SAT on the living room floor, his three-year-old niece Rose in his lap, an Xbox controller in his hands. Beside him sat his nine-year-old nephew Bruce with the other controller.

"Oohhh!" Joe's voice was echoed with a chorus from the rest

of the mostly male onlookers. "Rose, don't touch the control," he said, laughing. But his laughter just egged her on. She continued to press buttons while he tried to beat Bruce around the game's auto-racing track.

Joe wasn't used to losing to his nephew. "Hey, now, I've got a handicap."

Bruce laughed. "So not my problem, dude."

Joe's car crashed against the wall, breaking into a thousand bits. Bruce raised both arms in the air. "Yeah!"

"My turn, my turn!" yelled his nephew Chris.

Joe gave up his controller and pretended to eat Rose's fingers. "You made me lose!" he said as she shrieked with laughter. "Now what am I going to do with you, huh?"

"In the air! In the air!" Rose shrieked.

Joe stood and tossed her into the air, almost to the ceiling. After a couple times, the rest of the little ones were clamoring to be tossed.

"Look, guys, there's Uncle Bull. I bet he'll play toss the meathead with us."

Bull grinned and set down his pop can. "Make sure Tori and her folks stay in the kitchen, will you?" he said to Joe's sister Gwen. Bull charged the pack of kids who screamed with delight. "Who's a scaredy-cat?" he asked. He rolled around on the ground with them for a moment, then got up with half a dozen kids hanging on.

Joe did the same. Within a few minutes, screams of "Grandpa! Grandpa!" brought Owen into the game. Joe wasn't sure who liked this game better—the kids or the three grown men. He suspected it might be a tie.

After a while, the men had had enough. They leaned up against a wall with fresh cold drinks and watched their family.

"Happy wedding, son," said Owen. "Great party."

"Thanks, Dad," Joe said, taking another swallow of Heineken.

"Thanks for acting as Meat Master today. Good stuff." One of his dad's thousand and one talents.

"So, gotten around to telling your wife your secret identity yet?"

Joe choked on his beer. "Dad!" He looked around for Tori. Not here, good. Then he looked at the beer in his dad's hand. "How many of those have you had?" His dad had a reputation for being a great confidante. But in the last few weeks, Joe had begun to worry that Owen would tell Tori himself if he thought Joe tarried too long.

"Maybe not enough," Owen said. "If I tell all my secrets and blame it on the drink, it might clear up some problems around here."

Bull started laughing. "Want me to get you another one?"

Owen grinned at him.

Joe took another swallow. "You can't expect me to believe you tell Mom everything."

"She knew my secret identity before we started dating," Owen said pointedly.

"Hayley knew my secret identity before we started dating," agreed Bull. He lowered his voice. "Sort of dating."

Joe rolled his eyes. "Well, if you want to get picky, Tori knew about my secret identity before we were dating, too." They'd met when Joe—that is, Superhero X—rescued her from a mugger on Halloween night. It was love at first sight for both of them.

But when Joe casually walked down the street six or eight times until he saw her outside and introduced himself, Tori thought she was meeting him for the first time. When he dropped superheroes into the conversation, she said her family thought superheroes were nut-jobs. He hadn't figured out how to bring it up again in a more positive light.

"So you're not having any problems? No identity crisis?" Owen prodded his son. "You said you were going to tell her.

That's the only reason I agreed to marry you two without her knowing. Then you didn't tell her and—"

"I know, I know!"

Bull interrupted. "Hayley says this is all going to backfire on us, but she won't tell me what she means. I think something's happening."

Owen directed an enigmatic look toward Bull.

"I'm going to tell her," Joe said with more heat than he meant. He took a deep breath. "It's a tricky situation, what with her family hating superheroes and all." He heard the resentment in his voice and hoped his dad didn't.

Owen continued in a lighter tone. "I'm just saying, if you'd been upfront with your wife when you promised me you would —*before the wedding day*—we wouldn't be hiding in the living room in order to play with the kids."

Yeah, it would be hard to explain how they could carry around five or six kids without getting tired. Joe punched his dad lightly in the shoulder. "Lightly" for the three of them. The punch would bring a llama to its knees. "I betcha Mom doesn't tell you everything either."

Owen paused, beer bottle halfway to his lips. Then he said, "No more or less than your wife tells you, I'm sure."

Joe turned to watch his dad take another swallow. "What's that supposed to mean?"

Owen got up and brushed off his pants. "Oh, I think I've meddled enough for one day. Why don't we get everyone together and open some presents?" he said over his shoulder.

Joe shook his head at Bull. "My dad really shouldn't drink. He can't hold his beer."

Bull watched Owen leave. "So Tori's keeping secrets from you, too?"

Joe frowned and turned to watch his dad again. "She doesn't have any secrets." He thought about it for a moment. "At least, not any big ones."

Bull elbowed him. "You gotta tell her. Just say it. Like pulling off a Band-Aid."

Bull had picked up that phrase from Hayley. Joe leaned his head back against the wall. "Yeah, well, Band-Aids hurt like crazy when they pull off the hair, too."

"Whiner."

"Hey, guys." Joe's brother, Carl, plopped down next to him. "Congratulations, little brother," he said, socking Joe in the arm. An inch taller and four years older, Carl loved to play up the "big brother" role, even at thirty-three. The fact that he didn't have any powers and Joe could beat him up any time he wanted didn't seem to matter to him.

"Thanks, Carl." Joe clinked his beer bottle against Carl's. "How's life?"

"Good. Real good." They looked around Joe's house at all the people—from new babies to grandparents approaching eighty, almost the whole family was here. "Mostly good. There's something I could use your help with."

"Uh-oh," Joe said. "I think I'm donating a kidney that day."

Carl hesitated. He started to speak, then took a drink instead.

When he didn't continue, Joe prodded him. "What?" Carl had a thing about being the oldest. He thought it meant you never asked for help from anyone younger than you. The fact that he was asking, or trying, made Joe want to say yes. He hoped it wouldn't be something he really didn't want to do. Like donate a kidney.

"Katie's been having some...some issues." Carl picked at the paper label on his beer bottle.

"Everyone in the living room!" Owen called into the kitchen. "Come on, time for gifts!"

Carl started to stand. Joe put his hand on his arm, warning bells echoing in his head. "Hang on. What kind of 'issues'?"

Carl shrugged. His wife Brenda walked in with their youngest son, and Carl stood. Clasping Joe's forearm, he gave him a hand up. Carl didn't let go, speaking low and urgently so that only Joe and Bull could hear. "Joe, you're the only person I know to ask. Brenda is cool with Dad and you and everything, but...she never thought it might happen to us. We're feeling a little... unequipped." He clapped Joe on the back, making it look like he was giving his brother a congratulatory hug.

Understanding dawned. "Oh," Joe said. He looked at Bull. "About the right age."

Bull nodded. "Eighth grade. That's when it happened to me. I'll help, too, if I can," he said to Carl. "And I'm sure Hayley will be happy to talk to her any time."

"Can she come over here after school sometimes? Maybe spend an occasional weekend? She needs someone who understands. And..." Carl looked embarrassed. He spoke to his shoes, his voice even lower. "Brenda and I need a break."

Joe rubbed his head even as he promised his brother to help. He and Tori *really* needed to talk. How was he going to explain a niece who could do, well, whatever it was she was beginning to do? He kept his voice low. "You know Tori and her folks still don't know anything."

Carl chuckled a little. "I can't figure out how you've managed to keep her in the dark, man." Then he got Joe's point. "Oh. So Katie would..."

"I'm just saying I have to talk to Tori first. Katie is *not* to say *anything* to Tori until I tell her it's okay." How had life gotten so complicated? His dad was right, he should've told Tori when they met. "I'm serious. I won't even take her back to your place. She'll go straight to an orphanage!"

Carl laughed and hugged him again, pounding him on the back. "You got it! I really appreciate this. And if you need anything, you know, anything at all! Thanks, Joe!" Carl lowered his voice once more. "Oh, and uh, just...be careful."

Carl walked over to his wife and kissed her cheek. He looked happier than he had all day. Joe felt the weight of additional anxiety.

Bull chuckled beside him and slapped his shoulder. "Good luck, dude. You'll need it."

Joe laughed with him and forced the anxiety away. It wouldn't be so bad. Occasional visits from a niece he loved, hanging out with her sometimes and helping her to understand what was happening. Actually, it'd be fun. He'd never mentored a young person coming into their power.

Then Joe stopped. *Be careful? What did that mean?*

7

The events of the last week had Tori feeling weird and fearful and irritable when she wasn't excited and curious and eager to find out more about her power. The wedding reception Saturday had been a successful meshing of the two families. *Thank you, God!*

Sunday, she and Joe spent a quiet relaxing day together after doing a little cleaning up. The peaceful feeling persisted today, and walking now in the fresh crisp air the few blocks from her house to Lexie's apartment re-energized her.

Tori thought about what it would be like to return to Half TV tomorrow. Pam in HR had called this morning to say they needed one more day to get a temporary replacement in for Evan. Tori wondered if she would have to sit at the same desk. She hoped not. Janice at Totally Temps assured her that if it was too weird, to let her know and she'd look for a new assignment.

Joe had been great about the whole thing, telling her not to go back until she was ready. Considering that she needed a job to help pay the bills, he acted completely unperturbed about all the time she'd been off work. Three days was over half a paycheck.

Maybe he didn't want her to worry, but she was determined to pull her weight in their marriage, including financially.

She'd been asking God for career guidance for a while now, but the events of the past week weren't helping her make any decisions. She'd helped stop an armed robbery, found out she had a super power (as hard as that was to believe), and she'd found her dead boss under her desk. What was she supposed to be getting out of all these horrible experiences? Become a police officer? A superhero? A private detective? *Leave town?*

No matter how much she prayed about it, she kept getting the feeling that everything was under control. She wanted to trust that God had a plan for her life, but she wasn't sure yet if she would like it.

Tori knocked and walked into Lexie's apartment to the smell of pot roast and potatoes. "Mmm, I'll babysit for you anytime," she said when she joined her sister in the kitchen.

Lexie grinned and put the food on the table. While she poured two glasses of lemonade, she asked Tori if she'd told Joe yet.

Tori didn't have to ask about what. Unfortunately, she didn't have a good answer.

"How'd he take it? You're not in tears, so I assume it went well."

Tori hedged. "The party went till late Saturday and we spent most of Sunday cleaning up, so..."

Her sister put her hands on her hips and put on her "mom" face. "You have got to be the most anti-conflict person I know. Heaven forbid you should have an argument with someone."

"I argue with you all the time," Tori shot back. "I'm not anti-conflict. I just like it when everyone gets along and life is going smoothly."

Lexie raised one eyebrow. "Your life is going smoothly?"

Well, no, not really. But it would be worse if she were fighting with her brand-new husband. They were so happy. She didn't want to ruin it.

"Okay, well, what about work then? Has the temp agency found you someplace else?" Lexie sat down and gave Ben his rubber-covered spoon.

"I'm going back to the TV station tomorrow." Tori took a slice of steaming meat and a few small red potatoes. She needed to learn to cook better now that she was married.

"What? You can't be serious!" Lexie mashed some potato on Ben's plate with unnecessary force. "You're done there, Tori. It isn't safe. Call them back and tell them you're not coming."

Tori noticed Ben watching his mother with unease. "It'll be fine, Lex. Won't it, Benji? Aunt Tori is going to have a totally nice day tomorrow." She tapped his nose to try to get him to smile. He didn't.

"Tori, someone D-I-E-D and no one knows who did it! You already told me the parking lot is huge and half-lit. It's not safe!" Lexie attacked Ben's meat with the sharp knife she held, cutting it into smaller and smaller pieces, her emotions taking over.

The air swirled with fear and what Tori called Lexie's Mother Bear Quality. But now Tori was beginning to believe that Lexie's emotional energy was more than extraordinary empathy. She'd bet Lexie had a power, too. She wanted to ask her about it, but right now Mother Bear was scaring her cub.

Tori cleared her throat loudly.

Lexie glanced at Tori, then noticed her son's expression. Only Ben's quivering chin forced her to calm down. She ruffled his hair and smiled at him, getting the tiniest smile in return.

"I'm sure it's never been safer now that the police have been there, and with it being on the news and all," Tori said. She tried to think of anything to make the situation seem not so bad. "Besides, now that everyone is on high alert, nothing else can happen. Everyone will be watching." That actually sounded like a good argument. Tori decided to believe it.

The heated expression on her sister's face could boil water. Lex glanced at her son and tried to speak calmly—through clenched teeth. "Generally speaking, the argument for safety because the police are looking for a K-I-L-L-E-R is not a solid one."

Tori wondered how they would have adult discussions when Ben learned to spell. Maybe they'd use Pig Latin. That could be fun. She smiled a little, then caught her sister's frown as Lexie waited for a response.

Lex raised her eyebrows and tilted her head. That look reminded Tori of their mom. "Am I right?"

Tori sighed and took a bite of her food, talking around it after a moment. "Let's just see how tomorrow goes." She took another bite. "This is so delicious. It never turns out this way when I make it."

"Meat!" Ben cried out, tired of being left out of the conversation. "Meat an' 'tatoes!" He scooped some onto his spoon and held onto it with one hand while he pushed the spoon into his mouth. He watched Tori to make sure she noticed his accomplishment. Some of the potatoes fell off, and Ben turned his focus to trying to pick them up with his fingers.

Lexie sighed and lowered her voice. "You don't really know any of them. You don't have any reason to trust them. *Or* feel any loyalty," she added. "Someone killed that guy and until the police know who and why, you can't know who you can trust."

"I promise to be careful, okay?" Tori covered her sister's hand with her own and focused calming thoughts her way. "Meanwhile, you should get to your class before you're late. I'll take care of the dishes."

An hour later, Lexie was gone, Ben was in bed, and Tori sat on the couch reading the back of a DVD. Beside her sat a few more movies and several paperback novels. A whole night alone. Bliss. Tonight she would lose herself in another world, totally ignoring the troubling issues in the real world. But would it be a romantic comedy where the boy gets the girl? Tori liked those even more now that she was living her own romance. Or would it be a thriller where the monsters were either genetic mutations or lawyers?

She couldn't decide what she wanted, but she had the entire night to make up her mind. *Ahh, thank you, God.* She couldn't remember the last time she'd had a whole evening to herself. She closed her eyes and smiled in delight. Oh! She'd watch a romantic comedy *and then* read a thriller! Giggling to herself, she popped open a Hugh Jackman DVD and slipped it into the player.

Someone knocked on the door.

Tori frowned at the clock above the TV. Seven-fifteen. She hoped it wasn't Angela next door asking her to babysit. Tori hated to say no to people but, cute as Angela's kids were, she needed one night alone. She paused, considering not answering at all. But with all the lights on and a movie starting, whoever it was would know she was home.

She moaned and tramped to the door, working up an excuse to send whoever it was away. She flipped on the outside light and opened the door partway, trying not to let all the warm air out. A man she didn't know stood there. He smiled.

"Yes?" she said. She took in his expensive clothes, his well-groomed appearance, and decided he was lost. This was so not his neighborhood. She'd send him back to the west side of town where he belonged and get back to her movie. "Are you lost?"

He chuckled. "Hello, Victoria."

Tori blinked, taken aback. He didn't look at all familiar. She mentally ran through all the temp jobs she'd had lately but couldn't place him at any of them. He didn't look a bit like a mugger or a rapist, but Tori closed the door a little more anyway. She couldn't help it. She had a funny feeling, but she couldn't say what exactly she felt. She wished Joe had come over to babysit with her, but he'd decided to work late when she told him she'd be out.

"Do I know you?" She gave him a cautious half-smile, but inside she was praying for safety. She didn't want to know if she could handle one more over-the-top experience right now.

"I can see you don't remember me," he said with a smooth smile, "but yes, you know me. I'm your father."

Shock glued Tori in place. Her father? As in, "Luke, I am your father"? But she hadn't seen him since her pre-memory toddler days. Why would he show up now? If it was really him.

Tori glanced around the courtyard of the apartment complex. Empty. It was dark and freezing cold, having snowed a few inches earlier in the day. No one wanted to be out. And Tori wasn't so sure she wanted to invite this man in.

"Can I see your ID?" Tori felt as surprised by her question as the man now looked. It had just popped out. She reached for his proffered wallet. *Kane Curtis, 21 Matrix Court, Green Hills, Michigan.* Like she'd thought, the rich area of town. Well, that fit with what little she knew about her biological father, that and his name.

Looking up to compare the picture on the driver license with the man in front of her, Tori saw he was quietly laughing. She frowned.

"I'm not laughing at you," he said kindly. "I'm trying to decide whether I should be impressed with your safety standards or worried that you have to be so concerned with your surroundings." He looked around the courtyard and the street and raised an eyebrow.

That's when Tori knew he was telling the truth. Lexie had that exact same look.

"Please, come in," she said reluctantly, moving away from the door. She tried to smile on the outside while running through a hundred possible *why* scenarios on the inside. Why was he here? And how did he know her when she didn't even live here anymore?

Should she call her dad? He'd tell her what to do, probably even come over. Years of secrets and unanswered questions battled inside until Tori didn't know if she was more curious or uneasy. She braced herself. She was twenty-seven years old, plenty old enough to handle things on her own.

She watched this man, her father, as he wiped his feet on the mat and shrugged carefully out of his winter-weight overcoat. Silk probably, or perhaps some kind of micro-fiber, something expensive. She noticed that he glanced at their overcrowded and somewhat dirty coat closet and didn't hand her his coat. Tori didn't offer to take it.

She waved him toward the kitchen. "Can I get you something to drink?" She couldn't get over how tall he was, well over six feet. He looked like he worked out in the gym, too. His hair was quite stylish, graying around the temples. Tori did some quick math and decided he looked pretty good for a man nearing sixty. She could imagine why her mother found him attractive when they were young. Of course, that would be the problem. The women in her family and their choice of men.

Not that the family curse was going to affect her. She refused to allow it. She didn't make a mistake. Joe was perfect.

"Coffee would be fine," he said, looking around their small kitchen, moving his head to catch part of the living room in his gaze.

"Sorry, we don't drink coffee." She opened the fridge. "We have Diet Coke, apple juice, milk, hot chocolate..." She looked up and tried not to look apologetic. This was her home, well, Lexie and Ben's home. That he made her feel she should apologize made her determined not to.

"If you're having hot chocolate, that would be nice," he said.

He looked at the kitchen table and chairs, painted in a rainbow of colors by Lexie last year, complete with tiny Ben-prints. He wiped a crumb or two from a chair and sat down, carefully folding his coat on his lap.

"Is your nephew here? Ben, right?"

A man like Kane Curtis should not be inspiring such dread. He was rich, handsome, and somewhat charming. But Tori absolutely, positively did not want him near Ben. "He's asleep."

Tori microwaved two mugs of milk and tried to think of something to say. Should she launch right into twenty questions, or let him begin by telling her why he came?

"Did you choose to live here?" he asked.

Tori could hear the confusion in his voice. She turned to him with a frown as the microwave beeped. Maybe he didn't know that she'd moved out. But how could he not hear that his question was insulting?

"Your mother lives in a nice part of town," he said. "Why don't you live there?"

Tori pulled out the mugs and added the hot cocoa powder and spoons. "It's an *expensive* part of town."

Could he really be such a naïve rich boy? Mom talked about him so infrequently, and usually with a good deal of venom in her voice, Tori wasn't sure how to take his odd, somewhat *rude*, comments.

She set a mug on the table in front of him and sat down, moving a coloring book aside to put her own mug on the table. She watched him look around the kitchen. Two sinks, no dishwasher, the microwave and some other appliances taking up most of the counter space, a small butcher-block island where most of their meal prep took place.

Tori felt embarrassed as she saw her life from this man's view. And her embarrassment made her angry. Their home—and their life—was warm and cozy and full of a great deal of love. She and her sister had created a haven for themselves and Ben. They'd never felt safer than they did living here together. Even though she'd moved out a couple months ago, it was still a haven for her. She didn't expect other people to understand, but she didn't expect the man who dared refer to himself as her father to make her feel small.

Danny, her *real* dad, had never in all her life made her feel embarrassed or ashamed. Tori suddenly felt the need to call him and thank him for that.

Turning to Kane, that's what she would call him, she decided, she said, "Why are you here?" Ruining my perfect evening. She left that unsaid. For now.

Kane met her gaze, measuring and making mental notes. Tori could see it in his eyes.

"I came to find you and take you home, Victoria." He flicked his wrist at the apartment. "You deserve so much more than this. You and Alexia and my grandson. Your heritage demands it. It's time I became a proper father to you."

Tori laughed. In disbelief, not good humor. "*Really*?"

Kane looked surprised.

Tori searched his face, tried to read his eyes, to figure out what he was thinking. She decided not to correct him about where she lived. "We have everything we need here, thank you," she said firmly, using all her willpower not to succumb to his level of rudeness. "We're warm and dry and well-fed and perfectly happy." She couldn't help herself. "And we already have a dad."

She'd often wondered why her biological father had left them, why he had allowed Danny to adopt her and Lexie, why he hadn't made an appearance since then, even though they lived *in the same city*. But now she saw what good fortune that had been.

Kane took a deep breath and stirred his heretofore untouched hot chocolate. "I can see I haven't approached this correctly," he said. He met Tori's gaze with a sad look that made him look older. "I don't want you to feel I'm belittling what you have. But I can give you more than you ever dreamed. And I want to."

Tori leaned back in her chair a little and stirred her hot chocolate as well. She took a calming breath and watched him stir his drink. He had a manicure. She tried not to roll her eyes. A manicure. She didn't know a single man in her life with a manicure. There was something...ostentatious about it.

"Your grandmother died a few months ago," Kane said, his voice filled with quiet sadness.

Tori glanced up in surprise. Now that was something she *hadn't* thought of, that she had another family besides her mother's side and Danny's side. It had never occurred to her. She wondered if any of them had ever wanted to meet her.

"For the first time, I can see my own mortality," Kane continued, stirring but not drinking the cocoa. "Your grandfather died years ago, and my brother and I don't speak. I see all the mistakes I've made and I'm looking for ways to make them right."

Tori tried to imagine another grandmother besides Grandma Millie and Gramma Jean. She couldn't do it. All her sugar-cookie-eating and petunia-planting memories were of them. With them. But she did remember how it broke her heart when Gramma Jean died.

"I'm sorry about your mom." Tori met his eyes again. He smiled at her for a moment, then looked away.

"You and Alexia are the only children I have." His voice still sounded sad. "And Benjamin is the only grandchild I have."

There was something else in his voice now, Tori sensed. Was it hope? She wished Lexie were here. Lexie could read anyone. With 100% accuracy. Of course, it was a good thing she wasn't here because Lexie hated their father almost as much as Mom did.

Tori sighed. She didn't want to make Lexie or Mom upset, but they hadn't seen Kane in years. Here he was, right in their kitchen, not drinking hot chocolate with her, and he looked genuinely sad and lonely. She couldn't just push him out into the cold, could she?

After a moment she said, "What did you have in mind?"

KANE USED every bit of his willpower not to chortle in triumph. And his father called him weak. Ha! His father would have bungled this job before he'd even begun, forcing his will on others by brute strength. But Kane won because he used his head. He had finesse. It was an omen. This was merely the beginning of the victories coming his way.

He felt the energy burning in his chest and took a slow calming breath. This was not the time or the place to show his daughter what kind of bloodline she came from. Soon.

He thought quickly, revising his original plan. He'd hoped all three of them would be here tonight, that the girls would be thrilled to have a rich daddy walk in and make all their dreams come true. But he couldn't wait for his men to conduct a new inquiry into his daughters' activities. Their schedules had apparently changed since the last one. No problem. Maybe this would be better. He'd woo this one first, then get her to convince her sister, the one who had his grandson, and then they'd all be together. One big, happy family.

He remembered the last time he'd seen Alexia. She'd been little, maybe around kindergarten age. She'd stared at him like she could see inside, then she cried like the world was going to end. She'd been upset with him for leaving, obviously. He'd have to figure out how to make her forgive him soon. But for now, he would focus on Victoria.

Kane asked to look in on his sleeping grandson. Victoria denied him with an absurd excuse about waking the boy. He suggested they have dinner together tomorrow night. She liked that. When he asked if she thought Alexia would come, she insisted it was too soon. With Alexia it would take more time. There was a limit to how much time Kane would allow the girls, but he smiled and nodded.

He answered questions about his mother, sometimes telling the truth, and deftly sidestepped questions about his father and brother. If Victoria acted interested, he continued on the current topic of conversation. He told her about his mother's rose garden and the horses she used to ride. He left out the fact that he only knew about the garden after she died when he wondered to the housekeeper why no one brought roses into the house anymore. And he neglected to mention that the horses had been recycled into steaks and glue.

When Victoria seemed uninterested or repulsed—what had Dixie done to make the girl repulsed by talk of money and success?—then Kane turned the conversation elsewhere. Soon he couldn't think of anything else to say. The girl had a typical female's interest in relationships and people, and apparently no interest in taking her place in the richest, most powerful family in the state. No wonder she lived in this all-but-a-hovel. His mother would have fainted.

She wouldn't have liked the nicknames either. He'd chosen names of power for his daughters. He expected the girls to use them. But then, they'd never developed any powers so maybe it didn't matter anymore.

"What do you do?" he asked suddenly.

"I'm a temp," the girl said with a bright smile.

At his questioning glance, she continued. "A temp, you know, a temporary employee? I get to try out all kinds of jobs at all kinds of places so I can decide what I want to pursue."

Kane slowly nodded his head. "Ahh." No wonder she had no money, no career. "You should work for me, I pay better."

She laughed. She thought he was joking. And perhaps he had been. But the more he thought about it, the more he liked the idea. He'd keep reeling her in until he had what he wanted. Yes, this could be perfect.

"Then you could afford to live in a nicer area," he said. He thought about his grandson. Soon he would be living with Kane. "I own a beautiful condominium property you and your sister would like."

Tori waved her arm vaguely and chuckled. "Well, as far as I know, there's only been the one mugging around here, and I didn't even get hurt."

Kane's eyes sharpened on hers. Information was power. One power anyway. "What happened?"

Her eyes widened and she stuttered and stammered.

Obviously, she hadn't meant to share that fact. So she hadn't told her parents. Dixie, that is. Kane knew what role he would play now—confidante. Perfect. He'd share all her secrets.

He smiled the way ladies loved. "I can see you're unhurt. So what happened?"

"Just some teenagers dressed up so no one could see their faces," she said cautiously. "Gave them courage to be...adventurous, I guess. One grabbed my purse, then dropped it after I chased him."

"Really?" Kane wondered if his family had been wrong and she had a power after all. "How did you get him to do that?"

She laughed and blushed. "I didn't. I fell and some other guy found it and returned it to me."

Kane masked his disappointment. He shouldn't have expected anything. His mind worked to put together ways he could use tonight's information to achieve his ends. He looked at his watch and smiled graciously again. He had other things to do tonight.

"I really should be going. I've taken enough of your time, dropping by unannounced." He stood and carefully shook out the wrinkles in his coat, not letting it touch the undoubtedly dirty floor. He pressed her again. "May I see the boy before I go?"

She cleared her throat as she picked up the mugs and took them to the sink. "I'm sorry," she said. "It's really not a good idea."

What was she hiding? Children fell asleep at the drop of a hat. It shouldn't matter if the boy was awakened. He must already be displaying his gift and she didn't want Kane to see it. Kane's heart rate picked up speed. He wondered what the boy could do.

His daughter walked him to the door and he forced himself to calmly follow her.

"I hope you can be patient with Lexie," she said. "I'll try my best, but it's going to take time to convince her that you've changed."

"I've changed?" he said without thinking.

She turned to him, her face serious. "You know, since your mother died, wanting to be part of your family again."

He nodded and applied what he hoped was the proper expression. "Yes, yes, it's true, I really have changed." He had no idea what the twit was talking about, but she seemed reassured.

He buttoned his coat and opened the door. "I'll send a car for you tomorrow at 7:30," he said as he left.

"A car, well, oh, um," she stammered behind him. "I'd prefer to drive myself. Thanks anyway."

Kane ground his teeth. She had no respect for his position in this city. He calmed himself. She would soon.

"Fine, I'll have my secretary contact you with a location and directions."

He waved over his shoulder and hurried away. She really was clueless. Which would make his growing idea that much easier to implement. Soon she'd be begging to move into one of his condos. He just had to make sure her sister and his grandson came with her.

As Kane was leaving Lexie's place, Joe was pulling into a dark parking lot across town. He parked at the back of an unremarkable building in an unremarkable industrial park. Hiding in plain sight. Next to his eight-year-old black Dodge pickup sat a dark gray Ford and a gold or tan, depending on how dirty it was, Toyota. Both sedans were several years closer to their born-on date than Joe's truck. His fingers itched to write "Wash Me" in the dirt on the Toyota's windshield simply because it would make Mickey crazy. He restrained the urge, and let himself in the back door using the numeric keypad.

Just as the door started to close, Joe let the ten-year-old inside have his fun: he zipped over to Mickey's car and wrote on the back window. Chuckling, he admitted to himself that getting married hadn't made him a grownup. Back inside, he pressed his thumb against a panel on the wall and mockingly saluted one of the three video cameras in the tiny vestibule. Through that door and down a flight of stairs, another numeric keypad took his digits, and a final steel door opened.

Mickey looked up as Joe entered. He relaxed on one of the oversized leather sofas in the sitting room, reading on his iPad. None of them were willing to use the colloquial "lair" to refer to their secret office. Joe and Bull had dubbed it Bachelor Heaven, but Mickey liked people to call it the team office. More understatement. So Mickey. But Joe did find it funny that Mickey called this room by such an old-world name.

Mickey just looked at him the first time Joe had laughed. "It's the *room* where we *sit*," he'd said, as if Joe were a dunce.

Joe walked over and gripped his friend's hand in a warm hello as he felt a familiar contentment settle around him. He'd helped Mickey design this space, and Mickey had made it clear Joe was welcome any time. Even after he got married.

Mick's super ability lay with machines, computers, and inventions. A laboratory filled with his gizmo's lay behind a door near the kitchen. Joe found Mick's talents far more fascinating than

Joe's own ability to gain strength through metals or even his capacity to heal quickly. What Mickey could do was just plain *cool*. Joe missed hanging out and playing with the new inventions.

He cast a longing look toward the door to the gym and sat down on a couch. He needed to make more time to work out, get the softness of holiday eating and honeymooning out of his muscles. Due to their abilities, as well as their desire to stay under the radar, a public gym wouldn't work.

Being married was taking up a lot more of Joe's time than he'd anticipated. Though it did have its perks, he thought with an inner grin.

"'S'up?" Mickey said and went back to reading.

Joe relaxed into the leather. He felt a deeper sense of belonging here than he ever felt at home. The city had made him an offer—they would provide him a house rent-free in a neighborhood that needed to be cleaned up, and after five years they would give him the house. Joe was grateful, but he accepted the house only because it was part of the assignment. He could never make that falling-down building feel like home. And if he did, it could blow their cover. How many guys in their mid-20s have enough money to throw into home renovations? In that neighborhood?

Mickey's basement though, this was a place where a man could relax, take a load off. There were days Joe wondered if Mickey would be able to get him to leave. Of course, Joe frequently wondered how often Mickey stayed here all night, steps away from his work, miles away from his empty house.

Joe brought his attention back to the moment when the steel door opened again.

"Hey, guys," Bull called. "Look who I found outside."

Detectives Art Paredes and Casey Knox of the Double Bay Police Department, Superhero Liaison Unit, called out their hellos and sat on one of the couches.

"Hiya, Art," Joe said, shaking his hand. "Good to see you, Casey. You're looking wonderful." He gave her a casual hug.

Art sighed dramatically. "It's always, 'Hi, Art' and 'Hellooo, Casey.' I'm gonna get a complex."

Everyone laughed—because it was true. Gorgeous Casey Knox could've been a model if she were taller, and if she didn't have a passion for putting away the bad guys. Any of them would've dated her in a heartbeat, but she'd built a sturdy wall between her work and her personal life.

Art was a good-looking guy himself, but he knew it. The man had an obsession with clothes that would've been irritating if not for his sense of humor about it. If it meant catching crooks and killers, Art would wade through sewers—Italian loafers and all. Joe had been there that day. Casey had created "Art's Wall of Shame" in their office at the station—pictures of Art in various degrees of ripped, stained, and totally ruined clothing. Under each picture Art had written the name of the criminal nabbed that day. Joe had seen it; it was a wall to be proud of.

"All right, let's get down to business." On his iPad, Mickey opened an app he'd developed where he kept all his notes.

Joe patted his pockets in the vain hope that a pad and pen would appear that he hadn't put there. Mickey shook his head and pointed to the drawer on Joe's side of the coffee table. Inside were several notepads and pens. Joe grinned his thanks.

"You weren't a Boy Scout, were you?" Mickey grumbled. "Art, why don't you take the floor?"

Art pulled a file from his briefcase and opened it on his lap. He lay some photos on the coffee table. "I'm sorry to say Evan Ruffalo died sometime Wednesday night or early Thursday morning, and we've confirmed that it was not from natural causes."

Joe said a silent prayer for the man and his wife. He never thought Evan would get hurt. Threatened, yes; murdered, no. "Any leads yet?"

"Techs haven't found much. At this point, we're quietly looking for a Jack."

A person with powers was a suspect. Not a surprise, but not good news. Joe looked through the pictures while Art read from his file. Joe had seen dead bodies before, but nothing ever prepared him for it. He never got used to it, and that was probably a good thing. He flipped quickly through the pictures.

"His body was found by a new employee—under her desk actually. But we—"

"Yeah, Joe's wife," Bull interjected.

The last picture in Joe's hand was of a police officer interviewing a woman in her mid-twenties, a tallish brunette who looked semi-hysterical, flash-frozen on the paper.

"Tori." Her name slipped out as he looked at the picture. She looked much worse than he'd imagined when she told him about it last Thursday afternoon.

"What?" Casey exclaimed. "Tori Lewis. That's the woman in the picture."

"Tori Clarke," Joe said, still looking at the photo and feeling an urge to hit something. Hard.

"Tori Lewis is your new wife?" Art asked, his voice getting higher at the end.

Joe looked up to catch a look pass between the two detectives. "Her maiden name is Lewis. She hasn't gotten around to changing it yet."

"She's not a suspect, is she?"

Joe noticed that Mickey's tone was harder than was usual when he spoke with the SLU. It was nice to know Mickey had embraced Tori into their circle, even if he hadn't realized it yet.

Casey made a non-committal movement. "At first we thought she was our primary suspect because she kept telling officers on the scene, 'It was an accident, I swear it was an accident.' The officer who interviewed her eventually learned that she'd bumped his back with her foot a couple of times before she looked to see what was down there. Although she's on the list, we don't consider her a prime suspect."

"Tori didn't kill Evan." Joe tried to make his tone neutral, but everyone was staring at him. He tried again. "My wife isn't a killer. She was in the horrible position of being in the wrong place at the wrong time."

Again. Joe hoped the SLU didn't realize Tori was also at the convenience store robbery. It would be too coincidental for them to ignore.

"Of course, Joe." Art's voice took on the cadence of a police officer giving nothing away.

Joe started to say more, but Mickey interrupted.

"Did you find anything in Evan's office?" Mickey asked. "Anything to give you an idea of who or why?"

"Isn't it obvious why?" Joe jumped in before Art could answer. "He found out something about the missing kids, something important."

Art hedged. "Well, that's why we're here. Officially, the police don't have many leads. The security tapes are being analyzed, doors and desks are being examined to see what was broken into, what might be missing. But we found little physical evidence near the body—"

"Or, in fact, anywhere at the scene," Casey broke in.

"Right," Art nodded, "to shed much light on who killed him or how. The fact that a smaller group of us know Mr. Ruffalo is linked to another case... Well, it's time to send one of you in."

"Excellent. Evan works in finance and development," Mickey said. "Joe has experience in finance. He can be there tomorrow."

"What about Tori?" Casey asked. "Is she still working there?"

Art shook his head. "That won't work. No one will believe that a married couple just happened to start working in the same department at the same time. Maybe you should go in, Mickey."

Casey nodded.

"Since Tori is a temp, it won't be a problem. She can get reassigned to another company." Mickey made some notes on his tablet.

That was probably a great idea, actually. Joe didn't want her anywhere near a murderer. "She's supposed to go in tomorrow, but I'll ask her to stay home."

"No, you should both be there." Bull had been sitting quietly, but now he leaned forward. "You know how offices are, the women confide in women, men talk to men. You'll find out more if you're both there."

Mickey paused in his note-making. Joe could see he was considering the idea. Did it have merit? Theoretically, he agreed with Bull, but...

"I'm not sure how I would explain it to her." Joe tried to send Bull a look to make him understand what Joe was getting at without saying it in front of the SLU.

"You work for Mickey's security firm, right? As your day job."

Heads started nodding as they began to see where Bull was going.

"So you'll tell her that your firm was hired to do some under-cover work for the police," Casey said. "Do you think she could pretend not to know you and help us out?"

"They've only known each other for three months," Mickey said. "Can't be that hard to pretend they don't know each other."

Joe gave Mickey a disgruntled look. He didn't argue though.

"Do you think you can do it?" Art asked Joe. "Just because we don't have any leads doesn't mean the wrong word in the right ear couldn't destroy something we could've found."

Joe thought about what he did know about his wife. She was stronger than she looked. She had grit. And he absolutely trusted her. He began to nod. "I think we can do it. Let me talk to her tonight. If she doesn't want to get involved, I'll get her to change her assignment. Either way, set me up to start working there tomorrow."

The memory of their first meeting flashed in Joe's head. He

was dressed as Zorro at Halloween, patrolling the neighborhood, and found Tori after she'd just been mugged. The first time he'd heard that voice in his head insisting he protect her.

But also the first time he had the sensation that his powers were even stronger when she was around. She made him feel like he could do anything.

He nodded to himself. Bull probably had it right. He and Tori could make a good team.

8

Tori blew on her second cup of hot chocolate of the evening. She wasn't thinking about calories; she was thinking that Lexie's always tasted better. Tori was just too lazy to warm up milk and wash an extra pan. She let her thoughts drift to what she'd been trying so hard not to think about.

Kane Curtis.

Hugh Jackman hadn't been able to get Kane out of her head. Dean Koontz couldn't exorcise him. So Tori sat on the couch with a cup of cocoa waiting for Lexie to get home.

She picked a marshmallow from her mug and sucked on it until it dissolved on her tongue. The marshmallows made a big difference, too. She should buy some for Joe's house, that is, for home.

Tori heard the front door open. Moment of truth. She got up from the couch and met her sister by the door. "Hey, how was class?"

Lexie hung up her coat and scarf. "Great." She smiled. "I think I definitely want to start my own business. It's hard, but I think I'll like it. Now I just have to figure out something to do." She giggled.

Grr. Lexie didn't giggle that much. Tori didn't want to ruin the moment. Maybe she'd tell her about Kane's visit later. "Want some hot chocolate? I just made myself some."

"Sure, thanks."

Tori went in the kitchen while Lexie checked on Ben. She focused on being calm, relaxed, happy. She didn't want Lexie to pick up on anything negative in Tori's emotions. Calm. Happy. Calm.

She met Lexie in the living room and gave her a mug.

"So what's up?" Lexie asked as she blew on her drink.

"Nothing, just watching a movie." Calm. Happy.

"You wanted to tell me something." Lexie tilted her head expectantly.

Oh, blast it. She had to learn to manage herself better around Lexie. She might as well tell her since she was such a terrible liar. She wondered if maybe she should get a tiny bit better at that, too.

Tori looked toward Ben's room and lowered her voice. The three-year-old was asleep and couldn't hear her. He probably couldn't grasp what she was talking about anyway, but she didn't want him to know.

"I had a visitor tonight," she said, watching Lexie.

Lexie paused in her sipping and raised one eyebrow.

The man couldn't have been lying about being their father. Tori could see some of his features in Lexie's face and hands. She'd seen enough in the bathroom mirror to believe him after he'd left.

"It was our father, Mom's first husband."

The mug started to slip in her sister's hand, then was moved with unnecessary force to the coffee table. "And?" Lexie demanded.

"He wants to meet you and Ben." Tori rather wished she and

her sister beat around the bush a little more. Things like this wouldn't come as such a shock if they meandered a bit before getting to the point.

"Well, that's too bad." Lexie folded her arms over her chest and leaned back in the couch. She stared into space, her expression hardening.

The look on her face reminded Tori of what Lexie used to be like, angry and cussing and defensive about everything. She'd been the family wild child as long as Tori could remember. Even though she was two years younger, Tori always felt like she had to take care of Lexie, protect her, constantly beg God to keep her sister out of jail and *alive*. But over time, Lexie calmed down. She fell in love with a pretty decent guy—no needle marks, appeared to have a real job, and he didn't stare at Tori's breasts when Lexie wasn't looking. All pluses.

But apparently Mr. Wonderful wanted to do the deed without paying the price. By the time Lexie was four months pregnant, he'd moved out and Tori had moved in. Mom and Dad hadn't believed that not everything that happened in Lexie's life was Lexie's fault. Especially because she was going through a second pregnancy at age twenty-four with no husband in sight.

So Tori continued her self-appointed job of taking care of Lexie. Until Ben was born. The moment she held him in her arms, something changed in Lexie. Tori had seen it in her face. She just *decided* that she would be an excellent mom, and she went at it with gusto.

In a weird way, it was the perfect situation. Men couldn't be trusted. Their parents, wonderful as they could be, couldn't be trusted in the hard times. So Tori and her sister began creating their own safe environment. For the first time, both women began to blossom.

Lexie stopped swearing, stopped drinking, joined Tori in a decision to give up men. She cleaned up her body, her apartment, her life, one step at a time. She got a job bagging groceries, finished her GED, learned to cook. She'd been so focused on improving herself, had in fact done such an excellent job, Tori had started to feel a little envious.

Tori had worked two jobs those first two years just to keep Ben in diapers and baby food. She wanted to do more with her life, but Ben's needs were her priority. That meant supporting Lexie in whatever way she could to become the kind of mother Ben needed and deserved.

Tonight, Tori didn't want to be responsible for Lexie taking a step back. She couldn't tell what Lexie was thinking. Strangely, she couldn't really tell what her sister was feeling either. She'd expected waves of fury and righteous indignation rolling over them both. Instead, there was nothing but icy cold calm.

"That's all you have to say?" Tori looked at her older sister expectantly. She didn't even have to think about it—when she felt Lexie needed to be protected from something, she instinctively played the leader. Lexie did the same with her. But now, Tori wasn't sure which of them should push the other. Was getting involved in their father's life a good thing or a bad thing?

Lexie picked up her mug again and downed half of it. Tori wondered if she wished it was spiked.

"There's nothing else *to* say."

"But what about—"

"Tori, we made a pact. We don't belong to him. He has no right to us. He gave that up when Dad adopted us. Forever." Lexie leaned toward her. "You don't remember, but I do. There is something wrong with him. I could feel it even as a child. *That man,*" she spat the words, "never even showed up at the courthouse to say goodbye. As far as I'm concerned, he doesn't exist."

"You waited for him?" Tori asked.

"Of course I did. I was six years old. That's what children do. They expect their parents to show them undying love and devotion. And *Dad* does. The end." Lexie focused on drinking her cocoa. When she finished it off, she held out her hand.

"I'm not done."

Lexie stomped off to the kitchen. Tori heard dishes rattling in the sink, chairs moving around, cupboards opening and closing. Maybe she'd just give her a moment.

Lexie came back in, looked at Ben's snack bowl and a water glass on the table, reached for them and stopped, then sank down on the couch. Tori knew that her sister was far more rattled than she wanted to let on.

"What do you want me to tell him?"

Lexie sat quietly for a moment. Then she let her head fall against the back of the couch and closed her eyes.

God, help us make a good decision, Tori prayed. *Please make Lexie agree to meet him.*

A minute or two passed in silence. Then Lexie looked up, resolve firmly etched in her face again. "Tell him no. If he contacts you. Otherwise, just let it go. Don't get involved with him, Tori. No good can come of this."

A wave of disappointment washed through Tori, knocking her back into the cushions. "But he's our father. Don't you want to know his side?"

"No."

Tori thought about the relatives she'd heard about tonight. "What about the rest of the family? Our grandmother just died. I don't want everyone to die without ever knowing each other."

"They've all had plenty of time, Tor. If they'd wanted to, they could've called."

The more reasonably Lexie spoke, the more plaintive Tori felt. "We don't know if they contacted us. They might've called Mom and she told them to kiss off."

Lexie shook her head. "We decided what we were going to do a long time ago. It's done."

"But we were children then. What about Ben? What if we need to know about allergies or his medical history?" Tori felt herself getting wound up. She couldn't figure out what was getting her so bothered. Until tonight she'd been perfectly happy with her family situation. Or at least accepting of it. "What if he needs a transplant some day?"

Her sister just sat there, watching her, not saying anything more. That was Lexie. Once she'd said her piece, she was done. She simply waited for you to catch up.

Tori stopped. She rubbed her forehead, leaning her elbow against her knee. Finally she said, "I know. I know. I just..." She shook her head. "He sounded so...alone. Listening to him talk about his mother dying, it made me want to give it a try." She looked up. "I don't want to die with any more regrets than necessary."

"Then don't see him again," Lexie said.

Tori closed her eyes and ran her hands through her hair. Lexie was right. She knew it. Very simply, seeing Kane again would not be a healthy choice for any of them.

She wondered how she was going to tell Kane that when they had dinner together tomorrow.

Joe was pleasantly surprised at how easy it was to get Tori's help on his new assignment. She'd been upset when she came home from babysitting Ben, but she didn't want to talk about it. So he'd launched into his prepared speech on how the security agency he worked for had been hired to investigate her boss's death. Undercover.

Her eyes had lit up right away. "Can I help?"

He'd made her promise to act like she hadn't met him before. And when she started smiling that lovely smile, he told her she couldn't do that either.

She laughed and said, "I think it would be fun to pretend not to like you." Then she ran her hands down his chest. "But starting tomorrow."

Now at work, Joe tried not to think about the fun they'd had in the bedroom right after that. He had to focus on the task at hand, and on pretending not to know his wife. "Any questions, Lori?" Joe asked her.

He'd introduced himself around the office this morning as Evan's temporary replacement and noted the reactions of each employee. Could any of them be the killer? Might they know something that they hadn't told the police?

Tori sat quietly at a desk she'd said was *not* the one where Evan was found. She sat up straight and looked him in the eye. Her rather conservative business attire neither made her stand out nor look like a killer. Basically, she looked like all the other women in the office. But since the police had very little to go on, right now everyone was a suspect to Joe. Not because he believed any of them was the killer, but because he had no reason to believe they weren't.

"Uh, it's Tori. No questions. I understand." She smiled a bit from her perch on the edge of her chair. She looked like a bird about to take flight, a beautiful bird with lovely hazel eyes.

Joe mentally shook his head. He'd made Tori promise to act like a stranger, and here he was the one with the problem.

"Okay, let me email you the file," he said. "Sit tight and I'll be back." He rubbed his eyes as he walked away. Focus. He had to concentrate on Evan, on learning what Evan was investigating, what he had uncovered. Tori's former cubicle had been sealed up with plywood and police tape, but Evan's office remained open so that Joe could work there. That's where he would spend most of his time this week, looking through, behind, and under everything he could find. Of course, he also had to do some work for the station in order to keep his cover.

In Evan's office, Joe backed up an Excel spreadsheet he'd been working on. Joe's dad, a retired superhero himself, teased Joe that his aptitude with numbers was another one of his abilities. For Joe and Mickey, Joe's talent had been just another way to get him through a door in an investigation. Joe emailed the spreadsheet to Tori along with a document explaining what needed to be done with the file.

He'd spoken to Evan's boss earlier. Richard had been informed that Joe was working undercover, and he'd given him access to all the files Evan had been working on. As far as the station knew, Evan's death was linked to something work-related. Maybe. But Joe still thought Evan had hit a nerve with The Nine somehow.

He walked back to the cubicle outside his office. "Okay, the email program is..." Joe stopped. Tori already had the email open and the directions printed out. She saved the file to her desktop as he watched, then started reading the directions he'd sent.

"Yes?" She turned around when he stopped talking.

Joe paused, then shook his head. Richard's assistant told him the temp was all but useless. Chuck must've been thinking of someone else. Joe didn't know much about what his wife was good at, but she seemed pretty competent so far. "We need a cost analysis of each development deal over one, five, and ten years," he said. "For those who haven't been with us ten years, we need a future projection based on history."

"Okay," she said.

Joe waited for her questions. None. Well, if she was as good as she acted, he'd have time to go through some of Evan's papers. "All right, then," he said to her. "I'll be in Evan's office if you need me."

She nodded, thanked him, and went back to reading his directions. Acting for all the world like she hadn't met him before today. She was good.

Joe closed Evan's door and sat down behind his desk. He'd searched through the computer files quickly this morning. Whatever Evan knew, if he was keeping it on his work computer, he'd named the file something that sounded like work. The company used desktop computers for anyone under a certain level of responsibility, including Evan. The higher-ups all had laptops and docking stations so they could take their work home. If Evan hadn't saved files relating to his search on this computer, he must've saved them on his home computer. If that was the case, Art would have to follow up. Meanwhile, Joe would go through every single computer file Evan had access to.

Up until yesterday, neither Mickey nor the detectives had been sure Evan knew anything at all. His murder to the contrary. Joe's orders had been to not only look for anything regarding the missing children, but also any financial red flags. It was possible that Evan had been embezzling money, or found out someone else was. Both reasonable motives.

Joe pulled files from the stacks on the desk and skimmed through them. Then he opened the drawers and began going through the files there. Work-related, work, work, work. All work-related. Maybe it *was* embezzlement and Joe would have to start crunching numbers to find what he was looking for.

He opened the last drawer, bottom on the left. Kleenex box, cough drops, miscellaneous office supplies. A file folder hidden under everything else.

Joe pulled it out and opened it, praying he'd finally found something. The chubby cheeks and laughing eyes of a happy little boy, probably five or six years old, smiled back at him. Jason. The boy Evan and his wife were going to adopt. Until the boy suddenly disappeared.

Joe prayed the boy was alive and well. Jason reminded him too much of his nephew, Zack, not to be moved by his disappearance. He decided to risk taking the file to the copy room. Maybe Mickey could find something in the background that would help. Jason wasn't the only missing child. There were three public facilities for children in Double Bay, and all three had "lost" children in the last two years. Unexplained disappearances. And that didn't count the children reported missing by families.

Both the police and the superhero squads knew about the problem, and everyone was on alert, but no one could find a way to stop it. There wasn't any evidence that the missing children were even linked. Evan had been searching for the boy who would be his son since he'd disappeared four months ago. Joe heard that Evan had stopped cooperating with the police when they regretfully informed him that they had no new leads a few weeks back. Joe believed Evan had stumbled onto something on his own, but for the life of him he couldn't figure out what.

TORI OPENED the card that came with the pot of violets. Had Joe sent her flowers at work? Sneaky, tricky little—*Meet me at The Captain's Table at 7:30 p.m. I hope you enjoy shopping. – Kane*

A gift card holder from Nordstrom was taped to the side. Opening it, she gasped—one thousand dollars! *I guess he wants me to buy a new dress.* Tori's emotions tumbled between the excitement of going shopping and buying anything she wanted, and the disappointment that her father thought he had to buy her favor. Or that he didn't think she owned a nice enough dress.

The Captain's Table, though. One of the most expensive restaurants in town. It sat at the edge of Lake Michigan, a wall of windows on the waterside. That's all she knew; that's all you could see by driving by. She honestly didn't have anything appropriate for that kind of restaurant.

She tapped her finger on the card, thinking. Well, darn it, she wasn't going to embarrass herself because of her pride. And if she was going to accept the gift card, then she might as well enjoy the shopping.

Joe had told her this morning that she'd only be working

eight-hour days, but he'd be working overtime and then he'd have to go back to his security office to check in with his boss. She hadn't expected them to come back from their honeymoon and be so freaking busy all the time, but today she was glad. She didn't have to explain to him where she was going or why.

By the time she finished work at five, and hurried to find a new dress, Tori was both excited and nervous. What should she talk about? Should she try to keep Mom out of the conversation? What should she say if he asked about her? They hadn't spent that much time together—what if after a few hours in her company, Kane decided he was glad he'd left them?

Of course, at some point she'd have to tell him she couldn't see him anymore, that Lexie had refused to see him, that he'd never meet Ben. Somehow, she didn't think Kane would take that very well. She'd have to leave it for the end of the evening. And she couldn't think about it now, it only made her more nervous.

She checked her make-up and straightened her necklace. Smoothing the skirt of her black dress, she admired how svelte she looked in it. The neckline showed off her neck and shoulders —some of her assets, if she did say so herself—and the skirt swished as she walked. Assuming that the amount of the gift certificate was representative of how much Kane did not want to be embarrassed at her appearance at such an upscale establishment, Tori bought new shoes, a matching purse, and a luxurious black coat that came nearly to her ankles.

Excitement and guilt continued to wage war. These were the nicest clothes she'd ever owned. She'd never felt more beautiful. But the more she loved how she looked, the more convinced she was that *she* had just been bought as easily as she'd bought the clothes.

The only problem she could foresee with her attire was where in the world she'd be able to wear it all again. Certainly Joe wouldn't notice and ask. He had no idea yet what she owned and what she didn't. But a niggling voice in the back of her head suggested secrets were no way to build a good marriage. Even so, would he ever take her to place as nice as The Captain's Table if they were just getting by financially?

But she had tonight so, darn it, she was determined to enjoy it.

Checking her watch, Tori gathered up her things and locked up the house. It only took twenty minutes to get there, so she arrived on time. The Captain's Table was the kind of upper crust establishment that didn't have self-parking. Fighting embarrassment, Tori pulled up to the valet stand and smiled as she handed over her keys. Her Honda wasn't in bad shape for Northern Michigan, but the rust showed in the daylight. If she could *pretend* not to be embarrassed or unnerved at anything tonight, perhaps that would be enough.

The valet smiled back at her. A good sign.

Inside, the maître d' took her coat and escorted her to the table where Kane waited. Her father rose gracefully and leaned over to kiss her cheek. Tori pretended she was used to that type of greeting. He pulled out her chair and waited until she was seated to ask what she would like to drink. She pretended this was normal, too, and assured him water was fine. Kane nodded to the maître d' and sat down again.

A moment later, a glass of ice and a bottle of expensive water arrived along with a bottle of wine. Kane and the waiter went through all the motions of pouring, sniffing, tasting, and nodding that Tori had only seen in the movies. She reminded herself to keep smiling.

She tasted her wine when it was served and smiled graciously at both men. "Delicious, thank you," she said. She wasn't sure she really thought it was delicious, but it was the appropriate response. And she shouldn't be drinking if she was driving herself home. But the sip seemed necessary to keep up what was now feeling like a charade rather than a way to cope.

Kane smiled at her as the waiter left them. "You make me proud," he said.

Tori wondered why. Because she smiled and nodded a lot? She wanted to ask, but didn't know how to do so without sounding insecure. Instead, she managed to blush and reached for her water.

Kane watched her. "I don't know why I left you."

Tori didn't know why either. But she liked the idea that he wished he'd stayed with them, tried to make his marriage work. She wondered, if he had tried harder, if her parents would still be married.

"I should've taken you with me, no matter what she said. You're mine."

Okay, not really the line of thinking she'd been pursuing. She kept smiling. Her father must not understand that such a possessive tone wasn't normal.

He lifted his glass. "To family."

Tori lifted her glass to his, then drank a sip. Her romantic notions flew in the face of reality—at least as Kane perceived it. She should probably stop thinking about what might have been and start focusing on what might yet be. Maybe with time Lexie would bend, and Kane would learn how to act more appropriately toward his daughters.

"You haven't told your mother yet, have you?" he asked.

Tori's smile faltered. "Not exactly."

"Alexia will tell her."

It was a statement, not a question. Well, Lexie hadn't exactly made her feelings unclear. But how could Kane know that?

Tori wanted to argue that her sister always kept Tori's secrets, but she didn't know how to explain that to this man she hardly knew. She took another sip of water, needing an excuse to break eye contact. Her father stared at her as if he were reading her very soul. A bit unnerving.

"Loyalty well-placed is a good thing," he said. "Life would be easier on you if Dixie could continue in her make-believe world."

Tori wondered what that meant. If there was one thing Tori could not imagine her mother doing, it was playing make-believe. Not even when they were children.

Kane leaned toward her and lowered his voice a little. "Listen, Victoria, let's keep our relationship between us. Your sister and your mother don't understand. They don't understand me and they certainly don't understand you. Do they?"

Tori fiddled with her napkin and shook her head. She felt like she should speak, add to the conversation. But she was so uncomfortable, she didn't know what to say. Was he criticizing her family? She suppressed the fleeting thought that once again, it seemed to be on her shoulders alone to hold her family together. As always. And as always, to do so against everyone else's will.

"You've had a hard time, I know that."

Tori thought of the last couple weeks. "A hard time" was an understatement. "It wasn't so bad." She didn't want to add any more details than she'd already divulged. She certainly didn't want to bring up the possibility of super powers. That would really freak him out.

"You should've grown up safely ensconced in the arms of your family—"

What? Kane wasn't talking about her recent troubles. She tried not to frown—she did grow up safely. "I was—"

"But instead you were ripped away and kept away."

What was Kane was talking about? She was kept away from his family, yes, but they didn't live that far away, the other side of the city. They could've contacted her when she was older. So why hadn't they? Even if he'd been waiting until Mom couldn't interfere, she'd moved away from home five years ago.

"But I'm going to fix that now," Kane continued. "You just have to trust me." He smiled warmly at her. "Don't tell Dixie or your sister. Don't talk about me with your friends. Let's start over, father and daughter, and rebuild our relationship without anyone else's interference. Okay?"

Tori nodded. Not that she agreed so much as she didn't know how to disagree. Kane was kind of intimidating, even when he was being his version of warm and fuzzy. This was a little weirder than she'd anticipated, but...she didn't really have a frame of reference for reconnecting with a long-lost parent. So...maybe he was right. Lexie certainly hadn't taken kindly to Tori's wish to renew her father's acquaintance. And she did want to make a habit out of making her own decisions, something that her mother had taken from her for years.

They spent the rest of the evening eating expensive food and talking about Kane and his company and all the wonderful things he'd done. Curtis Enterprises had faltered for a bit after his father died, Kane said, but he had taken over and brought the revenues to record highs. He traveled around the world for business and had a second location in Las Vegas. When Tori commented that she'd never been there, Kane smiled and assured her she would see everything soon.

"In fact, come work for me," Kane said over dessert. "We have excellent benefits at Curtis Enterprises. You'll have your own office and a generous salary."

Tori blinked in surprise. "That's very kind, but I don't think I have the kind of skills that would—"

Kane waved his hand and interrupted. "You're my daughter. You'll get the best of everything. You can start next week."

Weird had just risen to a new level. Not only had Kane talked about himself for the entire evening, but he obviously had no idea what Tori did for a living. *She* didn't even know what she was good at, but she knew it wasn't something that deserved an office and a generous salary.

Come to think of it, he hadn't asked her a single question about herself tonight. He hadn't even congratulated her on her wedding. Did he know she was married? He must think she still lived with Lexie. But, wait, how did he know *that*?

"In fact, I have a block of magnificent condos facing West Bay. The view is excellent. I'll call the manager and tell him to set one aside for you."

Uh, that would be a *no*.

"Thank you, really, but no," Tori protested. "I'm not interested in moving right now." *Because I'm married* should've been the next words out of her mouth. But a lifetime of guarding her private life had turned a habit into an instinct. She suddenly didn't want to tell him anything.

Kane's face twitched. He seemed to be working hard to control himself. And thank goodness, because Tori didn't want to know how scary he'd look if he wasn't trying to control himself.

She felt goosebumps rise on her arms.

"Think about it," he said in a clipped voice. "I told you, I want to make up for lost time."

He held up his hand when Tori started to speak. "Just think about it. We'll talk later."

In minutes, the bill was paid and they were outside waiting for their cars to be brought around. Tori tried to smile up at Kane. She didn't want to end the evening with such hard feelings.

There were a few moments tonight when he seemed kind of wonderful—thoughtful, funny, interesting. She'd hoped to find out more about herself by finding out more about where she came from. But he was too controlling to feel comfortable around. Maybe he'd decide it was too much work and they'd drift apart as quickly as they'd gotten together.

Always hoping for the easy way out, she admitted to herself. If he was angry that she wouldn't move into his condos, imagine what he'd be like if she told him she'd promised Lexie to never see him again.

When the valet drove up in Kane's Mercedes, Kane walked

over to the driver side and tipped the man, then turned to Tori and waved. "I'll call you," he said. Then he got in and drove away.

Tori faltered in surprise, then waved at his taillights. She'd expected a hug or some kind of gesture. He'd kissed her hello, after all. She tamped down her disappointment. Maybe he wasn't the demonstrative type. That was fine.

She smiled at the valet who opened her car door for her. The man returned her smile with an easy grace, nodding to her, and wishing her a safe drive home.

Even a stranger was nicer to her than her father. Maybe Lexie was right. She should forget all about Kane Curtis and move on with her life.

9

Tori sighed and tried to focus on her work. It was Friday afternoon, and the numbers on the computer monitor blurred together as her mind drifted. The last couple days at work had been a combination of fun—pretending to dislike Joe—and boring. It seemed like Joe just gave her busy work. Create a spreadsheet using last year's numbers. Now do it again with this year's projections. Create one comparing the last five years. For heaven's sake, this couldn't possibly be real work that needed to be done. If so, this was *not* the job for her.

Nights were better because she and Joe had make-up sex. He pretended to be a tall, cool machine, buttoned up from the moment he arrived each morning. Not at all the fun guy she'd married. But the fun guy came home to her at night. She smiled a little, thinking about it. It was silly, pretending to have make-up sex, but it was fun. Maybe she'd have to get in a real fight with him at work and see what happened in the bedroom later.

She sighed and looked around the cubicles. Everyone, mostly women, hunched over their computers, not speaking to her. Since she couldn't sit at her old cubicle, she no longer sat by Joanie, her only friend. The woman in the cubicle to Tori's right glanced at her occasionally, but didn't show any signs of friend-ship. Even polite acknowledgement would be nice.

Joe asked her boatloads of questions about who knew whom and who argued with whom and tons of stuff Tori could have no way of knowing after four days. But she did her best to be friendly so people would want to open up, and so she could help Joe figure out what happened to Evan.

Today she'd finally gotten fed up and told him if he wanted gossip, he should talk to Joanie. Seeing the calculating look in his eye, she immediately regretted her words. Poor Joanie. She wouldn't like getting the third degree.

But it would be worth it to find the killer. Tori wanted to help but she was beginning to think she wasn't doing anything more than getting in the way. How many times in the past had Dixie thrown up her arms and told her, "You can't save the world, Victoria Joy. It'll just land you in trouble."

"You ready to go down?" Joanie's voice cut through Tori's thoughts.

She jumped in her chair and looked up.

"Sorry, I didn't mean to startle you," Joanie said. She looked at Tori with something akin to pity. "You hanging in there?"

Tori took a deep breath and shuffled some papers. "It would be a lot easier if people would talk to me," she said quietly so the woman next door couldn't hear, "instead of look at me like I might be the killer."

Joanie looked over her shoulder then leaned in closer to Tori. "He's fairly awful, isn't he?" she said in a low voice. "Joe. I mean, first of all, he walks around like he's got a stick up his butt. He's wound tighter than a cheap watch."

Tori looked around to make sure no one was listening, partic-ularly Joe. As much as she wanted to know what was going on, she tried to avoid gossip. She guessed she'd have to learn to see it as "work" while she was at this job.

"Then he starts asking me all about everyone in the office and do I think I know who did it." Joanie raised her hands to her shoulders. "As if *I'd* know."

Tori laughed in spite of herself, then pursed her lips in an effort to keep quiet. "But Joanie, you *do* know everything that goes on around here," she said.

Joanie laughed and stood up straight. "Yeah, well...are you ready yet? Don't tell me no one told you? The first Friday of every month we have cake for that month's birthdays. We didn't do it last week because of, you know." Joanie ran a finger over her throat and made a sucking sound.

Tori laughed in surprise, then covered her mouth with her hand. *"Joanie!"*

"If you don't laugh about it a little, it'll creep you right out," she said with a shrug. "Anyway, so long as you go down to the celebration, you can leave early. If you don't go down, you have to stay till five, so let's go."

Tori shook her head. A murder and a birthday party within a week. She couldn't keep up with this place. "Well, uh..." She looked at the work on her desk. "When does it start?"

"Four-thirty. You're going, so shut off your computer." Joanie tapped her hands impatiently on the counter that ran along the top of the half-sides of the cubicles.

"It's only 4:20," Tori stalled. Shouldn't she ask Joe first? No, wait, he'd left earlier. She couldn't remember where, but he'd made it sound like he wasn't coming back.

"We'll walk all the way around the building really slow then," Joanie said. "Come on, it's Friday. The work will still be here Monday."

It's not like she was accomplishing a lot anyway. Tori turned off her computer and followed Joanie to the kitchen where they pulled pop cans from the fridge. Walking and talking, Tori relaxed a bit. She wasn't a pariah. She had friends here.

She *was* a pariah.

Tori mingled with the others in the big conference room, picking at her cake and feeling like she didn't belong. She didn't. She was a temp. The temp who found her dead boss under her desk. Not really the sort of thing that made birthday cake conversation.

Joanie quickly got roped into a discussion about who was going to participate in the karaoke contest at the bar across the street. That left Tori pretty much standing alone against the wall, noticing people pretend not to notice her. She thought about wandering over to stand next to Joanie, but wondered at what point people would begin screaming and running for the door if she approached them.

She needed to be alone.

Tori moved some cake around on her plate, her appetite gone. She meandered over to the trashcan and dumped her plate. Wiping at the edges of her mouth with her napkin, she looked around the room and didn't catch anyone's eye. She dropped the napkin in the trash and snuck out the door.

Up at her desk, Tori glanced toward Joe's still-closed door, then grabbed her purse and coat. Hurrying to her car, she fought the urge to cry. Working undercover wasn't nearly as fun as she'd thought it would be. She needed her down comforter and one of her favorite chick flicks. And some hot chocolate with milk. And marshmallows.

Pulling out of the parking lot, she saw a car pull into traffic behind her and nearly broadside another vehicle. Great. A little snow sticks to the streets, and people forget how to drive. A few minutes later, Tori glanced in her rearview mirror. Was that the same car she'd noticed earlier? It was dark, blue or black maybe, and coated with the brown sludge that usually covered snow-country cars in the winter. She couldn't see much more in the fading light. At least he wasn't tailgating.

As she waited at a red light, her attention moved to a bill-board on the corner. A laughing, beautiful couple in expensive clothes celebrating with diamonds. She stared at the man in the billboard. Did he cheat on his wife? Did he cheat on his taxes? Was he interested in his kids? Did he put his career first? Was it worth trying to have a deep and meaningful relationship with him?

She was being silly. Kane Curtis might not be the kind of man Tori wanted to get to know better, and her mother and sister hadn't made wise choices with their first relationships, but Joe was warm and wonderful and decent and upstanding and...

The light turned green and Tori drove on. She brushed an errant tear from her face and turned the heater up. This was a seriously crappy day. Maybe it was hormones. Any excuse would make her feel a little better. All she wanted right now was to get home.

She made a left onto her street. A dark, dirty sedan turned left behind her. Tori stared at it in her mirror. She turned right into the alley that ran behind her house, and watched the mirror again. The car drove past. Tori let out her breath. She was losing her mind. No one was following her.

Pulling up to her parking space behind her house, she saw a big green SUV parked there. She stopped her car, looking around for the owner. Not only was he parked in her spot, but he'd parked at such an angle that he took up *both* spaces. Tori's knuckles tightened around her steering wheel. There was no place else she could safely and legally park back here. Aggra-vated, she hit the accelerator and drove on to the end of the alley. She'd have to look for street parking.

After circling for five minutes, she found a spot two and a half blocks away. Stinking lousy idiots who parked in other people's driveways! She was going to write a note and put it on his windshield. She stepped carefully around some frozen mud in the alley, cold and miserable, but nearly home. At least there wasn't much new snow. She hadn't worn her boots today.

A car passed her in the alley and Tori stepped aside to give it room to pass without splashing anything gross on her. That would really end her day on a high note. She looked up when she heard footsteps. A man walked her way, shoulders hunched against the cold. She nodded to him. She'd always thought if more people were friendly to their neighbors, there wouldn't be so much crime and hate.

After he passed, she opened her purse to pull out her keys. Suddenly, the strap pulled hard against her shoulder, knocking her to the ground. Her shoulder hit hard, but her arm tightened reflexively. She still had her purse, but so did her "neighbor." He yanked at the strap. Tori held on and was dragged a foot down the dirty asphalt. This could not be happening to her *again*.

Running steps caught her attention. "Help!" Her voice sounded garbled to her. She tried again. "Help m-uh—"

Tori felt the impact as the runner hit the mugger. She slid another few inches, then felt the purse strap release as the mugger let go. She struggled to her feet. Her eyes caught sight of a huge man in black throwing a punch at her assailant. She ran a few steps toward her back door, then turned again. The mugger was putting up a fight. Tori looked toward her house, then back again. She didn't want her rescuer to get beaten up. But could she help by...doing that thing she did? She hoped she could figure out *how*.

She ran, fumbling to get the right key, and unlocked the door. Leaving it open a crack, she ran back to the fight. She looked around, thankful for once that so much trash accumulated in the alley. She picked up a broken Crock Pot and swung it at the mugger.

"Get out of here, you jerk!" she screamed.

She saw the big man stop and look at her in surprise. The mugger pulled back his arm for another punch. Tori connected the ceramic pot with his fist. The man grunted and started to run. Everything that had been simmering inside, every bit of fear and anger and confusion, boiled to the surface. Tori took off after him. She swung the Crock Pot by its cord and missed.

She tried to catch up to the would-be thief. She wanted him punished. Now. Slipping on the damp asphalt, she hefted the pot over her head and threw it at him. She felt an animal sense of satisfaction when she saw it bounce off his shoulder.

"Yeah, you better run!" she yelled. "I'm calling the police!" Tori remembered Halloween Zorro and his claim to be part of the Neighborhood Watch. "I'll send the Neighborhood Watch after you, too!"

The mugger snatched up a piece of debris and turned toward Tori just as she felt strong arms wrap around her from behind. Her huge protector spun her around, her feet barely touching the ground, and pulled her tightly against his hard body. She felt something slam into his back as he pushed her head down under his chin.

He didn't even grunt.

The big man's body wrapped around hers, keeping her safe, but Tori struggled against him. More than anything right now, she wanted to do some serious bodily harm to that, that...*jerk* who'd tried to rob her. Only she wasn't thinking *jerk*. She made a mental note to put a dollar in the Cursing Jar.

She heard him running away. Still struggling against her savior, she shouted, "When I get my hands on you, you're going to regret the day you were born!" Tori looked down as her foot banged against something. A broken piece from a cement block wall, big as a cantaloupe. That's what the mugger had thrown? How was this guy not hurt?

"It's okay," the big man said, his voice deep and rich and slightly metallic. "You're okay."

"Let me go! I'm calling the police," she said, shaking in righteous indignation, all but ignoring her rescuer, focused only on justice. "He should be in jail!"

"He'll get what he deserves soon enough," the man said, his voice penetrating Tori's consciousness enough to sound familiar. "Right now we need to get you—"

A man's scream came from near the end of the alley. Tori and the big man turned toward the sound in time to see the mugger crash into the pavement as if from a fall. He bounced up and down on the ground several times at the edge of the light of a streetlamp, all the while screaming in pain. The last bounce tossed him away from the light.

Squinting, Tori tried to make out what was happening, but all she could see were shadows. The man flew up in the air again and came down hard. His last scream ended abruptly.

Tori's hand flew to her mouth to hold back a scream of her own. She felt herself crushed up against the man who'd saved her and she turned and threw her arms around his waist. *Did she just see a man die?*

"Is he—is he—?" She felt her teeth beginning to chatter. A chill climbed up through the cold pavement and sucked the warmth out of her bones.

Tori looked back. The man at the end of the alley remained still. The shadows didn't. Tori felt ice in her veins. She couldn't move, unable to pull her gaze away. *God, please don't let him be dead. I didn't mean for him to be dead. I just wanted him arrested.*

"Go home, get inside," the big man said.

Tori just stood there, frozen with her arms around his waist. She didn't think she could move. Not even if her life depended on it.

"Tori, go!"

At the sound of her name, she looked up. His face was hidden in his hooded coat. She *knew* she knew that voice. "Zorro?"

He'd saved her again. She'd needed him and he'd come. She

buried her head in his coat and started to cry. Her arms wrapped even more tightly around his waist. She felt her relief mingle with all the other emotions of the last several days and felt her cries merge into gut-wrenching sobs. A robbery at gunpoint. Learning she had some kind of strange power. A man murdered and left under her desk. A mugging. Maybe even another murder. Too much horror. Too much.

She felt him pick her up and her arms moved to wrap around his neck. The same feeling of safety she felt with Joe crashed over her now. That's what she wanted, what she *needed*—Joe. She struggled in Zorro's arms and he put her down near her back door.

"I appreciate your help, I really do." She tried to keep the tears out of her voice. "But I'm going to go inside and call the police and my husband." Her voice cracked on the last word. "Do the police know about you? Do I tell them you were here or...?" She trailed off, not sure what the protocol was for being rescued by a superhero.

"I've already contacted them," he said.

Tori heard the metallic quality in his voice again. He had something disguising his voice. Curious, she asked, "What's your name?"

He let a brief smile slip through his serious expression. "Superhero X, at your service."

"You're Zorro, right? We met at Halloween?"

"The same."

"You told me then that you patrol this neighborhood, but I've never seen you."

"That's part of the point."

Tori thought about her situation with the SLU. She didn't understand this whole "super power" thing, but she couldn't pretend it didn't exist. If she had someone to help her, someone *not* in the police department, someone who understood...

"You should get inside," Superhero X said. "You're shaking.

When the police get here, they'll knock on your door. I'll keep watch until they arrive. Okay?"

He was so nice. Maybe he'd help her.

He opened her door all the way and gently pushed her inside.

"If I need you, how do I contact you?" she blurted out before the door closed.

He paused, as if considering how to reply. He glanced at the outside of the door. "Hang a wreath or something on this hook. Then wait for me in Gaffney Park."

Tori let him close the door. She stood in the mudroom shivering. He'd help her. A real superhero would help her figure all this out. What a relief.

She pulled out her cell phone to call Joe. She hoped wherever he was, he'd answer. She wanted him home. Now. She felt safer around him. Kind of like she had around Superhero X, but better.

Joe's number went to voice mail. Tori did her best to keep her voice from wobbling when she told him there'd been a mugging and could he please come home as soon as possible. She ended the call and tried to think of what to do next. She really didn't want to be alone. She couldn't call her mother, and she didn't want Lexie to bring Ben over, not with what was happening outside. She looked out the back window, and made sure the door was locked. Who could she call?

She found the number she wanted in her phone's address book and dialed. "Hannah?"

HANNAH ARRIVED before the police did, for which Tori was especially grateful.

"My dear!" Hannah hugged Tori hard as soon as she walked in the door. "You poor thing! Are you okay? You're shivering.

Come, let's get you warmed up. I'll make us some tea while we wait for Joe."

In minutes, Tori was wrapped in blankets and motherly love in front of a struggling-to-catch fire, a hot mug clenched in her hands. Hannah sat next to her, patting her feet and asking questions. Tori told her everything that happened, every detail. Her mother-in-law was the easiest person to talk to she'd ever met.

Thank you, God. I didn't know I needed her, but thank you for giving me Hannah.

Hannah tsked and patted Tori's blanket-covered feet again. "You tell the police everything you told me. It will help them find the...the other person."

Tori gave her a wry look. "Exactly, Hannah. I can't even explain it in a way that sounds believable."

"You will. Joe will help."

Tori started to ask how Joe could help when he hadn't even been there, but a knock on the back door interrupted.

"That'll be the police," Hannah said, getting up. "I'll get it. You stay here."

Tori heard voices, several voices. How many people did it take to get her statement? She blew on her tea. She was getting to be a real pro at witnessing a crime. Too bad it wouldn't be useful on her resume.

A minute later, Hannah ushered two uniformed police officers and—oh, great—Detective Knox and Detective Paredes into the living room. Did they cover *every* crime in the city? They were going to start thinking of her as a suspect instead of a witness if she kept popping up everywhere they went.

Tori nodded to them. "Officers. Detectives."

Detective Paredes motioned to the uniforms to go ahead. One took out a pad and asked Tori a dozen questions about what had happened. They seemed satisfied enough with her answers. They shook the detective's hand and left the way they came.

Tori sighed in relief. That was easier than she'd anticipated. Detective Knox sat down in a chair near Tori.

"Hi, Tori, I'm glad you're okay."

Tori nodded and tried to add a polite smile. "Thanks, Detective."

"Casey, really." She motioned with her hand. "Well, Detective Knox in front of uniformed officers, but you can call me Casey when we're alone."

Apparently Hannah didn't count.

"Call me Art," said the other detective. "Why don't you tell us again what happened?"

Tori frowned. "You just heard me." Her unease returned. What did they want from her? Tori looked to Hannah, sitting beside her.

Hannah patted her hand. "You can trust them, honey."

That's what all law-abiding citizens say until the circumstances twist unexpectedly. Tori swallowed. Okay, just do what they ask and they'll go away. She hoped. So long as they didn't ask her again if she wanted to come work for them. Not in front of Hannah.

Tori began her retelling of tonight's events. But this time, Art and Casey interrupted a lot more. They asked her questions about the strength of the mugger, whether he said anything, under his breath or out loud, if she noticed any strange smells emanating from him. It dawned on Tori that they were trying to find out if her attacker had any super powers. Holy cow!

She looked at Hannah, then looked pointedly at Casey.

"It's okay," Casey said, "Hannah knows there are people in Double Bay with superhuman abilities. You won't shock her."

Tori looked at Hannah in surprise. "Really?" Hmm, maybe here was another person she could talk to about her situation. Her nerves eased a bit and she answered more questions, trying to remember everything. She told them that Superhero X had intervened so quickly that he probably knew more about what happened than she did.

"We've talked to him," Art said. "But we wanted to hear your account as well."

Tori tried to read Art's bland expression. She suspected they not only wanted to hear her side, but they wanted to know if she had used her power tonight. Even if Hannah knew all about superheroes, Tori had no intention of sharing her secret with her mother-in-law. Not tonight anyway.

"I didn't do anything," she said clearly, hoping they got the point and didn't ask any more questions. "I threw a Crock Pot at him. That's all." She'd tried to do more, but when she yelled at the guy to get away from them, he didn't listen.

Tori saw Hannah cover her mouth with her hand. She grinned at her. "It does sound pretty ridiculous, doesn't it? The only time I've been glad we have such poor trash service."

Tori heard a noise at the other end of the house. The back door slammed. "Joe!" She hoped it was Joe. She wanted everyone else to go away. Well, maybe not Hannah, but no more police. She was getting tired of running into "Call me Art" and "Call me Casey" all the time. And she really, *really* needed Joe to hold her.

Joe rushed into the living room. Hannah got out of the way as Tori threw herself into her husband's arms. Warmth and comfort and peace flooded through her. And the tears she'd been holding back spilled out. She squeezed him tight. Everything would be okay now.

A couple seconds later, she prodded his shoulder. "Joe!" she coughed.

He immediately loosened his grip. "Sorry! Sorry, baby. I was so worried."

"You don't know your own strength, sweetie," she said as he held her in slightly less than a bear hug.

Art coughed.

"I'm going to go make you two some dinner. I assume neither

of you have eaten." Hannah got up and left without waiting for a response.

Joe pulled back enough to look into her face. He looked concerned but not fearful. Good. She hadn't wanted her voice mail to scare him. Even though the whole thing had scared her.

"Are you okay?" he asked.

"I'm fine, really," she assured him. "Someone helped me." Did Joe know? Certainly he must if his mother knew. She looked questioningly at Casey, who nodded. "A superhero named Super-hero X was there. He kept me from getting hurt."

Joe grunted and held her close again.

A moment later, Art cleared his throat and said, "Well, this is touching but uncomfortable. Casey, any more questions?"

"We'll call you if we think of any," she said, looking from Tori to Joe.

Joe let go of Tori long enough to shake the detectives' hands. Tori did the same, and Joe ushered them out.

Whew. Glad that's over. Note to self: try to avoid the police for more than a few days at a time.

"Mom said spaghetti will be ready in fifteen minutes," Joe said when he returned. He sat on the couch next to her and pulled her, blankets and all, onto his lap. "You're a magnet for trouble, aren't you?" He rubbed her back.

"Mmm," she said. This was nice. Really nice. "Only since I met you."

They both chuckled. Then silence reigned as they watched the fire.

"Joe, I assume you have TV trays from your bachelor days?" Hannah looked around the living room. Joe nodded toward a corner and she pulled two from a cart.

"Mom, I'll do that. You've done enough for us already. Thanks so much for dinner."

Tori let them argue lovingly about dinner and Hannah's

ability to walk home alone. She nodded when Hannah said she'd call Tori tomorrow.

A few minutes later, Joe let go of her long enough to bring them each a steaming plate of pasta.

"Think we can turn on the TV?" Tori asked. "My thoughts are too loud right now."

They ate and watched a sit-com in companionable silence.

"I'm sorry," she said softly in the middle of it.

Joe leaned back against the couch and reached over to brush her hair away from her cheek. "For what?"

Tori shrugged and left her gaze on the TV. Why had so many weird things happened to her so suddenly? Weird *scary* things. She didn't understand it, but she wondered if somehow she was to blame.

Joe grunted and pulled her closer. "If you mean you haven't enjoyed being involved in three felonies in two weeks, I think you can be forgiven."

Tori snuggled closer to him.

"You just might be one of the strongest women I know," Joe said, his lips near her hair.

Tori grunted. "By being a magnet for trouble?"

Joe chuckled. "Well, the best magnets are the strongest. Maybe you've discovered a latent talent."

Tori froze. Was this the opening she was looking for? He knew about superheroes. He didn't seem to think they were weird. Would he be okay with a superhero wife though?

Joe laughed at something on the TV. The horrible evening was turning out okay. She relaxed in his arms. His voice and his touch continued to build a comforting hedge around her soul, protecting her from the evil outside. Maybe she shouldn't make things worse. She'd find a way to tell him tomorrow.

Please, God, don't let this destroy my marriage.

JOE HELD Tori as she fell asleep in his arms watching TV. He should tell her. If tonight wasn't an invitation on a silver platter...

But he didn't want to make a bad night worse. She needed a good night's sleep to deal with the craziness of finding out she'd married a superhero.

His thoughts turned to the last few hours. This afternoon he'd gotten the feeling he should get out on patrol. He checked out the park where there had been a rash of muggings lately. Nothing. Then he heard that voice again. *Protect her.*

He didn't know how he knew to come home, but when he ran up the alley and saw Tori being attacked, it was all he could do not to rip the arms off the guy and paint his name with the mugger's blood. The only reason he let him go was to get Tori safely locked into the house.

What would've happened if he'd given chase instead? Would the man still be alive? Who or what would he have found at the end of the alley? The dead man was the only one down there by the time Joe arrived.

The crushed face, the broken limbs at wrong angles, the blood. He shook his head and tried to put it out of his mind. This was the worst part of his job, but he had to deal with it.

Thank you, God, for protecting Tori. Thank you for...is that voice you? Are you the one helping me to know when and where to be? I guess I know the answer to that, don't I?

Joe prayed for peace, for distance from the images of dead people. He focused on the sci-fi movie and tried to lose himself on another planet. An hour later, when he felt himself nod and his eyes close, he turned off the TV and picked up his wife. He tucked her into bed, leaving her in her sweats only because it was a cold night and she was more asleep than awake. He looked forward to the summer when they could sleep together naked.

As Joe brushed his teeth, he thought about the three crimes Tori had been involved in. They must be coincidental. But he didn't believe in so much coincidence. Normally. Nothing had been normal in his life since he'd met Tori.

So how did she fit into this picture? Could someone be after her? Who? Why? She was a temp—where else had she worked? At the orphanage? Joe's mind churned with possibilities, coming up with possible links and discarding them, looking for loose threads to follow. He worked the puzzle from every angle his tired brain could come up with. No ideas enlightened him.

He got under the covers with his wife, her head near his shoulder. She looked peaceful for the first time in hours. He brushed his hand over her hair. Nice. Curly and soft. He did it again. She sighed.

Leaning closer, Joe kissed the top of her head. She smelled warm and wonderful. Sleepily, he wondered if he'd made the wrong decision about getting married. Maybe he was the reason she was in danger. He couldn't think of why, though. Too tired.

He snapped off the light and relaxed in the darkness. He'd tell her tomorrow. They'd get it all out in the light of day and deal with it. Somehow, they'd work it out.

Tomorrow.

Tori woke up slowly. She'd been waking up and falling back asleep for a while now. She figured it must be about time to actually get up. Something warm pressed against her back. She smiled and leaned toward it. "Morning, Joe."

Meow. The warmth moved. Snickers.

Tori twisted under the covers to face the cat. "Morning, Snickers. Where's Joe?"

Snickers purred and curled up close to Tori's face.

"You don't know, huh?" Tori moved the covers just enough to scratch Joe's cat behind the ears, then she pulled her hand back in. She loved waking up warm and toasty under a ton of blankets on a cold winter's morning. She yawned and stretched. Actually, it didn't feel that cold. Joe must've already turned the heat up.

She moved her head to check the alarm clock: 9:27. Holy cow! She'd never slept so late. No wonder Joe was already up. She should get up, too. They weren't getting a lot of "just the two of us" time, and she didn't want to waste any.

Snickers put his paw on Tori's nose. Tori giggled. It was soft and it tickled. She'd never had a pet before. Snickers was so cuddly and sweet, she realized she'd been missing out. She petted the cat and talked to him for a few more minutes, stretched again, and decided she really should get up.

Then she remembered. She'd promised herself she'd talk to Joe today. She sighed.

"I can do this," she mumbled to herself as she went to the bathroom. "It'll be fine. He won't mind. He might even think it's kind of cool." She remembered what he said about her being a magnet for trouble. She wondered if that could actually be true. A question she'd have to ask Superhero X. If you had a super power, did you just "find" problem situations to help with? How else had Superhero X found her last night?

Wait, so did she find Evan for a reason? But he was already dead. Was there something she could've done? And how would she have known what to do?

Tori was so focused on her thoughts that she didn't notice the note until she was drying her hands. She pulled it from the mirror and read the message. Her shoulders sagged. Joe was out on some emergency with work. He hoped he'd be home tonight, but he might be gone through tomorrow. Lots of love.

She sighed again. No point being angry, but she didn't remember him being gone all the time when they were dating. Maybe his company didn't have that many jobs in November and December.

Well, since he wasn't here... She grabbed the paperback she was reading from her nightstand and curled back into the still-warm bed. Snickers continued to purr. Tori grinned and joined him. "Purrrr, Snickers. Purr." She laughed. Snickers thrust his left ear under Tori's fingers and purred louder. Tori laughed again. There were worse things than a Saturday morning with nothing to do but read in bed with a friendly cat.

By Sunday morning, Tori had finished her book, baked some

cookies for Joe and his co-workers, and done a couple loads of laundry. She called Lexie to see if she wanted to walk to church together.

"We're skipping today. I have homework I need to do," Lexie said.

Tori tried to decide if Lex was still irritated with her. "Want to drive to lunch together?" They went to their parents' house twice a month after church for a family meal. They drove together unless one of them had some other errand to run.

"I'll meet you there. I don't know what time I'm leaving. Depends on how my homework goes."

Yeah, she's still mad. Totally lame excuse.

Tori tried not to sound miffed as she agreed and hung up. If anyone needed a nice sermon about controlling their tongue and their bad attitude today, it was her. She was cranky from hormones, cranky from Joe being gone with only the briefest phone call last night to say he wouldn't be home till tonight, and cranky because her cranky sister was still upset about Tori seeing Kane.

She'd tried to tell her that it was a polite dinner to say thanks, but no thanks. At least that's how Tori had now decided to look at it. The fact that Lexie might be right about Tori originally wanting to get to know Kane, well, that didn't matter because she didn't want to get to know him anymore. He was kind of weird.

She cuddled Snickers for a few minutes—someone loved her —and then walked to church. Another funny thing about her new life, Joe's dad Owen was the pastor of a little church a few blocks over. Tori and Lexie had said several times over the last couple years that they should give it a try. But with their hectic lives and multiple jobs and a-baby-becoming-a-toddler, they never made the time.

After Tori met Joe, she started going with him and really liked it. The people were friendly, and many were neighbors she didn't know, plus one or two she did. Lexie and Ben started coming a few weeks ago, too, which made the experience feel all the more like a big family.

In a city this size, it was kind of funny that Tori and Lexie lived just a few blocks from each other, and Joe and his parents lived just a few blocks from each other, all in the same neighborhood. Seemed like everyone else she knew was fairly scattered. She liked the community feel of her neighborhood, despite its less-than-appealing first impression.

The walk over in the cold, fresh air made Tori feel better. When she arrived, Hannah and Owen both gave her big hugs. Tori sat with Hannah and Joe's sister Melissa, a high school senior, same age as Tori's little sister Samantha. Owen's sermon wasn't on controlling your bad attitude, but it was good. The music was wonderful as always. Afterward, Hannah asked her over for lunch, but Tori told her she had plans with her family.

"Good," Hannah said. "I just wanted to make sure you weren't spending the day alone." She gave Tori a penetrating, motherly stare. "Are you feeling all right after Friday?"

Tori assured her mother-in-law that she was fine, not sure if she was lying or not, and hugged her goodbye. As she walked home, she waved to a few neighbors, some of whom were also walking home from church. Like her, many people hadn't buttoned up their coats. The midday air was significantly warmer, maybe even the high 40s today. She sighed and smiled. "Thanks for a good day, God."

Driving through her old neighborhood to her parents' house made the differences in the communities even more apparent. Not only were the streets cleaner where her parents lived, but the snow was cleaner, too. As if you could keep dirt from appearing if you had enough money. The houses were farther apart, the streets less crowded, the cars newer. And hardly anyone walked anywhere. Tori had known three of her neighbors when she lived there. Three. In six years. There was something wrong with that.

She parked in the driveway, next to Kevin's ten-year-old

Chevy. Lexie would have to park in the street. Tori clamped down on her uncharitable thoughts and apologized to God. Hardly out of church an hour. For goodness' sake.

She took a deep breath, knocked, and walked in. She hoped everyone here was in a good mood today. Yells rather than people welcomed her.

"Are you *blind*?"

"What an idiot!"

Tori peeked in the living room and relaxed. The football team Kevin and Dad were rooting for obviously wasn't doing well. Even with the Super Bowl a couple weeks away, Tori really, truly, honestly couldn't care less. She liked the party food; otherwise, it was just another reality TV show.

Samantha peeked out of the kitchen. "Hey, Tori! It's Tori."

"Hey, Samantha," Tori called as she hung up her coat and pulled off her boots. "Hi, Mom!"

"Dinner's almost ready. Is Lexie with you?" asked Samantha.

Tori shook her head. "Driving separately."

"I think she just pulled up," Kevin yelled from the living room.

Dixie organized her family into washing up and sitting down on her timetable like a general commanding her troops. It didn't matter what was happening on TV, or who was bleeding, Dixie made sure meals were served hot. Now Tori only had to keep Evan and the mugger a secret for another couple of hours and the afternoon would be a success.

"I don't understand why you and Joe don't move to another neighborhood," Dixie said as she passed the salad. "Will you pass me the potatoes, dear?" she said to Danny. "He knows you were mugged there a few months ago. And I've heard stories about drug dealers down there now. At least Lexie is working at getting out."

Calm. Just stay calm or it'll get a whole lot worse before this meal is through. She wished Joe were here. He was so good at light-hearted dinner conversation.

Tori spooned some salad onto her plate and passed it to her brother. It wasn't very often Lexie got to play "the good daughter." Even though she wasn't aware of any immediate plans her sister had to move, Tori should let Lexie enjoy the moment. "Joe's house is perfectly safe, Mom. There are three locks on the front door and two on the back. Plus an alarm system." That she kept forgetting to use.

Tori glanced at her dad as she took the potatoes from Dixie. He met her eyes and looked away, not saying anything. That meant he wished she'd move, too.

"Someone died at her work, too." Lexie stabbed a piece of meat from the platter without looking at Tori.

If looks could kill, Tori would be at the center of yet another murder investigation. What was Lexie thinking? Mom was such a worrywart, she'd never forget this. Of course, since Lexie was mad at her, that just might be the point.

"Really? Do the police have any clues yet?" Kevin asked. "Did they find fingerprints on your desk? Or run a toxicology test on the body? Maybe they should find out if he had a mistress."

Tori tried not to smile at him and mouthed *shut up*. Kevin was on his way to being a doctor, but he could be a real clown. He'd get her laughing about disgusting forensic stuff and then Mom would be mad, thinking they were mocking the dead or something. At twenty-one, he was a junior at the University of Northern Michigan, pre-med and making his parents incredibly happy. Under other circumstances, this might make a girl hate her little brother. But Tori and Kevin had been close since he was born. And they had the same tastes in TV. They'd been known to spend twelve hour days watching *CSI* and *Law and Order* marathons.

"Kevin, you're so gross." Samantha filled her plate with salad and passed the potatoes without taking any. She planned to go to

UNM in the fall, but as a fashion design major. She was the most girly-girl of anyone Tori knew. Slightly annoying, but still her little sister, so she loved her anyway.

"Yes, Kevin, you are," Dixie said, passing Tori the salmon. "Take some fish, Sam. You need some protein."

"Mo-om," Samantha moaned and rolled her eyes. Trademark move. As the baby of the family, she'd figured out *in utero* how to manipulate her mother, which meant she could manipulate everyone else as well.

"I'm sorry. *Samantha*, take some fish," Dixie repeated.

Sam had been a perfectly fine name until she'd become friends with a girl named Mercedes, also planning to major in fashion design, and suddenly *Samantha* was born. Tori hoped she wouldn't try to be one of those single-name super stars. If she did, Tori decided she'd have to start calling her Sam in public, just to keep her grounded.

"Do the police know anything yet?" Danny asked.

Tori hated to see her dad worry. She took a big bite of potatoes so she couldn't talk. She shrugged her shoulders at him and shook her head.

"Po-leee!" Ben screamed in delight. "Woo-ooo, woo-ooo!"

"Yes, that's right," Lexie crooned. "That's the sound a police car makes. Eat some fish, baby."

"Fish," he said, using his fingers to push some onto his spoon. "I waw un teatrhuh cackuh." He brought the spoon up, dropped half of the contents into his bib, and chewed seriously as he looked around the table.

"He wants cheese and crackers? What?" Kevin laughed.

"Guess who Tori met this week?" Lexie asked her mother.

Tori choked on her food and grabbed for her water glass. "Lexie!" she gasped. Really? Enough was enough!

Dixie looked from one daughter to the other, a vigilant mama bear ready to attack at the slightest provocation. The whole family stopped for a moment, watchful and quiet. Even Ben stopped babbling and stared at his grandma.

"Tell her, Tori," Lexie goaded. "You said it's not a big deal. So tell her."

"Tell me what?" Dixie demanded.

Tori glared at her sister. How could she do this? Their mother would go ballistic and Lexie knew it. Tori closed her eyes briefly and leaned back in her chair. She studied her sister. This was her way of making sure Tori never saw Kane again—to have their mother make sure of it. She shook her head. It wouldn't work. She was a big girl now. She wasn't letting Mom run her life any more.

To prove it, she turned to Dixie and said, "I saw our father."

Dixie stared at her, confusion in her features.

"Kane Curtis," Tori said. "We had dinner."

Dixie's face went from a healthy pink to deathly white to a furious red in a single moment. "No!" she roared. "I forbid it! I for*bid* it, do you hear me, young lady?"

"Nana?"

Ben's whimper cut at Tori's heart. Dixie didn't seem to have heard it, which kind of scared Tori. She looked at her sister. "Take him to the kitchen," she muttered between clenched teeth.

Both satisfaction and dismay washed over Lexie's features. She picked up the highchair, toddler and all, and fled to the kitchen.

Danny put his hand over Dixie's fist, a bold move as she was still clutching her fork. "Honey, let's discuss this after dinner."

"No! We will *not* discuss this!" Dixie screamed. "We are not having this conversation! Victoria Joy Lewis, you will *not* see him again! Are we clear?"

It had been over fifteen years since Kane's name had been mentioned in this house. Tori suddenly remembered why. Her mother turned into...*someone else*...when she talked about her ex-husband. The maternal family organizer disappeared, replaced by an angry, bitter ogre bent under a load of hatred.

"*Are we clear?*"

Tori stared at her plate. She loved her mother, and she wanted to make her happy. But agreeing with her now wouldn't make Dixie happy. It would simply end this conversation. Whether or not Tori agreed not to see Kane again, Dixie would never look at her the same. So why not be a grown-up and make her own decision, stop letting her mother tell her what to do?

Without looking at anyone at the table, Tori picked up her plate and headed for the kitchen.

"Answer me, young lady!"

"Tori," Danny called, "come back here, please."

Tori kept walking. She hated every step, but she kept going. She wanted to tell Dad that it had nothing to do with him. She didn't want to hurt him, but she knew she was cutting his heart out. She wanted to tell him that no one could ever replace him. But she kept walking.

In the kitchen, Lexie stood still as stone, a stricken expression on her face. "Tori, I—I didn't—I forgot how—"

Tori shook her head. At the movement, she noticed her eyes were full of water. Her mascara would run if she cried. She put her plate on the counter and gently blotted the corners of her eyes. Her appetite was gone. She laid the napkin on the counter and turned to leave.

"Tori, wait!" Lexie jumped and opened a cupboard. Taking out a plastic container, she scraped Tori's dinner into it, snapped the lid on, and pressed it into Tori's hand.

Lexie hated to be compared to her mother, but the food was such a Dixie thing. As if somehow it would help if everyone had enough to eat.

Tori kissed the top of Ben's head and walked out without looking at her sister. No sound came from the dining room. She wondered if no one thought she would leave. Had she never asserted herself before? Slipping on her boots, she thought about it. No. She didn't think she had. She grabbed her coat and walked out.

Why did standing up for herself have to be so difficult?

And so lonely?

TORI SAVED THE FILE, printed it, and emailed it to Joe. Then she took the printed spreadsheet to his office. She knocked and opened the door.

"Here's the annualized—" She stopped and frowned as she watched Joe jump up from under the desk and sit down.

"Is this a bad time?" she asked. "I can come back."

"No, it's fine. You startled me." Joe reached for the spreadsheet. "I was just…" His voice trailed off as he looked over the numbers. "This can't be right."

Tori walked to the side of his desk and looked over his shoulder. "What can't be right?" She tried not to be upset with him. He'd warned her he'd be working long hours on this case. But she hadn't seen him all weekend, and he'd left early this morning. Now she had to pretend she didn't know him.

She stared at his profile. Strong jaw, clean-shaven cheeks, thick hair—though with too much hair gel. He said he tried to look different when he went undercover so no one in his real life would recognize him. Apparently the hair gel and tie were the extent of his disguise. Wasn't too much hair gel a villainous faux pas? She should look around the office for someone with hair from the 1960s. And a thick mustache.

Or maybe she should do some non-prime-time-TV research on bad guys. It'd be nice to know if her life was in danger, or just her sanity. She turned her attention back to Joe's computer.

Joe clicked over to his email and brought up the file she'd just sent. Opening it, he clicked on various cells, checking her formulas. Tori set her teeth. She'd done exactly as he'd asked. She *bet* he was going to say this is not what he'd asked for. She *bet* he was going to ask her to re-do it another way. This undercover finance work sucked.

"The formulas look okay, but there's something wrong with this number." He opened a file on his desk and pulled out a different spreadsheet.

Tori went to stand next to him and looked over his shoulder. He smelled so good. She wanted to put her hand on his shoulder, run her fingers through his hair, kiss his neck. But she'd left the door open. Grr.

"Yeah, look, here is the number from the original spreadsheet. It's different than this one." Joe pointed to the paper, then to his screen.

"The nine rule," Tori said. Why hadn't she closed the door? She could've at least gotten a quick hug. Or put her hand on his back as she leaned closer. That probably wouldn't help people continue to believe their charade though.

"What?" Joe turned his whole body to face her, his eyes boring into hers. "What did you say?" he whispered fiercely.

If she didn't love and trust him, Joe would almost scare her right now. What was the problem? All accountants knew about the nine rule. "The nine rule," she said again. He must have his mind someplace else that he didn't remember it.

"Evan emailed me about it that last day. He was always reminding me of the obvious. I don't know what kind of temps he had before..." Tori choked. She hadn't known Evan very well, but it still brought tears to her eyes that he was dead. Violently dead.

Joe grabbed her forearm. "Show me the email. Now. Please."

Tori pulled her arm away, trying to understand what Joe was really asking. "I don't have it. I deleted it. Everyone knows that rule. If a number doesn't add up properly, you divide the difference by nine to see if it's a transposition error. I didn't have to be reminded," she said with more attitude than was necessary. Maybe if anyone around here thought she was smart and good at her job, she wouldn't feel the need to prove it.

Joe's gaze became unfocused. He didn't look like he was thinking about the spreadsheet anymore.

"Joe?" Tori whispered. "What?"

He blinked and met her gaze again. "Tori, I looked through all of his outgoing emails. I didn't find one to you or anyone else reminding you of a transposition issue. Can you remember *exactly* what it said? It could be important."

Tori thought about it for a moment. Yeah, it was only one line. There was no more to it than that. "He'd sent me another email just before, late Wednesday. Then this one was dated about midnight Wednesday. It said, 'If I'm not here tomorrow, remember the nine.' That's all."

Joe took a deep breath. He pulled a notebook from his pocket and wrote down what she said. "Do you remember if he used the word nine or the number nine?"

"The word," Tori replied. "I remember thinking it's weird when a numbers person spells out a number."

He looked at her, his mouth open a little, his face pale.

"This is important," Tori whispered. "Why?"

Joe shook himself out of his headspace. "I've got to call IT."

"Tell me." Tori tried not to beg. "I want to help." I want to help more than working on stupid spreadsheets.

Joe shook his head at her. He started to say something else, but IT picked up on the other end. "I need to access some emails sent last Wednesday," he said. They must've put him on hold because he looked up and said, "I just got an email from Mark that they also want to see last year's information on the reality show deals. You only used this year's information. I'll forward it to you."

Tori started to tell him Mark only asked for this year's information, but Joe interrupted with, "Yeah, I'm still here."

Tori ground her teeth. Why had she agreed to stay and work for these nincompoops? She closed her eyes. They were going to be the death of her. Her eyes popped open. Don't even think that! Someone around here really was a killer.

Joe was busy talking to IT, so Tori figured she'd been dismissed. Yup, today it was going to be easy to pretend she disliked him. She'd think of the people above him who were filtering down information in bits and pieces, and point her dislike of them Joe's way.

She had to pretend to dislike him. It was the only way she'd get through the day without throwing herself in his arms and begging him to kiss her. She wanted to hug him and tell him about yesterday's terrible family dinner. She wanted to be held and soothed and reassured that it would all turn out okay. She wanted Joe to be the husband he was on their honeymoon.

Tori walked out and closed the door. Heads turned. Okay, so maybe that was a little more like a slam. She marched to her desk. She didn't care what the others thought. They didn't like her anyway. As far as she could tell, none of her co-workers showed even the slightest hint that might indicate killing instincts. She didn't particularly care what they thought of her if they weren't planning on taking her to lunch. Or taking her out.

"Being an idiot, is he?" Joanie asked. She paused at Tori's desk with a fresh cup of coffee.

Tori growled in her throat. She threw the papers down on her desk and slammed her body into the chair.

Joanie chuckled. "I don't know why they hired him. I guess they had to do something, but still. It irks me that he's a temp and he can tell me what to do. I've been here nineteen years. I'm old enough to be his mother!"

Tori swiveled in her chair and let her frustration out. "I'm telling you, if he doesn't figure out what he wants, there's going to be another murder around here! How difficult is it to decide how you want to see the numbers? Maybe I should just ask him what

he needs to know and *I'll* decide how they should be presented."
Her fingers twisted into fists. She needed to control her anger.
Especially until she knew how her power worked. She only knew
it happened sometimes when she was angry, but she couldn't
seem to make it work on command.

Destiny, in the next cube over, snickered. "Trust me, girl, I've
been here long enough to know where they hide the bodies. I can
help you get rid of one."

Joanie laughed, but Tori was too wound up. "Does anyone
know if this is a capital punishment state? If it is, I'll have to lure
him away somewhere where I won't get the electric chair." Come
to think of it, luring him away sounded wonderful.

"I'll Google it for you," Destiny said.

Jennifer, two cubicles away, stood up with her hands on her
hips. "You guys are *sick*. Someone just *died* around here and you're
making jokes about killing people!"

"Who's joking?" Destiny said with a straight face.

That finally broke through the tension Tori was feeling. She
laughed. Good. Much better. She was really beginning to like
Destiny.

"Ugh!" Jennifer huffed. "I can't believe you animals! I'm going
to HR and complain about each of you. You better hope they
don't call the police." Jennifer strode off to the elevator.

"Oh great," Joanie groaned. "We're in for it now. I'd rather
have three Joe's than one Jennifer. At least he tries to be nice.
Even if he is an idiot." She walked back to her desk.

Tori turned to her computer and leaned her head on one
hand. Maybe she should quit. She wasn't herself. She wasn't
normally hard to get along with or mean-hearted. Was this the
best she could behave, stressful situation or no?

She sighed. *God, please help me to be more understanding, more
helpful, and to see what I'm not seeing.*

Opening the last spreadsheet, she started reformatting it to
get ready to dump in last year's information. She didn't hate her

job. What she hated was feeling like she was wasting her time, that she was just being kept busy for eight hours a day, just collecting a paycheck.

She wanted *more* from her life. She wanted to achieve something, be good at something she enjoyed that had meaning. But what? That was the million dollar question. She'd thought this super power thing would be the "something," but she didn't know who to talk to about it, or how to use it. She was afraid to talk to Casey and Art yet. Maybe she should make an appointment with Owen. Privately. As a pastor, he should know all about the meaning of life.

Her phone rang twenty minutes later. Pam in HR needed to speak with her. As she walked down the stairs, Tori wondered how much meaning she could derive out of making license plates.

LEXIE HADN'T TALKED to Tori since yesterday's mealtime fiasco. She knew she needed to apologize, but convincing Tori to listen to her was more important. She shoved her homework into her backpack with an apple and a bottle of water. If it were anyone else, she might worry that Tori was too upset with her to come over tonight. But Lexie had class on Monday nights and Tori babysat. That was the deal. They'd lived together raising Ben long enough to do what needed to be done regardless of whether they were happy with each other.

So when Tori walked in at the usual time, Lexie didn't even let her take off her coat before she thrust a sheaf of papers at her sister's face. "Read these," she demanded.

Tori ignored the papers while she took off her boots. "Geez, Lex, let me get my coat off, will ya?"

"I told you he was trouble, didn't I?" Lexie continued. "I knew it. But no, you wouldn't believe me." She rattled the papers at Tori's head. "But now I've got proof! Read these and promise me you'll stay away from him, Tor."

"I'm not going to be able to read them if you give me a paper cut on my cornea."

Lexie backed up a step and waited for her sister to hang up her coat. She didn't know much about Kane Curtis as a man except that something about him frightened her, had since she was a little girl. She could *feel* things about people. She couldn't explain it, but sometimes she seemed to know things about them that she couldn't know.

She'd spent all yesterday afternoon on the Internet researching Kane Curtis the businessman. She printed all of it so she could prove to Tori that it wasn't just a feeling. Kane was not a good man. Her sister believed the best about people, and normally Lexie found that to be an endearing quality. But in this case, it was dangerous.

Tori rolled her eyes before she finally took the papers. She scanned the first page and put her hand on her hip. "Gosh, Lex, you hate our father. Not exactly breaking news. Doesn't mean I have to." She headed for the kitchen.

Lexie took her sister's arm and pushed her into a chair in front of a cup of hot chocolate. "Drink and read." She knew how much Tori loved the way Lexie made hot chocolate, so she'd made Tori a mug that was extra rich with extra marshmallows.

Tori heaved a dramatic sigh and read the first page. "*Curtis Enterprises Investigated by SEC*. They aren't the only ones." She flipped the page face down on the wooden table and took a sip of her cocoa.

"*Whistleblower at Curtis Enterprises Murdered*," she read. She pointed a glare at Lexie. "Sorry, but murders are losing their shock value."

Pretend all you want, little sis, but that one hit you. I can see it in your face. Lexie waited for Tori to read the next one, one of the worst of the stories she'd found.

"*Genetic Experimentation on Children Shut Down.*" Tori looked up and shifted in her seat. She took a big swallow of the hot chocolate and shot a surreptitious glance toward Ben's room.

"Read the highlighted part." Lexie crossed her arms and waited.

"Alpha Genetics had recently been purchased by Curtis Enterprises of Double Bay, Michigan." Tori met her gaze again, fear creeping in around the edges this time. She turned back to the papers, flipping through them, reading headline after headline, and highlights of what Curtis Enterprises was accused of being involved in.

Lexie felt a shiver go down her back as she saw Tori turn to the last page. "That's a printout from my bank account. See the highlighted part?"

"Fifty thousand dollars? What's that from?"

"Exactly what I asked my bank this morning. Blood money? Drug money? Bribery? I don't know. It happened last week. *After* he visited here. *Here! My home! Ben's home!*" Lexie's hands cut through the air as she spoke faster and faster. She could feel her emotions spilling out like a bucket of snakes. She tried to hold them in as she continued.

"I called the bank," she told Tori, "and you know who they say the deposit came from? Guess! One guess!"

Tori grabbed one of her hands and held it between them on the table. Lexie could feel her sister focus on calmer emotions, reflecting them back to Lexie. She felt a little better.

"Curtis Enterprises!" Lexie squeezed Tori's hand, trying to physically hang onto the peace. "I asked them how someone can deposit money into my *private* account without my permission, without me giving them my bank account number, and they said they don't know. I told them to take it out and they said they can't, that it's a bona fide transaction. They told me *I have to accept it!*"

Lexie's other arm knocked her mug. Hot cocoa spilled across the table. She jumped up to get some paper towels. "I'll tell *you* what I'm going to accept or not accept!" she fumed. "That is *my* account and I will *not* accept his dirty money! *Regardless* of what the bank says."

She scrubbed furiously at the hot cocoa. Tori moved back to keep from being hit with chocolatey paper towel bits. "So you know what I did, Tori? You know what I did with that scoundrel's money?"

Lexie's laugh grated through the air like bits of hail. She threw the dirty paper towels in the trash and turned to her little sister, arms akimbo.

"I wrote a check for $50,000 and drove it down to St. Silvia's Orphanage. I mean, where would a creep like that be *least* likely to give his money? They were shocked, let me tell you. And think how shocked *he'd* be if he knew!" She stood tall in triumph when she finished her tirade.

Then she noticed her sister's face. Tori was a little freaked out. Lexie prided herself on her control, but ever since Kane Curtis had walked back into their lives, she'd lost it more times than she had in the last few *years*. She couldn't remember the last time she'd scared Tori.

Lexie's shoulders sagged. "The thing is," she said, wondering if her voice was shaking the way her insides were, "if Kane could make a deposit in my bank account, he could probably track where the money goes. That, more than all the news articles, scares me. That he can track us down, even the most intimate details of our lives, and interfere in whatever way he wants."

Her privacy was more than normal expectations of confidentiality. It was the key to protecting Ben. If their father could meddle with her bank account, what else could he meddle with?

The sisters stared at each other for a moment. Lexie wiped her hand down her face and leaned toward Tori. She grasped her hand and squeezed. "You see, don't you?"

Tori closed her eyes and leaned back, pulling her hand away. "He doesn't deserve to be hated. Maybe he just didn't realize he was overstepping his bounds? He hasn't had any practice at being a father. Maybe I just need to explain to him..."

Lexie slumped in her chair as her sister trailed off. She stared across the table, but Tori wouldn't meet her gaze. Lexie shook her head. "Oh Tori..."

For the first time since she was sixteen, when her naive little sister had come to save her from a life on the streets, Lexie felt completely alone.

11

Meanwhile, in the underground team office, Joe and the rest listened carefully while Art and Casey explained what they had learned so far.

"It looks like Evan Ruffalo might have found something after all," Art said. "Joe found a file with Jason's information in it, and another file with names and dates and locations for over a dozen more kids. Most of them are in our missing persons database. There were also printouts about biological research companies in Vegas, Chicago, and here in Double Bay."

"We think Evan was trying to link the disappearances," Casey interjected.

"Joe also found a ticket stub in Evan's desk. Looks like he flew out to Las Vegas the weekend before he was killed." Art tapped his pen rhythmically against his knee. "Maybe he found his link and someone didn't like it."

Joe felt a shiver run down his spine. "You know whose headquarters is in Vegas."

Mickey whistled long and low. Bull massaged his temples. Hayley sat back hard in her seat.

Vegas meant a lot of things to a lot of people, but for Joe, it always meant one thing—The Nine. An organization with nine leaders who called themselves The Fathers, the members all had super powers. But in the exercise of free will, the members had chosen to use their powers for personal gain. Not for the protection of the human race.

"Who?" Art and Casey asked together.

"I've told you there's a criminal element among the super-heroes," Mickey said slowly. "There's a group headquartered in Vegas called The Nine. If Evan talked to someone connected with them—and we have no reason to suspect—"

"We have every reason to suspect them!" Hayley argued. "One of their leaders used to live here in Double Bay. The city became a much better place when that Thriller died!"

Bull patted Hayley's knee in an effort to calm her. In typical Hayley fashion, she folded her arms over her chest and pulled into herself. Joe wished she could let go of her demons, whatever they were. She rarely talked about her past, but he figured she must have been mistreated in some way, probably because of her abilities, and that's why she'd built such thick walls around herself.

"What's a Thriller?" Casey asked.

"Someone who gets a thrill using their powers to subjugate others. You need to talk to Owen," Mickey said. "These are not people you want to stir up. Fighting The Nine would be like Peter Pan and the Lost Boys fighting the U.S. Army. They're highly organized and well equipped, with extreme powers. Paladins—well, we generally aren't. Our policy has always been to spread out and try to protect as much territory as possible."

"Joe's dad, Owen Clarke? What does he have to do with it?" Casey looked to Joe for an answer.

"My dad is the local Paladin Guild Leader," Joe said. "That's our official name, Paladins. The superhero nickname started after comic books became popular in the early 1900s, though we've been called heroes for as long as anyone can remember. In fact, the Bible stories of David and his Mighty Men—they were Paladins. The Guild was started in the early thirteenth century. There is one guild worldwide, with hundreds of local chapters like ours."

Joe met the eyes of his teammates, but more than that, his family. "We've all sworn to live by a simple set of rules whereby our number one priority is to protect the areas we live in. For the most part, anyone with powers not affiliated with the Guild is considered a potential enemy."

Art frowned. "Why? I thought you guys had kind of a live-and-let-live policy."

"*Potential* enemy," Mickey said. "Because left unchecked, those who live outside the rules can become too powerful to stop. Like The Nine. Unfortunately, they've experienced a huge growth spurt in the last thirty years, particularly in the United States, their base of power. Their policy on Paladins—ignore, recruit, or destroy. We've heard stories that would curdle your blood. I have no doubt they would execute an Unmarked who dared question them."

"An Unmarked is..." Art looked around the group.

"A person unmarked by powers," Hayley said quietly. "These powers are a curse from God because Cain killed his brother Abel."

"Not a curse," Joe interjected, looking at Hayley. She'd always considered her powers more curse than gift. Sometimes he just wanted to shake her until she understood that God did *not* have it out for her. Since that probably wouldn't be the best way to get across *God loves you*, he'd refrained. So far.

"The Bible calls it a curse," Hayley murmured, picking at lint on her jeans.

She had him there. But trying to explain to her that the curse had become a gift, a physical and spiritual responsibility that could open her heart to a deep, foundational joy...well, those conversations hadn't gone well.

"I beg your pardon?" Art's eyes widened. "I thought powers had to do with genetics."

"When Adam and Eve's son Cain killed his brother," Joe turned back to the detectives, "God's punishment was to give Cain and his descendants supernatural powers that they were to use to protect humankind. They were to travel the earth, keeping people safe from the forces of evil. It was a way to constantly remind them how precious human life is, particularly to God."

"Learn to protect that which you've destroyed." Art nodded. "Some people believe rehabilitation works that way."

"I've never heard any of this." Casey made notes in a small spiral notebook. "So much to learn."

"We like to keep the details close," Mickey said, looking pointedly at her notebook. "It's one way to protect ourselves."

"But you're the superheroes," Casey said, closing her notebook. "What do you need protection from?"

"You know, he could've just been gambling," Bull suggested. "Isn't that the big reason people go to Vegas?"

Joe took advantage of the opening and pulled out a folder. "I found something else." He passed around copies of Evan's email to Tori. "Tori told me about this today. Evan sent it just before midnight Wednesday."

If I'm not around tomorrow, remember the Nine.

Hayley gasped and paled. "Joe! Is Tori in danger?"

Joe felt a shiver run down his spine. "Of course not! She was just a temp. No one could possibly think..." Could they? She was Evan's assistant, if only for a few days. Surely no one would connect her to Evan's personal investigations.

Art tapped his pen harder against his knee. His lips pressed into a thin line.

"Let's not be too hasty in making any assumptions regarding The Nine," Mickey said, leaning his elbows on his knees. "That includes you two." Mickey pointed at the detectives.

"If you're saying they're homegrown terrorists, Homeland Security is going to want to know," Art insisted.

"A dog doesn't..." Mickey paused with a glance toward Casey. "Poop where he sleeps."

"But a dog does return to his vomit." Casey met Mickey's unwavering stare with one of her own.

A quote from Proverbs. Joe wondered if Casey believed what she was hearing about superheroes and the origin of their powers. Maybe. That could be helpful. Or maybe she grew up in a church where she'd memorized a few now-meaningless-to-her Bible verses.

"The Nine is more like organized crime on steroids. And no," Mickey interrupted himself before Art could, "I don't think you should call the FBI yet. We don't know for sure that they're involved."

Art looked at him coolly. "Not really your call."

Maybe inviting the police into their meetings hadn't been such a great idea. Joe wondered, if push came to shove, if they would respect Owen's authority.

Joe watched Mickey clench his teeth, fighting to stay calm before he continued. "Let's find out who we can pin some evidence on first. We won't be finding any of The Nine to arrest, I can tell you that. I know a couple of them, and I'm not too keen to meet them in a fight. They're..." Mickey clenched his fists and didn't finish. "There's a good chance they sent a footman. Someone you can actually send to jail."

"You know some of The Nine?" Bull looked as shocked as Joe felt.

How could Mickey know them? Did Dad know? This whole thing felt like it was spiraling out of control. Joe had never worked a case like this. For a moment he wished he were back on street sweeper patrol, picking up petty thieves and helping little old ladies and lost cats.

Mickey continued without answering. "Do you know anyone on the police force in Vegas? Personally?"

Casey cleared her throat. "I'm checking to see if a woman I went to the academy with is still there." She shook her head and met Art's worried eyes. "We don't know if anyone in Vegas understands exactly what they're dealing with over there. Or that they even recognize a problem. And I'm not sure how to tell them."

Joe rubbed his hands over his face. "Do you know who Evan met with?"

The detectives shook their heads. "We're still investigating the lead. You'll be the first to know."

"Okay, can we please get back to Tori now?" Hayley swung her foot impatiently on her knee. "She's been in a robbery, found a dead man, and got mugged, all in the last two weeks. Uh, *duh!*"

Everyone stared at Hayley.

"It sounds a lot worse when you say it like that," said Bull.

"Thanks, Bull." Joe cracked his knuckles on both hands. Tension built inside, needing a release. He eyed the door to the gym.

"I still wonder if it has to do with you." Bull looked at Joe. "She gets married to a superhero and doesn't know it, then suddenly — pandemonium."

The pounding of his heart stopped Joe's breath. He coughed to clear his throat. He'd pretty much ignored Bull the last time he brought up this idea. And Mickey had agreed that there was no connection. But Joe was her husband, her protector; he had to look at all of the possibilities.

Protect her.

Was the voice in his head a sign telling him that what Bull said was true? Could Tori be in danger because she'd married him? Now he wanted to punch Bull instead of the bag. His fists clenched as his body responded to the adrenalin in his system. His muscles trembled. His skin tightened. He knew that if Art shot him right now, the bullet would do nothing. But Tori was defenseless.

"Easy, Joe," Mickey said. "Two of those things happened at work or after work. It could be related to Evan."

"Not making me feel better if Evan's involved with The Nine." Joe scowled at his friend.

Casey flipped some pages in her notebook. "Okay, where else has Tori worked? Has she worked for St. Silvia's? Volunteered there? Has she ever worked at a school or a daycare?"

Hayley shook her head. "I don't think so. But her nephew goes to preschool. She lived with him and her sister till she married Joe." She told Casey where she thought the preschool was located.

"What else?" Casey asked.

"I can't see how she's involved," Mickey said, leaning back against the couch.

"I can't either." Joe let his head fall back against the leather, his eyes sliding closed.

In his mind, he saw Tori getting mugged on Halloween, saw her shaken and pale after finding Evan, saw her attacked again in the alley behind their house. "Do you really think it could be a coincidence?" He opened his eyes and looked at Mickey. "All those things happening in just a few weeks?"

"Ugh!" Hayley huffed on the couch. "Sometimes you guys are so *stupid*." She crossed her arms and glared at the ceiling.

Mickey stared at him for a moment, thinking. "I rarely see coincidences anymore. Eventually, I see connections." Mickey rubbed his chin. "It doesn't help that you have secrets. Makes it hard to find patterns."

"What secrets?" asked Art.

Everyone looked at Joe. "I've been meaning to tell her about this," he waved his arm around the room, "but I haven't had a chance to do it yet."

Mickey coughed in a way that sounded like "coward."

Joe tensed, trying not to fidget. "As Hayley mentioned," he ground out through clenched teeth, "it's been a little busy around here."

"Just talk to her," Art suggested. "How bad can it be?"

"And *listen*," Casey added. "Maybe she can tell you something that will help." She looked at Art, who nodded at her.

Joe saw the others nodding, too. It's true that he and Tori had had a busy couple of weeks since they'd returned from their honeymoon. But maybe, just possibly, he was scared to tell her. What if she didn't like the idea of being married to a superhero? What then?

Well, he was going to have to man up.

At the next convenient moment.

HAYLEY'S FEARS WERE UNFOUNDED. Just because her best friend rushed into marriage with someone she barely knew—someone Hayley knew pretty well and had to pretend she didn't when Tori was around—that didn't mean Tori wouldn't want to hang out anymore. Hayley was so excited when Tori called and asked to come over tonight, she spent time working on some of her plants to make them flower, even though it was out of season. Flowers made people feel welcome, made them want to come back.

On the other hand, she wasn't sure her fears for Tori's safety were baseless. She wanted to help her friend figure out her powers so she could protect herself if anything else happened. But it would be a lot easier to teach her by showing her Hayley's own powers. Which she couldn't because she'd promised to let Joe tell Tori everything. Which he hadn't.

Grr.

Maybe last night's conversation would spur him to action.

Otherwise, she was going to tell Tori anyway. Hayley was her best friend and best friends protected each other.

When Tori arrived, they ordered a Hawaiian pizza and curled into the couch for a long overdue girly chat. So relaxing. Better than hanging out with the boys. Hayley even took a third piece of pizza. It was like a vacation day, her and Tori hanging out alone.

Tori studied her water glass. "Have you ever *seen* a superhero, Hayley?"

Hayley choked on a piece of pineapple. She took a moment to catch her breath. Was this an opening she should take advantage of? Remembering her stupid promise, she decided probably not. "Sure. They're on the news."

"I mean in person."

"I saw Sonic once. At least I'm pretty sure it was him." Hayley hoped that didn't count as a lie. It *was* him. They'd been having lunch. "No one else can run that fast."

She watched Tori trying to piece things together. Her friend had never believed in superheroes before, so it'd been kind of easy to pretend to be normal around her. But now Tori not only believed they were real, the police had convinced her that she had a power herself. But she had no one to talk to about it. She didn't know that both her husband and her best friend had super powers, too.

Dang it. Promise or no promise, she wasn't going to let her friend flail around alone. "Does this have to do with the superhero you met at the robbery?"

"Spook? No. Well, maybe. I don't know."

Yeah, that was clear as mud. She tried again.

"Is it about the one you met on Halloween?" No one said Hayley couldn't confirm a direct question if Tori asked her anything. She'd only promised not to tell.

Tori folded her cloth napkin into some form of origami. "Um, maybe, yeah." She let go a wicked grin. "He was totally cute!"

Hayley smiled. Joe was okay.

"Of course, not nearly as handsome as Joe," Tori hurried to add.

Hayley laughed. If she only knew. She wondered if she should tell Joe how loyal Tori was to him. Nah. He was being a turd. Maybe later.

"He showed up last Friday when I was mugged, too."

"Yeah," Hayley said. How hard could it be to tell her, Joe? You go around saving her enough, just tell her already. Too bad Hayley didn't have any psychic powers or she could berate Joe all she wanted right this minute.

"What do you mean, yeah?" Tori asked. "I didn't tell you that."

Hayley paused. She took a bite of pizza to buy time. Did Joe tell her then? Ugh! This whole thing was getting ridiculous. "You must've," she said with her mouth full. "How else could I know?"

Tori nodded and bit off the last of the stuffed crust on her piece. Then she laughed. "How'd he come up with that name, anyway? Superhero X. Not very creative, is it?"

Hayley chuckled. Names were the worst. Coming up with one that halfway described you and wasn't lame and wasn't already taken. Tori had no idea that Joe inherited the name. His dad was Superhero W; his son would be Superhero Y. Bummer for him.

Tori looked at Hayley expectantly. "What?"

"Nothing. It's just..." It's just that I'm great at lying to men, but I suck at lying to my best friend. I'm going to choke Joe. Wrap philodendron in layers around his neck and squeeze. Bring an unnatural spring to the oak tree in his front yard and wrap one of the branches around his chest until he cries uncle and *tells her*.

"Have you heard of him?" Tori asked.

"Well—I—uh, yeah, sort of. I've heard of him."

Tori sighed. "I wish I understood more of this. I asked Superhero X how I could reach him. I think I'm going to try to get his help figuring out what to do."

Hayley grunted. Yes, he should absolutely help you, the idiot.

"What? You think that's a bad idea?" Tori asked. "I know I'm married, and I shouldn't be hanging out with—actually, I have no idea if he's single or married."

Hayley started to comment when Tori paused, but then Tori plowed ahead before Hayley could form a reply.

"No, there's nothing weird about it. I *love* Joe. I adore him! I would never do anything to endanger our marriage." Her face fell a little. "Though all this crazy overtime isn't helping. I haven't told him yet, Hayley." She stopped, as if waiting for a rebuke.

Hayley wasn't sure what to do. She should probably press Tori as hard as she was pressing Joe. If one of them started the conversation, surely they'd both confess and be done with it. "Well, you're right that the timing hasn't worked out well yet." Grudgingly, she admitted that maybe she could give Joe that much. "But you really need to tell him, sooner rather than later."

"Yeah, I know, I know." Tori took a sip of her Wild Cherry Pepsi. "He said that things should ease up after this week, that we'd get some down time together by the weekend." She took a deep breath. "I'll tell him then." She looked Hayley in the eye. "I promise."

"You better."

"I will. I just have to figure out how to say it. I mean, I don't want to come off all Amazon warrior woman—"

Hayley started laughing. Definitely not the way she'd ever pictured herself. She couldn't imagine Tori that way either.

Tori laughed. "You know what I mean. I want to appear strong, not weak. I want to learn to help people, rescue people, you know? Just because Superhero X rescued me on Halloween, it was only because I couldn't run in Lexie's stupid high heels. And the other night, I was doing okay until..." She thought about it, then scrunched up her face. "Actually, I'm glad he showed up then."

"Me, too!" Hayley agreed heartily. She'd read the report. Tori might've been killed if X hadn't been there. "Being personally attacked sounds worse than accidentally walking into an armed robbery."

Tori nodded. "I just don't want Joe to think I'm the kind of girl who needs saving. I want him to admire me, respect me. And I don't want him to be repulsed by me either."

Hayley dropped her paper plate to her lap and leaned forward, her hand on Tori's knee. "Tori Lewis Clarke, J—" Hayley cursed in her head. She almost screwed up. "Superhero X is not like your parents. First of all, he *is* a superhero so he's not going to be repulsed by superheroes."

"Right, I know," Tori agreed. "But I was talking about Joe."

Hayley wanted to slap her forehead. This was so confusing. "Yes, Joe. Well, he's a great guy! You've told me so, right? So he's going to love it!" That may or may not be a lie. She had no idea.

Tori looked up, her eyes bright with sudden tears. "I liked Joe from the moment I met him. I don't want to say or do anything to lose him."

Hayley laid her hand on Tori's arm, at a complete loss as to how to help her. Infatuation she understood. She knew the danger and the attraction of lust. But Tori seemed to be genuinely in love. Hayley didn't know what to do with that. But she did understand about losing people.

"And you're afraid your husband might hate superheroes like your mom. So you think you can't tell him that you *are* one."

"Hayley, I *force* people to *do* things. And I don't even realize it! How does that not scare you? Aren't you afraid I'll try to force you to do something?"

"Tori, you've been my best friend since the second grade. If you force me to do something I don't want to do, I'll kick your butt."

Tori let out a burst of relieved laughter.

Hayley wasn't sure she'd even realize it if Tori was "making her" do something. Could a person tell? Could they fight it? But at least Tori was smiling again.

Then Tori gasped and dropped her plate. "Oh nooo!"

"What? What?" Hayley tossed her plate on the floor and grabbed Tori's hands.

Tori shook, trying not to cry. "Oh Hayley! I just thought of something horrible!" And then she broke down into a sobbing mess.

It took Hayley a minute or two to get Tori to stop blubbering and say what she was thinking in words that made sense. All she got out of it was "so in love" and "Thanksgiving" and "marry me." Hayley already knew they were so in love that Joe proposed at Thanksgiving, less than a month after they'd met. Crazy kids. But what was Tori so upset about? She was crying so hard that sympathetic tears washed down Hayley's face as well.

"Tori, calm down, I can't understand you." Hayley handed her a clean napkin, dabbing at her own face with another.

Tori wiped her eyes and took a couple of shuddering breaths. "The day before Thanksgiving, we were having such a great time together and I was just dizzy in love with him and I just—I just—"

"Don't cry," Hayley begged.

She took another sobbing breath and said, "I just blurted out, 'Marry me, Joe!' Hayley, *what if I made Joe marry me?* The next day he had a ring and told our families and everything!"

Hayley sat in shock for a moment. Could Tori really do that? That was way bigger than "put down the gun." We're talking making a *permanent* change in a person. Joe still acted like he loved Tori nearly two months later! That was *crazy*. Could a power like that really come from God?

She tried to focus on her sobbing friend. She patted Tori's back and said, *there, there, of course you didn't, you just go home and talk to him,* all the time wondering if her friend's marriage might be over almost before it started.

Tori picked up groceries on the way home from work, planning a special dinner with Joe tonight. She had a half-thought-out plan to seduce him and then try to find out if he'd never intended to propose. It's not like she had much experience in that department, but she was hoping that if the seduction was successful, Joe might, at worst, say, funny, I never meant to marry you but I'm so glad I did!

Ugh. What was she thinking? Would that even work?

But there'd also be the really nice dinner. Isn't that what they said? The way to a man's heart? Surely that would give her bonus points. And maybe, just maybe, if the whole thing went off without too much of a hitch, it'd be the perfect segue into, oh and by the way, honey, I'm thinking about becoming a superhero.

After the lovemaking, in case it was their last time before he left her.

Last night, Hayley insisted she was wrong about Joe not wanting to marry her. Did she, Tori, know how her power worked? How long the effects lasted? Whether the person ever realized what had happened? No, no, and no. She didn't know the answer to anything! Hayley's point somehow being that Tori shouldn't worry about it.

That sounded comforting last night. Now, with the possibility that she was living the last few hours of happily married life, Tori wasn't so sure.

So while she cooked, Snickers winding around her ankles, she hoped that somehow her friend was right and her impulsive words so many weeks ago *weren't* the only thing keeping her and Joe together. At the same time, she resigned herself to the knowledge that tonight might be the last night she lived with the man she loved.

By the time Joe arrived, dinner was sizzling and double-fudge brownies cooled on the counter. Tori waited for him to put his briefcase down before she kissed him. Afraid it might be one of their last kisses, she ate him up like dark chocolate on a warm day.

"Oh...well...mmm," Joe murmured as he slid his hands under her shirt and around her ribs, pulling her closer. Warm lips and hot tongues collided.

Tori couldn't help but grin as Joe nibbled his way down her neck. So far, the seduction scene was playing out even better than she'd hoped.

The sound of water hissing and spitting brought Tori halfway back to her senses.

"Oh, the potatoes! Hang on. Honey!" Tori giggled up a scale of notes, Joe's hands playing tantalizing music on her skin.

"You have ten seconds to get everything turned off or turned down, then you're mine."

"Joe!" Tori wriggled under his touch. "It'll ruin everything if I just turn it all off."

"How long until it's done?"

"Fifteen minutes." Tori felt her body temperature creep up. Maybe she needn't have started a fire when she came home.

"Set the timer. We'll be done in fourteen and a half."

Joe slapped her behind as Tori giggled again. She turned down the heat on the boiling potatoes, checked the roast in the oven, and set the kitchen timer.

Another thought—that things were heating up just as she had to let him go—zoomed through her mind, but she pushed it out. Tears would be *so* not sexy.

When the kitchen timer went off twelve minutes later, the exhausted, sated couple gave each other one more kiss. Then Joe smacked her bottom and said, "Woman, get me my dinner."

As Tori prepared their plates, she wondered how she should bring up the subject. Honey, would you like to be married to someone else? Sweetie, why did you marry me? Darling, I love you so I'm packing your bags and letting you go.

Yeah, none of those were going to work. She'd have to think about it some more during dinner.

They ate on the living room carpet, dinner plates on the coffee table, backs against the couch, thighs and shoulders touching. If this were a regular, happy marriage, it'd be, well, *perfect*. Maybe she could just pretend for a few minutes. Let Joe watch the news in peace before she...well, whatever it was she came up with as a plan.

Her words to Hayley came back to her. Tori wanted to be a woman Joe would admire for being able to handle any situation. Fine. She would be. Even if their marriage was practically over before he saw it.

She glanced at Joe, then back at the TV screen. "Have you ever seen a superhero?" She hoped having a non-plan worked as well as a real plan.

"Mmm-hmm..." He was completely engrossed in the sentencing of an actor in L.A. who'd apparently bought drugs for another underage actor.

Ah, the beginning of a plan. If she talked to him while he was watching TV, maybe he'd give up some useful information without even knowing it. "Have you ever met one?"

Joe grunted.

In their twenty-eight days of marriage, Tori hadn't yet decided if grunts were always "yes" or always "no." Perhaps non-yes-or-no questions would work better.

"How many have you seen?"

A commercial came on. Tori waited for Joe to give her his attention. But this one was for that video game he wanted. The one she bought at the mall earlier this week.

She sighed. What would she do with their wedding presents? And they'd already had a party. How would they explain to their friends and family that they weren't married anymore?

"Have you seen more than two?"

He admired a sleek BMW motorcycle on the screen. "I've gotta get one of those."

Tori looked askance at the husband she wanted to keep. Alive. "You must be joking," she said, veering off course for a moment. "You don't even know how to ride one, do you? And I don't want to be a widow." Of course, she didn't want to be a divorcée madly in love with her ex-husband either.

"It's not that hard. Two what?" Joe changed the subject.

Tori lost him for a second, deep as she was in contemplating the rest of her lonely life. "Oh. Superheroes."

"I guess."

"When? Where did you see them?" She tried to keep her voice light. Maybe he *liked* superheroes. That would be good. So long as he didn't mind too much a superhero forcing him to do something, and so long as he was happy with the outcome... maybe this could all work out.

He finally looked at her. "What?"

Tori met his eyes for a moment and turned away, as if the question weren't important. "I just wondered how many there are. I've only seen a couple in my whole life. Hayley's seen two. I wondered how many you've seen."

"Hayley said she's seen two superheroes?"

Tori felt the weight of Joe's stare. He seemed remarkably interested now that she wanted him *not* to be engaged in the conversation. It'd be easier to grill him for what he knew if he were still focused on the TV. She waved her hand in a nonchalant manner and succeeded in knocking her fork to the carpet.

"Yeah, I'm not sure up close or what," she said, stacking their plates and piling all the silverware on top. "She said she's seen them on the news, but that's not what we were talking about at the time."

Joe narrowed his gaze on her. "Did you tell her about the one you saw?"

"Well, she knows about the one that stopped the mugger on Halloween." Tori stalled. Was there anything wrong with admitting she'd told Hayley? This was where a good plan would've come in handy. Now she was going to have to do this by the seat of her pants. Only she wasn't *wearing* pants.

Joe frowned as he waited for her reply.

The hairs on Tori's neck were prickling.

The news came back on and Joe turned to watch. How could she tell him now? A frown didn't bode well. She needed him to be in a good mood so he'd be more accepting of this unlikely situation. I mean, really, how many people find out *after* they get married that they've just married a superhero? She felt like crying again, but she reminded herself that she could handle this. She could handle anything.

"Would you like some dessert?"

Joe grunted, still watching the news. Tori blew out a sigh as she spooned ice cream on top of two brownies. It's hard to think of a plan for something you don't want to do. As she walked back into the living room with absolutely no acknowledgement from her husband, Tori thought maybe she should just come out with it. Deal with the consequences later. She'd ruined their perfect evening anyway.

A reporter stood interviewing a young family as their house burned in the background. Firefighters worked to keep the fire from spreading, but this house was history.

"Now why wasn't a superhero there to help?" Tori mused aloud as she gave Joe his brownie.

"They can't be everywhere," he said, digging into his dessert. "Half the time it's dumb luck, being in the right place at the right time."

Tori prayed for the family. Even if she'd been there, she couldn't have done anything. She couldn't just demand that the fire stop burning.

Another reporter talked to a laborer who'd been fired from his job and rehired at a lower rate.

Now *that* was something Tori could've stopped. She thought about Joe's "dumb luck" comment. "How do you know? Maybe there's a signal or something, you know, that calls them."

Joe looked at her. "Like in the Batman movies?"

"Yeah."

He leaned over and kissed her forehead. "Those are movies, honey."

Was he being condescending? "Well, how do you know?"

He pointed at the TV. "See any signals?"

Tori clamped her jaw to keep from saying something biting. Here she was trying to have a conversation with him and he wasn't taking her seriously at all. "Are you done with that?"

Tori grabbed his plate without waiting for a reply and marched into the kitchen. She scraped the rest of her brownie into the trash. Maybe he wasn't interested in having a conversation with her because he'd never really meant to marry her. She had to find out for sure. If she *hadn't* forced him to marry her, and he *was* glad they were together, she didn't want to start a fight over nothing.

When everything was in the dishwasher, she returned to the living room and began tidying.

"What are you doing?"

"Just cleaning up." She started folding a sweatshirt, and couldn't resist the urge to verbally smack him. "You're not paying attention to me anyway."

He pulled her down into his lap before she could finish. "I'm not done with you yet."

"You're watching TV." Tori struggled half-heartedly. He didn't act like someone who wished he were somewhere else.

"So? I can pay attention to you while I'm watching TV." He nuzzled her neck as his gaze flicked back and forth between her and the news.

"Oh, Joe," she sighed. "That's so romantic." She fluttered her eyelashes at him, her lack of smile surely enough evidence of her irritation.

Joe made it through the first hour of prime time before he lost focus again. During a commercial she crawled onto the couch and sighed loudly. "Don't you get tired of watching the same stuff all the time?"

"I always watch this show." He turned toward her and frowned. "You told me you love this show, too."

"Yeah, but it's a re-run. Don't you want to do something else?"

"Like what? Go look for superheroes?" He laughed.

Tori frowned. Was he mocking her? "I'm serious, Joe. We could..." But it was January in Northern Michigan. They certainly weren't going outside. And they'd already done the most fun indoor activity.

"We could have a baby," she blurted out. If he wanted out of this marriage, his reaction to her as a superhero was moot. If he wanted to stay, he'd say, let's have a baby later. Tori held her breath. Both her mom and Hayley had brought up the baby thing recently. Maybe it was a sign.

"Sure." Joe kissed her again, but it felt like a kiss-to-shut-you-up kiss. Unfortunately, it worked. Joe was a great kisser. "Show's on."

Tori sat on the couch to the left of where he sat on the floor. She watched him bite his nails. What did "sure" mean? Sure, let's stop using birth control? Sure, someday when I'm ready? Sure, anything to get back to my show?

"Why don't you use nail clippers?" she asked him. "I don't remember seeing you use anything besides your teeth."

Joe grinned at her over his shoulder. "You should see my pedicure."

Tori grimaced, but it turned into a laugh. Her heart fluttered a bit, reminding her that she didn't want to lose him. Among other things, he was funny. Even if sometimes he was disgustingly funny, he could always make her laugh.

Okay, let's say that he's *not* in love with someone else. He *doesn't* want to leave. Then...

Tori groaned—that meant she couldn't tell him! Not now anyway. First she had to convince him that she believed super-heroes were real, and were good people. He'd already gleaned from her mother that her family wasn't exactly pro-superhero. She'd build up the whole notion so that when she dropped the bomb, it would go off with a little poof instead of a big bang. Maybe Joe would even get a little kick out of it. The thrill of finding himself married to a superhero.

Tori saw herself standing arms akimbo, cape blowing in the breeze, on top of a roof somewhere. Eight months pregnant. Yeah, that wasn't going to work. She'd have to tell him before he wanted to follow through on the baby idea.

She leaned her head back on the couch and closed her eyes. At least the seduction had worked. That had been *great* fun. Because she was keeping a secret?

She smiled. If that were the case, maybe she'd *never* tell him.

12

Tori shifted in the wrought iron chair and focused on her deli sandwich. Kane had called this morning and insisted on having lunch together. She tried to tell him no, but he sounded so reasonable when he said he wanted to apologize for upsetting Lexie, it was easier to agree. The apology wasn't really an apology, though. More like, I understand Lexie didn't want Ben to have the money I sent him.

Kind of a jerk thing to say. And it all but proved that Lexie was right—Kane knew she didn't have the money anymore. If he was actively monitoring their bank accounts, he was way beyond any Fatherhood 101 lessons Tori could come up with.

Too bad. She would've liked to have gotten to know him a little better. For now, she tried to think of some neutral small talk to engage in until they finished eating and she could leave. She'd have to apologize to Lexie later.

It occurred to her that if her mom was so anti-superhero, to the point where she insisted they didn't exist, maybe Kane knew why. Maybe Dixie had told him about it at some point.

"Something on your mind?" he asked.

"Huh? Oh, well, sort of." If they were going to sit here

together, she might as well get one question answered before they said goodbye. Still, she hesitated.

"You going to let me know what it is or just fidget all day?" His mouth smiled, but his fingers tapped the table. "You never know, I might be able to help."

Tori took a fortifying breath. "I was just wondering...do you know anything about superheroes?"

Kane's face froze. Oh geez, she shouldn't have asked. She should've kept—

He burst out laughing. "Why?"

Tori shrugged. She didn't want to tell him she'd met one. And she really didn't want to tell him she might be one. She just wanted to know more about her mom's aversion to them.

"Mom hates them. I wondered if you knew why."

His face darkened and he shook his head. "I hate to even think what she's told you. Though I'm surprised she ever mentioned it at all."

"She hasn't really said that much."

Kane leaned forward, eyes glittering. "I've been wanting to talk to you about this anyway. I'm not a superhero, Victoria. I'm *better* than a superhero."

What? She fell back in her chair. That was so not what she was expecting.

"My gifts are more powerful. I can do so much more with them. And you, my dear girl," he picked up one of her hands and held it between both of his. "You are part of my bloodline. You and your sister and Ben."

Holy smoke! A bloodline? A "better than a superhero" bloodline. Not a random accident. Why hadn't her mother told her? Tori's head spun as she tried to wrap her mind around this news. Kane not only didn't act surprised or embarrassed by this bizarre conversation, he seemed unnaturally excited about it.

"So...what's better than a superhero?" Tori stumbled over the words. Kane gripped her hand tightly. She tried to pull away, but he wouldn't let go. A voice in the back of her head told her something was wrong here, but she wasn't sure what.

"*Our* family are better than superheroes," Kane said, his voice low and fierce. "*Our* family have gifts and abilities that put so-called superheroes to shame. They're not heroes anyway. They took the name Paladin thousands of years ago. But they're not protectors; they're weak. *We* don't pretend to be saving the world, telling other people how they should live. We take care of each other. We protect our families." He gripped her hand tighter. "I'll never let anyone get away with hurting you, Victoria. You'll always be safe with me."

Tori shifted in her seat to hide her shudder. His protectiveness sounded menacing, frightening. But Tori couldn't help but wonder how leaving your family behind was protecting them. How had letting someone else adopt his daughters protected them? She let the question slip out.

Kane's expression turned fiery. After a moment, he carefully composed his features like he was putting on a mask. He let go of her hand. "Your mother doesn't understand. She said she did. She promised to support me in my work when we were young, but she failed me. She failed me, and she failed my family."

Tori heard long-held anger in his voice. She wished she hadn't brought up the topic. But she wanted to know about her parents, understand her past. Her nerves were getting to her, uneasiness dripping like a cold tap into her blood. But she kept listening.

"She was going to ruin me if I didn't let that *bottom feeder* give you his name." Kane's revulsion for Danny tainted the very air. Tori felt herself leaning away from Kane. She'd heard lawyers occasionally referred to by that term, but Danny was a real estate attorney and the least likely person to deserve such a derogatory term.

Kane continued. "If I'd stayed with her, I knew I'd never

succeed at the level that I could. She wanted to pull me down to her level. She couldn't even give me children who—"

He stopped himself. He turned a cool smile to Tori. "It's not your fault. There are other ways..."

Tori didn't know what to say. What wasn't her fault?

Someone was a few fries short. He didn't sound obviously crazy, especially when he tried to be charming, but Tori was beginning to be glad she hadn't grown up with him. He scared her.

Kane took a deep breath. "Excuse me. Divorce is a difficult thing. Now, what did your mother tell you about the Paladins?"

Tori shook her head. "Practically nothing." Absolutely nothing. Tori had never heard of Paladins before. She surreptitiously glanced at her watch. Blast. Not time to go yet.

Kane shook his head. "I explained to her that my family and the Paladins came from the same group of people given supernatural powers thousands of years ago. But *we* evolved. We learned to use the powers in every way imaginable. Sometimes we made mistakes, but we learned from them. We became an extraordinary group of people, particularly my family." Kane smiled at her. "*Your* family."

"The Paladins didn't evolve?" Tori asked. This was the craziest history lesson she'd ever had. She wondered if she could verify any of it on Google.

"They formed a guild, created rules, and stifled their own power. My family refused to join the guild. We could see what it would do and we refused to be a part of it. Because of that one decision, we thrived."

Kane leaned forward. Tori forced herself not to lean back any further. She wasn't sure the spindly-legged chair could take it. But she really, *really* didn't want to irritate Kane. Or show any weakness.

"Victoria, you are part of one of the greatest families the world has ever known," he said. "That's why I want you to come home with me. Let me show you everything you've been missing. Let me train you to become part of a great legacy. You'll never regret it!"

Tori tried to smile politely, but her lips felt stiff. For years she'd struggled between wanting more in her life, wanting to *be* more, and wanting to fit in, be liked, conform. But Kane's earnest speech leaned a little more toward the fanatical than she was comfortable with.

Still, listening to this man whose blood she shared, she wondered if that secret desire to be more was encoded in her genes. It was certainly obvious now where her strange power came from. Lexie's ability to influence people's emotions must come from this bloodline, too. Assuming it was all real and not a figment of a madman's imagination. She wondered if Lexie knew. If not, she was going to be livid when she found out.

"You feel it, don't you?" Kane smiled at her. "Your blood is stirring right now just thinking about it."

Tori forced her smile. She didn't want him to suspect anything. She was afraid of what he'd do, what he *could* do. "I'm sorry, but I don't have any special gifts."

"You might," Kane said. "You're my daughter. The Curtis family has never had children without powers." A flash of terrible anger swept over his face before the mask covered it again. "We just have to find out what your powers are. Can you think of anything you've noticed that's strange?"

Tori shook her head. Don't react. Don't move.

"Something that always made you feel like an outsider?"

She shook her head again. She hoped her body language wasn't screaming, *Liar!*

Kane thought for a moment. "Strange dreams? Dreams that you can fly, or talk to dragons, or understand any language?"

Tori couldn't help but laugh. "Talk to dragons?"

Kane shrugged. "You never know, especially in a dream. It could mean anything."

Tori took a drink of water to hide her growing unease. "Nothing," she said.

"Anything that gives you a strange feeling deep in your gut?"

Oh yes, that one she was quite familiar with. And she desperately didn't want him to discover it. She chewed on her lip as she thought about how to reply in a way that he'd give up.

"Stop that," Kane said abruptly.

"What?" Tori asked, surprised.

"Taking your lip in your teeth." He swore harshly. "Your mother did that all the time. Bothered me to no end. What?" he asked sharply.

Tori shook her head, embarrassed to mention it.

He schooled his features into a smile. "Go ahead, you know you can tell me anything."

Well, that wasn't true, was it? She picked at a trailing thread on her sleeve. Maybe she could lighten the mood, change the subject. "We aren't allowed to curse at our house. When we were kids, we had to pay a fine from our allowance. Now that we're adults, if we mess up, we have to put a dollar in the Cursing Jar. Of course, now we're pretty well trained not to do it. I was just thinking about how much money you'd owe my dad." She smiled, trying to make a joke of it.

Kane stared at her, only partially hiding his temper. "He's not your father, Victoria. I am."

Uh, yeah, but... To keep the peace, she said, "Of course." But she couldn't smile at him, not even to diffuse his anger. Danny was her dad. Not this mercurial stranger.

"He has his own children, Victoria. Children of his own blood. You'll understand when you're a parent."

Tori felt desperate to change the subject again. She knew her dad loved her. He couldn't fake it. But Kane's words hurt. They picked at old insecurities Tori tried to suppress.

She openly checked her watch. "Listen, I have to get back to work."

"Speaking of which, have you decided when you'll start?"

Tori blinked. "Start what?"

He chuckled and the sound grated down her nerves. "Your new job at Curtis Enterprises. They've already started repainting the condo I've chosen for you. You'll love it."

Tori took a deep breath. A narcissistic control freak with super powers. Great. Nothing left but the direct approach. She hoped he couldn't shoot laser beams out of his eyes. "I'm not coming to work for you, Kane." She tried to be gentle about it. "I appreciate the offer, but I have a good life. I'm not moving. Thank you, but no."

Kane stared at her. He had a light in his eyes Tori didn't like. If she were willing to use the term in reference to her father, she'd say the light felt *predatory*.

She gave an involuntary shiver and hid it by stretching her shoulders a bit.

He leaned closer. "I want you to explore *all* of your gifts, Victoria. I want you to find out who you really are. The world is waiting for you to make a choice! I'm here to help you choose wisely."

"Thank y-you, but—"

"Did nothing I say penetrate? Do you not understand your giftedness?"

"I don't have any gifts, not in that way, but—"

"I don't have time for this," he said impatiently, waving one fist in the air.

Tori cowered a little before she realized it. She straightened and lifted her chin. He wouldn't hit her, would he? Certainly not in a busy restaurant.

"If you want to be part of this family, show up for work tomorrow." Kane took a fifty dollar bill out of his wallet, threw it on the table, and marched toward the door. He turned and growled, "What use are you if you don't have a power? Dixie's to blame for this, just like everything else. I should've known. A son will be better than a daughter any day..."

He was still muttering as he stormed out, a few restaurant patrons watching him curiously.

Tori felt cold in her bones. Whoever he was, whatever he was, she was beginning to understand Dixie's refusal to talk about him. He made Tori feel like *she* was the idiot, like *she* was the crazy one.

A few fries short, indeed.

TORI PULLED her coat closer as she walked to her car after work. What a week. What a month, actually. It had crossed her mind once or twice since her lunch with Kane yesterday that just maybe her mother had done her a favor by keeping her too drugged up to understand her situation. Not that it was the best solution, but she was beginning to realize Dixie had been trying to protect her.

Tori almost wished for a little of that oblivion right now. She wouldn't have to think about her upcoming talk with Joe. It was Friday night. She'd promised herself she was going to tell him.

But...

There was always a *but*.

But she didn't want to tell him what she'd learned yesterday, that she knew where her powers came from, that there were at least two groups of people out there with powers and she came from the nut-job side. She needed to process that first, figure out how she was going to handle Kane if he didn't leave her alone. She decided she would tell Joe she'd found out she had a super power, but she planned on leaving the details as hazy as they'd been a couple days ago. No point in scaring the poor guy more than was necessary.

Hearing footsteps, she picked up her pace. It hadn't snowed for the last couple days and the parking lot was plowed clean. In the cold dark, sound seemed to echo. She'd be at her car in a minute—ah, the joys of being so low on the totem pole that her assigned spot was in the next county—and her ridiculous nerves could take a break. The conversation with Kane bothered her more than she'd like to admit.

The footsteps got closer. Tori turned and jumped when a shadow turned out to be a man in some kind of dark suit. Then she recognized him. Superhero X.

"You scared me!"

"Sorry," he said. "I want to be sure you get home safely."

"Well, giving me a heart attack isn't going to help." Tori knew her anger came from nerves, but she had to learn to control it now. Always. Her power had something to do with getting angry, she was pretty sure. Which reminded her, she wanted to talk to him about helping her with all this. Ah, but not tonight. She just wanted to get home to Joe. She missed him with all the long hours they were both keeping.

She stopped and turned to X. "Thanks, but I'm fine. My car is right there." She pointed fifty yards in front of her, in the right corner of the lot.

"Great, I'll walk you to your car and when you're home, I'll go about my business," he said with a grin.

She shook her head at him. He had a nice smile. She'd give him that. "I don't need any help, I don't need protection, and I don't want you following me," she said. "I'm fine."

But the big, strong hunk beside her didn't take the hint. "You've been in a few difficult situations lately."

Wasn't *that* an understatement? Tori started walking. The quicker she got to her car, the quicker she'd be home.

"We want to make sure you're safe." He strolled along cheerfully beside her as if he had no place better to be.

"We? Who's we?"

"My team and I."

Tori stopped and stared at him. His team? Did that mean he was watching her? That they were tracking her movements? Did they know about Kane? Did they know more than she did about Kane? Maybe she should ask him to coffee so he could answer all her questions.

But she was tired and Joe would be home soon.

Maybe Superhero X could help her figure things out, but not tonight. She sighed again. "I do want to talk to you sometime, but not now. Go away, please. Go home. I don't need you to—"

BAM!

The sound of an explosion startled them both.

WHA-BAMM!

A second explosion, louder and bigger than the first, knocked Tori to her knees. For an instant, she thought she saw her car on fire at the far end of the parking lot. Then Superhero X's body wrapped around hers, protecting her in a cocoon of muscle. Tori could feel the warmth of the explosion whoosh around them.

X crab-walked them behind another car, a big black Mercedes with a spot much closer to the door than Tori could ever hope to have. She looked up over the trunk toward the blazing inferno burning red against the black sky. That certainly looked like her car.

"What the—?" Tori stared in frozen fascination at the fire. She turned to Superhero X and saw the same shocked look she imagined she had.

"You didn't know about this?" she asked. She couldn't shake the feeling that he knew something he wasn't sharing. And she couldn't shake the fear that thought spread through her mind and body. What if he was more like Kane? She didn't know him after all. Both men professed to have her best interests at heart.

Tori jumped up and started to run.

A car length later, strong arms grabbed her, swinging her off her feet. She yelled. A big hand covered her mouth as she was pulled behind another car.

"Quiet," X whispered in her ear. He peeked out behind the bumper, scanning the parking lot.

The shivers running down her spine weren't the type she got when reading the good parts of a romance novel. This was real. This man could break her in half. Perhaps he'd been involved in blowing up her car. Perhaps he'd killed Evan. Perhaps he'd kill her.

Wait, her mind struggled to catch up. *Wait!*

Tori struggled to get out of the superhero's grip. Instead of letting her go, he pulled her closer. A sense of safety battled with the cold rush of hysteria that threatened to sweep over her. She fought her panic, still clawing at his arms.

"Shh," he said in her ear. "I know you're scared, but we have to get out of here."

Tori sobbed behind his hand. She struggled not to give in to her fear. What was happening? *Why* were these things happening to her?

She watched Superhero X look around the parking lot. He pulled his hand away from her mouth and tucked her body in close to his, smoothing her hair and whispering to her, his chin tucked over her head, still protective.

Thoughts of Joe holding her close like this flitted through Tori's mind. She felt herself relax slightly. Killers didn't try to comfort you. The feeling of safety encompassed her, calming her. As surely as she knew there were bad people in the world, she knew there were good people, too. Superhero X was one of the good guys. She was willing to bet her life on it.

She rubbed the tears from her eyes. She could hear a few people's voices. She started to stand, but Superhero X held her back.

He looked down at her. "Trust me."

No explanation. No commanding tones. Just a request.

Tori gave him the tiniest of nods.

Superhero X pointed to a black king cab pickup halfway between their hiding spot and her burning car. She heard more yelling near the studio doors. Taking her hand firmly in his, the superhero ran for the truck.

Shouldn't she be running for the safety of the crowd? The fleeting thought disappeared as he opened the driver side door and helped her in. He gave her a push and she slid all the way over to the passenger door. She cast a surprised look at him but he didn't notice.

He climbed in behind her, started the truck, and drove to the exit without the lights on. Tori frowned in the dark. The interior light hadn't come on when he'd opened the door. Most of the parking lot lights were out. He was driving around the outer edge of the parking lot as if he were trying not to be seen. Why?

Fear gripped her gut again. She eased closer to the passenger door.

At the street, Superhero X took her hand before he came to a stop. He pressed a button on his fancy watch, flipped on his lights and his turn signal, waited for a break in traffic, and turned left into the street.

"I know you're afraid, Tori," he said in a low voice, soothing even with the metallic sound under it, "but try not to be afraid of me. I'm here to protect you. I promise."

She closed her eyes and tried to think. *God, please help me know what to do, who to trust.* As she focused on listening for his answer, she felt a growing peace. With it came that strange sense of safety that she felt around Joe. She glanced over at Superhero X's masked profile. Nuts or not, trusting Superhero X seemed to be the best plan.

But they should go to the police, make a report. Or not. The police didn't seem to think of her as an innocent bystander in Evan's death. Perhaps less so after that mugger had been killed in front of her. But at least the police weren't planning her imminent demise.

Not as far as she knew anyway.

X made another turn, then another, and hope flared in Tori's chest. "Are you taking me home?"

"No."

Sprayed with the emotional equivalent of liquid nitrogen, the hope froze and shattered. Tori tried to let peace fill the void rather than fear, but fear gained a foothold.

Superhero X glanced over and saw the fresh tears. He sighed and turned back to the road as Tori held her bottom lip between her teeth. She could feel her chin quivering like a flag in a breeze.

"Why not? My husband will be expecting me soon. He'll keep me safe." She ignored the quiver in her voice. She needed to be stronger. She simply *had* to buck up and keep her wits about her.

"I'm taking you someplace where no one can hurt you. I'll make sure he meets you there." His voice was calm and soothing. It eased Tori's nerves even though her mind still struggled to make sense of the last few minutes.

"You *are* taking me home," she said as she recognized her neighborhood.

He didn't say anything as he drove past her street. He turned down an alley and drove a few blocks, checking his rearview mirror. He pulled up behind a big white house and parked.

Tori knew she was close to home, though from the alley in the dark she couldn't be sure exactly where she was. She opened the door and hopped out. She considered making a mad dash for home when she heard a familiar voice.

"Is that you, Tori?"

From out of the darkness materialized Joe's dad. That's where they were, in the alley behind Owen and Hannah's house and the church.

Tori stared as Owen walked up and clasped Superhero X's hand, slapping him on the back. Then he moved to Tori.

"Are you okay, honey?" he said kindly. He put his arm around her shoulders and Tori hugged him tight. He led her toward the house. "Hannah is just putting dinner on the table."

Tori looked over her shoulder at Superhero X. He knew Pastor Owen? He'd brought her to a church. Did he think he was giving her sanctuary, or did he know these were her in-laws?

The gears in Tori's mind stopped turning in their usual fashion. In fact, they ground to a downright halt. She thought she could smell the burning oil as she finally and completely lost the ability to process what was going on around her.

But she did remember her husband. "We have to make sure Joe's okay." She spoke urgently to Owen.

"Don't worry, X will bring him back here."

"Are you sure? Owen, something strange is happening. You don't know the half of it, but I don't want Joe—"

"He'll be here in a few minutes. You'll see. Everything will be a lot clearer soon." Owen looked over his shoulder at Superhero X.

Tori saw them exchange a look. Well, for crying out loud! Everybody seemed to know what was going on around here except her.

She let Owen lead her up the three stairs to the back door. After dinner, she would take him aside and tell him what had been happening. She'd ask for pastoral confidentiality and tell him *everything*. Owen would help her know what to do next.

13

Joe let go a mental sigh of relief. His parents would take care of Tori. He drove the few blocks home, called Mickey, changed into street clothes and drove back to his parents' house. If it were anyone else, he'd be back at the fire, he thought as he walked in the back door. But it wasn't anyone else, it was his wife. And he was hearing that voice again.

God, if that's you, you have to tell me what to do. In-the-nick-of-time rescues are fine, but not when it's Tori. We've got to protect her better.

Inside, his dad pointed him toward the hall bathroom where Joe heard female voices. A quick look at his hands showed they'd healed enough that Tori wouldn't notice. Just scratches now. He found his mom putting ointment on Tori's skinned palms. She'd probably have the tear in Tori's jeans mended before dinner. He smiled. Hannah always made things better. Tori was clean and dry and looked much calmer. She looked up when he leaned against the doorway.

"Joe!" The look of relief and pleasure on her face lifted his heart. "You're okay."

She started to pull away from Hannah, but Hannah stopped her with, "Hang on, let's finish your hands, he's not going anywhere."

"'Course I'm okay. How about you?" He couldn't decide if he was surprised or not that she wasn't curled up in a little ball crying. She was stronger than she sometimes appeared. Joe relaxed a little. When he told her about his family, she'd probably be okay about it. Probably. He hoped.

Hannah finished with Tori's hands and Tori jumped into his arms. Ahh. He held her close. Hannah patted his shoulder and walked back to the kitchen. In the semi-privacy of the hallway, Joe pulled Tori off the ground so her face was next to his. Her arms wrapped around his neck. They stood like that for a moment, cheek to cheek. She was okay.

But he was going to get the cretins responsible.

"You smell like smoke," he said.

She pulled back. "You, too." Her brow crinkled. "Why? Did you go outside? Did you see my car? It's the one that exploded, isn't it?"

Joe floundered, trying to figure out which question to answer first, how to answer with the least amount of lying. "I'm not sure," he began. "I saw the fire but I'm not sure how it started or—"

"It started with an *explosion*," Tori exclaimed. "Twice! A very big, very loud—Joe, I think my car blew up! I do! How can my car just blow up? And then Su—"

She stopped and studied his face. Joe could see she was trying to decide how much to tell him.

"I heard Superhero X was there." That should make it easier for her to go on.

"Yeah," she said. She shook her head. "I don't know how I've never seen a superhero my whole life and then suddenly one is popping up everywhere."

Joe could explain it to her but—

"Dinner!" Hannah called. "Everyone in the kitchen. Time to eat."

Saved by dinner.

Joe led Tori into the kitchen, trying to remember not to hold her ointment-covered hand. Seeing a hot lasagna cooling on the stove, he used a finger to pull a piece of cheese from the corner. It burned his finger, but he loved hot melted cheese.

"Ach!" Hannah swiped at his hand. "Where are your manners? Don't put your fingers in the food."

Joe grinned at his mom's back and sat down at the table. He pulled Tori into a chair next to him.

"Owen!" Hannah called. "Joe, find your dad. Dinner's ready."

"Da-ad!" Joe shouted toward the living room. "Dinner!"

Hannah turned and gave him that mom look that said, *that's not what I asked you to do, I could've done that.*

Joe chuckled and shrugged his shoulders.

Tori rolled her eyes at him and said to Hannah, "I'll get them for you."

A few seconds later, a burst of laughter came from the living room. The sound of the TV went off and everyone filed into the kitchen. Owen was explaining something to Joe's younger brother Stuart, and Stuart was laughing and arguing. Melissa exclaimed over Tori's hands and asked questions about the explosion. Tori had an arm around Joe's niece Katie.

D'oh! Joe slapped his forehead when he saw Katie. He'd promised she could visit him and Tori. He was going to help her, but he couldn't do that openly until Tori knew. Ugh, he was losing track of everything that needed to be done.

His mom caught his eye when she put the salad on the table. "We're taking care of it," she whispered, and nodded toward her granddaughter.

Joe sighed in relief. "Love you, Mom."

Finally everyone sat, Owen said grace, plates were passed,

and the family dug into the lasagna, garlic bread, and salad. Everyone but Tori.

"Tori, honey, eat something," Hannah said.

Joe glanced at Tori sitting next to him staring at her plate, fork idly pushing at her salad. "You okay? You want to lie down?"

She looked up at him. Joe couldn't ignore the rush of warmth as he held her gaze. Her hazel eyes were clear but troubled. "I can't believe Bill is dead. I haven't even finished paying for him yet."

At his family's shocked faces, Joe hurried to add, "Bill is her car."

"You named your car?" Katie laughed. "Cool."

Tori looked at Owen and Hannah, then back at Joe. "I'm going to have to talk to the police again, aren't I?" It wasn't a question.

"Not during dinner. Eat something," Hannah urged. "Then we'll talk this all out. Trust me, you're going to need your strength."

"We don't know if it was your car yet, do we?" Owen asked.

Tori looked skeptical. "It sure looked like my car. It was parked where I park."

"Well, when the police figure it out, they'll call. Meanwhile, eat while it's hot." Owen pointed his fork at Tori's plate.

She picked up a piece of garlic bread and took a bite. Then she groaned.

"I know, it's great, isn't it," Joe said. "Mom makes it fresh."

"I had two library books in the back seat!"

"Oh, man, that's terrible," said Melissa, the bookworm of the family.

"And my iPod," Tori said morosely.

"That sucks!" Katie exclaimed.

"Katie." Hannah raised her eyebrows.

"Stinks," she amended. "I'd die without my iPod."

"But she didn't die, and that's the important part," added

Stuart. "Why don't you want to talk to the police? Pass the salad, please?"

Tori wrinkled her nose at him. "I've talked to more police in the last ten years than most people do in a lifetime."

"Why?" asked Katie. She twirled melted cheese around her fork and ate just the cheese.

"It's a long story."

"I like long stories," Katie said. "Uncle Stuart's going to be a police officer, so that's why he wants to know."

"How's school going, Stuart?" Joe asked, changing the subject to give Tori some space. "I haven't seen you much lately."

The rest of dinner passed easily, the younger three talking about school, Hannah pushing food on everyone, Tori finally eating. Joe looked around the table and knew he was luckier than most. His family not only loved each other, they liked each other, too. He hoped he and Tori would be so lucky when they had kids.

Kids. Was she serious about getting pregnant? They'd just gotten married! Joe looked at Tori out of the corner of his eye as he ate. He had no intention of leaving his work as a superhero. If he didn't have his abilities and could lead a normal life, he'd probably let Tori talk him into starting a family right away. He loved what his parents had, and he wanted it for himself. But his dad had quit working as a superhero at his mom's insistence when Joe was born.

No, he wasn't ready to quit. He wasn't even sure how serious Tori was anyway. She'd been kind of hot and cold that night. Maybe she didn't really mean it. One of the long list of things they needed to discuss. Sooner rather than later.

"Tori and I will clean up the kitchen, Mom," he said. It would give them a little bit of alone time. They needed to regain some of their newlywed excitement, shake off the stress of the last few weeks. Then they could have the talk.

"Yes!" Stuart exclaimed.

Tori laughed.

"I get the remote!" said Melissa.

"I'll help in the kitchen, too," said Katie.

"That's very sweet of you," Hannah told her. "But why don't you sit in the living room with us so they can have a little bit of time together, okay?"

"You two should stay here tonight," Owen said.

Joe met his dad's eyes. Yup, that's what he was thinking. No telling if their house was safe tonight or not. "Sounds great," he said. He turned to Tori. "It'll be fun. We'll stay up late and make popcorn and watch movies." He hoped she didn't guess the real reason. He needed to get his house wired with Mickey's security system the way his mom and dad's house was. This place could be a fortress when necessary.

As people finished eating, they cleared their places and headed to the living room.

Joe considered what to say to Tori about her car blowing up. He was pretty sure it was hers. If things ever quieted down, they needed to go car shopping now, too.

He was still trying to figure out which events were linked. They all seemed so random. But Bull and Hayley both worried that maybe Joe was the link. Great! How? He hadn't been doing anything big enough to make enemies yet. And how would they find out his real identity anyway? That would be the only way to find Tori.

He scraped the plates while Tori loaded the dishwasher. He was lucky. His wife wasn't a weepy, needy, girly type who fell apart when life got rough. And since she'd never acted like a throw-caution-to-the-wind type, he felt confident that he could put her someplace safe and expect her to be there when he was done fixing the problem. That's the kind of woman he wanted, someone he could rely on. Someone who understood he had a job to do and wouldn't get in the way.

TORI USED her thumbnail to scrape a bit of cheese off a plate before she put it in the dishwasher. She didn't know what it was about Joe's family, but she felt calmer here than she did at her parents' house. She felt like she didn't have to hide anything around them. They didn't have any secrets from each other.

She rinsed out a glass and placed it in the top rack. Joe handed her some silverware, the touch of his hand sending a shiver of warmth down her arm. They shared a smile.

Tell the truth. The words echoed in Tori's mind.

Not now, with all his family around. She heard them laughing in the other room, a comforting sound. She wanted to tell Joe this weekend, sooner rather than later. Maybe when they were in bed. Just not with an audience. She'd gotten herself too riled up about whether he would accept it.

And now that she thought about it, she probably *was* too riled up. This family knew at least one superhero and had no problems with it. They accepted her exploding car with little more than concern over her welfare. Joe would handle her news as calmly as he did everything.

Tell the truth.

She looked at her husband, her head cocked as she tried to understand this funny urge to tell him *now*.

"You okay?" he asked, concern on his face.

Tori wondered if this was something weird having to do with her power, something she didn't know about yet. The urge overwhelmed her and she said, "Do you trust me enough that I can be honest with you?"

Joe frowned. "What do you mean, do I trust you? You're my wife. Of course I trust you."

Tori finished with the dishes and wiped her hands on a towel.

"No matter what?" Tori crossed her arms. Her hands squeezed into fists. She didn't really want to do this now. Not here in the kitchen.

Joe cocked his head and narrowed his eyes. He suddenly seemed very uncomfortable. "Uh, maybe."

Oh, that was *so* the wrong answer.

"Maybe?" Tori took a step toward him. She wanted to stop this conversation right now but she couldn't and it was making her fighting mad. "You want me to be honest with you, right? Tell you everything that comes into my head without knowing if it will be something you do or don't trust me on? That's ridiculous!"

Joe shook his head and took another half step back. "I didn't say I wanted to know everything that came into your head."

"Ugghhh!" Tori turned back to the cupboards. She felt scared and angry. What was happening to her? "Joe, that's not what trust is! You don't get to pick and choose. You trust me or you don't trust me."

Tell the truth.

She opened the refrigerator and pulled out butter. She went through some more cupboards looking for the popcorn.

"Why would you think I don't trust you?" Joe's voice was raised now, too. "What shouldn't I trust you about?"

Why was Joe upset? He never raised his voice. She was the one with the big secret about to pop out. And now she was more worried than ever about how he would take it.

"You don't have a reason?" he yelled. "You're just mad at me for no reason?"

Tori turned to see Joe shaking his head and walking away. Forget it. She'd obviously picked the wrong time for this conversation.

Tell the truth.

"Okay, you want to know how I expect to be trusted?" Tori felt a growing panic. This was *not* the right time for this discussion, but she couldn't help speaking. "Here's an example for you. I trust *you*. I trust you with my heart, my life, my secrets, my everything. Ready? I have a super power! *I might be a superhero, Joe!* There's the truth! There's honesty!"

She waved a bag of popcorn in the air like a mad woman. "And I'm going to fully expect you to trust me on whatever decisions I make in that regard. Because I don't know what the heck I'm doing, but *I'm doing it!*"

Tori watched Joe's expression go slack-jawed. Her hands flew to cover her mouth. They stood and stared at each other, silent, processing. All Tori could think was, *what did I just do?*

Then she noticed Katie standing slack-jawed as well near the hallway.

Oh great. She'd scarred her niece for life, too.

Tell the truth. Tori could still feel the urge to speak, but she clamped her jaws together as hard as she could and put both hands over her mouth.

Joe opened his mouth. He closed it and cleared his throat. "Okay, the truth is..." Then he frowned as if he were listening to something. He looked around the kitchen, then abruptly turned around to see Katie watching them, eyes wide.

"Katie Clarke! Get in here!"

KATIE COULD NOT BELIEVE her ears.

Aunt Tori was a superhero? And Uncle Joe didn't know?

She'd wanted to hang out with them, so she leaned against the wall outside the kitchen with her iPod turned down so she could listen. They weren't whispering so it wasn't like she was eavesdropping. If they saw her and were under the impression she was listening to music and not to them, well, they were half-right. Then when they started yelling at each other, she was too stunned to even think about giving them some privacy.

"Now!"

She jumped and hurried toward her uncle. She felt herself chewing on her lower lip. She'd worried it to bleeding a few times at home. Her uncle would understand better than her dad, right? Way more than her mom.

She looked at her aunt. Aunt Tori would surely understand. But why had everyone been keeping the family secret from her aunt if *she* was a superhero?

Katie cocked her head at her uncle and folded her arms. She was tough. She had nothing to be afraid of. And she *would not cry*.

Her uncle imitated her pose. Inside, she shrank back. He looked much more intimidating than she probably did. She couldn't hold his gaze. She looked at her aunt, hoping she'd find relief in that corner.

"Katie, I'm so sorry," Tori began. "Don't worry. Everything's going to be—"

"Is there anything you'd like to tell me, young lady?" Joe interrupted, his voice reminding her of the rumbling of a volcano she'd heard in a movie in science class.

Katie didn't have to think about that one. "No," she said, trying not to sound timid.

"Joe!" Tori frowned, looking from Joe to Katie and back.

"You're sure?" Joe asked.

Oh yes, *very* sure. Not when he glowered like that. "Yes," she said in a stronger voice.

"What did your dad mean when he told me to be careful?"

Katie felt her mouth fall open in shock. Her dad *said that*? How *rude*!

"Joe, why are you grilling Katie?" Tori moved closer, stopping halfway between Katie and Joe.

Katie looked from one adult to the other and made up her mind. She'd come in here seeking solace and understanding, but she didn't realize she'd picked the wrong adult. "Aunt Tori, I haven't done anything wrong. Honest."

She sidled over to her aunt, keeping an eye on her ferocious-looking uncle.

Tori put her arms around Katie and squeezed. Katie felt a sense of relief so strong she almost leaned into her aunt and wrapped both arms around her. But then she remembered her dignity. If she wanted to grow up to be the kind of person people loved and respected, thirteen wasn't too early to start. Nobody respected a wuss.

"Katie, do you know what I'm asking you?" Joe's expression softened infinitesimally.

Katie swallowed. She hated questions like this! What could she say? How could she answer? Slowly, she nodded her head. As she continued to meet his gaze, she beseeched him in her mind to tell the truth first. If Aunt Tori knew about him, too, then it wouldn't be so hard. They could be one big, happy family. A super freak family, but...

"That's you, isn't it?" he asked.

Tori pulled away enough to look at Katie's face. Then her eyes widened. "Oh my gosh..." she breathed out on a whisper.

Katie's insides were cramping up. But she couldn't let them know she was scared. She pulled away from her aunt, lifted her head and stared into the kitchen, not looking at anyone or anything.

"Oh, sweetie," Tori said as she hugged Katie again. "It's okay. Don't let your grumpy old uncle scare you. You and I are going to be *okay*, understand?" She pulled back and looked into Katie's eyes.

Katie tried for a moment to act cool, act like an adult, but then she fell into her aunt's embrace. She could act like a kid for just a minute. She closed her eyes and hugged her back. The first adult who didn't look at her funny. Besides her grandparents, but they loved everyone.

"So you can talk to people in their heads?" Tori asked.

Katie shrugged. "Um, I don't...I don't think so."

"She makes people tell the truth," said Joe. "Right?"

"Maybe," she mumbled, not looking at him. She let her aunt hug her and felt better than she had in months.

Tori led Katie over to the kitchen table and made her sit. Then she pulled a pitcher of lemonade out of the fridge and brought it over with two tall glasses. Katie thought it was a little funny that her aunt didn't get a glass for her uncle, but she didn't say anything.

"So," Tori said as she poured, "you didn't know till recently that you had a super power?"

Katie sipped her lemonade and shook her head, not meeting her aunt's gaze.

"Me neither," Tori said with a smile. "Do you know how it works? What you can do? How to do it?"

Katie kept her eyes on the table and shook her head again.

"Same here," Tori said. She put her hand under Katie's chin and lifted it so Katie was looking at her. "Don't worry. I met someone who's going to help us figure this out. Well, I mean, I haven't asked him yet, but I know he'll help us." Tori smoothed Katie's hair away from her face and said, "We're going to be fine. You'll see."

Katie finally smiled at her. Maybe her aunt was right. Maybe everything would be okay.

Her aunt frowned at her uncle. Katie peeked over her shoulder to see his reaction. He didn't look like a thundercloud anymore, but it wasn't good.

He cleared his throat and moved to pat her on the back. "Tori's right. You'll be fine."

She turned back to her aunt. If only Uncle Joe would tell Aunt Tori and get it over with. She hated having to keep secrets. She peeked at him one more time, wishing he would—

"No!" The way he looked at her when he said that, Katie thought lightning might come out of his ears.

Joe stood in his parents' kitchen staring at his scowling wife and his miserable niece wondering what he'd ever done to deserve this. How was he going to keep any secrets from Tori if Katie was around?

Then he caught himself. He didn't want to keep secrets from his *wife.* He let a growl escape into the back of his throat and ran one hand through his hair. He needed to get control of the situation.

"Tori, we have to talk. You can't do this. You're going to get yourself killed." Joe sighed, closing his eyes. It was one thing to put himself in danger. There was no way he wanted his wife in harm's way.

The silence in the kitchen was deafening. He looked up to see what the problem was. His sweet-tempered wife had murder in her eyes. For him? Because he wanted her to be safe? He groaned again. "What?"

"*What?* You're asking me *what?*"

It looked like Tori was grinding her teeth. Joe figured keeping his distance would be prudent.

"Katie, would you mind giving us some privacy, please?" Tori smiled tightly at Katie, who grabbed her lemonade and fled the room.

Joe hoped she wasn't telling her grandparents. He needed a minute with Tori first. What had gotten into her head that she thought she had a super power? Who told her that? He wondered if she hit her head tonight when the explosion knocked them off their feet. He took Katie's seat and reached for Tori's hand.

"Let's start at the beginning," he said in his best customer service voice. Calm, cool, collected, he'd get to the bottom of all this. What did Tori know about super powers anyway? She was probably confused about...about something. But he'd help her figure it out.

Tori eyed him with a distrustful gleam in her eye. She let him take her hand, but it lay limp in his. "All right," she said cautiously.

Joe rubbed her hand between his. Calm. They'd both stay calm. He cleared his throat. "So when did you find out you had a..." He hesitated, but when her eyes narrowed to razors, he finished. "A super power."

"A few weeks ago," she said, "after the convenience store robbery."

"And you didn't tell me?" Joe heard his voice rise and Tori tried to pull her hand away. "Sorry, sorry," he said in a softer voice, not letting go of her hand. "So...you found out...something, and then what?"

"Joe, you not believing me is the same as you not trusting me," Tori said. She sounded disappointed in him. Which really steamed him up under the circumstances.

"You throw this at me—*honey, I think I'm a superhero*—moments after a superhero rescues you *again*—"

"I don't *need* rescuing!"

"And I'm supposed to say, *Congratulations, let's watch a movie*?" Joe shook his head. "Huh-uh, it doesn't work that way. I can't switch gears that fast."

Tori ripped her hand out of his and marched over to the stove. "I don't expect you to not be surprised," she said. She opened drawers until she found scissors and cut open the top of the popcorn bag. "But you should know me well enough to know I don't make up outrageous stories!" She poured oil into a frying pan and turned the burner on high.

She turned back to face him. "You think this didn't shock the socks off me? You bet it did! The SLU tried to convince me—"

"The SLU? The Superhero Liaison Unit? They're involved?" Joe slammed his fist down on the table causing everything to jump. Grimacing, he looked down to see if he'd damaged his mother's table. A bit of a dent, but no cracks in the wood. He needed to calm down or he'd have to explain why he could crack an oak table in half. Now was not the time.

"They've been helping me get acclimated—"

"Acclimated to what? You haven't done any fighting, have you?" Joe raked his fingers through his hair, his heart pounding. Memories of some of the thugs he'd battled in the past assaulted him. Tori would be torn to pieces!

"Not fighting, saving!" Tori poured popcorn into the heating oil. Her delicate hand clenched a spatula. A hand that could so easily be broken. "That's what I'm trying to tell you. I stopped that robbery and—"

"What do you mean you stopped the robbery? How?" Joe couldn't stay seated any longer. He paced over to the stove and leaned against the counter, hands clutching the counter edge to keep them still.

Tori explained about the robbery, the talk with the SLU, how she realized she could use her power on herself. She could control people with her mind? That's incredible! Unbelievable! And she'd done it to him. It couldn't be true, could it?

"The only people I know who can do that are villains!" Joe burst out. A chunk of the counter broke off in his left hand.

Tori gasped. A long intake of breath accompanied by a look of mingled pain and anger and disbelief.

He looked at the piece of countertop in his hand. "Don't worry, I'll fix it." He saw her face and realized she was upset about the villains comment, not the counter. Crap. "No honey, honey, I didn't—" Joe dropped the piece of countertop and reached for Tori as she turned on him with the spatula.

"Villains?" she shouted, hitting him with the spatula. "*Villains?*" She hit him again, leaving a second oily splotch on his shirt.

Joe smelled burning oil. He grabbed Tori's wrist before she hit him again. "I didn't say *you* were a villain."

She kicked him in the shin. He grabbed her other wrist as she lunged for him. "I meant people who make poor choices and—" He held her at arm's length. "And end up on the other side of the law." She twisted and bit his wrist.

"Ow!" Joe let her go and stepped back, looking at his arm in shock. When he wasn't touching some kind of metal—his wedding ring only helped a little—and focusing on his power, his body was far less resistant. His wrist *hurt*. "I can't believe you bit me!"

Pop! Pop-pop! Bursting kernels of corn bounced out of the pan and onto the counter and floor. Oil splattered onto the burner and burned with black smoke and a foul odor.

"What's going on in here?"

Joe and Tori looked up to see Owen and Hannah rushing into the kitchen. Owen turned off the stove, Hannah handed him a lid, and Owen covered the exploding popcorn, flinching as hot oil flicked onto his skin.

He turned to them. "*Well?*"

"She bit me!" Joe hadn't meant to say that. Seeing that stern look on his parents' faces sometimes caused him to revert to adolescent behavior.

Tori looked contrite for the three seconds it took for her to see she hadn't broken the skin. Then she puffed up with anger again. "He called me a villain!"

"I did not!"

"You better watch it or I'll *make you* do something you don't want to do!"

"Oh, come on," Joe yelled back, his patience at an end. "You make me do things I don't want to do all the time! Honey, take out the trash! Honey, my car needs an oil change! Honey, come to brunch with my parents!" He leaned closer and pointed his finger in her face. "Trust me, babe, every woman gets that power when she puts on a wedding ring, and that don't make her a superhero!"

Tori's face contorted with rage. "Aarghhh!"

Joe jumped away and headed for the door. Why had he said those things? He was out of control, he knew that, and it really bothered him. But not half as much as thinking about Tori in danger. He grabbed his coat and slammed the door behind him. He needed to leave before they hurt each other again.

Before we hurt each other more than we already have.

14

Tori trudged over to her house the next morning. Alone. Joe had stayed out late, long after she'd gone to bed. She didn't know where he went, but she felt the bed move when he climbed in. He didn't spoon her, though, and he was gone before she woke up.

She had to face the fact that her worst fears might be coming true. Joe was okay with other people having super powers, even his own niece, but not his wife. Especially if she might be a villain.

Tori tried not to cry. The tears would sting her face in the cold morning air.

His parents had been far more supportive, though not very helpful. They asked her questions and listened to her calmly, reassuring her that she'd figure it all out in time. They knew some other people with super powers, they said, and it was never a quick or easy process, figuring out what you were capable of.

They tried to reassure her that Joe would come around. That one was harder to believe. Tori was smart enough to know that it was because her heart was involved that she was so scared. She'd much rather not have a super power than not have Joe. But neither of those things seemed to be up to her. Still, Owen and Hannah were unwilling to step in and offer any guidance until she and Joe talked. That seemed to be their primary piece of advice.

Her in-laws were wonderful, optimistic people, but Tori didn't know how long it would be before Joe was willing to discuss their new reality. She needed to talk to someone who really understood. She ditched her plan to tell Owen everything in favor of a better idea.

She let herself into her house—oh dear, would it be just Joe's house again soon? Don't think about it. Don't! She blinked rapidly. Then she found the Christmas wreath she'd put away. She hung it on the hook on the back door.

Would he see it? How long would it take for him to notice?

She went upstairs and put on her long underwear under her clothes. She found a pair of chemical hand warmers and some protein bars and stuffed them in her pockets. Grabbing her warmest outerwear and her wallet, she set off for the bus stop. Now that she didn't have a car, she'd have to memorize the bus schedule again.

Forty minutes later, she walked into Gaffney Park. Now what? She should've brought a book. She could listen to podcasts on her phone for a couple hours before the battery died.

"Are you going to fix this, God?" She believed everything eventually worked out for good, not necessarily for the best as she saw it, but good. She'd been around the faith mountain enough times to know that you had no idea how or when bad times would turn around. You just had to believe they would, and they did.

She opened an app on her phone and found one of her favorite radio shows, a woman preacher.

"Consider it pure joy," the woman said now, "when trials come your way because the testing of your faith produces character."

Tori sighed and shook her head. "Don't I have enough character yet, God?"

She sat and listened to the podcast for an hour, but he didn't show.

She walked around and ate one of her protein bars. She watched some children building a snowman. But he didn't come.

She hurried across the street to a fast food restaurant so she could use the bathroom. She bought a hot chocolate and hurried back to the park. It didn't look like he'd been there.

She ate her last protein bar and tried to figure out what she should do if he didn't help her. Another hour later, after four hours alone in the cold, her heaviest winter clothes weren't keeping her warm enough. She had to face the fact that Superhero X wasn't coming. So she made the only decision she could.

She'd go it alone.

Tori woke up Monday morning to her cell phone ringing in the otherwise empty guest room at her in-laws'. She and Joe had barely spoken over the weekend. Of course, she'd hardly seen him. Everyone but Tori agreed they should continue to sleep at Owen and Hannah's "just in case."

"Just in case, what?" she asked. "Joe's house explodes next?" She laughed, but the others only smiled. For goodness' sake, what was going on? She had a right to know.

She hit the button on her phone and tried to say hello like she was awake.

"Tori, hi, it's Janice. Listen, I have good news and bad news. The good news is, you can take some time off and enjoy this beautiful day."

Tori covered her eyes with her hand. More character, huh, God? "The bad news is I'm fired?"

"Well..." Tori waited as Janice tried to find a positive spin for the situation. "You've been through a lot there, and Pam feels you probably need some time to..."

Yeah, I think I need time to...too.

"Okay, thanks, Janice."

"Oh, honey, I'm so sorry. I'm glad you're okay, though. Call me when you're ready to look for another job."

Tori lay in bed thinking. What should she do? She didn't feel like trying to sleep until life got better. That might require a cryogenic sleep tank. Most everyone she knew either wasn't talking to her, or was at work or school. She didn't have a car to go anywhere. That left hanging out here or going someplace she could get to by bus.

She showered and got dressed, then went downstairs to find something to eat for breakfast. She felt Snickers rub against her legs. "Morning, baby," she said, picking the cat up. Joe had brought him over sometime Friday night. "Are you enjoying all the extra attention?" She scratched the cat and looked around to be sure no one was around to listen. "That makes one of us," she whispered.

Snickers purred in reply.

Tori made a quick breakfast of peanut butter and jam on toast and ate it standing at the kitchen counter. "What do you think, Snickers? Do I seem like the superhero type to you?"

Snickers turned his head and listened to an imagined noise in the living room.

"Don't worry, everyone's at work." Tori took another bite of toast, Snickers tucked under her other arm. "I don't know. What would I do? And where? And *how*?" She rubbed her chin over the top of the cat's head.

Licking the last of the peanut butter from her fingers, Tori stared at the cat. Even if she wanted to—and wasn't *that* the million dollar question—she wouldn't know how to proceed.

"I think we should take the easy way out and ignore the whole thing," she said to the cat.

Snickers stared up at her, unblinking.

"What? You think I should ask someone? Like a superhero? I tried. Didn't work." Tori scratched his head and tried not to think about it. Maybe Casey could introduce her to another one. If she was a superhero liaison, she must know lots of superheroes. "You're not coming up with many good ideas, mister," she said to Snickers.

Tori sighed and put the cat on the floor. She finished off her orange juice, put the dishes in the dishwasher, and grabbed her purse.

"God," she said, stopping on her way out the door and looking expectantly at the hallway ceiling, "I could use some direction here. Just in case you weren't aware of it."

As it turned out, her prayers were answered before she could get to the mall. Tori was walking from the bus stop toward the mall entrance past the parking garage when a young woman hurried up to her.

"Excuse me, but can I get a ride with you? There's a man following me and I'm afraid to walk to my car." The girl was a few years younger than Tori, wide eyes, shaking hands.

"I don't have my car here, but I'll walk you to your car." Tori looked around as the woman moved closer. "Where is he?"

Following the other woman's gaze, Tori caught sight of a poorly dressed man with a scruffy beard heading their way.

"I thought he might be following me so I walked past my car and up a level. But he *is* following me. That's my car he's passing now. The red Camry."

"C'mon." Tori walked with the woman around the outside of the parking structure and back in the other side. No security guards around. They both tried to keep an eye on Scruffy. He was still following, but not quickly. They reached the Camry and the woman dug her keys out of her purse and unlocked the door.

"You should get in, too. I'll drive you back to the entrance."

Tori looked up and followed the young woman's gaze. Scruffy was jogging toward them.

He laughed. "Ain't this my lucky day?" he called out.

Tori glanced quickly around the garage. No one else was around to help, and if Tori was going to try, she didn't want an audience anyway. She told the woman, "Get in. Lock your door and unlock my side." Just in case.

Her heart was racing. She felt her breath coming quickly, clouds of white puffing around her face. She tried to control her breathing. Now was not the time to get cold feet. Now was the time for action.

And that would be...?

Her mind froze for a second as the man jogged closer. He was only three parking spaces away. She had to *do* something.

"*Stop!*" That worked last time.

His steps faltered.

"I said *stop!*" An emotion that felt like both anger and fear and something else welled up inside. It felt vaguely familiar. But what should she say to scare him? "One more step and you're going to wish you'd never met me!"

Whatever *that* meant. She sounded ridiculous. She narrowed her eyes at him. She had a super power, darn it! She'd *force* him to listen to her.

If she could figure out how.

The man stopped. He stood staring at her, looking a little confused...and more than a little scary. He stood about Tori's height, five-eight or nine maybe, and lean. Tori couldn't tell if he was lean and strong, or lean and thin. But he looked hungry, and that couldn't be good.

She thought of some of the reality police shows she and Joe watched. They made perps sit down while they questioned them.

Perps? So now she was going to think in terms of reality cop shows?

Tori focused her thoughts and energy at him, hoping that's all she needed to do. "Sit down. Now!"

The man dropped to the cement. Still staring at her with his watery eyes.

Wow, it worked. She tried to contain her surprise. Now that immediate danger was delayed, Tori tried to think logically. She couldn't just tell the woman to drive off. Then Tori or someone else might be in danger next. What would the police do?

Tori mentally smacked her forehead. Police! Exactly!

She pulled her cell phone out of her purse. Keeping one eye on Scruffy, she hunted for the card Casey had given her. She felt embarrassed to call 911, but she definitely wanted police to come. And Casey was the police.

"Casey Knox."

"Oh, thank you! Casey, this is Tori Clarke. We spoke a week or two ago?" Tori tried to calm down. Now that the moment was here, the moment she should be acting like a superhero, she wanted to appear in control, not hysterical.

"Tori, yes, how are you?"

Fake it. *Pretend* to be the person you want to be until it becomes second nature. Her seventh grade gym teacher had told her that.

"Uh, I'm good," she said with a little false cheer. "But I need your help. Now, if you please. I found a situation and I need backup, er—" Oh geez, too much TV! "What I mean is, there's this guy, he's on the ground right now, but—"

"Okay, give me your location and I'll send a squad car over. Are you in immediate danger?"

"Uh," Tori stared at Scruffy and tried to decide if she was in danger. "Depends on how long this—*effect* lasts, I guess."

"Okay, I'll send a car over, and Art and I will be there as soon as we can."

"Great. Thanks." Tori told her where to find them, then dropped her phone back into her purse. Wondering if she had anything useful for catching bad guys, she dug through the rest of the contents. Nope. Not unless safety-pinning his sleeves together or stuffing Kleenex tissues in his mouth would help. She could always get in the car and lock the door, if necessary. But she didn't want to get away, she wanted to help.

Tori opened the door and told the young woman that the police were on the way. The girl relaxed a smidgen and nodded. Tori closed the door, leaving it unlocked in case she needed an escape route.

She walked to the end of the car so she could see Scruffy better. Hadn't he sat down by the green Honda? Because now he was sitting in back of the gray Ford. As Tori watched, his feet inched out a bit, then his butt slid forward.

So that's how you're gonna play it, huh? Well, so far he was doing what she'd told him—sitting. She just wasn't specific enough, apparently.

An image of a family picnic of long ago popped into her head. Her aunts yelled to get all the kids to behave, but her uncles intimidated.

"What are you afraid of?" Tori tried to imitate her uncles' tone of voice. "Tell me, Scruffy."

Scruffy stopped moving and his eyes lost focus, seeing something behind Tori perhaps. "Snakes."

Tori glanced over her shoulder, then back at him. "You mean, big nasty snakes like those?"

Scruffy began to tremble. His eyes bulged and widened, and his mouth moved soundlessly.

He was really seeing snakes? "You don't want to get bit by snakes like that, do you?"

The man started inching backward.

"If you sit still and don't move *one inch*, they won't bite you." *Totally* making this up. Tori hoped the girl in the car couldn't hear her. She could barely believe she was making him see things. But she could feel a hot churning in her gut and in her head. It must be her power working.

Scruffy stopped, then looked behind him.

"You don't want to know how many snakes are in here. *A lot.* Snakes to your right, snakes to your left, in front of you, behind you."

Drool dripped from Scruffy's mouth as his eyes skittered around the garage.

This was *fascinating.* Tori tried to gauge how far was far enough to keep the man in line. She didn't want to give him a heart attack or anything.

"Hey, *hey!*" She snapped her fingers to get his attention. Scruffy looked at her. "I promise not to let a single one of them near you if you stay exactly where you are. Okay? Don't move and I promise you'll be fine."

He nodded vigorously, pulling his body into as small a space as he could.

He was so petrified that Tori looked around a little uneasily to make sure there really weren't any snakes. She couldn't make things appear. Right?

Of course not. She mentally shook herself. She couldn't make things appear, except in people's heads. Well, that's a new fact to file.

She turned when a car screeched up the turn leading to the second floor of the garage. A police car rolled their way and two men in blue got out.

"Tori Clarke?"

Safety! Tori's grin rivaled the size of the Grand Canyon. "Yes! Boy, am I glad to see you guys!"

One of the cops walked closer to the blubbering Scruffy. "Homeless guy?"

Oh dear, what had Casey told them? Would they think she was a freak when they saw what she'd done?

"Uh, no, maybe. He was following this girl," Tori pointed to the young woman hesitantly emerging from her car, "and she asked me for help. It looked like he was going to try to attack us both, but I made him...stop." Tori finished lamely, glancing nervously from one cop to the other to Scruffy and back to the first cop. She didn't sound like a superhero when she babbled.

Both officers looked at her. "Good," said the younger one looking back at the quivering man on the ground. "What'd you do to him?"

"Hel-help me," Scruffy blubbered to the cop.

"He's, uh, apparently afraid of...snakes." Tori glanced at the cop nearest her and back at Scruffy. "So I let him believe that they wouldn't bite him if he didn't move."

Tori was unprepared for their laughter. It bounced off the walls of the garage. Looking at them, she realized they didn't think she was a freak. Relief washed over her.

The first cop reached over to shake hands. "Sergeant Chas Richards." He nodded to the other cop. "Officer Dick Nelson. Knox and Paredes should be here any minute."

Nelson nudged Scruffy with his foot. "Calm down. Put your hands behind your back."

When nothing happened, Nelson looked at Tori. "Can you help us out here?"

Tori cleared her throat. This was totally surreal.

"Hey! Scruffy!" Tori snapped her fingers. He looked at her, then beyond her, and shuddered with fear. "I promised I wouldn't let them get you if you sat still and you did, so now I'm making them go away." She swept her arm broadly around her, focusing on what she was telling him. "See? They're gone. No more snakes. Now just do what the nice officer says, okay?"

Feeling self-conscious, Tori crossed her arms over her wool coat and turned away to see Casey and Art pull up behind the squad car. She hurried over, feeling a strange sense of belonging as she approached. Here were two people who wouldn't think anything strange was going on.

"Hey, Art. Hey, Casey." Going for cool and in control.

"*Hola*, what's up?" Art got out and walked to Tori, shaking her hand as he took in the scene.

Tori wanted to hug them both, but she controlled herself. "Well, uh, Scruffy here is afraid of snakes, so..." Tori told them what happened as concisely as possible.

Art and Casey watched Officer Nelson cuff Scruffy while Sergeant Richards talked to the young woman. Tori studied each one of them, the four police officers, the girl, the bad guy. What did all of this look like from their perspectives?

'Cause to her it was freakin' weird!

Now that it was over, Tori's mind filled with doubts about this whole thing. What if Joe or her parents saw a picture of her in the paper or on the news? What if her friends or her coworkers found out? And what did she think of the looks cast her way by the young woman she'd just helped?

Not that she expected gratitude. Okay, a little gratitude. But she didn't expect to feel like the new girl in high school—lots of staring, little in the way of welcome.

"Good job." Art clapped her on the back. "You're learning how to use your power creatively, that's for sure."

"Nice work, Tori." Casey smiled at her.

Okay, *now* she felt better. Tori took her first deep breath of the hour. She did it! She helped someone by using her head, without holding back or pretending she couldn't. Whatever the cop was saying to the woman by her car, it probably wasn't, "That woman you asked for help is actually a superhero with scary powers."

"So you're in, huh?" Art asked.

"Well," Tori took another deep breath, "let's see how it goes."

HAYLEY FINISHED COUNTING and wrote a number on her re-order form. Even the boring parts of owning a nursery made her happy. If this were the only thing she did in life, she'd be content. Well, this and being married. That's all she wanted.

Okay, she *really* wanted a baby, but maybe that wouldn't be a good idea. On the other hand, she wasn't always as careful as she should be, so who knows? She didn't know if she did the things she did hoping she'd get pregnant, or to punish herself, or because she really didn't care.

She heard someone hurrying up behind her and turned. She smiled. "Hey!" she said to Tori.

"Hey!" Tori said with a grin. "I did it!"

Tori pulled on Hayley's arm and headed for the office. Inside, she shut the door and turned to Hayley. "I really did it!" she said again. Her voice went up in a squeal at the end. "I helped someone!"

"You—? Ohhh." Hayley sank into her chair. "Wow. So soon?" Hayley fought off a sense of dread. Tori shouldn't be out there on her own with no mentor. Hayley remembered how badly she'd screwed up when she had no one to ask. She wanted to be happy for Tori. But having a super power wasn't all fireworks and parades. Joe should be helping her. Well, if he wasn't going to, Hayley would.

She smiled at her friend. What's not to be happy about? Tori was alive and well. She hadn't been thrown off the top of a forty-story building. She hadn't been shot with a semi-automatic weapon. Apparently, she hadn't divorced her husband. These were all good things.

"I feel *high* or something," Tori marveled, pacing the tiny office. "I mean, if this is what it feels like to be high, to take drugs, I *definitely* see the appeal."

"Oh dear," Hayley laughed. "Please don't."

Tori whirled at one end of the office. "Not that I'm going to take drugs or anything! But Hayley, I *helped* someone. I *saved* someone. Do you think doctors feel this way? Firemen? Lawyers?" Tori whirled again. "*Parents.* I bet parents feel this way when their kids are small and doing all sorts of death-defying things. It's no wonder superheroes want to be superheroes!"

Not all of them did. But Hayley was part of a team now. They counted on her to be there for them and she didn't have a good reason to quit. Bull pulled his share of the load with a full-time job, so she did, too. But if Hayley ever got to be a parent, she'd feel much more high than she'd ever felt saving people. That would be the ultimate high.

Tori continued to babble for a moment while Hayley tried to arrange her thoughts. Had she been this way? Ever? She was happy to help people, generally happy to help the team, but she couldn't remember ever feeling the way Tori did now. It was all about the plants for Hayley. Everything else was icing.

And she didn't always like icing.

"I wish I could tell Lexie." Tori shook her head. "Later. She wouldn't understand yet."

Hayley allowed herself to be pulled into her friend's enthusiasm. She so wanted to jump in and say, I have a super power, too, we can be superheroes together! But it appeared she had no option but to ride this out until she could convince Joe to tell his wife his secret—*everyone's* secret. Grr.

"It was amazing!" Tori said. "I've never done anything like that before! He totally believed there were snakes all around him, and he just sat there shaking and drooling until the police came."

"I wish I could've seen it," said Hayley. "It sounds amazing."

Tori threw her hands up in the air. "I feel *great*! I'm on an adrenaline rush or something. Total euphoria. I feel like I could go do it again right now!"

Hayley laughed. "You sound so happy, Tori."

"*I am.* But all I could think about when it was over was what if a newspaper photographer had been there and my parents saw a picture? I didn't even have sunglasses on or anything." Tori pulled a comical worried face. "I have to tell you, I'm more worried about that than anything else. It's one thing that keeps me second-guessing whether I should really be doing this. You know my parents."

Don't worry, Hayley thought, I'm doing enough second-guessing for both of us.

"I'm happy that you've had such a great first experience," she said, determined to help Tori since no one else would. "But what about all the situations you'll find yourself in that you never considered?"

Hayley tried to act like she'd just thought of these things, not like she'd been dealing with them for years. "The potential for violence? The long hours and missed birthdays? The fear when a Jack tries to hurt someone you love?" Hayley bit her tongue and hoped Tori missed the fact that Hayley had just used a word she shouldn't know.

"Oh. Right." Tori paused in her manic pacing.

Hayley didn't want to bring her down. Not today. Today Tori was alive and well and had a successful episode. Now was the time to celebrate.

"Are you doing anything tonight?" Hayley asked. "I don't suppose you and that blockhead of yours are speaking to each other yet?"

"He's not a blockhead, Hay, he's..." Tori struggled to find a way to express herself.

Hayley laughed. "He's a blockhead."

Tori grinned. "Maybe a little." Her smiled faltered. "What would I do without you? You're my only true friend."

Though it sounded kind of nice, Hayley dissented. "That's not true. I'm just the only person you know who's not easily surprised."

That brought back Tori's smile. "Do you really think that's all it is?"

"Tor, a teenage girl used a super power on you and she didn't even know what she was doing. It went horribly wrong. Who knows what was happening inside your heads or how long the effects will last. Maybe it's long over, maybe it's not." She shrugged. Then she had another thought. "But knowing Joe, I'd guess you haven't seen him because he's out bustin' a cap in some guy for blowing up your car."

Tori laughed. "I could see that being a possibility."

"Now back to you. We have to celebrate your first bust. What do you want to do?"

"Owen and Hannah seem to be trying to make every night wonderful and entertaining," Tori said. "I think they're trying to make me feel better about everything. Since we're staying with them, why don't you come over? It's way more fun there than at my house."

Hayley loved Joe's parents. In her dream world, she'd be one of their daughters: loved, supported, encouraged. "Sure, why not?" she said. "Should I bring some wine?"

"Sure, I'm not driving. Ever." Tori laughed. "Ooo, stay over! It'll be fun!"

"Uh, we'll see." Hayley wanted to say yes. It did sound fun. "I'm not sure how your new husband would feel about a sleep-over. But maybe we can sneak off somewhere and talk about how to keep you safe. A costume or something."

"Okay, cool."

Hayley played one more mentor card. "This superhero thing isn't an exciting new job, Tori. You have no idea what's going to happen next. You've got to ask yourself if you're willing to totally change your life, leave your current life behind. Forever."

And tonight she was going to find Joe and remind him the same thing. Last month he was just a superhero. Now he was going to have to accept and embrace that he was half of a super-hero couple, whether he liked it or not.

15

Apparently the criminal set weren't morning people.

Tori liked mornings. She could talk to God, pet the cat, make love with Joe—when they were speaking to each other—and still be ready to go by eight. Aside from ignoring her husband as she pretended he wasn't glaring at her, mornings were good.

It wasn't even that hard to ignore him when they were at his parents'. Their house always seemed to be full of people at all times of the day and night. Besides Stuart and Melissa who lived there, Katie seemed to be there a lot, and the other kids and grandkids were always running in and out. When Owen wasn't working at the church, he had people over at the house. It was kind of fun.

But Tori couldn't find anyone who needed a superhero in the morning. That blasted robbery happened in the afternoon. She met Scruffy close to noon. She heard about a purse-snatcher on the news, and even he snatched in the afternoon.

Last night, Hayley had come over and the Clarke family had tried to teach the two of them how to play poker. Turned out Hayley was shockingly good, and Tori had no poker face at all.

Hannah had patted her hand and said, "That only means you aren't a good liar, and that's a good thing."

But everyone got up this morning and went to work or school or wherever they were expected. Tori wanted to do something important with her day, too. So she went looking for trouble.

Once again, she couldn't find it until the afternoon. She was walking past Pete's Deli & Liquor and found herself faced with another "situation."

"Let me *go*!"

Tori saw an older man sitting on the sidewalk holding onto the bottom of a woman's coat. This guy made Scruffy look clean and respectable. His long white hair was tangled and matted over greasy skin. His clothes were cement-gray and fraying around the edges. He sat huddled on a pile of sleeping bags.

"Just some change," the old man said. His fierce grip seemed incongruous with his rheumy eyes. "You got change. You just bought something. Share your wealth with a sick old man."

The woman pulled at her coat, her anger boiling over into a slew of curse words.

Tori considered telling the woman to apologize. She understood—she was tired of men who don't listen, too. But that's no reason to be acerbic.

Problem was, she hadn't earned her assertiveness badge yet from the Superhero Scouts. So she walked over and spoke to the old man instead. Since it was winter, she'd decided to put off her costume problem for a little while and just use her hat and scarf for cover. "Let her go, sir," Tori said without preamble.

"Wha—?" His bleary eyes turned to her. Now that she was closer, she could smell alcohol and body odor wafting up like an anti-perfume.

The woman pulled part of her jacket free, but the drunk still had the belt caught in his fingers.

Maybe her power wasn't strong enough when her mouth was covered. Maybe people couldn't hear her well enough. "Let go of her jacket, sir," Tori repeated more firmly, too nervous to pull the scarf away from her face.

His fingers relaxed somewhat and the woman jerked free. As Tori fought the urge to call out, "You're welcome!" to the ungrateful woman's back, the grasping hand caught her wrist.

"Spare some change?" The man's breath was too close for comfort.

Tori turned her head away, trying not to breathe any more than she had to. The man *reeked*. She twisted her wrist, trying to free herself without being obviously rude. "Maybe, let me check."

Better to give him some money than be caught in his grasp. The man obviously had issues, bigger problems than Tori could help. She'd helped the woman regain possession of her coat. Perhaps that was all she could do today.

The old man wouldn't release Tori's wrist, so she pulled a dollar out of her pants pocket with her other hand. He'd have to let her go to take the money. "Here."

He grabbed it with his other hand, and pulled her closer with her captured wrist. "Give an old man a kiss." He puckered up and tried to move closer.

Tori bounded back in surprise, trying to hide her disgust.

"Let go of me!"

This time her voice must've carried more weight because he let go. Tori took a quick step back and rubbed her wrist against her pants leg.

A businessman in a trench coat walked out of the store and the old man grabbed the hem of his coat. "Spare some change?"

The man shook his head without meeting the drunk's gaze and pulled away.

The drunk let loose a string of curses at the other man's retreating back.

"Hey!" Tori was too shocked to keep the reprimand back. Her natural tendency to try to help had been reinforced by her parents' urgings to "do the right thing" and "be a good citizen."

But they'd also taught her that cursing was both rude and a lazy way to communicate. "Do you live somewhere? Can I call someone for you?" she asked.

"I live with *you*. I'll kiss you all you want." The man tried to stumble to his feet.

"Sit down!" She needed to relax and think, but he was making her nervous. The Tori from last month would've given him the money and darted away, praying for him whenever she thought of him. But the post-robbery Tori, the one who knew she had a super power...maybe she could find some added confidence if she *pretended* she was a superhero who knew what she was doing. If only there were a handbook. *In this situation, refer to page 73.*

If only.

Well, much as she didn't want to bother her *yet again*, Casey would know what to do. As the drunk sagged back to the sidewalk, Tori dialed her number.

And got her voice mail.

"Casey, it's Tori Clarke. Sorry to bother you, but I've got a drunk here accosting people on the street and I wasn't sure—do I call the police? Which department? I'm at Lincoln and 22nd Street in front of"—Tori looked up at the sign—"Pete's Deli & Liquor. Call me on my cell phone if you get this in the next half hour or so. Thanks."

Tori ended the call and slid her phone back into her pocket. She looked down at the mess of humanity at her feet. She didn't understand how people came to this. Or how they got out.

"Come on, pretty girl, give an old man a little kiss." He started to get up again.

"*Sit!*" Tori half-yelled at him.

In her peripheral vision, she saw people watching as they passed. She fought embarrassment. Okay, sure she sounded like she was ordering a disobedient dog, but he wouldn't *listen*.

He reached for another passerby. "Spare some change?"

"Hey!" Tori snapped her fingers in front of his face. When he was looking directly at her again, she said, "*Sit still, do not move, do not speak. Understand?*"

Her cell phone rang. Casey's name flashed onto the screen. Relief washed over her. She stepped farther away from the old man so he couldn't grab her when she wasn't looking, then pressed Talk.

"Hey, Tori. Casey. I was on the other line. What can I do for you?"

Tori explained the situation, and Casey assured her they'd send a unit right over.

Putting her phone away, Tori folded her arms over her chest and stared at the drunk. Sitting quietly for a change.

She looked around the street, hoping the police car would come quickly. She was getting embarrassed, people staring at her as if this old man were her problem. She was just trying to help. Instead she was beginning to feel harassed herself. Was she even supposed to call the police on drunks and homeless people? Well, she only did it because they were assaulting people.

A hand closed around her ankle. Tori jumped—half a jump, as the other half of her was connected to the trapped ankle.

"What did I just—"

"I believe the lady told you to sit."

A tremor shook Tori's stomach as she turned. She knew that voice.

And much as she'd desperately wanted to talk to him on Saturday, today she wanted to prove that she could do this superhero thing on her own.

"You're late," she said, letting a little heat creep into her words. "I don't need you anymore."

Pedestrians slowed on the sidewalk, staring as slack-jawed as the drunk.

It occurred to Tori that she'd never seen Superhero X in the daylight. The man was huge. He must've stood close to six and a half feet tall, arms folded like ax handles over his chest, feet planted like trees. He flicked his gaze over to Tori and back to the drunk. Who gaped at him and slowly released Tori's ankle.

"He did that because I told him to, by the way," she said, nodding to her foot and stepping away.

His eyes moved in such a way that Tori knew he raised his eyebrows under his mask. He didn't even have the courtesy to believe her. His gaze was intense, but with an underlying sense of humor. Tori tried to decide if he was laughing at her.

He was bigger than she remembered. Broader. When the word "handsomer" began to cross her mind, she gave herself a mental shake. It wasn't even a word. And she was a *married* woman now. Not like when they met at Halloween. Maybe, possibly, she'd been infatuated with him for, like, a *day*. But that day was long gone and she shouldn't be thinking about it now.

Irritated with herself, she took it out on him. "What are you doing here?" She shook her ankle like she'd stepped in something nasty and glared at the drunk. Who knew what was on his hands?

"Helping. What are you doing here?" His neutral tone irritated her even more.

"I found him," Tori motioned vaguely toward the sidewalk, "harassing people. I'm trying to get him some help."

Superhero X didn't take his eyes off her as he lifted his right arm and pushed back a flap of his costume exposing what resembled a wristwatch. She'd noticed it last Friday after her car exploded. He pushed a button and spoke.

"Patrol car needed at Lincoln and 22nd Street. A drunk harassing pedestrians. Situation under control."

Tori glared at him. "*I* already called the police. *I* have the situation under control."

A tinny female voice came from his watch, or whatever it was. "Acknowledged, Superhero X, car on its way."

Tori fumed. A voice in her head suggested her reaction was unreasonable. But he acted like she was incompetent. She was *totally* competent.

"*I have it under control.*" The gathering pedestrians caused Tori to pitch her voice at a teeth-grinding stage whisper. She crossed her knotted fists under her arms and kept her back to the crowd. Why didn't he tell people to move on, nothing to see?

Though he truly was something to look at. His eyes were the rich brown of Godiva chocolate. They radiated both authority and compassion.

"You're huge," the drunk whispered in alcohol-inspired awe.

"He didn't seem to be listening to you." Superhero X tilted his head and raised his eyebrows in question. His voice was as deep as the harbor at the end of the pier, deep and dark and slightly metallic sounding. Tori tried not to think about what it did to her stomach.

No, what she needed to focus on was his costume, his watch, his thingy that changed his voice. Those were things she needed help with, needed to get for herself. But no, he had to make her feel like she couldn't take care of one single drunk on her own. She was disappointed in him.

"No one listens when they're drunk." Tori noticed people openly staring at Superhero X as if she weren't even there. He ignored them, focusing on her and the old man. Tori felt her heart racing. She tried to remember if this was what it felt like when her power was building. Or maybe this was what it felt like to be around this superhero.

Weirdly, he reminded her of Joe in a lot of ways. Especially in the daylight. But this guy was bigger than Joe, tougher, scarier. Only she wasn't scared around him. In fact, she felt a little like she felt around Joe. Safe. She remembered she felt a little safer with him after her car blew up.

But today she was also a little angry. Why did he think she couldn't...ohhh.

She'd never told him. He didn't know.

She moved closer to him, back still to the pedestrians, and whispered, "There's something you need to know." She looked up at him, but couldn't hold his gaze. She moved her scarf a little so she could lower her voice even more. "I can..."

Wow, how exactly do you word it? Hey, I'm part of the fraternity. Hi, I can do *super* stuff—wink. That song from *Annie Get Your Gun* shot through her head and she wanted to sing, "Anything you can do, I can do better!" But that probably wouldn't ingratiate herself to him.

She finally went with, "I can convince people to listen to me." Yeah, that sounded good. Not as scary as Joe made it sound the other night. Not as villainous as, I can control people with my mind.

His silence intimidated her so she glanced up. He seemed to neither believe nor disbelieve her. Fair enough. He hadn't seen her in action yet.

The drunk looked at Tori, interrupting her thoughts. "He's a lot bigger than *you*."

"Size isn't everything," Tori snapped back at him.

Superhero X grinned. Disconcerted Tori frowned at him. He had a lovely smile, what she could see of it. She turned abruptly away.

And ran right into the police officer walking up behind her.

"Whoa, careful now." The officer put his hands on her shoulders until she regained her balance. "What's going on here?"

Tori pulled her scarf back over the lower half of her face.

The cop and his partner looked at Tori, the drunk, and Superhero X. The first cop spoke directly to the obvious leader. "More work to keep us busy, huh?" he said to Superhero X.

The superhero grinned. "Somebody needs to keep the city safe."

The male bonding made Tori grit her teeth. She stepped between them. "Did Casey send you?" she asked the cop, trying to get her "sincere, yet professional" face in place.

"Yeah, she did. So you're the new girl, huh?" The three men looked at each other and shared a smile.

For a moment, Tori wished her super power were something more useful. Like the ability to turn men into slugs.

CASEY AND ART watched the exchange from their car just down the street from the action.

"She said he didn't take it well," Casey said, "but she's the one who's angry."

"Can you tell what they're arguing about?" Art asked.

"Yeah, Art, 'cause I took that lip-reading class last week," Casey said with an annoyed look at her partner. The pressure from the top was getting to her. Their leads in Evan Ruffalo's death didn't lead to an actual person to arrest, and they were no closer to finding any of the missing children. Their other open cases were almost as frustrating.

Casey had a strange thought. "She said she told Joe about her power. But what if he didn't tell her about X? What if she doesn't know it's him?"

"How can she not know it's him?" Art asked.

"I—she—he's got his super suit on...?" She shrugged.

"Wouldn't she recognize his voice? I'd recognize your voice anywhere."

Casey looked at him in surprise. Really? "He disguises it, remember?"

"Eyes? Mouth?"

"Mask."

Art turned to look at her. "But she lives with him. She *sleeps* with him. How could she not—?" Art shook his head, unable to find words.

Casey rolled her eyes. "If one of the women you slept with walked up to you on the street in a costume with her face covered, you're telling me you'd recognize her?"

Art frowned at her, exasperation in his voice. "One would certainly hope so."

Count on Art to always surprise her.

They watched for another minute, then Art said, "Well, we might as well join the party, try to figure out what's going on."

They walked across the street to the group on the sidewalk. There were two uniforms, two superheroes, and a gaggle of looky-loos. Oh, and the original reason everyone showed up—a single, drunk old man.

Tori turned at their approach. "Casey! Art! Thanks for coming." She shook their hands vigorously. "Actually, thanks for sending someone to take care of this. I knew if I called you, every-thing would be completely under control." She directed the last part over her shoulder at Superhero X.

Oh yeah, she was mad. Casey eyed X. He was glaring at his wife. If the stakes weren't so high right now, this would be better than a soap opera.

"Hello, Art, Casey." He walked over and shook hands.

Casey caught the slight shake of his head as he squeezed her hand. So Tori *didn't* know. And he was keeping it a secret because...? This was getting more interesting by the minute.

"How's it going?" Art asked pointedly.

Superhero X kept his voice neutral. "Just helping out a new friend."

"Interfering is more like it," muttered Tori. She took Casey's arm and moved a step away from him. "Can you set up a lunch with one of your superheroes this week? I really need a mentor, someone to help me figure this out, not try to outdo me."

Tori kept her voice loud enough to be heard, but actively turned her back to Superhero X. Casey glanced over to see him scowling at them both. He shook his head slightly. "Sure, I'll call you with a day and time." Casey knew she shouldn't be, but she was enjoying this.

"That'd be great!" Tori brightened up considerably.

Another pair of cops walked up. "Must be one dangerous drunk," one of them said to the group at large. "Or are we having a party?"

"*Mine* showed up first, proving that I had it under control," Tori shot toward Superhero X without facing him.

"And when you were pulled off your feet and into his smelly lap, would you still be insisting you had it under control?" he muttered back at her.

"You two fight like an old married couple," laughed one of the officers. "A bit territorial, aren't you?"

Art burst out laughing. Casey elbowed him. He tried to feign a cough, but it didn't work.

"If you fellas would handle this," Casey looked from the uniforms to the drunk. "X, would you fill them in?"

Casey saw Tori stiffen and took her arm. "Art and I need to talk to you," she said quietly.

Art flanked Tori's other side as they walked across the street to their car. On the sidewalk, Tori looked nervously from one detective to the other.

"What's wrong?" she asked.

"Do you know him?" Casey nodded to Superhero X across the street.

Tori wrapped her arms around herself defensively, her eyes flicking to X and back. "Except for a couple times when he's helped me out—you know about that—I don't *know* him. Why?"

"Listen, Tori," Art began, "we appreciate you helping out.

But there are several good reasons why we ask superheroes to register with us. Some of them for your protection, some of them for the public's protection. If you're going to actively work as a superhero, you need to register." Art's charming "aw shucks" attitude was gone. His features hardened along with his voice.

Tori turned to Casey, looking panicky. "But you didn't mention this yesterday. What'd I do wrong today?"

Casey used her most soothing voice. "I understand. And we don't mean to pressure you. But there are other factors here you may not be aware of. Factors that could lead to your arrest unless—"

"*What?*" Tori screeched.

"We don't really know what you can do," Art said. "We don't know who you might be working with, working for—"

"I'm a *temp*! You think I'm a criminal?" Tori's hands flew to cover her mouth and Casey could see her eyes watering.

"I don't want to arrest you, Tori," she said. "Personally, I don't think you're doing anything other than trying to help, but it's our job to keep track of the superhero teams."

"And you don't seem to be on any of them," Art said. "We have a lot more important things to do than arrest the homeless."

Superhero X elbowed his way between Art and Casey. Casey had seen him coming out of the corner of her eye, had counted on his interference. He towered over all of them, took one look at Tori's terrified expression, and narrowed his eyes at the two detectives.

"You need us for anything else?" he asked.

"I think we've got it," Casey said, meeting his gaze, not allowing him to intimidate her. "We'll be in touch."

Casey watched Tori. She was off balance, scared. But there was no sense that she knew she was standing next to her husband. What game was X playing?

X took Tori's hand and marched down the street. After a few

steps, Tori pulled away, but X put his hand on her back to keep her going.

Art moved closer to Casey as they watched the other two walk away. "Does that beat all or what?"

"You about scared the crap out of her."

"Just wanted to give her a little push and see where she lands."

"What I wouldn't give to be a fly on the wall when she finds out." Casey shook her head and smiled wryly at her partner. "X may be bigger, but I'd lay odds on Tori."

SUPERHERO X LED Tori around the corner and down the street, ignoring the stares of pedestrians. If Hayley hadn't called and berated him for not telling Tori about the team, he wouldn't have known what Tori had started doing with her free time. At an alley, he grabbed her arm and pulled her in.

When she started to protest, he covered her mouth with his hand. His blood was pounding. He was furious for a dozen reasons and all of them began with "T."

"If you don't want the whole city to listen in," he growled, "follow me. We need to talk."

Her eyes widened and after a second, she nodded her head. As Joe, he would never have wanted to bring fear to his wife's eyes. But as X, he was downright overjoyed. If she were afraid, she'd put this foolishness behind her.

He marched down the alley to where a fire escape ladder hung down.

He pointed up. "We're going to the roof. Give me your foot." She hesitated, then grabbed the bottom rung of the ladder hanging at her shoulder height. She put her foot in his hands and he boosted her up.

He followed her closely in case she slipped. Gritting his teeth, he tried to ignore her shapely behind as he climbed. He hadn't seen much of it since their fight a few days ago.

When they reached the top of the three-story building, he walked to the center of the roof.

"Okay, go ahead." He turned to face her, crossing his arms over his chest.

She looked at him warily. "Go ahead, what?"

"You wanted to talk. Let's talk."

"Here?" She looked out over the city.

"Where else do you think we can talk? You want me to invite you back to my place?" The thought sent ideas through his mind of all the super creative things they could be doing. He wanted her to say yes. He shifted his feet uncomfortably. Focus.

She swung her gaze back to him and scowled. "No. This is fine."

He returned her scowl and waited.

She cleared her throat. "Listen...Superhero X..." She paused. "Is that what you want me to call you? It's kind of long..." She waited.

He grunted, then said, "My friends call me X."

"Is that...is that an invitation?"

He waited, still entirely too angry to speak. The things that she'd been through already and she had the audacity to go out into the city looking for more. She could *die*. How could she not understand that?

She sighed and her features relaxed. "Listen, X." He didn't say anything, so she continued. "There's a lot going on in my life right now. And as of about five minutes ago, it just got a whole lot worse. So I'm sorry if—"

Superhero X felt his scowl soften a bit as Tori's eyes filled with tears. "What do you mean? What got worse?" He'd been afraid Art and Casey had called Tori over to tell her about him. That didn't seem to be the case.

She hugged herself and shook her head. "You helped me after I got mugged on Halloween. I was wearing a Pirate Wench costume." Her comment hung like a question.

X drew in a ragged breath. She'd looked amazing in that costume. He'd fallen in love with her that night. "I remember every detail."

Tori stared at him in surprise. She started to speak, then changed her mind and shook her head again.

"What?"

She looked like she was doing battle inside to speak or be quiet. "I thought something happened between us that night. I mean, the things we said and...I guess it meant nothing to you, then."

She looked angry, which was ridiculous. *He* was the one with everything to be angry about. *He* was the wronged party here. *He* was the one who changed around his entire life for her.

"You made it very clear you wanted nothing to do with superheroes," he ground out. "So I stayed out of your way."

Tori huffed in indignation. "I did not! And you *kissed* me. The best kiss I ever had! Then you never came back!"

The best kiss she ever had? That mollified him somewhat. "You said you hated superheroes."

"I said no such thing! That must've been some other girl you kissed and left!"

X grunted and walked a few steps away from her, confused for a moment as to what she had said and to whom. Then it occurred to him—she'd told *Joe* she hated superheroes.

He turned to face her again. "I never kissed any other girls after you."

She brushed her hand across her face, surreptitiously wiping it on her pants. It half-killed him to stand there and pretend he didn't notice she was crying. "It doesn't matter anyway," she said. "It's too late."

It *did* matter, but X had to cover more territory first. He suspected Tori wasn't going to feel like talking to him again for a while once she found out her husband had been keeping a secret from her. He had to take advantage of the moment.

He tried to focus. "Let's start with the more recent past. Tell me more about your super power."

She stared at him for a moment. He could see she was weighing the wisdom of confiding in him. He tried to look open and friendly.

"What are you smiling about?" she asked suspiciously.

He rolled his eyes. So much for trying to win her over. He resorted to what worked for X. He invaded her space, hands on hips, and stared down at her. "*Please.*"

She took an irate step forward, imitating his pose, nearly chin-to-chest with him. It almost made him laugh.

"Apparently I can make people do things," she said. "But I don't know how it works, how to turn it on and off. I don't know why it worked on a drug addict, or why it didn't on a mugger, or why it only sort of did on a drunk."

Joe wanted to interrupt and ask who *were* all these people. But she was working herself up and he was a little afraid to stop her.

"I don't know why it worked *exceptionally* well on Scruffy. And I don't know why I can even use it on myself!"

She was yelling now. X took half a step back, hoping no one could hear her on the street.

"There! That's everything! Happy? I have no idea how to be a superhero, or even if I want to be one!" She advanced on him. "*And nobody will help me figure it out!*"

"I'm going to help you if—"

"Really? Really? Because you said, hang something on the back door and meet me in Gaffney Park, and I did, but you didn't show up! I waited for you for hours!"

What was she talking about? "When?" he asked, allowing

some belligerence into his voice. Of course he would help her if she asked him.

"Saturday!"

He shook his head. "Saturday we weren't even—" He snapped his mouth closed before he finished his sentence: *we weren't even home.*

He put his palms out, placating her. "Okay, just calm down. I only—"

"Don't tell me to calm down, Mr. Big Strong Superhero! If I don't figure out how I got down this rabbit hole, *I'm going to jail!*"

X let his hands drop, along with his jaw. Jail? "How could you go to jail?"

"They said since I'm not on a superhero team, they don't know who I'm working for, and I might be a criminal, and they don't want to but they'll *arrest* me! Even my husband thinks I'm a villain!" Tori turned and covered her face with her hands.

Without thinking, he pulled her into his arms. Why would Art and Casey threaten to—then he remembered. He'd told them at the last meeting that anyone with powers not associated with the Paladins Guild would be considered a potential enemy. Apparently, they'd taken him seriously.

He didn't know what to say, where to start. "I'm sure your husband doesn't think you're a villain." Was his protestation too little, too late? No, he'd make sure she believed him. He'd find a way to convince her. He couldn't lose her. Not now.

Tori pulled away. Wiping her hands over her wet cheeks, she said, "I'm stronger than you think I am. I don't need to be rescued. I didn't need to be rescued those other times, and I don't need it now."

"That's not what it looks like from my perspective."

Apparently the wrong thing to say.

She lashed out at him again. "Having my purse stolen isn't the worst thing that can happen. Yes, I need to try harder to avoid walking alone at night in my neighborhood. But I didn't need some overly-macho super-savior to come rushing in and start tossing muggers around like bags of apples. A simple 'Excuse me, ma'am, may I escort you home' would've done the trick."

"I didn't toss—"

She poked him in the chest with her finger. "And I *don't* need to be humiliated by another superhero when I'm in the middle of —of—whatever it is I'm doing."

"I didn't hum—"

"You *did*! You rushed in *again* and acted like I'm completely incapable of handling the situation!"

X clenched his fists. He wanted to throttle her. "Again, from *my* perspective," he tried to speak calmly, to be the better person here, but he heard his voice shaking around his clenched teeth. "It looked like a woman was being accosted by a man. Again. I was raised not to let things like that happen."

She poked him in the chest again. "But you act like I can't take care of myself. You did it today." Poke. "And you did it last week" —poke—"and the week before that!" Poke, poke.

"Well, excuse me for trying to impress you!" X grabbed her hand and shoved it away. *"Heaven forbid I try to take care of you and keep you safe!"* X shook with suppressed emotion. She might be a little right. He might've been a little overbearing. But only because he wanted to keep her out of harm's way. She didn't realize he had a voice in his head scaring him, making him wonder if she was in danger.

She sighed and shook her head. "I can't believe my mother was right," she said softly. "I really didn't think she was, but..."

She turned and walked away. Not a few steps this time. She was nearly to the fire escape before he realized she was leaving.

"Wait! Tori, come back!" In a few strides, X was at her side. He started to reach for her arm, but stopped himself. It occurred to him that manhandling her wouldn't force her to respect him.

He prayed for wisdom, unsure how to proceed.

"What is your mother right about?" He knew the answer

though. Joe knew. "About superheroes? You think they don't try to help? You think they aren't real? Tori, if you really have a super power, if you've been trying to help people yourself, you should know. Sometimes you have to walk in someone else's shoes to understand their life."

X paused, ashamed by the realization that he hadn't tried looking at things from Tori's perspective. "Maybe I've tried too hard to impress you. Made some assumptions about what would please you. I thought women liked to be taken care of."

Tori didn't move.

X waited. "I'm sorry."

That seemed to be what she was waiting for. She sighed heavily and turned around. She held out her hand. "Maybe we can start over. I'm Tori, I think I have a super power, and I could really use a friend."

16

Tori smiled as she drove the car she'd borrowed from Hannah through the post-rush hour traffic. She could still feel the bear hug Superhero X had given her when she'd offered a handshake. But then X's wrist-thingy had started to beep. He told her he had to be someplace, but that they needed to talk, so they agreed to meet at seven o'clock tonight at Pacific Park.

When Tori called Joe's cell phone to tell him she'd be out till late tonight, she got his voice mail. She'd let out a breath in relief. Then promptly felt guilty. But hey, they weren't talking to each other anyway. And with any luck, X would help her figure out how to handle Joe.

She pulled into the park at ten to seven. Superhero X was already waiting. That fact made her happier than it should have. They exchanged a smile as she got out, and together they walked to a bench tucked away in the middle of the park. Snow crunched under her boots as they left the path, the sound conspicuous in the quiet night.

Tori felt a little shy now that she could ask all her questions.

What if he thought they were stupid? Hadn't Hayley said that she heard people realized they had powers in their teens? And Kane had said something about powers revealing themselves in childhood. What if X didn't believe her? Would she have to use her power on him to prove it?

"So..." he said. He chuckled, sounding self-conscious to Tori. "Now that we're here, I'm not sure where to start."

Tori smiled in agreement. She tucked her legs underneath her on the bench and faced X. "Maybe we could start with 'how in the world does this work?'"

"Your power?"

She nodded.

"It's hard to say," he said with a shrug. "It's different for everybody."

Tori played with the zipper on her down coat. She hoped he'd be more helpful than *that*. Maybe she should tell him what Kane said. But if it turned out Kane was some kind of bad guy, she didn't want X to know she was related to him until she could prove that she wanted to be one of the good guys.

"What?" he asked gently.

She looked up, surprised that he seemed to be reading her expressions and body language in the dark. Something had changed since their rooftop fight earlier today. The compassion she found in his face helped her to relax. She really did need a friend.

"I told my husband about this, about my super power," she said, fiddling with her zipper. "He said..."

He gave her a moment, but when she didn't continue, he prodded her. "Tell me."

"He said only villains have this power," she said quietly, keeping her eyes on her coat. "Is that true?"

He didn't say anything. Tori finally raised her head to try to see what he was thinking. X was staring out into the park. After a moment, he met her eyes and said, "Maybe he doesn't know everything. Think you can forgive him for that?"

The right side of her mouth quirked into a half-smile. "Sure. If we ever start talking to each other again."

X smiled back at her. "I bet he feels as bad about that as you do."

Tori raised her eyebrows dubiously. "I doubt that. Not only did he say I have a villain's power, but he told me I *can't* be a superhero, and that I probably don't have any powers anyway."

She sighed, her thoughts zig-zagging around until they landed on her mother. Tori never would have believed she'd end up repeating her parents' mistakes, marrying the wrong man and ruining her life. Only now she was the bad guy and Joe was the wronged party.

"If you don't mind my saying so, I don't think you should do it either," he said.

Tori's hands stilled as she looked at him in surprise. "Be a superhero? Why not?"

"Because you could get yourself killed, that's why," he said with some heat. "I'm serious, Tori. Do you have any idea how easily you could be hurt or killed? My powers physically protect me from most things, but if they didn't, I'd've been dead about ten times now."

"Well," Tori paused, thinking. "I wouldn't get into the same kinds of situations you would. And I've already been doing really helpful things." She told him everything that had happened since the robbery. "I'd have to choose situations where my power is what would be the most useful. Don't you do that?"

"Maybe," he said, and Tori could tell from his expression that she'd scored a point there. "But I'd be—" He rubbed his hand over his jaw. "Your husband would be devastated if anything happened to you."

She didn't want to tell X, but her marriage had other problems. The chances of her getting hurt in a fight were infinitesimal compared to the chances of her getting divorced if she and Joe couldn't come to an agreement. Family history proved it.

"You look like you don't believe me," X said, sounding angry. "I'm serious. This can be very dangerous work. I feel like I keep repeating myself and you keep ignoring me. I thought you wanted my advice."

Tori didn't want to fight again, so she teased him. "You seem keen on stopping me. Maybe you're a villain and you don't want me to join any fights where I'd beat you."

X didn't smile. "Why do you feel you have to do this? What's wrong with your current life?"

Tori propped her elbow on the back of the park bench and leaned her cheek on her fist. She sighed. "I don't know if I *do* want to do this, but I'm not doing anything *important* with my life. I don't want to sit safely on the sidelines and watch life pass me by. I want to have a purpose. My husband is great, but...we could be so much *more*. I don't know how to explain it, but I really think it's true."

She shook her head, frustrated that she didn't know how to put it in words. "We're good people, but we don't do anything to make the world better. We could do more. We *should* do more. But now..." She didn't want to cry in front of him, but her world was spinning out of her control.

"Today I may have lost the ability to choose a workable option. If I pursue this superhero thing, there's a very good chance I'll lose my husband. That's how my parents got divorced. If I don't pursue it, there's a very good chance I'll be arrested for a crime or crimes I didn't commit. I don't even know what the crimes *are!*"

Tori sniffled and glanced up at X. He stared at her in consternation.

"Your parents aren't divorced. Why would you think *you're* getting divorced?"

Tori frowned at him. Had he researched her? If so, not very

thoroughly. "It's complicated." She didn't want to talk to a stranger about Kane. And it was hard enough to tell even her best friend about some of the complexities of her relationship with Dixie.

X stumbled over his words. "Are you—do you think your husband—you just got married, didn't you?"

"I don't want to talk about it," she said, looking away into the darkness. She did, though. She really did want to talk about it with someone who would understand. But her mother had insisted on absolute secrecy. Only Danny knew everything.

That's what she'd do. She'd call her dad tomorrow, see if he had time for lunch. He always gave good advice.

"Tori," X shifted closer, his thigh pressed warmly against her knees.

It felt good, her coat wasn't keeping her legs warm. How did he stay warm in his superhero suit?

"Obviously, all these things are related somehow. Tell me. Let me help." He rested his arm near hers on the bench, his hand on her elbow.

Tori went over her options. Owen didn't seem keen to help until she talked to Joe. Joe was so upset about the whole thing that he wasn't speaking to her. Hayley was willing to talk about anything Tori wanted to tell her, but how could she help if she didn't know anything about superheroes? Casey and Art might want to arrest her more than help her. Her dad would help however he could, but she didn't know how much that would be.

Maybe a superhero would be the best option. Of course, when he found out about Kane—if any of what Kane said was true—he might despise her and want nothing to do with her. Ever.

She felt his leg pressed warmly against hers. But if she did get divorced, maybe she and X could hang out. She squeezed her eyes shut. She didn't want to get divorced! She loved Joe! Where was the guidebook for this messed up situation? *How to know if your spouse is a louse—or is just afraid of you, page 134.*

Brushing tears from her eyes, feeling X's other hand rubbing her knee, Tori gave in. "My mom says my real father, my biological father, said he was a superhero, but he was a bum. He wasn't really a superhero, he just couldn't hold down a job."

"Your father was a Pretender?" X didn't try to hide his surprise.

Tori sniffled. "If you mean—yes, he pretended to be a superhero. They're actually called that?"

"It's kind of a nickname. Pretenders, Pop-Ups, Players, Thrillers, Flyers, Jacks." He interrupted himself. "Forget about that. Are you sure he didn't have any powers? That could explain..."

She thought about her last conversation with Kane. He obviously believed he was king of the universe, but what had she seen him do? Threaten and intimidate. That's it. "Mom hates to talk about him. She said he didn't have any powers. I don't know. He's very strange, and *he* says he has powers, but I've never seen him do anything unusual. Apparently, he loved the spotlight, but he was incapable of taking care of a family. That's what Mom said. He left when I was two."

X took her hand and laced their fingers together, squeezing it reassuringly. "But you're not him. You're not a Pretender who's going to leave her husband in search of fame."

"How do you know?" Tori cried. "My husband was mad at me before—imagine what would happen if he knew *everything*. And even if I can keep all this a secret, and agree not to be a superhero, it won't save my marriage because Casey said I'll go to *jail*!"

She knew she was borderline hysterical again. So much for practicing strength and control. No wonder Joe didn't respect her if she was always falling apart. "Is that even possible? Do they put unregistered superheroes in jail?"

"Of course not." X pushed Tori's knees to turn her sideways, then pulled her up against him.

"Because that's discrimination. Bigotry! I could use my power to make laws so they can't arrest people just because they don't want to register with the police." Tori's self-pitying tears turned to righteous indignation. She *could* use her power for good.

X chuckled against her hair. "No one's going to jail. I think the SLU was trying to scare you. I won't let any of those things happen," he said as he held her close. "I promise."

Tori felt such relief, such comfort, that she allowed herself to lean into X. For once, she wasn't alone. There was finally one person in the world from whom she had no secrets. After a moment, she pulled away, a guilty voice whispering in her head about being in another man's arms. She reached into her purse for a tissue.

"I guess I know why your family hates superheroes, huh?" he asked gently.

She sighed and leaned her elbows on her knees. "Actually," she said, not looking at him, "it wasn't that strong an emotion for me until you kissed me and never came back." She noticed X lean forward on his knees, too, but she wouldn't look at him. "It's no big deal anymore because my husband is an even better kisser than you." She laughed a little and pushed his shoulder with hers, trying to break the tense moment.

"Is that so?"

She heard the teasing in his voice. Good. Difficult moment behind them.

"It is," she said, feeling a little lighter. She turned to look at him as she laughed. "He's probably better than you at everything." The moon had gone behind a cloud and she couldn't see very well in the dark. She could feel X's breath. A heartbeat later, she felt his lips touch hers. White-hot lightning mixed with a flashing red alarm. The kiss was slow and warm and wet. Funny how after three months, his kiss could still feel so familiar. He kissed sort of like Joe.

Tori pulled away, gasping as she met his startled gaze. "I'm sorry—I shouldn't have—I'm *married*," she said, trying to control her breathing.

So *this* is how it began. She'd heard people say, "It just happened," but she couldn't believe they didn't see the signs. Now she saw them all—in retrospect.

"It's okay," X said, reaching for her. "Trust me."

Tori saw red again and slapped his face. "You have the morals of a snake!"

She jumped up from the bench to put some space between them. Wow, did that hurt. She rubbed her palm.

Glaring over her shoulder at him, she narrowed her eyes and looked closer. "Are you *laughing*?"

"No," he laughed. He coughed and cleared his throat and rubbed his cheek. "No, I'm not laughing. I'm shocked, that's all."

Tori watched him. If he thought this was funny, there was no way they could be friends.

"Seriously, Tori," he said. "A man has a tendency to react that way when he's kissing a beautiful woman one moment, and getting slapped the next." He paused. "I'm sorry."

Tori felt emotionally shaken. She couldn't trust herself to know if he meant it or not. "We can't be friends if you think that's ever going to happen again," she said firmly.

"It won't," he promised. A different kind of smile spread over his face. "I respect your loyalty. Honest. Your husband's very lucky."

Tori grunted. "Tell him that," she said under her breath as she turned away.

"Maybe I will," X replied, standing but not coming closer.

Tori watched him uncertainly. Where was her life headed? And why was Superhero X here now when her life seemed so messed up? Maybe superheroes really did show up when you needed them.

"I better go," she said.

"Wait," he said, taking a step closer.

She glared a warning and he stopped, his hands raised in front of him.

"I'm going to do some research," he said, "and find out if the SLU really thinks you could be involved in a crime. Then we'll meet again tomorrow and come up with a plan, okay?"

Tori thought about it for a moment, then nodded. "Where? Here?"

X shook his head. "I'll call you and we'll decide where to meet based on what I find out." He paused, thinking, then he smiled at her. "Maybe we'll do a little recon together. Would you like that?"

She smiled down at her shoes. "Maybe." She met his eyes again. "Yes." She turned to leave, smiling to herself, her step a little lighter.

"Tori," X moved another step closer, right next to her, but he didn't try to touch her. "You told me your secrets tonight, and I appreciate that." He hesitated, clearly worried.

Tori tilted her head, concerned at his tone.

"I have secrets of my own that I want to—need to—share with you. Please—*please* try to understand." He waited.

She didn't know what to make of that confession. Did he work alone, no superhero friends to talk to? She couldn't very well say no. And she did want to be his friend. "Okay," she said finally with a teasing smile. "I promise we can be friends if you promise not to kiss me anymore."

He grinned. "It's a deal."

As Tori walked away, she wondered if it was her imagination, or if she heard X say, "For now."

TORI ARRIVED at her dad's office with a bag of Subway sandwiches and a long list of questions. "Hey, Dad!"

"Hi there!" Danny came out from behind his desk and gave her a big hug before accepting his sandwich. "Your call was a wonderful surprise. The loss of your temp job is my gain."

Tori laughed and closed the door. She hadn't told him any details about why her job ended. He didn't need to know someone had blown up her car, despite his promises a couple weeks ago that he wouldn't have a heart attack.

They cleared a spot on his desk and laid out their lunch. "I can't remember the last time we had lunch together," she said.

"So what's the occasion?"

Tori shrugged. "No occasion. I just wanted to see my dad."

He gave her a long look, reading her face as she tried to act nonchalant. Tori's shoulders sagged as she struggled between knowing she couldn't hide much from him, and hoping he could figure some of it out without her having to say it out loud. She was afraid it would sound worse if she had to verbalize it.

Danny leaned over and hugged her around the shoulders. "What's the matter, little girl?" he asked.

He'd called her "little girl" for as long as they'd known each other, as long as Tori had any memories. As she grew older, he used it mostly when she was upset about something. Danny knew her that well. He was her *dad*. Kane wasn't.

She let him hug her for a moment, then sighed and pulled away. "How do you do that? Know when something is wrong?"

"It's a gift you're given when you have kids. You'll get it, too."

He finished unwrapping his lunch. He chuckled, but Tori could feel him watching her out of the corner of his eye. Another thing parents were good at, watching you when you thought they weren't. They bit into their sandwiches.

"Mmm, mine's really good."

Tori nodded her agreement.

"So?" he prompted.

"I need advice," she said to her sandwich.

"On?" He took another bite, chewing while he waited patiently.

"Oh...marriage. Family." She opened her chips and looked sideways at him.

Kane was wrong. Her dad loved her. She could tell.

Of course Danny loved her. But did he love Sam more because she was his own flesh and blood? That was what Kane meant, that it was some kind of genetic thing that you couldn't help. She wanted to know if it was true, but she didn't. She wanted to ask, but she *really* didn't.

"How is marriage?" he asked.

Tori wished she could get advice without having to spill the details. "It's not as easy as I thought it'd be."

Danny chuckled. "It never is."

Tori looked at him in surprise. "It is for you."

He chuckled again and shook his head. "It's an illusion."

Tori opened her mouth to argue. She shook her head, hoping...surely her parents' marriage wasn't in trouble, too.

"No, no, our marriage is fine. Your mother and I love each other very much. The fact that it looks easy, that's the illusion."

"Oh." Tori wasn't sure that was helpful at all.

Danny pointed a chip at her. "The key is to keep making a conscious effort to choose your spouse above everything. Well, except God. But everything else—children, career, friends, money. If you keep on choosing your spouse first, you can get through anything."

"Hmm. Maybe."

She felt him looking at her. Tori kept her head down. She

didn't want her dad to think she was a failure if she got divorced. That would be the second worst part of this whole awful situation. Losing Joe still came in first.

"I didn't say it'd be easy." He rubbed her shoulder. "Just don't give up."

"What if he doesn't choose *me* first?" Tori tried not to let her voice wobble. What if Joe wasn't willing to choose her—the whole, real Tori with all of her faults and quirks and abnormalities—over having a nice, normal wife, a nice, normal life?

Danny sighed. "Despite the fact that you two got married so fast, I know you're a level-headed young woman, and Joe seems like a level-headed young man. I think it's far too soon for you to be worried."

Tori tried not to disagree.

"One thing to consider," he said after a moment, "ask yourself if you've put him in the position of having to choose something other than you. Are you not compromising on something that is damaging your relationship?"

Tori looked up then. She stared at her dad thoughtfully. Maybe she was forcing Joe to choose her as a superhero or not at all. Maybe she needed to back up a step. Maybe she needed to be willing to walk away from that potential life in order to save and nurture her marriage.

She thought about Superhero X's question asking what was wrong with her current life. There would definitely be something wrong with it without Joe. She'd lived this long without being a superhero, she could live without it. She would just need to find a way to hide her abilities and live a normal life. Tori suspected Lexie might know how to do that.

She kissed Danny's cheek. "You're good, Dad."

He smiled and ruffled her hair. "Next question."

Tori's smile faded. "This one's harder. A lot harder. I don't even know if I..."

"Maybe I can help if you tell me," he said. He finished his sandwich and sighed. "Is it...about Kane?"

Tori heard her own uncertainty reflected in her dad's voice. She nodded her head. Maybe they both needed to talk about it.

"He wants to renew a relationship with you." Danny's voice tensed. "Is that right?"

She nodded. "Yeah..."

"And?"

She played with the straw in her drink. "I love you, Dad."

He put his hand on her shoulder, tightened his grip, then relaxed it again and rubbed her arm as he had before. "I love you, too."

Tori held her breath for a moment. "But different from Samantha?" She heard a waver in her voice though she'd tried to sound nonchalant. She hoped Danny would tell her the truth, not just what he thought she wanted to hear.

"Of course," he said. "I love you all differently because you're four different people. I admire different things about each of you."

"But...you love Kevin and Sam more...because they're your own, you know, genes or whatever." She didn't wipe at the tear falling down her cheek so Danny wouldn't realize she was crying. She didn't want comfort as much as she wanted the truth.

Danny pulled away, which increased the flow of tears. Tori kept her face averted, but Danny took her chin and forced her to look at him. She knew her heart showed clearly on her face, but Danny's face began to turn red. Tori saw the muscles bunch in his jaw and knew he was angry. At her?

"Is that what he said?" Danny's voice was fierce. He let go of her chin and took both of her shoulders, shaking her a little. "He told you I love the others more? Or did he just come out and say I don't love you at all? Did he say I'm only acting, but it's not real, not the way *he'd* love you?" Danny sneered.

Tori tried not to cry, but more tears fell when she nodded her head.

Her dad jumped up and pulled out his wallet. He hadn't gotten the twenty-dollar bill all the way out before he started calling Kane all kinds of horrible names.

Tori's eyes widened. Her hand covered her open mouth. Danny was the calmest, sanest man she knew. A rock. But right now he was almost scary. She'd never seen him like this, quietly cursing with enthusiasm and imagination. She didn't recognize some of the words and phrases he used, but she certainly got the idea. It was quiet, but ugly.

When he finally stopped, he leaned heavily against his desk, breathing like he'd run a race and lost. Tori felt her tears well up again. She stood and walked the two steps between them. This was a turn-around. Danny had always been the comforter. She didn't know how to comfort him.

She closed her eyes on a prayer and hugged him. After a moment's hesitation, Danny hugged her tight. Finally he pulled away, fire still burning in his eyes.

"That man did the kindest thing he could when he walked away twenty years ago," he said. "I ignored his barbs because I didn't think it would ever come to anything. He may have fathered you, but you are *my* daughter. If I believed he was a good man, I wouldn't stand between you if you wanted to get to know him better. But Tori, listen to me."

Danny gripped her shoulders. "*He is not a good man*. He's telling you lies to pull you away from your family. He wants you to choose sides. He wants you to choose him."

Tori frowned and nodded. "I think you're right. But what about honor your parents and love your enemies? I want to do the right thing. I'm just not sure what it is."

"And God will help you do the right thing. But remember the Bible also says to be both as innocent as a dove and as shrewd as a snake. Don't let him pull you down to his level—lies and self-ishness and anger. Don't trust him. Be very wary, Tori. He—"

Danny stopped and took a breath. "I have good reasons for what I'm telling you. I do. But I don't want to scare you or...break any promises."

"To Mom." Tori could figure that one out on her own.

Danny nodded. "He's trying to buy you, honey," he said, his voice gentling. He sighed. "He's trying to buy your love and loyalty. That's why he's implying that I don't love you as much as he does. The man doesn't understand love at all, so he doesn't see that it could have been possible for you to love us both."

He pulled her into a hug, then held her at arms' length again. "Tori, you are a very special girl. I've known that for a long time. Don't tell your mother I said that because it will upset her. I know you can figure out the truth about Kane. Have Lexie help you. I can't say any more, but I know the two of you can figure this out."

"You're not going to help me? Daddy, I—" She started to argue but he stopped her.

"I am helping you. Think about everything you know about your past. Talk to Lexie. Do some research on Kane. I know you're not taking your medication anymore. You must have noticed some changes by now."

Tori stared over her dad's shoulder, unable to hold his gaze. She nodded mutely. He *knew*. But did he know more than she did? She started to tell him what had been happening, but Danny held up his hand, shaking his head.

"Don't tell me anything you don't want your mother to know," he said. "Please. In this matter, my loyalty lies with her and she doesn't want to acknowledge any of it."

Tori nodded. Another marriage lesson.

Moving his hands to cup her face, Danny smiled gently at her. "Listen to your old man for a minute. It's time for you to stop letting other people tell you who you are, and who you aren't. I was so proud of you when I heard you'd fired that darned doctor."

But her wholesome dad didn't say darned.

Tori's eyebrows rose in surprise.

Danny looked a bit sheepish. "I'll put another twenty in the Cursing Jar after I go to the bank. I'm serious, though. You'll find your strength in knowing the truth. Be safe." His voice became fierce again. "Promise me you'll be safe."

"I will, Daddy. I promise."

"Pray for wisdom, little girl, then *use* it." He ruffled her hair a bit. "Okay?"

Tori nodded. "Okay."

She wasn't sure she understood everything her dad had said, but as she walked to the bus stop she wished she'd had the "record" feature going on her phone. She was pretty sure Danny had answered more questions than she'd asked, questions she didn't yet know. She hoped she would remember his advice when the time came.

17

J oe looked around the clubhouse at his friends and went straight to the point. "Tori is in trouble."

Hayley sat up straighter on the couch where she sat next to Bull. "What happened?"

"I'm not entirely sure," Joe admitted. What he wasn't entirely sure about was how to explain to his friends that his wife might have a super power. He figured Tori had already told Hayley about how Katie had forced her to tell the truth a few days ago. But it was time to let the rest of the team know. "She may or may not be a suspect in one or more ongoing criminal investigations."

"*What?*" Hayley leapt to her feet. "Joe! I *knew* something like this would happen! Where is she? Is she okay?" Bull tugged Hayley back down to his side, holding her hand.

"She's fine," Joe said. "She's at home."

Mickey cleared his throat. "What else?"

"That's all I know right now." Joe leaned forward on his knees, steepling his fingers together. He didn't want to meet Mickey's gaze. It sounded ridiculous to his own ears—*Tori may be a super-hero*. How would it sound to real superheroes?

"What else, Joe?" Mickey pressed.

"I don't know." Joe kept his head down. Mickey had an uncanny ability to read people, to know when they were hiding things. "I don't know what crimes or why. Maybe it's a scare tactic. All I know is we need to help her, and fast, before the S—before the police arrest her."

Hayley put her head in her hands and moaned. Bull rubbed her back and looked confused.

Mickey perked up like a watchdog smelling fresh meat. "The SLU wants to arrest her? Why?"

"I didn't say the SLU wan—"

"Joe," Hayley interrupted. "Tori needs a mentor. She's been weeks without one and you know how crucial—"

"Wait, you *knew*?" Joe sat up straight, staring at Hayley in shock. "Before a couple days ago, you knew and you didn't tell me?"

"Knew what?" Bull asked.

"She made me promise not to," said Hayley. "Just like *you* made me promise not to tell *her*."

"How long have you known?" Joe bellowed. Was he the last one to know?

Hayley moved closer to Bull. "Since the day after the robbery," she said in a small voice. "But—"

"How long have you known, Joe?" asked Mickey.

Joe looked at him. "Don't tell me you know, too? I found out Friday." He looked at Bull. "I think I figured out Katie's power."

"You knew Katie has a super power and you didn't tell me?" Hayley asked Bull.

"Oh, I might've forgotten," said Bull. He looked at Joe. "What is it?"

"She can make people tell the truth. It's very weird, trust me." Joe could still remember the feel of those three words in his head —*tell the truth*—urging him to speak against his better judgment. Thank goodness his training had helped him recognize it before he gave in.

"I didn't know about Katie, but I wondered if she would find an ability," Mickey said. "Since the SLU told us they had a Pop-Up, I've been trying to find out who it might be. And with Tori showing up at every crime scene recently..." He shrugged. "I wondered. So why didn't you bring her with you tonight?"

Bull frowned at him. "We agreed no one can come down here except—oohhh." He looked at Hayley. "Is that what you've been trying to make me guess for the last few weeks? Tori's a super-hero?" He laughed his surprise as he looked at Joe. "Dude, that rocks! Doing it with a superhero is—"

"Bull!" Hayley slapped his shoulder.

Joe clamped his mouth shut. He wouldn't know. The last time he and Tori did the wild thing was *before* her big revelation.

"If we're going to help her clear her name," Mickey continued with his earlier thought, "she needs to be here so we can figure out what happened."

"She knows about X, right?" asked Hayley. "You finally told her?"

Joe stared down at his flexing hands. "Uh, yeah, she's talked to X a few times. In fact, she's waiting for him to call her tonight."

Mickey slapped his hands together. "Excellent!"

"Thank you, God," Bull said to the ceiling. "Now I don't have to worry about what to say around her." He sighed in exaggerated relief. "You know how hard it would be to keep a secret from someone for *years*?"

All three of them looked at Bull with varying degrees of *you've got to be kidding*. Keeping their identity secret from most people was part of their everyday life.

"Oh, right," Bull said. He grinned and picked up a 25-pound free-weight, tossing it easily from one hand to the other. "Well, I think Joe's trying to impress someone. She likes you in your suit, huh? I wear mine to—"

"Bull!" Hayley slapped him again. "So if you told her," she said, "if you both know each other's secrets, why isn't she here?"

Joe looked at each of them while he chewed his right thumb-nail. "We're not exactly talking right now. So," he paused, wondering if his great plan would work. "I thought maybe X and the gang could tell her. I could call her and have her come down—"

A chorus of disbelief and outright refusal went up.

"So you *haven't* told her? Geez, Joe, if you're so scared, send her an email. Send her a voice mail." Mickey scowled at him. "What can you possibly gain from the secrecy?"

Bull snickered loudly.

Mickey looked at him, then rolled his eyes at Joe. "You must be joking," he said, shaking his head. "Like you don't get it enough at home, you're doing it in alleys? Rooftops?"

"I am *not* doing it in alleys." But he would've enjoyed doing it on that rooftop. Or in the park in the moonlight. Snow or no snow, it would've been *hot*.

"But..." Hayley's face twisted in total confusion. "If she doesn't know Superhero X is you..."

Bull howled with laughter. "Your wife's having an affair with your alter ego!" he roared. "Oh, that's priceless!"

Even Mickey chuckled. "Tori is seeing X and not speaking to you?"

Hayley tried to hide her laughter behind her hand.

"Stop laughing, Bull," Joe growled. "Tori is not having an affair. She even made me, er, X promise not to kiss her."

Mickey and Bull laughed harder.

"Whatever." Joe ran his hands through his hair. "The point is, I have a plan."

"Do tell," said Mickey.

Joe took a deep breath. "We'll all put on our suits and call her down here and explain together. That way everything will be cleared up at once." It really was a good plan. No more secrets, just like his friends had wanted for weeks. He nodded in encour-agement to Hayley. She'd been bugging him longer than anyone.

"No way."

"No."

"Huh-uh."

Joe sighed and leaned his head back, eyes closed. "Come on, guys. Help me out." Good thing he liked this couch so much. He might be spending a lot more time here.

"I'll help you out," Mickey said.

Joe met his gaze warily. "Yeah?"

"This is your new plan. Stop being a baby and go home and tell her right now. Coward."

Joe shook his head and started to explain why that wasn't going to work.

"It wasn't a suggestion, it was an order."

Joe felt a little sick to his stomach. While he was home, he might as well grab his pillow and toothbrush.

Tori tried to read her book while she waited in front of the fire for Joe to get home. Superhero X hadn't called yet to tell her what time to meet. But Joe had called half an hour ago and asked her if they could talk. Even though he wanted them to stay at his parents' a little longer, he wanted privacy, so he suggested they talk at their house.

Tori was tired of fighting. And after talking to Superhero X last night and her dad today, she wanted to try harder to get this argument behind them. She loved Joe and she wanted to be married to him. If it was so untenable for him that his wife was a superhero, maybe she was going to have to do something else. The superhero thing could be just another temp job that ended.

She'd better think of something fast, though, because now she needed money to buy another car, too. Sheesh. She wondered how tight their finances were. Would Joe feel threatened if she asked him outright? She had seventy-eight dollars in her savings account. Not even enough for a monthly bus pass. So many things they hadn't done yet—paperwork to create a joint checking account, paperwork to change her name, paperwork to change life insurance beneficiaries. Ugh. She wanted a job with no paperwork. She wondered if she could Google that.

Come to think of it, what would she do for money if she worked as a superhero? Another question for X. She wished she could make a list, but she was afraid Joe would find it and get mad again. Or still.

She heard the back door open. Her stomach jumped a little. She was nervous about how their conversation would go, but she knew part of her butterflies were from missing the man she loved.

He walked into the living room in his stocking feet and paused. He wore jeans and a flannel shirt with the sleeves rolled above his wrists. He looked nervous. Tori only had a small reading lamp on in addition to the light of the small fire. Maybe the soothing lighting would help them talk calmly.

"Hi," she said, determined to meet him halfway. It occurred to her this afternoon that she might have been ignoring him more than he'd been ignoring her. If the argument was partially her fault, she was going to do her part to fix it.

"Hi," he said. He walked over to where she sat on the couch. "Mind if I sit down?"

She shook her head. After he sat, she pulled the blanket she'd tucked around herself over his lap as well. He scooted an inch closer.

"So," she said.

"So." Joe stared at the fire.

For someone who wanted to talk to her so badly, he didn't have much to say. Tori tried to decide what she needed to confess. One thing was obvious and long overdue.

"I love you, Joe."

He turned to her, surprise and pleasure and worry chasing

over his features. "I love you." After a moment, he turned back to the fire.

She sighed. Fine, she'd go first. "I'm sorry. I had no idea. I think I've figured out what happened. My parents have had me on medication since I was four. I think they knew or suspected what was happening to me and were trying to hide it. But they never said anything to me."

She looked away from the fire to find him watching her. "When I met you, I just..." She shrugged, not sure what words to use. "I felt invincible when I was with you. I stopped taking the drugs and seeing the psychiatrist only a week or so before we met, but you made me feel like I could do anything." She smiled a little.

He frowned. "You were seeing a psychiatrist?"

Oh great. Not another thing to argue about.

"Because you have a super power? That's *wrong*." Joe reached for her hand. "That's fear and paranoia and—and bigotry."

Tori had used that word last night with Superhero X. She wondered if Joe and X could be friends. That might make life easier on her.

"They had their reasons," she said. She'd been thinking about the next part for the last few hours. She wasn't ready to offer, per se, but she was willing to have the conversation. "Would you," she cleared her choked throat, "would you feel more comfortable if I went back on the drugs?"

"No!" Joe whipped around to face her. His hand pulled her closer, off balance. "Absolutely not! I don't want you to take drugs for something that's a natural part of your makeup."

Tori regained her seat by sliding a little closer. Joe took advantage and pulled her all the way over to him. He wrapped his arm around her shoulder and stared into the fire. Tori felt like she'd been holding her breath for the last ten minutes and she could breathe again. She nestled her head into his shoulder. This felt so much better. Dad was right, choosing Joe over being a superhero was the right decision.

"Okay, well, I appreciate that. I can try to find someone who can help me control the power so I don't use it. I have a couple ideas of people to ask." She hoped that her friendship with X wouldn't make Joe jealous. She didn't know who else to ask. "I'll find a way to turn it off."

Joe sighed. He kissed the top of her head. After a moment, he said, "I didn't say you had to do that either."

Tori sat quietly thinking. She didn't know what else she could do. She was deeply relieved he didn't want her to go back to Dr. Huntington and the meds. But she didn't have any ideas about what was next until she talked to X. It didn't look like he was going to call tonight. Just as well. The conversation with Joe was going better than she could've hoped.

She approached the topic from the other side. "Just so you know, I'm not saying I have to be a superhero to be happy. I don't even know for sure what that life would be like. I'd have to find a way to save the world while holding down a nine-to-five job? *And* —bonus here—I get to hang around murderers and criminals just like the police, but I don't even get paid for it? We just got Disney Plus, Joe. When am I going to have time to watch it?" She added a little laugh.

Was she trying to talk him into this or out? She felt like an idiot that she didn't seem to know what she wanted.

"Then there's the problem of what to tell our friends," she continued when he didn't say anything. "My family isn't like yours. We don't have any superhero friends. There's the freaks— that's me and my sister—and there's the normal people. Luckily for us, the normal people have chosen to love us anyway. They just ask that we don't show our freakiness to the whole world and ruin their dinner parties."

Tori felt herself breaking down. She hadn't thought about all the secrets and lies she'd have to deal with. Forever. She clenched her jaw and told herself to buck up, be strong. If word got out, it could ruin her relationship with everyone she knew except her dad. Tori felt tears running down her face. She wished she could go to bed and hide. And watch Disney movies.

"You are *not* a freak." Joe held her close, speaking quietly, vehemently. "You have powers that you can—"

"You don't understand because *you're* not a freak," Tori exclaimed. "You're *cool*." She felt Joe chuckle. "You don't understand what it's like. Even on the drugs, and looking back I can see it now, even on the drugs I was scared people would find me strange or be afraid of me. It's a horrible way to live!"

"You're wrong. I do understand," he said. She shook her head, embarrassed that she was crying harder. "I do, Tori. I was shocked when you told me about your power because—"

"Because Katie made me!" Tori remembered how uncomfortable that had felt. Did she make people feel that way? "I was going to tell you, but I was going to say it much nicer than it came out. I'm so sorry, Joe. I'm sorry! I didn't mean to yell at you and say those horrible things."

Tori felt the pressure building inside. The stress of the last few weeks along with the fear that she was losing Joe and the overwhelming relief she felt right now that maybe she wasn't—it all churned inside her until she burst out—*"I just want you and me to be okay again, to be alone together! I want everything else to go away!"*

A bright flash of white light burst around them. Tori gasped and clutched at Joe. He was still with her, staring in shock at her and at the white nothingness around them. He pulled her closer, protectively. The air shimmered for a moment, then stilled. The living room was back. Or they were back in the living room.

"*What* was *that*?" Joe breathed.

Tori sat open-mouthed beside him. Oh, no. No no no no! She didn't just do that! *How* did she do that? "I'm sorry, Joe. Oh, I'm so sorry! I don't know what I did, but I swear I'll never do it again. I'll get help! Superhero X can help me. I'll—"

Joe turned her in his arms and kissed her soundly.

In her surprise, Tori didn't resist. After a moment, she kissed him back. She'd missed this so much. The feel of his lips, his tongue, his hands made her feel like an electric current ran through every nerve in her body. She felt more alive, more aware, more—

He pulled away.

She moaned in protest.

He laughed.

She opened her eyes. He was laughing? At her? No, he looked...excited.

"You are the coolest girl I know!" He swung his arm around her neck and looked around their living room again. "I can't figure out what you did, but it was *wild*. You're not only the coolest girl I know, you're the coolest superhero I know!"

Joe laughed again and squeezed her. Tori kept blinking as if she would be able to see what was happening here if she could just focus.

"Tori, I'm sorry for everything I said. I really am. I didn't understand. Will you forgive me?"

"Um, yes?" Okay, so they weren't breaking up then. She felt so tired. She leaned against Joe. The clock on the mantel pointed to five-thirty. If Superhero X called, she'd take Joe with her to meet him. "I've met someone who can help," she said. "He's—"

"I know." Joe kissed the top of her head.

"What do you mean, you know?"

"You're expecting his call, right?"

Tori sat up suddenly. "Joe, it's not like that, I swear."

He put his finger over her mouth, cutting off her protests. "I know. You think Superhero X can help you."

Tori paused, then nodded slowly.

Joe pressed his lips together in a somewhat rueful smile.

"Remember last night when he told you he has secrets he needs to tell you?"

Tori frowned. How could Joe know that? Unless he was watching them. But she was sure no one else was around. So how... Her eyes bugged out and her mouth dropped open. "No way," she breathed.

"I've been wanting to tell you since before we got married!" he exclaimed. He leaned back in the couch, his arms stretched over his head. "Ugh! I know what you mean about being afraid the other person won't accept you." He leaned forward, his elbows on his knees. "I was terrified. Your family isn't keen, and what if they convinced you not to marry me?"

Was he saying what it sounded like he was saying? Had she *married* Superhero X?

He raked his fingers through his hair. "I couldn't live without you. My dad threatened to not go through with the wedding if I didn't tell you. I tried! I don't know if you remember, but you told me to talk to you later, in bed."

She did remember that part. She'd felt so risque mentioning the bedroom on their wedding day.

Joe cupped his hands around her face. "I was crazy for you, and the idea that someone, *anyone*, could keep us apart only made me crazier. So I lied to my dad."

Tori finally found words. "You *lied* to Owen?"

He pulled her into his arms and laughed. "I did. He asked me if I talked to you and I said yes. I did talk to you. I just didn't tell you what I'd promised to." He leaned back and searched her face. "So you see, I do know how you feel."

It finally occurred to Tori that Joe was nervous. Nervous that she'd be angry. About him being a superhero, or withholding the information, she wasn't sure which, but he was just as scared as she'd been. And that made her feel a whole lot better.

She was about to tell him it was fine, she forgave him, when she had a shocking thought.

He saw her expression and his eyes clouded. "What?"

Staring at him for a moment, she reached up and pulled his head down for a kiss. It was tentative at first, then that amazing feeling of safety and strength permeated the kiss until they were pressed up against each other, fingers in each other's hair, hands beginning to roam, just like their very first kiss. Their first kiss when Joe was Superhero X, dressed as Zorro on Halloween night.

She pulled away and this time it was Joe who grumbled a protest. She smiled a little and then shook her head at him, her teeth worrying her lower lip. "I don't know," she said with a sigh.

He looked stricken.

"Now I'm not sure which of you is the better kisser."

It only took Joe a moment to get the reference. Then he was on top of her, Tori screeching and twisting and melting into him.

It was an amazing two minutes. Then Joe stopped with a sigh of disappointment. "We can't."

"Joe!" She tightened her arms around him. They were finally making up and he was *stopping*?

"I know, I know." He kissed her neck but moved his weight off her. "But one, I need to explain more about why we're staying at my folks' place, and two, Mom thinks we'll be back for dinner by six."

"Ugh! Call her and tell her we'll be late," Tori whined. She tried to pull Joe back down, but he leveraged her back into a sitting position instead. She pretended to sulk. Then she pulled her open shirt closed.

"That's reason three. It's cold in here. I want to see every inch of you, *not* covered in goose bumps." He rubbed one of her arms to warm it. Then he tucked his shirt back in and helped her with her clothes.

Tori sighed heavily. "Fine. But I'm just saying, Superhero X wouldn't have stopped like this last night. And that was in the snow."

Joe barked his surprised laughter. A second later, he tackled her.

After a fabulous minute of roving, caressing hands and hot, wet kisses, Tori's phone beeped that she had a text message.

"Ignore it," Joe whispered in between kisses.

Tori pulled her husband closer. Oh yes! She'd missed him so much.

The phone beeped again.

"Let me make sure it's nothing important." Tori kept kissing him as she tried to find her phone. Two texts from Lexie asking if she'd picked up Ben from school. Tori texted "no" and went back to what she was doing. She wondered for a moment if she should worry about her power doing something weird right now.

Two minutes later, her phone rang. But they weren't ready to stop.

They were still kissing and tasting and touching when Joe's phone rang. He looked at the caller ID and growled.

"Yeah, Dad?" Joe frowned and looked at Tori. "Yeah, she's with me. We're at the house." He pulled away from Tori and motioned for her to get up. "We'll be right there."

18

The moment Joe stopped the truck, Tori ran through the snowy yard and into the house. The connection between her and Lexie had always been strong, but when her sister lost control of her empathic abilities, the bond became a stranglehold.

She tripped trying to get her boots off. She pushed past Owen and Hannah as she raced through their kitchen into the living room. She didn't have to be told where her sister was. Lexie pulled Tori like steel to a magnet.

Lexie huddled on the floor against the couch, rocking back and forth. As soon as their eyes met, a wave of torment hit Tori like a physical force. She stumbled and fell, scrambling the last few feet on her knees, crying the whole way. At Lexie's side, Tori tried to remember what to do. Her sister's anguish rolled through the room in waves. Tori could barely think past this over-whelming despair.

The last time Lexie had a reaction like this was the day their parents made her give up her son Charlie for adoption. Tori closed her eyes against the pain in that memory. She didn't want to feed her sister's anxiety. Lexie wasn't telepathic, she couldn't read people's thoughts, but she could read their emotions. She could also direct her feelings toward those around her. That's the crushing weight anyone nearby would feel.

Tori took Lexie's hand. She smoothed her sister's hair away from her face. Calming, gentle touches. That's right, she remembered now. She sniffled and wiped her face on her sleeve. She had to stop crying. Tori took a few deep, cleansing breaths. She focused on the calm center in the deepest part of her heart, the place where she believed with all her being that God had a plan for them, strange abilities and all.

Please help us, Father God. Please, please, please.

Tori settled in closer and leaned her forehead against her sister's temple. "We're going to find Ben, Lex," she whispered. Joe had told her Ben was missing, but sitting here near her sister she knew it was worse than that. He was still close enough for Lexie to feel him, including his pain.

"We'll find him," she murmured, "but first we have to relax. Shh... Remember how we did this before?"

Lexie had a wall up around her misery. Tori could feel it like a barrier between them. The only way she could get Lexie out of her fortress was to go inside and lead her out. Tori pushed aside the fear that threatened to surface, a memory of the bad times after Charlie was taken away. She took one more deep breath and knocked on the wall.

"Lexie, let me in."

Pain ripped through Tori's chest. She cried out with the shock of it. She began to weep in earnest. A door in the wall started to open, then slammed shut. Someone wrenched her away from Lexie and the pain eased dramatically.

Tori opened her eyes to find Joe holding her close. The muscles in his face tightened as he struggled against his falling tears. That was Lexie's doing. Her emotions radiated out and affected everyone within twenty or thirty feet. Tori vaguely remembered that Hannah and Owen were crying when she pushed past them in the kitchen.

"It's okay, Joe," Tori said. She tried to sound soothing, fighting her sobs. "We've done this before."

"I'm not leaving you." Joe tightened his embrace. "What's happening?"

Tori had done enough research to find a word for it. "She's an empath."

She looked up to see a tough-looking, dark-haired man standing nearby, the muscles in his face tight like he was grinding his teeth. He was trying not to cry.

"I'm Mickey, Joe's friend. How can we help?" he asked.

"Just leave us alone. Please. I know what to do." Tori struggled out of Joe's grip.

Joe shook his head. "No. I'm not leaving. She's hurting you."

Tori started to argue, then conceded. "She doesn't mean to."

"Can we absorb some of the energy?" Mickey asked. "Will that help?"

No one had ever offered to help before. This man seemed to understand the problem in a way no one else had. His idea had merit. The more Tori thought about it, the more she thought Mickey might be onto something. If Tori only had to deal with a third of Lexie's pain...

"It'll hurt."

Both men nodded.

Tori motioned for them to kneel next to her sister. She took one of Lexie's hands, and Joe took the other. Mickey laid his hands on Lexie's shoulders. All three of them shuddered against the pain as soon as they touched her. The intensity of emotion pushing against them was the same as a moment ago, but Tori could feel it spreading out among them. She wondered how much Lexie could understand.

Closing her eyes, Tori leaned her forehead against Lexie's

temple. The wall of anguish still stood between them. Tori knocked.

In her mind, as if she were dreaming, she saw a door open in the wall. It opened more quickly than it had a moment ago. At some level, Lexie was reaching out. Tori walked in and the door disappeared. Before her was the alley where Lexie had lived when she was sixteen. It was dark and dirty. The distinctive odor of homeless people filled Tori's nose. Something moved in the dark and Tori shivered.

"Lex?" Tori walked down the alley, searching amongst broken pieces of furniture, behind the dumpster, in a cardboard box. She found her sister curled into herself at the end of the alley, sitting on a wadded up old blanket, arms wrapped around her knees.

Tori swallowed against the filth and sat down next to her. Lexie looked sixteen again. Skinny, scared, alone. Tori wondered if Lexie saw her as her fourteen-year-old self. In the bad years, Tori had come looking for her twice a week, bringing food, clothes, blankets, begging her to come home. Lexie's re-creation looked and smelled the same as Tori's memory of the reality.

Lexie had been able to feel Charlie with a frightening intensity even though he and his adoptive parents lived on the other side of the city. The police had arrested Lexie for stalking. She said she couldn't stay away from him. The couple had gotten a restraining order. Lexie refused to go back on the medication that would cloud her mind. She didn't want to lose the link to her son, and she couldn't forgive their parents for forcing the adoption.

In the dark alley, Tori took her sister's hand. It was different, clean. Tori looked around and noticed there were no empty wine bottles, no used needles. Lexie may have returned to a refuge of the past in her mind, but she'd come here as her new, cleaned-up self.

"Who's out there?" Lexie asked. Her voice quivered with fear, but her eyes had a shine of hope that they'd never had when she was sixteen.

"Joe and his friend Mickey. They want to help. We're going to find Ben."

A rock hit Tori in the chest and she sucked in her breath at the pain. Suddenly a shower of rocks pelted Lexie. At first Tori didn't understand. Then it dawned on her. Lexie had found a way to punish herself—and others—in her mind.

"Lex, stop! Stop it!"

The assault slowed and finally ended. Lexie began to sob. "I can't go through that again. I can't!"

The alley morphed and became a ledge. Goosebumps raised over Tori's skin. Vision or not, it looked and felt real. She darted a glance down, but all she could see was darkness. She closed her eyes and tried to swallow against a choking feeling. She couldn't tell the difference between Lexie's fear and her own.

A sense like a strong hand on her shoulder brought a small but instant measure of peace. Where...who...the real world. Joe was giving her strength in the real world.

Unsure whether the alley and the ledge were figments of Lexie's imagination or if there could be real-life effects to falling, Tori decided it was time to leave. They didn't have all the time in the world like they did when they were teenagers. Ben needed them. She could feel through Lexie that he was alive and scared.

On the ledge, Tori eased her arm around Lexie and pulled her close. She focused on feeding peaceful and calming emotions to her sister, a corner of her mind praying passionately for help. Images of Joe and Mickey helped Tori focus on getting back into the real world. When she focused on Joe, the sense of peace and strength deepened. It was weird but wonderful. She whispered and soothed and cajoled her sister into a calmer place.

The ledge became the alley again. The alley became lighter. Tori looked up to see the walls dissolving. A few moments later she opened her eyes in Joe's parents' living room.

"Lex." Tori heard her voice sound more firm now that the pain was receding. "You're not alone anymore. Feel it. There's four of us now. We'll find Ben together. Calm down, okay, and we'll help you figure out where he is."

Lexie opened her eyes. For a moment Tori wasn't sure how she was going to respond. Then she reached for Tori and hugged her hard. Tori held her close. She looked at Joe and Mickey. Both men were pale and sweaty. They must have absorbed a huge amount of Lexie's energy. Tori met their eyes—first Joe, then Mickey—and mouthed, *thank you.*

She turned back to Lexie. Both girls wiped at their tears. "We can do this, Lex," Tori said. "We'll drive around and you'll let us know if we're getting closer or farther away, okay?"

Lexie nodded. Her hand shook as she wiped her eyes with her sleeve. Mickey handed her a box of tissues. Tori would've sworn the two shared a look, but that couldn't be right. Lexie had vowed to keep all men at a distance after Ben's father had left her.

Joe put his hand on Tori's arm. His touch and his presence soothed her fears, as it had since the moment they'd met. "Let's go," he said.

Tori felt her legs shaking as she stood up. She let herself lean into Joe. The difference between walking a hard road alone and walking it with friends overwhelmed her with hope. She noticed Melissa and Stuart sitting near the top of the stairs, faces wet. They both tried to smile when they caught her eye. Tori didn't need telepathic powers to know they were rooting for Lexie.

The four walked through the kitchen to the back door and the pile of boots and coats. The kitchen was filled with people now, half of whom Tori didn't know. A hooded man stood beside Owen. He nodded at Tori as she passed. Three women sat praying together at the kitchen table, holding hands, their lips moving silently. A very old Asian man with a cane made Tori think of Obi-Wan Kenobi. Art and Casey stood shell-shocked in a corner. Most everyone wiped at their tears.

A few minutes later, the four were back in their winter coats and ready to go. Hannah patted Lexie's shoulder and pressed a stack of dish towels into Tori's hands.

"In case you need them," she said. Her voice sounded rough, like she'd been crying for a long time. She gave Tori a quick, hard hug.

Tori held Lexie's hand when they went outside. A cold winter wind buffeted the group as Mickey led them to the white Chevy Tahoe in the alley. Tori shivered. Her damp cheeks burned in the wind. At least it wasn't snowing.

A huge white Chevy Suburban with dark tinted windows pulled up behind the Tahoe. Hayley jumped out of the passenger seat and ran over. She grabbed them and the three girls held each other tight. Tori didn't know why or how Hayley was here, but she was glad to see her.

A blonde man about Joe's size stepped out from the driver side of the Suburban and waited.

Mickey stood in front of Lexie, his hand on her shoulder. "You ready?"

Lexie turned slowly in a circle and stopped. She stared without seeing.

"That way?" Mickey pointed northwest.

Lexie nodded. "Yes," she whispered. She cleared her throat and nodded again.

Tori studied Mickey's face. He looked intimidating but sounded so gentle. And Lexie seemed, inexplicably, to trust him. Maybe only because he was helping her find Ben. It probably wouldn't last longer than that. Tori knew her sister too well.

"You two follow us." Mickey nodded at the blonde man and Hayley. He opened the door of the first SUV and helped Lexie inside.

"We'll take our car," Art said to Mickey. "As soon as you have confirmation—"

Tori heard him pause, almost stutter, as he looked at Lexie. She wondered if he'd ever encountered anything like what had just happened. Chalk up another new experience for the Superhero Liaison Unit.

"—we'll have additional units heading your way."

"Joe," Owen called from the back door. "Call me. We'll do whatever is necessary."

Tori shivered. She'd never heard Owen use quite that tone before.

Mickey drove. He followed Lexie's directions, even anticipated them sometimes. Tori wondered if something had happened to him and Joe when they'd been connected to Lexie earlier.

They moved predominately northwest through residential areas and business districts, backtracking at the occasional one-way street or cul-de-sac. They drove up the peninsula between West Bay and East Bay. They circled down around the southern end of West Bay and continued west. Lexie mumbled that she felt Ben was farther north. Tori saw her look out over the expanse of water separating them from the unseen northern shoreline. Lexie began to cry.

Within moments, everyone in the SUV was crying, everyone fighting against Lexie's power. Tori tried to send Lexie peace, but she was exhausted. She felt like a wet sponge, unable to absorb any more. Mickey pulled over and wiped his face with one of the dish towels. Without saying a word, he got out and climbed into the back seat, moving Lexie into the middle.

Mickey reached for Lexie's hand, grasping it firmly in both of his.

"No, Mickey, don't—"

But it was too late. Tori saw him flinch. She grabbed Lexie's other hand to keep Mickey from feeling the full effect. It was the oddest sensation. Like she was privy to a wordless conversation. Tori could feel him help Lexie focus. Ben became a beacon, a homing signal in all their minds. With that single focus, all three of them turned their heads to the north.

Mickey's voice broke the thick quiet. "Joe, drive north around East Bay up toward Culver Lake."

Joe slid across to the driver's seat and pulled out into traffic. The SUV spun its tires in the snow for a moment before it gained traction on the blacktop. Tori looked out the back window. The second SUV and the unmarked police car had stopped behind them, a blue light flashing in the police car. They followed Mickey back onto the road. The sedan fish-tailed as it struggled to get back on the pavement. The blue light went off.

Twenty-five minutes later, they were traveling down a two-lane road with woods on the right, the occasional farm on the left. It was full dark outside. No streetlights out here in the country. Tori couldn't remember seeing such deep night before.

The headlights reflected off the snowbanks creating strange shadows. Tori tried not to shiver even as the heater blasted from the dash. She looked at the dashboard clock. It was only 7:23. Nothing scary happened at 7:23.

Lexie clutched her hand more tightly. Tori turned to her, an inexplicable fear rising in her throat. She wished she could hold Joe's hand. As if he could sense her unease, Joe caught her eye in the rearview mirror.

"We're close?" Mickey asked.

Lexie nodded.

Now there were woods on both sides. When the headlights hit the snow just right, Tori thought she could make out a fence inside the tree line.

"Wait," Lexie whispered. She sat forward in her seat. "Stop! Here, here!"

Joe pulled to the side of the road. Woods. Just woods. Tori's jaw ached. She was clenching her teeth. She tried to relax, but in a moment she was tense again. She stared through the trees on the right side of the road. Ben was in the woods somewhere, and he didn't want to be there. He wanted his mommy.

It took Tori a moment to understand why she knew this. She

still held her sister's hand. Lexie knew where her son was and what he was feeling. For a moment, Tori understood the burden Lexie had been forced to carry when Charlie was taken from her.

"I think there's a bit of light up there," Joe said. He drove forward on the shoulder. Snow and gravel crunched under the tires. Finally, a driveway appeared. A sign stood partially covered in snow. Small outdoor spotlights illuminated the sign from under the snow, creating more shadows.

CURTIS ENTERPRISES, Research Fac...

Tori felt her stomach drop. It couldn't be. He wouldn't. *Why?*

She looked at Lexie. A look of horror washed over her sister's face. Tori noticed Mickey in the dim light. She yanked Lexie's hand from his. He couldn't know. She didn't want him to know. He'd tell Joe and Joe would...

Tori didn't know what Joe would do. How would he react when he found out he'd married into the villain's family? There was no other way to look at it: Kane was a villain, he must be, and she was his daughter. Tori choked as she tried to hold in a sob.

"Joe..." Mickey said.

Joe turned in his seat. But he faced Tori, not Mickey. His usual superhero confidence was missing from his expression, replaced with uncertainty and questions.

"Tori, do you know where we are?" he asked.

She couldn't answer him. Her mind spun trying to find an answer that wouldn't destroy her newly happy life.

"I'll kill him," Lexie said with deadly calm. Her tears had dried. Something darker filled her expression now. For the first time, Tori was a little bit afraid of her sister. Afraid of how her power had grown over time without either of them realizing it. Afraid of how Lexie's fear and hatred could destroy the almost normal lives they'd built over the last few years.

"*Lexie, do not speak,*" Tori ordered quietly.

Her sister turned to her, anger flashing through her expression. It radiated out into Tori through their clasped hands. Tori shook her head. "Later."

Joe turned to Mickey. Tori watched his face. It changed back into the superhero-at-work expression she recognized. He wouldn't ask questions now. They'd find Ben first. But when it was over... Tori couldn't be sure of anything after that.

"Are you sure?" Joe asked Mickey.

Mickey nodded. He glanced sharply at Lexie and Tori. "Do you know who Kane Curtis is?"

Tori gripped Lexie's hand, warning her. They both stayed quiet, meeting Mickey's gaze then looking away.

"What's going on?" Joe asked from the front seat. He frowned at Tori. "If you know him, just tell us."

Tori couldn't decide if Joe's building anger was his own or in response to Lexie's power. Her sister was pulsing with rage. She pushed at Tori, trying to loosen Tori's hold.

"*Do not speak.*" Tori's anger and fear poured into her words. She felt her power grow.

But Lexie's anger was pushing Tori hard. When Tori got angry, she tended to lose some control. Lexie knew that. She pushed harder, trying to make Tori so angry she'd release her command. In Tori's mind, images of Ben crowded out the images of her and Joe.

Her sister was making her choose. The images of Ben became colored with Lexie's fears for her son. Blood and dirt and darkness and tears and—

"Okay!" she cried.

She ripped her hand out of Lexie's and wrapped her arms around herself, pulling away into the corner of the seat. She wanted to look away, but she couldn't help but stare at her husband when Lexie said the words out loud.

"He's our father."

Joe turned to Tori, his eyes widening, his face going slack. And Tori watched her perfect life slip away.

19

L exie felt her emotions transforming inside of her. The overwhelming pain of loss morphed into single-minded focus. Fear solidified into anger. Confusion became clarity. For the first time in her life, she embraced the curse she'd inherited.

When she'd stopped taking the medication that repressed her emotions, she'd had to learn how to control herself in order to survive. She'd built a safe, normal life for Ben through monumental self-discipline. No one would've guessed that freak blood ran in her veins.

Until now. Now she would use it to destroy the man who had cursed her life and taken her son. Sitting in the SUV, Lexie felt a pang of regret for the lovely life she was about to lose.

"Let's go," she said to Tori. She nudged her sister's thigh and Tori opened the door and got out.

Lexie closed her eyes and focused on Ben. Something in her chest pulled tight, like her heart was trying to reach out for a piece of itself somewhere in the woods. She followed the pull. She stepped onto the shoulder of the road into a couple inches of soft snow.

"So, what's the plan?" asked the man driving with Hayley.

Lexie spared him a glance as he and Hayley walked over from their vehicle. She heard others talking as she struggled up the snowbank.

"Tori, wait," called Joe.

Lexie heard her sister stop behind her. The frustration inside grew. She pushed it down. Her brother-in-law was a good man, and his friend was... Lexie looked at him. She'd never let anyone but Tori in her head before, but she'd seen inside these two. Integrity. Faithfulness. She wondered when the word "dependable" came into her head. She let herself slide down the snowbank and waited impatiently.

Mickey motioned to her from the back of the vehicle. Everyone gathered there—her sister and Joe, Mickey, Hayley, and the blonde man. Lexie joined them. Mickey put his hand on her shoulder. She started to tell him she didn't like to be touched, but when she looked at him and opened her mouth, she knew he already knew that. And she knew he wasn't going to let go of her, even if he took his hand away.

He squeezed her shoulder and turned to the others. Lexie continued to stare at him. Who was he?

"This is Bull," Mickey motioned to the blonde, who nodded to her. "He's part of our team. We're going to get your son back, but we need to work together. If Kane Curtis has your son, it's going to take all of us to get him back."

Lexie glanced around. "The six of us? We can do it?" She felt better already. Six was better than one.

Mickey shook his head. "No, all of us. Joe, call Owen and tell him where we are."

Lexie felt a warning in his words that chilled her more than the cold wind still blowing. Before she could ask him any more questions, the three men disappeared behind the second SUV.

She turned to Hayley. "What are they doing?" She felt Hayley's worry, but it wasn't worry for Ben. "What?"

Hayley looked like she was fighting within herself. "Please don't be mad," she said, looking from Lexie to Tori. "Secrets keep us safe. You two know that more than anyone." She looked like she was begging them.

"Hayley, what's wrong?" Tori asked. Her voice firmed as she said, "We're your best friends. You can trust us."

Hayley's features composed themselves from worry to relief and into a face of strength. "I know," she said. "And you can trust me." She looked at Lexie. "I'm going to help you get Ben back."

She walked away as three men in dark clothing strode out of the dark. Lexie felt her eyes widen. The smaller one approached her but didn't speak. His suit looked more like body armor, but in a flexible material. She reached out her hand to his chest. Hard, warm. She met his eyes, and for the first time, he grinned. They stared at each other for a moment, then she looked at the others.

Tori stood close to the taller one, holding his hand and gazing at him with adoration in her eyes. There was only one man her little sister looked at that way.

"Joe?" Her brother-in-law was a...a... She couldn't say "freak" when she looked at these capable-looking men gathered of their own free will to help Ben. If they succeeded, if they put Ben back in her arms tonight, she decided she would start calling them by the other name.

A woman in a similar suit solidified out of the night.

Tori gasped. "Hayley?"

The woman shook her head. "Green Thumb." She moved her hands in a beautiful dance, and vines started growing out of her pockets. As her hands swayed, the plants defied gravity, moving up into the air and curving around.

Lexie rolled her eyes and let herself smile for a moment. Green Thumb had made a heart shape around Tori and her husband.

Everyone turned to Lexie, a variety of smiles and grins on their faces. She didn't like being the center of attention. She looked at the man beside her. Shocked, she whipped her hand away. Her blood rushed as embarrassment swept through her. This whole time she had her hand on his chest like, like—

At her side, the back of his hand touched hers lightly. "Focus," he said quietly. "Control your emotions. Don't let them control you."

She breathed deeply and calmed. He knew the mantra she said to herself. But he'd made it stronger, made it work quicker. She wondered how. More than that, she felt that despite his warnings about the difficulties they faced, it was going to work.

She looked at the group around her. Never before had she been a part of something that was greater than the sum of its parts.

"My name is Tick Tock," said the man next to her. He pointed. "That's Powerhouse, Green Thumb, and Superhero X. Remember those names. Use them. You *cannot* use our other names. Understood?" He looked at Tori, too.

Lexie nodded at the blonde man, Hayley, and Joe.

"I'm the team leader," he continued, "but you're the key to this operation, Lexie. You'll stay with me, and I'll coordinate with the other teams."

She nodded. His tone was a not unpleasant combination of gentle and inflexible.

"You're going to find Ben and we're going to get him out."

Control your emotions. Don't let them control you. Lexie had been telling herself for hours that she would find Ben. But when the words were coming out of someone else's mouth... Last time she'd failed. What if it happened again?

"You can do it," Tick Tock said again.

She nodded.

"X, pull up the layout of the facility." Tick Tock ushered everyone to the back of the Suburban.

Lexie saw a sedan parked on the shoulder of the road thirty feet away. Two people sat and watched.

Tick Tock nodded at them and said to Lexie, "Superhero Liaison Unit, Double Bay Police Department. They can't enter without cause." He grinned. "That's us."

When the back door of the SUV opened, Lexie gasped. It looked like one of those rolling crime labs on TV, like something the FBI used. The men discussed entry strategies, potential threats, and best and worst places to be in a fight. The conversation left Lexie's head spinning. Who *were* these people?

Listening to them plan a rescue operation for Ben, a feeling came over Lexie that she hadn't felt very often in her life.

Gratitude.

TORI FOLLOWED the team up the driveway, the sound of their movements covered by the blowing wind. The decision to avoid the woods because the snow was too deep made sense. But walking up the open lane, visible to anyone driving, soon visible to anyone looking out a window... Tori shivered. She was scared, and it had nothing to do with Lexie.

They paused at the edge of the well-lit parking lot. Lexie closed her eyes and searched for Ben.

"That way." She pointed to the far end of the multi-building complex.

It looked as though most of the employees had already gone home for the day, but the team kept to the edge of the parking lot as they made their way around two buildings.

Tori watched Lexie stop and focus again, reaching inside with that part of herself she didn't understand. Tori felt her sister's fear build to anger and then to hope. Everyone tensed.

Lexie gasped. "Second floor. He's on the second floor of that building."

"Do you know where?" Tick Tock whispered.

"The room behind the corner one." Lexie pointed.

"I have an idea," Tori said. She told Tick Tock and he nodded.

"If it doesn't work, stay behind us. It may get messy."

The six of them walked up to the entrance of the building, Tori in the lead. When they walked in, the receptionist looked up in surprise.

"I'm sorry. We're closed." The woman looked over Tori's shoulder and frowned. Four people in masks would make anyone nervous.

Tori smiled. "Oh, it's okay, I'm here to see my father." She felt the tension in the others gathered behind her, but she kept her friendliest smile in place.

"And he is?"

"Kane Curtis."

Was it Tori's imagination or did the woman blanche under her makeup? She glanced nervously at the signage on the wall behind her and picked up the phone. "I'll see if he's available."

"Oh, I think he's expecting us," Tick Tock said, the metallic sound of his voice harsh in the echoing lobby.

Tori turned to him and followed his gaze. A small camera was tucked into the middle "r" of the Curtis Enterprises sign on the wall. Tori's smile faltered.

Lexie stepped up and stared directly into the camera. *"Give me back my son."*

If Kane were a regular person, Lexie would probably scare him into complying immediately. If only, Tori wished. Her hopes that he was simply a socially maladjusted, control freak, business tycoon had evaporated a few minutes ago when she realized where they were.

She had a thought. Probably wouldn't work but she might as well give it a try. She focused on the camera. *"Bring us Ben."*

She waited a moment, then looked to the receptionist. "Is he there?"

The woman turned away and stared at her desk. "We're closed. Please don't hurt me," she pleaded.

As the receptionist began to cry, Superhero X heard another sound off to his left. As he turned to look, he saw a dark shape flying toward them. Then another and another. "Powerhouse!" he shouted.

So Kane had his own private army. Shouldn't be a surprise. X raised his arm to flip the closest attacker over his shoulder, but not before he got a kick in the face.

Powerhouse turned just in time to grab an ankle as an assailant tried to kick him in the chest. He let him go as the third attacker knocked Green Thumb to the ground.

With a bellow of rage, Powerhouse picked the man up and threw him into a wall. Green Thumb finished tying up the first two, wrapping cords of ivy around the men, and rushed toward the third.

Tick Tock pushed Tori and Lexie under the receptionist's desk, and fought off two more men. X looked around the quiet lobby. Where were they coming from? A shadow of movement caught his eye just as he heard a quiet "sschtk" sound above. "The ceiling!" he yelled.

The others looked up as more ninja-looking attackers jumped silently from the ceiling tiles.

X pulled a man out of mid-air and tossed him to the ground. "Green Thumb!"

Philodendron shot out of her pockets as she ducked under one of Powerhouse's fists. She sent the ivy spinning wildly around the downed man's wrists, then his ankles.

A kick in his chest sent X back a step. A short man stood in a martial arts pose in front of him preparing to attack him again. X crossed his arms and motioned for him to make his move.

The man jumped in, aiming for X's knee. X brought it up into the guy's face without losing his balance. He heard the click of the man's teeth hitting together, then saw him trip as a long piece of growing vine wrapped along his ankles. By the time the creep hit the floor, the vines had him neatly tied up.

Green Thumb and X turned toward the rest of the fight. Whoever these guys were, most of them knew how to fight. And there were more of them coming out of the shadows.

X hit, kicked, and threw men, one after another. The three men tried to toss the attackers close to the left wall for Green Thumb to tie up. X turned from tossing one toward Powerhouse and found another with a knife at his throat.

"Drop the knife!" Powerhouse yelled. The small man turned his head toward the voice and X clocked the guy, the knife clattering to the floor.

Two more men began to apply their fists and feet to his body. He fought back in a frenzy. He didn't usually feel angry in a fight, but he did now. Lexie, he thought, as he threw another man at the front window. He could feel her growing panic that they needed to find Ben *now*. Where was their backup? They had to get out of this brawl and search for the boy.

More men, more fighting, more knives. X kept a firm grip on the short steel pipe in his right hand. He felt a knife slice across his upper arm as he swung his fist at another guy. It cut his suit, but not his skin. He kicked the knife away, then kicked the assailant wielding it. The offender flew ten feet, tripping another mug sneaking up behind Tick Tock.

"Tick Tock! Behind you!" X shouted. He saw one of the downed men stagger up and toward Green Thumb. X felled him like a tree and pushed Green Thumb out of range as another came at them with a knife.

A rush of cold air and voices. X glanced up. Two more superhero teams joined the fray. X heard someone yell his name. He ducked and rolled as another knife cut across his thigh. Adrenaline shot through his system as he focused on the metal in his hand. The new attacker reached and slashed toward X's gut, keeping eye contact with X. More focused than his comrades.

They circled each other, the man slicing out, X looking for an opening.

In his peripheral vision, X saw Tick Tock and Powerhouse fighting. Green Thumb tripped a pair of ruffians with her vines. The Cowl and Káwal from Superhero W's team cut a swath through their enemies without physically touching any of them. X wished he could watch those two fight. They were legends in the Paladin Guild. But he still had to take down his current opponent.

The masked man made a move, and X jumped out of range of the knife. Circling, waiting, another jump. Shouts of "Police!" didn't distract the man intent on bringing X down. The cops who had waited for Tick Tock's signal had arrived. The wave of new attackers slowed.

X normally treated all weapons as capable of hurting him. If he ever lost his power, he'd be less likely to be mortally injured if he continued to be careful. But he felt Lexie's intense need to find her son, so he changed his game and stood still. The attacker lunged, his knife at X's throat.

Before X could grab the knife, the man's arm broke with a loud crack. Another crack and his legs went out from under him. Down he fell.

X turned to see The Cowl standing silently nearby, his hands pointed at the fallen enemy. He nodded to X and turned to his next opponent.

Mouthing a silent *holy cow*, X rushed over to where the girls were hiding under the receptionist's desk. Only they weren't hiding. They were using their powers on the older woman to tell them where to find Ben. X heard Tori force the woman to tell them where Kane's office was before the police hustled the woman away from the fighting.

The woman turned back to the hidden camera, screaming, "They made me! They made me!"

Tick Tock hurried over. "Where is he?"

The team ran up the stairs as the skirmish continued.

TORI HEARD MORE YELLING, more fighting below, as she ran down an upstairs hall. Everyone followed Lexie until she suddenly stopped.

"Here?" asked Powerhouse. He shoved the door next to him and it came off its hinges. Empty.

Lexie shook her head. "No, he's gone." Her face twisted as she focused harder. "It's like he's not here. He was and then he *wasn't.*"

"We don't know what Kane's powers are," Tick Tock said, "but he may be hiding the boy somehow."

Tori squinted down the hall. A thick mass of twisting shadows moved toward a steel door. The shadows coalesced into a form, two shapes, and then she could see Kane. And Ben!

"Mamaaa!" he screamed as the door shut behind him.

Everyone ran. It took X and Powerhouse both to take down the door. The second hallway looked medical in nature, white and stainless steel, doors with small windows and keypad entry. They looked through the window of every door. Nothing.

At the last door, the window showed nothing, almost as if it opened into dark space. As Tori stared, the darkness shifted, as if it were looking out at them. Her fear fed Lexie's, and Lexie's fear fed her anger.

"Let him go!" Lexie screamed. "Let him go!" She beat her hands against the door, twisting the door handle, pounding until Tick Tock pulled her back. She fought him, trying to get to Ben.

As Tori watched, X and Powerhouse kicked at the door, pulled at it, ran their shoulders into it. Nothing happened.

Completely nothing. The door didn't dent, didn't shudder, didn't move at all.

Supernatural. Somehow Kane used a supernatural power to protect himself in the room. How did you fight that? Tori set aside her fear and tried to use her mind. How could you fight something supernatural? There must be a way.

With something else supernatural, of course. But that wasn't working. They all had supernatural gifts, yet Kane seemed impervious.

Danny's words came back to her. Work with Lexie, he said.

How could anger and fear help? Tori shook her head.

The darkness swirled and pulled back. Shadows undulated and dissolved and reformed. As they watched, natural darkness filled the space and they could see a medical laboratory. Kane and Ben solidified at the back. Ben screamed. He kicked and fought and, as they watched, Kane forced him into a chair with metal cuffs at his wrists and ankles. His crying increased.

Lexie screamed and beat against the door. It shuddered normally this time.

"X! The door!" Tori pointed excitedly. "It's a normal door now. Try again!"

Tick Tock and Green Thumb pulled Lexie away as X and Powerhouse pounded their bodies against the door. It dented. The frame cracked.

Kane looked up at the sound and became shadow. In a moment, the door was supernaturally solid again.

"Get him out of there," Lexie screamed at Tick Tock. "What's he doing to my baby?"

Tick Tock shook his head. "Nothing." He looked at the team and shook his head again. "He can't," he said, thinking it through out loud. "He can't *do* anything as a shadow. He had to solidify to put Ben in that chair. Ben's still screaming, so he's not a part of the shadow now."

X nodded. "So we need him to stay in human form to get through the door."

"But in human form, he can do whatever it is he's trying to do to Ben," Green Thumb argued.

"Ben may be safer when Kane is a shadow, but then we can't get in," added Powerhouse.

Tori sucked in a breath. Could she do it again? Her dad had encouraged her to pray for wisdom and then use it. Was this wise?

God, help me to know what to do, and help me to do *it.*

X looked at her. "What?"

"He's creating or using some kind of supernatural darkness," she said. "What if we could fight him with supernatural light?"

X's expression moved from confusion to understanding to hope. He clasped her shoulder. "You could do it," he said, his voice laced with excitement.

"Maybe," she shook her head a little. "But how?" She thought it might work. She wanted it to work. But she had no idea how she made it happen before.

Tick Tock broke in. "Tell me."

"She created this bright white light earlier today. It was—I don't know what it was." X looked toward the door and back to Tick Tock. "But it was bright enough to chase away any shadow."

Everyone turned to Tori. "I was really upset," she said. "I don't know how I did it. I don't know how to make it happen again."

Tick Tock's mouth formed a grim smile. "Well, I know just the thing to make you upset." He patted Lexie's back.

Of course! Work with Lexie! Maybe together they could do it. She looked into the darkness at the window and felt her own fear and anger. She let it burn. Let him try to make her more afraid. She'd feed on his power to grow her own.

Tick Tock laid out a plan and everyone got into place.

Tori and Lexie clasped hands and faced the darkness. Tori felt her sister's anger grow. It became a monster in the hallway, then a monster in the room. Tori felt Lexie's rage and her desire for destruction. It was terrifying.

She focused on Ben locked into that chair. She focused on his screams. Lexie fed her images of her worst fears for Ben. Tori trembled under the assault and felt a burning rising in her chest.

She remembered that the first time, the whole room disappeared. Tori concentrated on creating light inside, not wishing the room away. She didn't want to lose Ben somehow.

"Focus, Tori," X encouraged her from his position near the door.

Tori felt Lexie's pain, felt Ben's pain, felt her own pain that a man who should have loved her more than his own life had betrayed her in such a vile way. She released the churning and cried, *"Light!"*

Bright white light flashed and hovered in the hall. It filled the room in front of them. Tori focused on keeping it in the room while Powerhouse and X broke down the door. After three tries, the door flew back and against the side wall.

Lexie ran for her son. Tick Tock followed her, pulling something from his suit to pick the locks on the chair.

Tori felt the light shimmering. No! Stay! *Light!* She fixed all of her energy on keeping the darkness at bay.

Green Thumb and X and Powerhouse searched all the shadows of the room, trying to find where Kane hid. But the shadows increased as the light faded. Someone flipped a switch on the wall. The room brightened for a moment.

"There!" Someone shouted and pointed.

Tori fell back against the wall, letting go. Her light dissolved. Her head pounded. Her legs shook as she tried to stay on her feet.

A sharp series of pops and sparks flew from the light fixtures. Seething darkness settled in the corner where Ben and Lexie and

Tick Tock had been standing. Ominous silence shrouded the area.

The rest of the team stood in shock for a moment. Then X shouted to Tori, "Again! We'll grab them and get them out!"

Green Thumb ran to Tori. She stood behind her and clasped her shoulders. "It's all because of him," Green Thumb said. "Focus on that, Tori. They called you crazy because of him. They made you take pills because of him. And Lexie! She became an addict and a drunk and lived in an alley *because of him.*"

Her friend knew how to push her buttons. Tori stood straighter, felt a renewed rush. She thought of every awful situation she'd been in because of her freakishness. She focused on every moment her mother acted afraid of her instead of holding her tight.

Light blazed out.

Green Thumb kept reminding her of all the bad times. Then she told Tori the worst details of growing up a freak in her home. The verbal abuse, the beatings, the nights she spent locked in a closet.

The light vibrated around her.

She saw Lexie and Ben. Tick Tock had them in his arms as he rushed for the door. As they came through and ran for the exit, a dense black cloud moved along the floor and out the door.

Tori saw it. She didn't want Kane to get away. She didn't want him to have another opportunity to kidnap Ben. He should pay. She pushed the light to grow, to leave no corner for Kane to hide. The cloud moved slower, became denser.

She felt herself shaking, burning. A piece of the ceiling fell. Glass exploded behind her. Green Thumb cried out and let go of her shoulders.

Focus!

The shadow became denser, smaller. Another chunk of the ceiling came down on the shadow. No! She couldn't let him hide.

She forced the light brighter, shining partially under the debris where she last saw the darkness.

"Tori!" X yelled, shaking her. "Stop! You're bringing the ceiling down!" More glass exploded and he tried to shield her with his body.

Sudden intense pain. She used it to focus the light even more. Why wouldn't he stand up and be a man? She wanted him to be punished, to go to jail. But she couldn't force him to change back to his human form.

"Tori, stop!" X ducked as a light fixture fell and swung by his head. "You're bleeding! Stop!"

X was going to stop her. He was bigger and stronger and she couldn't fight him. Kane would get away. He'd get away with everything. Unless she could make him disappear so he couldn't hurt anyone anymore. It was the only option she had left. She focused with all her strength.

"Kane, go away!" she screamed.

She heard an explosion, X tackled her and covered her with his body, then darkness took her.

reen Thumb watched the organized confusion outside. This might be the first superhero-police joint bust in the history of Double Bay. Though from her perspective, parts of it looked more confused than organized.

She let the EMT finish bandaging her left hand, then hopped off the back of the ambulance as a child was carried over. Could it be true? Kane had kidnapped more children than Ben? She remembered hearing twelve or fifteen kids had gone missing. She ran back in the building. She needed to help find them.

As she hurried in, Superhero X was carrying Tori out. She had cuts on her face and upper body. Blood flowed from her nose. Her eyes were closed and Green Thumb couldn't tell if she'd passed out or something worse.

"Tori!" Green Thumb rushed up to them. "Is she okay?"

"I think so." X's voice was tight. He didn't look like he believed his words.

"Tori?"

Tori opened her eyes. "Did we save Ben?" She looked like she'd just done seventy-two hours on her feet with nothing but

Cheetos and Red Bull. But she didn't look like she was about to die.

I know I don't talk to you much, but thank you, God.

"We did, girlfriend." Green Thumb smoothed her friend's hair. "He's safe with Lexie now, and Tick Tock isn't letting anyone near them." In a lower voice, she said to X, "Someone brought out another child. I'm going to see if I can find any more."

He nodded. "If she's okay, I'll come help."

Green Thumb went back upstairs toward the laboratory area. She was about to turn down a hallway when a redheaded woman in a lab coat almost ran into her. She carried a small boy toward another door.

"Hey! Put him down!" Green Thumb pointed her hands toward the woman, ready to trip her with her vines if she tried to take the child anywhere but downstairs.

The woman looked at Green Thumb's costume and lay the boy none too gently on the floor. Nice thing about a super suit, no one knew what powers you had, so they assumed the worst.

"I'm trying to help him, to get him out of here," the woman pleaded.

Green Thumb paused. She'd known enough liars and cheats to recognize one, but she was supposed to let people explain themselves before she tied them up. Tick Tock was trying to teach her the rules of fair fighting. "Who are you?"

"I work for Curtis Enterprises, but I've been trying to get the children out when no one was watching," the redhead said. "Come on, Teddy." She reached for the boy.

He whimpered and shrank back. That was enough proof for Green Thumb.

"Liar!" She threw ivy at the woman at a furious rate, tripping her when she tried to run. When the woman started to yell nasty things, Green Thumb wrapped ivy around her head, effectively tying her jaw shut.

Satisfied the redhead wasn't getting away, Green Thumb

crouched down next to the boy. She was careful not to touch him. Was he hurt? Afraid of her?

He looked up, hope and hopelessness battling across his perfect little features. He lay quietly, waiting to see what Green Thumb was going to do to him. She knew the feeling.

"It's okay, sweetheart," she whispered. "I'm here to take you home."

He studied her for a long moment. Green Thumb was torn between grabbing him up and getting him out to safety, and giving him a chance to take in the situation. Her patience paid off. His chin began to quiver. Then the tears welled up and fell across his chubby cheeks. Her heart broke when he lifted his arms up to her.

Gently, she picked the boy up, cuddling him to her heart, murmuring comfort. She didn't want to let him go. This is what it could be like if she were normal. She'd have a child cuddling in her arms and—

Green Thumb cut off the thought. Not gonna happen.

She carried him outside, telling a pair of police officers about the woman tied up on the second floor. She found the EMT who had bandaged her hand. It took a minute for the boy to let go of her and go to him. Green Thumb almost decided not to relinquish him, but she reminded herself there were other children who needed to be rescued.

Upstairs, she headed toward the labs again. She looked down the hallway where they'd rescued Ben from Kane. Lights hung by wires, broken glass covered the floor, a huge section of the ceiling had buckled in several feet. Green Thumb stopped and stared. Tori did all that?

A cop brought another boy out from a hallway farther ahead. Green Thumb took her search in that direction. She found some rooms with open doors, empty now. This must be where the children were kept. She headed for the closed doors but paused at an open doorway when she caught movement inside.

A little boy lay strapped down on his bed. Drool fell from his lips. When he saw Green Thumb, he tried to leap at her, growling and baring dozens of razor sharp teeth. The boy had straight dark hair, olive skin, and huge black eyes with no white showing. He might've been five or six, though it was hard to tell. She looked at his hands and feet and saw claws twisting against the bands holding him down.

A sob burst from her throat. The others in the room—two paramedics, Powerhouse, and Superhero X—looked up at the sound.

Powerhouse and X stood to either side of the boy. The paramedics went through their paces, but their faces registered their shock as they tried to figure out how to help, staying out of the way of the clawing hands and sharp teeth. As they leaned over him, he opened his mouth again and growled with an inhuman sound.

"It's all right, little one," Powerhouse murmured. He lay his hand on the boy's shoulder. The growling stopped, but the boy tried to bite him. Bull pulled back and placed his hand on the boy's head instead. The boy twisted for a moment, then lay still.

Finally, one of the paramedics shook his head. "I don't know what they've done to him," he said, "but he's dying."

Even as he spoke, the boy's chest moved, expanded. The boy cried out and Green Thumb heard tiny pops and snaps. His body was growing before their eyes, bones breaking from the pressure. The second paramedic bit his lip and tried to remain stoic, but tears rolled down his face.

Green Thumb found Powerhouse's gaze across the room. This was all wrong. They were supposed to rescue the children, not arrive in time to see them die! She heard him say something to X about calming the boy. X pulled off his mask and the top of his suit. He tightened his grip on the steel pipe in his hand.

Was he going to—? That boy could tear him to pieces if X's power failed, even for a moment.

"Move back," he spoke quietly to the paramedics.

The boy screamed in agony again. This scream sounded much more like a little boy. Green Thumb felt her chest convulse on another sob.

The second paramedic moved back against the wall, taking his equipment with him. "He's dying, Pete," he said to the first man. "Let them do what they can."

Green Thumb watched her friends. What could they do?

Nodding to Powerhouse, X unstrapped the boy's feet. They kicked out at him, twisting and pounding on the bed. One foot made contact and ripped the left leg of his suit. Powerhouse placed one hand on the boy's head and one on his chest, trying to calm and sooth the child with quiet words. The stretching and cracking had stopped for now.

X loosed the boy's hands and picked him up from the bed, holding him gently and crooning to him. The boy kicked and clawed and scratched and bit. X's skin remained unmarked. After a few minutes, the boy calmed down and looked up at the man who held him. The two stared at each other for a moment.

X's face was compassion itself.

Green Thumb felt years of useless wishes and dashed hopes from her childhood rise up inside. Her friends did have something to give.

Holding the boy close to his chest, X sat down on the bed and rocked him. Slowly, he pulled in the boy's hands and feet so they faced X's body. Then Powerhouse slid onto the bed and stroked the boy's head and back.

The child calmed some more. He relaxed against Joe, his head falling back into Bull's touch. Over the next few minutes, his body would spasm and the boy would cry out. Then he would curl into his protectors and whimper.

Green Thumb leaned against the wall, her heart breaking, her tears falling unchecked. It wasn't until the boy finally stopped moving that the men holding him allowed themselves to cry. X held the child a little longer, then let one of the paramedics check his pulse. When the man shook his head, X gently lay the boy on the bed.

The two men stood side by side, gripping each other's shoulders, brothers-in-arms, watching the paramedics perform final checks. Powerhouse motioned to Green Thumb and she stepped under his other arm. When X moved to pull his suit back up, Powerhouse pulled her tightly against him, his tears mixing with hers. Green Thumb ignored her "no public displays" rule and soaked up the comfort.

The three of them wiped their faces as they left the room. The rest of the rooms had been opened. If any children had been imprisoned in them, others had retrieved them. Green Thumb's shoulders sagged in relief. She couldn't do this again.

It was one thing to destroy marijuana plants, or to tie up the "bad guys" for the police to retrieve. Since when did this job she never wanted involve putting a face to an evil so far outside of her imagination? She would never forget watching a little boy die in such a cruel and *inhuman* way. It was almost unfathomable that the man behind this was Tori's father.

They walked out of the building and over to the ambulances. The night sky was lit up with floodlights. A helicopter hovered somewhere above. Two ambulances had given way to a row of them in the last thirty minutes. The trio looked for Tori and Ben, and found Tick Tock and Lexie, too.

Tick Tock nodded to the three of them. "Everyone's fine," he assured them.

"Not everyone," Green Thumb said. "I quit."

TORI SIGHED against Joe's hand, pressed against her cheek, and let the soothing sense that all was well permeate her being. She hadn't wanted to let go of him since he climbed into the ambulance with her. But he'd been quiet, scary quiet. Lying here in her hospital bed, doctors and nurses finally gone, Tori knew they needed to talk. But where to start...

"Does our insurance cover a hospital stay?"

Joe stopped staring at the floor and turned to her. "What? Sure, I guess. Don't worry about that right now, baby. Get some rest."

The clock on the wall said 11:35. Maybe he didn't want to talk right now. Maybe he wanted to go home. Maybe he was mad at her, thought tonight was her fault, hers and Lexie's.

"You should go home," she told him. "You need your rest, too." At least she wasn't crying and carrying on. That was something. She was determined to learn how to be a stronger person.

"No." Joe's voice was hard. "I'm not leaving you."

Surprised, Tori raised her eyes from her knees back to her husband. Or maybe he wasn't mad at her. This marriage thing was harder than she thought it would be. There was a lot more guessing than she'd expected.

"Mickey is upgrading the security systems at our house. Until he's done, we're staying with my parents." Joe looked around the hospital room, a private room in a small wing away from any other patient rooms. "This is a special wing built especially to cater to people like us. The security is good, but I'm not leaving until you do."

Fear crept back up Tori's stomach and lodged in her heart. "Because of...?" She didn't even want to say his name. She hadn't been able to process the activities of this evening yet. It all seemed too unreal.

Joe's shoulders shook like the weight of the world rested there. "Tori, Kane Curtis is one of the foremost villains in the Midwest. His father was part of a group called The Nine. They're..." He struggled to find the right words. "I don't understand what happened tonight, but I am *not* letting him hurt you or your sister or Ben. You don't understand how..." He stopped and shook his head. Then he kissed the back of her hand hard. "I can't lose you."

"You won't." Tori wanted to soothe him somehow, but he had shadows in his eyes she'd never seen before. "Joe, I'm sorry about all this. I didn't know any of it, I swear! Besides..." She was afraid to say the words out loud. What if...? "Maybe he's...gone. Forever."

They stared at each other, thinking through the possibilities, but unwilling to say them out loud. "We'll see," was all Joe said.

Tori was eager to forget about Kane for now, so she let it go. More important to her was what the future held for her and Joe. "I need to ask you something, Joe. And please be honest. I'm worried that somehow I... Are you sure you want to be married to me? Of your own free will?"

The words were barely out of her mouth before he climbed up on the bed with her and pulled her close. "Of course!"

"Are you sure I didn't make you?" Her heart clogged with hope as she waited for his answer.

Under her ear, his chest rumbled as if he chuckled, but his voice didn't sound lighthearted. "I've never wanted anything as badly as I want you, Tori. You didn't make me marry you. I couldn't wait. There's something between us. I can't explain it. Something that pulls us together. I know when you're in trouble. I can see it and feel it. It's horrible."

Really? How? She wanted to ask but he continued.

"Did you know that I can be as strong as any metal I touch? And I heal quickly, usually within a few hours. But ever since I met you, I feel stronger. I don't know if it's real. Maybe it's my imagination. But I feel different when we're together."

Tori snuggled closer. "Ever since we met, I've felt safe with you in a way I've never felt before. I was afraid you'd think it was some girly, clingy thing, so I didn't want to tell you." She thought about the feeling, how it came and went. "Even when I'm scared, like when my car blew up, there's something about you that makes me calmer. I feel stronger in that way. I think you're right, we're connected somehow."

Joe rubbed his chin on the top of her head. "Something."

"Do you know of anyone else like us?"

She felt him shake his head.

Weird. All these things were so weird. And somehow, it all tied back to Kane and the Paladins.

"Am I one of the bad guys to you?" She wished she could take the words back. She didn't mean to think out loud.

Joe pulled away and stared into her face, his hands cradling her head. He took his time, studying her like he was trying to understand a puzzle.

Tori didn't take offense. She really wanted to know. Would she have tendencies one way or the other? Would the others accept her, or would they worry that she couldn't be trusted? Joe would know the answer.

"I think we all are who we choose to be," he said finally. "Some days, it's hard to be good and easy to take the wrong path no matter who you are. I think you want to be one of the good guys."

She smiled softly at him. "I choose to believe that God made me on purpose, for a reason. And that he brought us together for a reason." Not that she wasn't scared something in her blood could make her do something horrible. Kane scared her more than anyone she'd ever met. But she believed that Good was stronger than Evil, even when Evil won some of the battles.

Joe smiled, but she could still see the shadows. Something was still bothering him.

"Did something happen tonight? Something I don't know about?"

He pulled her close again, his chin resting on her head. His embrace was almost painful. Her heart felt like it was breaking a little for him. Something bad *had* happened. She knew it.

"Hayley said there were more children." Tori tried to guess, but Joe stayed silent. "Did something happen to one of them?"

After a moment, he nodded. Tori felt something wet drop on her cheek. Tears. Oh no. She closed her eyes. Maybe she didn't want to know right now. She searched for something else to talk about.

"I'm glad we're living in the version where Peter Parker and Mary Jane both know. You know, so we don't have to keep secrets from each other." She felt his grip relax, so she continued. He needed to think about something else.

"Chad at the comic book store told me that there are different versions of many of the origin stories. I like the *Spider-Man* one where they get to be together. Don't you?"

Joe chuckled. This time, Tori could tell his mood was easing. She was catching on to this marriage stuff, after all.

"I know we don't have a lot of money, worse now since I'm unemployed and car-less, but I bought some comic books so I could do some research and—"

Joe chuckled more. "Tori, that's fiction, not research."

She poked him in the bicep. "Well, it was all I had. *Somebody* hadn't gotten around to making time to help me yet."

She felt better, too, now that they weren't talking about the scary stuff anymore. She tried to make him laugh. "Maybe Super-hero X will make time for me now."

Then she had another thought. "And *Hayley*! How long has she been Green Thumb? How long have you worked together? You pretended not to know each other when I introduced you at Thanksgiving."

"She's been on the team a few years," Joe said. "I get the impression she's had her powers since at least high school, maybe earlier. She doesn't talk about it much."

"And I thought Hayley was the normal one of us girls." Tori recalled some of the things Hayley had said tonight, horrible things about her past that Tori had never known. Sure, she knew Hayley's home life was pretty bad because Tori's parents had actually allowed Hayley to live with them when the girls were seniors in high school. But Hayley was better at keeping secrets than Tori would ever have imagined. She'd never had a clue.

Joe laughed. "Hayley is definitely not normal."

"Hey!" Tori poked him again. "That's my best friend you're talking about." Well, almost. "My second-best friend, that is."

Joe kissed the top of her head. "Don't worry, sweetheart, I like taking in rescues. Just ask Snickers. Found him sleeping under my porch a few years ago. Look how good he's got it now."

Tori laughed and pulled away. "Hey! I am *not* a rescue!"

"I beg to differ," Joe protested. "First, I rescued you at Halloween..." Joe went on to list all the times Superhero X had rescued her, embellishing the stories to the point of absurdity, making Tori laugh until her cheeks ached.

Once again, light had chased away the darkness. Tori kept up the banter as long as she could. When she started nodding off, Joe kicked off his shoes and got under the blanket with her, muttering about hospital rules and who was going to be able to make *him* move anyway.

Tori fell asleep in his arms. Despite the small bed, the aches and pains, and the darkness she now knew waited for them both, she slept well. Her heritage notwithstanding, she wasn't a super villain. She could handle anything else.

FOUR DAYS LATER, Tori and Joe stood in his parents' kitchen sneaking hot chocolate chip cookies off the cooling rack when his mom wasn't looking. When Hannah finally caught Joe, she whacked his hand with her spatula.

"She made me do it!" He pointed at Tori.

"Hey!" She gave him a mock affronted look. "You can't use me as your excuse if you don't get a cookie for me, too."

He laughed and kissed her. "Sorry."

"Kiss me again," she said quietly, pulling his shirt to get him closer, "and I'll let you blame me all you want."

"Hand check!" Bull called from where he sat with Hayley, holding her hand.

They all laughed, and Joe and Tori pulled away from each other. A little bit away.

The big kitchen, filled with a mish-mash of chairs, was getting crowded as more people arrived. Tori tried not to be nervous. This would be her first Paladins Guild meeting. Today she might get an idea of whether she would fit in with this world, or if everyone would consider her an untrustworthy outcast.

Owen sat down at the table, which Tori had come to learn meant it was time to settle down. She took a seat and Joe sat next to her. She squeezed his hand. It would be okay. It would. She took a deep breath.

"I'd like to get through everything before our other guests arrive for the big game," Owen said. "I'll try to be quick. Duke, Mickey, Bill, great work Wednesday night. Your teams worked effectively together, and with law enforcement. The SLU complimented you all on the scene, and other agencies have contacted them with kudos and questions about how they can work with us as well. Great job, everyone."

Everybody nodded and smiled at each other. Tori chuckled at a couple of high-fives.

Joe whispered in her ear, "Excellent job, wife."

She grinned and kissed his cheek.

"Unfortunately," Owen continued, "no one has seen Kane Curtis since Wednesday night. He has not been arrested and is considered at large."

Tori looked down at her lap. Everyone knew that was her fault. Either she hadn't stopped him and he escaped, or she...*did something* to him. Either way, he'd gotten away with a long list of crimes. Tori couldn't stop thinking about it. How could God let him go unpunished? It wasn't right.

"Altogether, we had a very successful episode," Owen continued. "Now before any rumors start clouding up the truth, I want to make a formal announcement." He waited until he had all eyes on him.

Tori waited curiously.

"Many of you know that Hannah and I were happy to welcome a new daughter-in-law into our home." He smiled at Tori. "What you may or may not be aware of is that Tori has discovered she has a super power, probably more than one. The circumstances around why she only just found this out is her business, but I would like you to welcome her to the Double Bay chapter of the Worldwide Order of Paladins."

Everyone clapped. A few people cheered. Tori tried not to slide down her seat in embarrassment.

"In addition," Owen's voice gained a degree or two in intensity, "I want to be clear that *no one* here will talk to anyone outside this room about Tori's affiliation or lack thereof with the Curtis family. You are not to confirm or deny anything. You are not to participate in gossip among yourselves. Your only answer to questions is 'I don't know.' Does everyone understand that?"

Owen looked to each person individually, waiting for them to say yes before moving to the next person. Tori thought he would skip over her. She did, after all, know some of the answers to the questions, so how could she lie? But he spoke to her last.

"Tori, you and Joe and I will discuss this in more detail later, but this goes for you, too. For the safety of our teams, we cannot let rumors grow about a Paladin's link to The Nine. Do you understand?"

Tori nodded her head. Wow. She hadn't realized how the ripples in one person's life could brush up against so many others'.

Owen smiled slightly and nodded. He talked about other chapter matters, and closed the meeting on time, keeping to his thirty-minute schedule.

"Any questions before we adjourn?"

Tori looked around and tentatively raised her hand. Joe cleared his throat, getting Owen's attention. She wasn't sure if she was glad about that or not. What if her question made Owen upset? Or upset the others? This was her first meeting, after all.

"I hope you don't mind but...earlier you said that Wednesday night was successful. Just Wednesday night, or everything related to it?"

"We call a single event or multiple related events an episode," Owen explained, not appearing to be annoyed. Yet.

"And you said it was successful."

Owen nodded.

"But," she looked at Joe, then looked to her other new team-mates, "we didn't find Kane. He's not going to be punished for kidnapping or child abuse or illegal genetic research or anything."

"But we found Ben, the reason we went in," Owen said, "and we rescued seven other children as well."

"But if we're looking at the multiple related events, we didn't find Evan Ruffalo's killer, or his son Jason." Tori's voice strengthened as she found the confidence to speak out. "We don't know who killed that mugger that we think Kane sent. We didn't find the car bomber. That's a lot of things we didn't get done. I don't really understand how that is successful."

"We look at our work differently than law enforcement," Owen explained. "Everything that you mentioned is important, and law enforcement agencies work on those kinds of issues every day. They relate to justice. Our work is ancillary to law enforcement. We helped them find Ben and other missing children that they couldn't find before. The events of Wednesday night should curb additional illegal genetic research here in Double Bay."

He nodded to the people gathered. "The city and some state and federal agencies have had another good experience with professional Paladins, which means we and Paladins elsewhere will be more likely to continue working harmoniously with, instead of in contention with, local and outside law enforcement. And, hopefully, we've kept The Nine from expanding their reach here."

Tori saw a lot of heads nodding.

"I understand your question, Tori." Owen smiled gently at her. "It's hard to feel like you've done enough. We've all felt that way. We'll support you and your sister as you both decide how to proceed with your lives, and we'll help you through the difficult times. But we all have to learn to accept that we can't do everything. Our abilities do have limits."

Joe put his arm around her shoulder. Tori nodded, but she was going to need more time to understand. Whether it was too much TV watching or what, it was hard to see things differently than how she'd always perceived them before. She'd always thought the good guys won. Every time. She was going to have to re-think her view of the world.

"Okay, if there's nothing else," Owen looked around the room with a grin, "welcome to our Super Bowl party. Please make yourselves at home."

Chairs rattled as people got up and moved around. A few people patted Tori's shoulder and welcomed her to the chapter. She thanked each one and tried to remember their names. She saw Owen speaking privately to Hayley. She hoped Hayley wasn't really going to quit. Tori needed her no-nonsense friend to help her navigate this new world.

Joe leaned close to her ear and whispered, "I know a love seat with our name on it."

Tori giggled, glad that Joe was trying to distract her from her thoughts. "Excellent. Lead the way." Today she would chill out with her friends and family. She'd think about serious matters tomorrow.

Stuart and Melissa were already sitting in front of the TV. "You guys done?" Stuart asked. "Dad asked me to set up the upstairs TV in the kitchen."

"All done," Joe said. He sat in the love seat and pulled Tori down next to him.

She snuggled into his side, content. What a relaxing day this was going to be. Exactly the kind of day she'd anticipated when she got married.

Well, life was an adventure, that's for sure. But not today.

"I can't believe I'm saying this," she said to Joe as other people starting filing in to watch the pre-game show, "but I've never been so happy to sit down and watch a boring old football game in my life."

A PEEK AT MY BULLHEADED SUPERHERO VALENTINE

AN ADVENTURES OF LEWIS AND CLARKE NOVELLA

Read the next story in the timeline
Available now at most online retailers

There had to be a way. He was a superhero, for Pete's sake. Surely he could get a woman to go out on a date with him. One woman in particular.

Bull Kincaid lay on his oversized leather couch tossing a throw pillow in the air. He stared at the ceiling, thinking. *I Love Lucy* played in the background, but even Lucy Ricardo couldn't get his mind off his troubles today.

He'd come straight home from his day job as a history teacher and wrestling coach at Glenview High School so he could figure this out. His superhero team had the night off, so he had plenty of time before Hayley got home to come up with a plan.

Valentine's Day was four days away.

He couldn't woo her with a bouquet of flowers because a) she owned a nursery so she could get all the flowers she wanted, and b) she preferred live flowers to cut ones. She had the supernatural ability to make plants grow and multiply in the blink of an eye, and she'd made it clear she preferred that the flowers continue to flourish.

Maybe he could give her a potted rose bush and put a big, red bow on it. But where would he get one of those in February in Northern Michigan? Besides at her nursery.

Okay, not flowers. She liked chocolate as much as anyone, but she didn't go ga-ga over it like some women. So that was out.

He bounced the throw pillow off the ceiling.

Think, think. Once again, he was hampered by his tiny brain.

"You may be big, but you're dumb, dumb, dumb!"

He closed his eyes tightly and imagined himself pushing his father's voice out of his head. Joe's dad had taught him that visualization trick a few years ago. Not that it helped. He wasn't getting any smarter. He couldn't even get this one girl to go out with him.

Previous attempts to coax a date from Hayley had been met with a variety of responses from "not on your life" six years ago to "I'm not hungry" last night. Sure, he could keep coasting on the crumbs she gave him, but he wanted more. Even a little bit more — like one real, live date — would make him happy. At least it would show progress.

Okay, come on, you can do this. What would make her go on a real date with him rather than just use him for sex and comfort?

He'd worked with Hayley on the same superhero team for going on eight years. He'd probably been in love with her for seven and a half. And for the last six years, if she was lonely or upset, she came to him and they had the most amazing nights. She always left before breakfast, breaking his heart each time. But he knew she had come to love him. At least a little. He was almost positive.

Watching his best friend and fellow superhero Joe Clarke fall in love with his new wife Tori and seeing them together these last few months gave Bull an idea of what married love was like. And it made him believe he wasn't imagining things. Hayley Addison loved him.

If she were just using him for sex, for instance, she wouldn't give him gifts. Not that she used that word. But she brought him things he didn't know he needed "to make this house livable." She gave him a tie last year before parent-teacher conferences because "you can't wear the same tie every year." After he said he liked ferns and ivy, green plants that he couldn't kill and that didn't drop flower blossoms he'd have to clean up, he found several potted plants in his house.

But the most obvious proof that she loved him happened in December when she went to the mall with him and Joe and Tori and *she let him hold her hand.* She'd only allowed this public display of affection during the last couple months, and only when they were with their two closest friends, probably because she felt safe with them. Nonetheless, it occurred before the Curtis Episode, so he knew it was real, not a by-product of that horrific experience.

She loved him. She was just scared.

He stilled, pillow gripped in his fists. So it wasn't that he needed to convince her that she loved him and should marry him and live happily ever after together. He needed to take away her fear.

But how could he erase years of anxiety and abuse for her when he couldn't get his own father's voice out of his head? He'd gotten counseling from Joe's dad, a retired-superhero-turned-pastor. He prayed regularly and asked God to heal him, and he'd found great relief from the worst of his past hurts. And he poured his heart into the hurting kids around him, trying to give his students the encouragement and support he never had.

But still his father's taunts would pop up like a jack-in-the-box and startle him into feeling like he wasn't fully human, like he was half a man — and not the good half.

So how could he help Hayley? He couldn't force her into counseling, though he knew Pastor Owen had tried to help her. He couldn't make her believe that God trusted her with this gift to help mankind if she insisted on seeing it as a curse. He couldn't force her to relax and let her guard down when she believed her defenses were all that protected her.

When she felt safe, then she'd open up.

He threw the pillow at the ceiling, his grin reappearing. He knew *he* made her feel safe. How could he expand on that? Maybe he could make his house and yard a plant oasis like her nursery. Then she'd always want to be here. He wouldn't use his powers at home, and he'd make sure none of his friends did either. If she wanted to quit being a superhero, fine. He'd try to keep the superhero world all but invisible to her just as it was to most of the people of Double Bay.

And he'd make sure she never had to deal with the kind of despicable people they'd all fought last month at Curtis Research Facility. He couldn't imagine what it would be like to find out your best friend's biological father was Double Bay's biggest villain. Not only that, but that he performed genetic experiments on children, even kidnapping his own grandson.

Bull wiped his eyes, trying to wipe away the images of that night. It was the kind of horror that made you quit or forced you to re-double your efforts.

While Hayley hadn't exactly moved in afterward, she hadn't gone home much either. She slept in his bed all night, showered here, ate here, watched TV here. He knew she stopped at her apartment every few days because she would have different clothes or a new book, the previous things disappearing.

Maybe things had already turned in his favor.

His grinned slipped. No, if she were feeling safe, she wouldn't be having the nightmares. He crushed the pillow against his chest, staring at a watermark on the ceiling. His heart hurt for her, actually ached in his chest. Seeing those children had sickened everyone, but especially Hayley. She'd quit the team that night and had been hiding out in Bull's house ever since.

Only their immediate team members knew, but no one had said a word. They couldn't fault her for running away. But Bull didn't think anyone realized how desperately Hayley wanted to be a mother with a normal life. He didn't think even Tori realized the depth of Hayley's maternal instincts. He understood, though. He considered the boys on the wrestling team "his boys." He'd do anything to protect them, to protect any child.

Bull scrubbed at his eyes. He stood over six and a half feet tall and tipped the scales at nearly 300 pounds of muscle before breakfast. His supernatural strength had saved dozens, maybe hundreds of people. He'd caught crooks, stopped robberies, and once he'd pulled a sewer drain apart with his bare hands to rescue a puppy caught inside.

But he hadn't been able to do a thing to help that dying boy.

He threw the pillow across the room. He'd had a few nightmares of his own.

He jumped off the couch and paced the living room. *Hayley. Come on, focus.*

Okay, what about other women? Some of the female teachers at school flirted with him. They complimented him on his friendly smile and laid-back personality. How could he use that to his advantage? Maybe try to make Hayley jealous somehow? No, knowing his Hayley, that would just push her further away. Plus, she knew he hadn't dated anyone else. Not really. A few meals here and there. He hadn't so much as taken another woman to the movies in the last...what had it been, three years? Four?

He shook his head. She knew he was mad for her, was waiting for her to change her mind, but she was about as bullheaded as anyone he'd ever met.

He'd never considered himself stubborn, but in this case he would outlast her. Whatever it took.

He looked around the living room and tried to see it from a woman's perspective. First, he needed to pick up the pillow he'd thrown and straighten the lamp that now teetered on the edge of a side table. He folded the blanket that he usually kept stuffed at one end of the couch and stepped back.

He rearranged the throw pillows so they were equidistant apart. Nothing more he could think of there. He moved the TV remote and the stereo remote to a side table and straightened a stack of papers, mail, and magazines piled on the coffee table. Another step back. Nope. He grabbed the pile and looked around for a place to put it. Where would a woman put the mail she hadn't read yet?

He wandered into the kitchen. The table, right? But it still had this morning's breakfast crumbs on it. He started to put the mail on the counter, noticed crumbs there, too, and finally set it on the floor. He got out cleaner and a handful of paper towels and wiped everything down. Then he put the pile from the living room in a neat stack in the middle of the table. It didn't look right, but he didn't have a better idea.

He grabbed his coat and scarf from the back of the kitchen chair where he'd tossed them and hung them on the iron coat rack on the inside porch. Back in the kitchen, he debated mopping the kitchen floor for about three seconds. Then he looked at his watch and hurried to the bedroom.

He made the bed, put his dirty clothes in the hamper, and neatened the bathroom as best he could. He stood in the middle of the bedroom looking around. Neatness and cleanliness, that's what women wanted, right? He'd have to start making those things a priority.

Was Hayley's place neat and clean all the time? He hadn't been there enough to remember. He wasn't sure if she was a neat freak in general, or if she was just trying to leave a small footprint here. Go unnoticed.

Ha! He'd notice her wherever she was, no matter how unobtrusive she was trying to be.

He checked his watch again. Any minute she'd be home. If she didn't stop by her apartment or the grocery store. Where should he wait? He heard the TV in the living room and headed that way, then paused in the doorway. He turned around and pulled off his GHS Wrestling T-shirt and hurled it at the hamper. Pulling a clean shirt from a drawer, he started back out, checked his stride and turned around, and put his dirty shirt in the hamper rather than leaving it on top.

Satisfied, he strolled nonchalantly back to the couch and turned his eyes back to Lucy's black and white adventures. He put his arm on the back of the couch and tried to relax. He twisted around and put his legs up on the cushions, getting comfortable. Then he sat up straight again, listening to outdoor sounds more than the TV.

Finally, he heard the outside door slam shut in the winter

wind. He rushed to the kitchen, then leaned against the counter trying to look casual.

He couldn't stand the suspense. He walked over and casually opened the door to the back porch.

Hayley noticed him with a brief "Hi" and pulled off her knit hat. Her straight dark hair danced in the air with static electricity. He watched as she hung her hunter green wool coat and matching scarf on the coat rack. She leaned against the door frame, pulled off her snowy boots, and danced the two steps into the kitchen in her stocking feet.

Bull backed out of her way a few steps, admiring her long legs and graceful movements. She was beautiful.

She leaned through the door and picked up a plastic bag and her purse from the floor of the porch, then straightened and shut and locked the door.

Bull wanted nothing more than to march over to her, wrap his hands in her hair, and kiss her senseless. He still wasn't sure how to get her to say yes, but maybe she'd agree to a date if he could keep her from overthinking it. He folded his arms over his chest and fought to control himself.

"I brought Chinese for dinner," she said, holding up the heavy plastic bag. "All your favorites."

Maybe he should go with his first impulse. He didn't have a better plan. What could it hurt? In two long strides he closed the distance between them, moved the bag from her hand to the floor, and let himself do what he wished. Just this once.

The feel of her flooded his senses. One arm pulled her close, while his other hand tangled in her soft hair. His mouth came down on hers with the passion he normally kept hidden. He felt her surprised gasp and took advantage of the moment, exploring her mouth with abandon. She smelled like wild fruit. She tasted like spearmint. She was everything he wanted in the world.

After a moment, Hayley responded, pressing up against him, kissing him almost as thoroughly as he kissed her. Her hands slid up his chest and through his hair, eliciting a groan he couldn't hold in. When she wrapped her arms around his neck, he picked her up, bringing their mouths to the same level. He took a step forward and braced her body against the door. With one arm holding her up, he used his other hand to explore the contours of her face, the graceful length of her neck, all the while kissing her like it was the end of the world.

Bull's heart swelled to a giant ache in his chest. He wanted her to feel how much he loved her. She needed to know, to really understand how much she meant to him. Then surely she would finally allow herself to be loved.

They held each other close, kissing and touching and letting themselves get carried away. When the kisses finally ended, they were both breathing heavily.

"I should bring you Chinese more often," Hayley panted.

"I want to take you out, a *real* date, on Valentine's Day." Bull surprised himself with his outburst. He'd treated her like a scared, wounded fawn for so long, he was afraid his demand would send her packing. But now that it was out there, he wouldn't back down.

He let her slide down so her feet touched the ground, but he didn't let go. "I'll make reservations, we'll get dressed up, I'll drive, and I'll pay." He wanted to make that clear. She rarely allowed him to treat her and often insisted on driving her own car.

His tone sounded unnaturally firm to his ears. Would she be offended? While he was trying to decide if he should soften his demands, she answered.

"But, um, it's this Sunday." Hayley stumbled over her words. She didn't sound argumentative, just unable to think coherently.

Bull's heart pounded in his chest, a kind of testosterone-induced satisfaction. He'd kissed her so well she couldn't think. He needed to remember to add that to his arsenal.

Arsenal. For a fight. *That* was something he understood. Maybe it was time to take her to the mat, force her to fight or tap out. No more careful handling. Ever since he had come into his power of superhuman strength, he'd been trying *not* to fight, afraid he might hurt someone. He taught his boys at school how to wrestle fairly, playing by the rules, keeping "fights" on the mat.

However — it occurred to him now — he *did* teach his boys to fight to win. But he hadn't been fighting as hard as he could have for Hayley. He'd been playing carefully, trying to be a gentleman, a *gentle* man.

Well, that ended now.

Let the war begin.

"Sunday night," he said with new confidence. "We'll leave here at seven."

Hayley studied his face for a moment, and Bull readied himself for battle. Her eyes dropped to his lips. He knew she thought of their kiss when she wet her lips with the tip of her tongue. She cleared her throat and turned away.

"Fine," she said, reaching for the bag of steaming Chinese food resting on the floor.

Thank goodness she'd turned her back. Bull needed a moment to pick his jaw off the floor.

She said yes!

A SNEAK PEEK AT SUPERHERO IN THE MAKING

ADVENTURES OF LEWIS AND CLARKE

Check out a scene from the next book in the Adventures of Lewis and Clarke series

Coming Soon

THE ADVENTURES OF LEWIS AND CLARKE BOOK TWO

"Combines down-to-earth humor, tense mystery, and sweet romance."
- GVR Carcillo

Superhero in the Making

KITTY BUCHOLTZ

Halfway through the fourth ring, Tori grabbed the phone and pressed Talk. "What do you want?"

Jade's laughter came through the receiver, but Tori shivered when she heard it. "I want you to work for me. I think I've made that very clear. And to show you I'm serious, I enlisted the aid of your husband. Say hello, Joe."

Tori's heart clenched as Joe's laughter echoed through the line. "Hello, Joe," he said. But it didn't sound right.

"What have you done to him?" Tori's voice was tight and hard. She could hear it. She needed to stay calm, needed to keep Jade calm. "Let him go and we'll discuss this."

Katie pressed close against Tori's side, listening.

"I'm offering you power and wealth beyond your wildest dreams," Jade said, her voice sounding breezy on the outside but hard on the inside. "It's a win-win situation. Why don't you see that?"

"You're right," Tori said. "I hadn't realized the extent of the opportunity. We should talk about it. How about I come over and you let Joe go? We can talk then."

Jade laughed again. "Oh, it's not that easy now. But you come on over and we'll work things out."

Tori grabbed for a pen and paper. "Where?"

Katie held the paper still while Tori wrote down the address.

"And no police. You come alone." Jade's voice was hard. "If the police show up, you're going to have to live with the consequences. Alone."

Jade hung up.

Tori stood with the phone in her hand for a moment, trying to think. Trying not to shake. She slowly replaced the receiver.

"Aunt Tori, she's lying," Katie cried. "I heard her, she's lying! I *know* it. We have to call Grandpa!"

Tori closed her eyes and tried to think. Joe didn't sound right. He sounded...high or something.

"Call Grandpa!" Katie pulled on Tori's arm.

"No, Katie. We can't call anyone. I'm afraid she'll..." She didn't want to scare her niece, but Tori was afraid Jade would follow through on her threat.

"Then let's call Bull," Katie insisted. "He'll help us."

Tori remembered seeing Bull work as Powerhouse last night. Bigger than Joe and built like a tank, no one could take him down. But Jade's warning rang in her head. She rubbed her eyes to keep from crying.

Okay, first she had to take care of Katie. Then she would find Joe. "Get your backpack, I'm taking you to Julia's house. I want you to—"

"No!" Katie pulled back.

"Katie, you heard her," Tori said, ripping the paper off the pad and stuffing it into her purse. "She's not right in the head, and I'm *not* leaving you alone."

Katie wiped her tears with her sleeve. "I'm coming with you."

"Absolutely not!"

Katie took a deep breath, obviously trying to stop trembling. "I can do this. I can help you get Uncle Joe back. I can make her tell the truth about where he is and what she's done to him, and you can't!"

Tori started to protest. But she couldn't ignore the idea that Katie could help even the odds, if only a little. If she were any other teenage girl, Tori would pack her over to Julia's in a heartbeat.

Katie stood straighter, looking taller and older. "You need me," she said, picking up the phone. "And you need Bull. Trust me, I've lived with superheroes my whole life. This is how it works. We stick together." She handed the phone to Tori.

Tori considered the thirteen-year-old's argument. She had been looking for a friend and a mentor. But she hadn't expected to find one in someone who wasn't even old enough to drive.

A NOTE FROM KITTY

I hope you enjoyed reading *Unexpected Superhero*, the third story in the Adventures of Lewis and Clarke series. I had such a blast writing it—and not a little trepidation! There is such an amazing array of excellent writing and storytelling in the world of comics.

I have to admit, I used to be a comic book snob. I made my husband miserable for the first few years we were together, complaining about how much money and time he spent on comic books. But recently we hit a milestone. For the first time, I was the one who spent the most money at a comic book store!

If you've never read one, ask me or a friend for a recommendation based on the kinds of stories you like. You might be surprised!

Now that you've read the first three stories in the series about Tori and Joe, if you love Bull and Hailey and want to learn more about them, *My Bullheaded Superhero Valentine* is the next piece of their story, and follows *Unexpected Superhero* in the timeline.

My books are available as ebooks and in print at most online retailers. *Unexpected Superhero* and *Little Miss Lovesick* are also available as audiobooks. All the ebooks, print books, and audiobooks will be added to my own web store over the course of 2024.

Purchases there support me and my work in a significantly greater way so I'd love it if you'd like to buy from me directly (kittybucholtz.com/books)!

You can also join my free or paid membership community over on Patreon (links at the end of About the Author). Read chapters early before the books even come out, discuss the stories with other readers, see fun art about the settings of the books, and more!

You might also try my romantic comedies in the Traverse City in Love series and the Strays of Loon Lake series. You can read *Cherry on Top* for free. It's set in the same town as *Little Miss Lovesick* during the famous National Cherry Festival. It's my gift to you when you join my reader newsletter at kittybucholtz.com/freebook.

If you really want to make my day, I'd love for you to post your thoughts in a book review. Thanks so much!

And just so you know, I rebranded all my books in 2024 to be "sweet" — so no swear words or overt sex scenes. I hope you enjoy the change.

Happy Reading!

ACKNOWLEDGMENTS

Unexpected Superhero has been a long time in the making. I've talked to dozens of people about comic books and superheroes, and I've learned something from each of them. I did my best to remember everyone I talked to—thank you to everyone who answered questions, gave an opinion, shared an idea, or read part of the book.

Thank you to Mike Akerley, Jill Bandemer, Janet Batchler, Brie and Jared Bryson, Bridgette and Don Coleman and Snickers the cat, Stephanie and Darrin Dennis, Dave Derus, Ben Drake, Fran Ervin, Ruth and Luke Flanagan, Catherine and Sean Gaffney, Sergio Gonzalez, Kahle McCann, Jonathan McDonald, all of my friends at the Orange County Chapter of Romance Writers of America, John Olson, Anthony Platipodis, Lisa and Steve Rowe, Janinne and David Schell, Stephanie Shackelford, Shonna and Mike Slayton, Rachel and Simeon Taylor, Mel and Andrew Turnham, Jessica and Ray Westcott, and Debbie White.

Special thanks to Jane Barton, Bronwyn Bates, Jean Bedford, Laura Brierley-Newton, Barbara Brooks, Kim Buddee, Kate Butler, Emily Cantrill, Luke Corbin, Sarah Cottier, Mathilde de Hauteclocque, Denise Doraisamy, Brielle Evans, David Eyles, Delia Falconer, Deborah FitzGerald, Susanna Freymark, Georgina Gamble, Sarah Goldstein, Ellie Graham, Luke Habib, Marilyn Harris, Emma Holst, Bridget Hoskins, Judy Hutchison, Jennifer Huynh, Jennifer James, Madeleine James, Amy Jenkins, Catherine Johnson, Geraldine Johnson, Kurt Johnson, Jannali Jones, Blae Levy, Thang Luong, Anthony Macris, Jade Maloney,

Ari Mattes, Roslyn McFarland, Dawn McGuire, Mathilde Minnie, Alison Monaghan, Jacqueline Moreno-Ovidi, David Morris, Kay Nankervis, Margot Nash, Marianne O'Reilly, Nicola O'Shea, Amy Paterson, Ian Pettit, (super duper thanks to) Betsy Pickering, Jen Reid, Helen Richardson, Natasha Roberts, Brigitte Ross, Aimee Scott, Rosie Scott, Noor Shehabi, Howard Shih, Sarah Stone, Dominique Sweers, Kylie Taylor, Jen Vermeulen, Scott Wilson, and all of the rest of my friends and fellow students in the Master of Arts in Creative Writing program at University of Technology, Sydney. I miss you guys!

Thank you to my friends in my Australian writer's group, The Writer's Coven—Deborah Allen, Jennifer Brassel, Coleen Kwan, Bernadette Magee, Margie Mason, Ann McCutcheon, Judy Neumann, Paula Roe, and Shannon Stein.

And thank you to Cathleen Armstrong, Janice Cantore, Ceil Higgins, Cecile Knowles, Susan Lawson, Wendy Lawton, Bonnie Line, Sue Massey, Lauraine Snelling, Marcy Weydemuller (who is also my wonderful editor!), Kathleen Wright, and the rest of the awesome Reunioners.

Like dessert, I like to save the best for last—and you're the best, John! You've always been my hero, so it's no surprise that the hero of this story has a lot of your qualities. If you'd never given me a copy of the graphic novel, *Kingdom Come*, this book would never have existed. Thanks for introducing me to this strange and wonderful world.

And to the superhero who keeps rescuing me from all the messes I get into—thank you, Jesus. You really are the greatest superhero the world has ever known.

ALSO BY KITTY BUCHOLTZ

CONSIDER BUYING BOOKS DIRECT FROM
KITTY! GO TO KITTYBUCHOLTZ.COM/BOOKS

Adventures of Lewis and Clarke

Superhero in Disguise

A Very Merry Superhero Wedding

Unexpected Superhero

My Bullheaded Superhero Valentine

Also...

Adventures of Lewis and Clarke: The Beginning (the first three books)

The Strays of Loon Lake

Welcome to Loon Lake

Love at the Fluff and Fold

Traverse City in Love

Cherry on Top (free short story)

Little Miss Lovesick

Death and Tacos (coming soon!)

ABOUT THE AUTHOR

Kitty Bucholtz writes sweet romantic comedy and superhero urban fantasy, often with an inspirational element woven in. Her stories feature women whose sense of humor and nervous gutsiness get them into and out of all kinds of trouble. She grew up forty miles east of Traverse City, Michigan—a town that is a smaller but surprisingly similar version of Double Bay, Michigan, the setting of this book. She went to college there, met and married the love of her life, and waved goodbye to everything she knew when she and her husband, John, struck out for parts unknown.

Their romantic adventures have included a scolding at Parliament House in Belfast for canoodling, three trips Down Under where her handsome hubby made animated movie animals look real, and a delicious taste of European life living in Sweden. After earning her M.A. in Creative Writing in Sydney, she formed Daydreamer Entertainment and began self-publishing. Founder of Write Now! Workshop and Write Now! Workshop Podcast, she loves to teach and coach writers.

Only God knows where they'll wind up next – but they're pretty sure it will be another cool chapter in their adventure!

If you enjoyed this or any of Kitty's books, please leave a review—they are a tremendous help to both writers and readers!

Connect with Kitty today!
kittybucholtz.com
kitty@kittybucholtz.com

Get your copy of the free short story *Cherry on Top* at kittybucholtz.com/freebook today!

patreon.com/kittybucholtz

tiktok.com/@kitty_bucholtz

facebook.com/kittybucholtzauthor

bookbub.com/profile/kitty-bucholtz

amazon.com/author/kittybucholtz

x.com/KittyBucholtz

instagram.com/kittybucholtz

goodreads.com/kittybucholtz

youtube.com/kittybucholtz